WILLOW MAN

JOHN INMAN

DSP PUBLICATIONS

Published by
DSP PUBLICATIONS

5032 Capital Circle SW, Suite 2, PMB# 279, Tallahassee, FL 32305-7886 USA
http://www.dsppublications.com/

This is a work of fiction. Names, characters, places, and incidents either are the product of author imagination or are used fictitiously, and any resemblance to actual persons, living or dead, business establishments, events, or locales is entirely coincidental.

Willow Man
© 2014 John Inman.

Cover Art
© 2014 Aaron Anderson.
aaronbydesign55@gmail.com
Cover content is for illustrative purposes only and any person depicted on the cover is a model.

All rights reserved. This book is licensed to the original purchaser only. Duplication or distribution via any means is illegal and a violation of international copyright law, subject to criminal prosecution and upon conviction, fines, and/or imprisonment. Any eBook format cannot be legally loaned or given to others. No part of this book may be reproduced or transmitted in any form or by any means, electronic or mechanical, including photocopying, recording, or by any information storage and retrieval system, without the written permission of the Publisher, except where permitted by law. To request permission and all other inquiries, contact DSP Publications, 5032 Capital Circle SW, Suite 2, PMB# 279, Tallahassee, FL 32305-7886, USA, or http://www.dsppublications.com/.

ISBN: 978-1-63216-349-3
Digital ISBN: 978-1-63216-350-9
Library of Congress Control Number: 2014945075
First Edition January 2015

Printed in the United States of America
∞
This paper meets the requirements of
ANSI/NISO Z39.48-1992 (Permanence of Paper).

A NOTE FROM THE AUTHOR

IT WAS a day I will never forget. The crash took place at 9:01 on a beautiful September morning in the crystal skies over San Diego. With a boom that rolled across the city like thunder, PSA's Boeing 727 Flight 182 collided with a small Cessna directly in my line of sight as I stood at my dining room window looking east. The stricken airliner crashed less than a mile from my home, spewing bodies everywhere. Just as the city darkened that day with billowing smoke, so too, I think, did my mind darken a little bit, and has remained so ever since. *Willow Man* comes from that darkness of imagination. I dedicate this story to the 144 souls lost on that long-ago day in 1978. May they rest in peace.

—John Inman

PROLOGUE

THROUGH ALL the long eons, like a great festering wound, the canyon gouged a path for itself through the barren hillside leading down to the sea. When man arrived, driven to the continent's last horizon in his search for wealth and freedom in this new America, a city grew up around it. What was once desert scrub and parched stone and empty, endless vistas became, with man's magic, a promised land. A mecca. Man planted the seeds he carried here from other lands, and what was once desert became green. What was once dead became a torrent of life.

They came first in tall ships through the treacherous South American straits. Then, as the continent was conquered, in covered wagons drawn by teams of sturdy oxen. Centuries later they still came, soaring across the sky in sleek airliners, making what was once a journey of months, a journey of moments, to settle in this place where even the most fantastic of dreams, they had heard, could become reality. Every year the city stretched out its arms a little wider, and every year, with winter's rains, the wound that tore through the heart of the city grew a little deeper. A little more oppressive. Man did not go there. He lived out his life on the verge of this long winding canyon, admiring its beauty but rarely venturing into the depths of it to seek out its secrets.

The foliage that brooded deep in the shadows of this great wound became wild and, in places, almost impenetrable.

Thickets of brambles and scrub grass ranged low to the ground, brittle in the summer months, sepia-toned and listless, greening and coming alive only with the rains of winter. The smell of sage, carried over the lip of the canyon by the endless wind that seemed to forever tear through this place on its way to the sea, sweetened the air around the homes man built to perch like sentinels upon the canyon's edge. Soon the land surrounding the canyon became so overbuilt that the scent of sage and ocean were the only remnants left of its true self.

Looming above the brambles and sage along the canyon walls, stood tall eucalyptus trees, immigrants from another land. They had taken Southern California as their own, thriving here as all immigrants seem to do, human or otherwise. Soaring high, reaching ever upward, they lifted their proud leafy heads above the canyon walls, as if turning their backs to the shadows on the canyon floor to seek out the company of sun and man.

And in the deepest parts of the canyon, down in places where only the noontime sun ever reached, stood the billowing willows and pepper trees. Lush the year round, they cared nothing for man, cared nothing for seasons, their roots buried so deep in the earth that water could always be found to feed their broad canopies. Their long, graceful limbs never seemed to rest but continually swayed like dancers moving to the music of the never-ending wind that whistled and sang around them. Their long, elegant leaves, as slender and thick as prairie grass, billowed continually about their heads, and if man took the time to look down from the canyon's edge to see them there, he was reminded of ocean swells and cool moving water.

But beneath those billowing treetops that moved continually like wind-tossed hair upon a human head, the shadows lay deep and forbidding. There was life there, man knew, but it was not a life that he cared to witness, that he cared to be a part of. Inevitably he turned away from those shadows, uneasy, and raised his eyes to the sky, back to the light, back to the place where no secrets were ever kept.

And in this Eden he created, this perfect city by the sea, man lived out his life in peace and contentment, until the day the creature that brooded there, deep among the shadows beneath the willows, rose up from the canyon to seek what it had long craved, replacing man's search for the great American dream, in one thudding heartbeat, with a fight for his very survival.

And more importantly, the survival of his children....

CHAPTER ONE

"*Woody?* My God, is that *you*? How long has it *been*?"

Woody wasn't exactly sure just *how* long it had been, but to his way of thinking, it certainly hadn't been long enough.

He remembered Crystal, of course. Hell, who wouldn't? She had been gorgeous once. Still was, pretty much, although she did appear to have considerably higher mileage on the old odometer these days. Woody could still recall the way she used to whisk her pom-poms around at basketball games, wiggle her tight little butt, and aim her perky pubescent tits up at the grandstand as if to say, "Here they are, boys. Come and get 'em." Well, it looked as if, at some point between then and now, somebody had indeed come and got 'em, and loosened up the chassis considerably in the process. She was a raging airhead then, and judging by appearances, she was a raging airhead now. Maybe some things you simply don't grow out of.

"High school?" he said, wishing he had been a little quicker getting to the alley for his after-set cigarette.

Tonight, he knew, his set had been a good one. His voice in tune. His fingers adept on the guitar strings. The crowd congenial. They even seemed to be listening to him, which was a nice change of pace for the club he was currently working. Usually they just sat out there in that dark netherworld behind the spotlight, swilling beers and downing shots of tequila until they didn't know where the hell they were and certainly didn't give a shit where the hell Woody was or give two hoots for the fact that he was trying to entertain the ungrateful bastards.

No, it had been a good night. Until now.

The airhead squealed like a pig being disemboweled and gave his arm a playful slap, sloshing the beer from his glass onto his pant leg. "Well, of course it was *high school*, silly! But what year was that? When did we graduate?"

Woody was wondering if beer would stain khaki. He was also wondering how many shots of tequila this broad had poured down her throat during the course of the evening. "You mean you don't remember?"

She giggled, like being stupid was the asset she was most proud of. "What year is it now?" she asked, looking honestly thoughtful.

Woody dragged up a smile and pointed it at her like a gun. "Doesn't matter. Having a good time tonight? You don't seem to be feeling any pain."

Ha. Ha. She laughed the same laugh a hyena might laugh after finding a nice tasty zebra carcass lying on the savannah. A long series of hoots and haws with a couple of snorts scattered around to give it texture.

"I'm having a *wonderful* time! But, I didn't know you could *sing*, Woody! Gee, I mean, you're a real *singer*!"

"The matter is still up for debate."

Whoosh. He imagined his words flapping across the top of her head like dying pigeons and splattering in a burst of feathers against the far wall, stunned into oblivion, uncomprehended by anything or anyone in between. Least of all her.

"Really?" she asked, suddenly sincere. "Well, I thought you were *great*!"

"Thanks," he said, leaving his smile thumbtacked to his face like a poster.

"Buy me a drink?" Crystal asked with a flirtatious leer that promised more than drinking company if he played his cards right.

Woody was used to that look. It was a look he had seen time and again over the years. He supposed he was handsome enough, coming in at a little under six feet and as trim as a runner, with a sprinkling of soft hair across a well-defined chest and sporting long, elegant fingers—a guitar player's fingers, his mother once told him. No moles, no scars, no Adonis, but with shoulder-length, reddish-blond hair that framed an open, expressive face, which in moments of repose seemed to wander toward the forlorn side, there was something about him, Woody knew, that certain women, and certain men, seemed to enjoy looking at. Sometimes that knowledge amused him. But not tonight.

Woody's smile faltered. "Sorry, kid. Not allowed to fraternize with the customers. Club rule."

It took her a minute to absorb this. "Gee, honey, I'm not asking you to fraternize me, whatever *that* means. Sounds kinky, though. Oh, wait, I think I know what it means." Rusty wheels turned inside her tequila-glutted brain for all of five seconds before she said, "Well, maybe I don't. So how about that drink?"

Woody glanced over her shoulder at nothing whatsoever and announced, "Oops, there's my boss. Gotta run." And with that, he took off like a bat out of hell toward the back door, aiming a last "Have fun tonight!" over his shoulder at the decidedly disappointed-looking ex-cheerleader behind him.

Once outside, he breathed in the cool night air and then replaced the freshness of it inside his lungs with a grateful puff from a Pall Mall.

Glad to be alone, Woody gazed up at the moon, which hung like a streetlight above his head. Where the hell was he? Oakland? That's right, Oakland. His agent had booked him this gig right after Del Cerro, with no waiting in between jobs for a change. That was nice. His three days here ended tonight after his next set. Then he had a two week run in a club called Strikers, which was part of a gigantic bowling complex in San Diego—more than a hundred lanes, or so he'd been told—again without any dead time between gigs.

He supposed he'd be singing to the accompaniment of strikes and spares and rumbling bowling balls, but what the hell, he could always crank up the mike. *San Diego,* he thought. *My hometown.* Supposedly every entertainer's dream, playing their hometown. Woody didn't quite see it that way, but what the heck. The money was good. Or sort of good. And how many of his old cohorts would be hanging around a bowling alley? Not many, or so he hoped.

He knew he should be happy to be leading the life he'd once dreamed of, but somehow his dream had lost a little of its pizzazz when it made the transition to reality. Maybe they always did. Maybe fiction was always better than fact. Too bad, that. It was a good dream. Not that his life now was bad, exactly. It just wasn't as good as the dream. After all, two weeks in a bowling alley in San Diego didn't quite measure up to a run at the Palace, now did it? Actually he didn't even know if the Palace still existed, or if it was still the holy of holies that up-and-coming young performers aspired to. Maybe it was a Kmart now. Wouldn't surprise him.

He stomped out the Pall Mall and immediately lit another. Damn cigarettes. Not good for his voice. But he wasn't exactly doing opera here. Sometimes a little cigarette hack in the middle of "Drop Kick Me, Jesus" added depth to the rendering. Or maybe it didn't. Who the hell cared anyway? And actually, "Drop Kick Me, Jesus," even by country-western standards, was a bit too banal for his playlist. He stole most of his material from George Strait, George Jones, and Willie Nelson. Not that they would mind, he was sure, since none of those august entities had ever in their lives heard of Woody Stiles, yours truly, or if they had, they had forgotten about him two minutes later.

He wasn't exactly in the fast lane to stardom, he had to admit. Here he was, pushing thirty. After years of struggle, his gigs were getting closer together and being fairly well received of late, but that elusive recording contract seemed to be nowhere on the horizon that he could see. Against the advice of his agent, he had dumped his band a couple of years back. He had been soloing ever since. Just him, his God-given voice, and his Gibson acoustic. Without a band, his gigs were a little more limited—no dance clubs to be sure—but on the other hand, he didn't have to split his pay five ways either. So all in all, going solo was a smart thing to do. Lonely, though. Jeez, it got lonely sometimes. He missed getting drunk with the guys after a show and playing till dawn for no one but themselves in some seedy motel room, surrounded by a mountain of takeout Chinese cartons and empty beer bottles, until the neighbors started pounding on the walls and screaming at them to "Shut the hell up, for Christ's sake, people are trying to sleep over here!"

The band had picked up another lead singer somewhere, he had heard, but what happened to them after that was anybody's guess. Flying under the radar somewhere, he supposed. Back to hustling for tips in the dives they had worked themselves out of while he was at the helm, maybe. Or maybe they were finally working themselves up again. He hoped so. They were nice guys. Good musicians. A little too dependent on outside stimulants, maybe, but how many working musicians weren't?

Woody himself had locked his sorry ass in a hotel room in Dallas for two weeks and weaned himself off crystal meth along about the time he'd dumped the band, and it was the best thing he'd ever done for himself. Wasn't easy, mind you. He still remembered dropping an issue of *Variety* on the floor and leaving it there for five days before his petrified muscles limbered up enough to allow him to bend over and pick it up. But there's no point in plucking away at your guitar strings until your fingers bleed and singing every insipid request that the drunken louts in the audience throw at you if you're just going to turn right around and suck the night's proceeds up your nose through a rolled-up dollar bill. No wonder so many country western singers were ex-druggies. It kind of went with the territory.

Lately, Woody had even been trying to wean himself away from country as well, going for a more Jackson Browne sound, but he supposed his voice just wasn't built for it. He could get an audience jiving pretty good with a little Mel Tillis or Clint Black, but when he shot for Billy Joel or Sting, he could see the bar patrons go glassy-eyed and start fiddling with their car keys. Not a good sign.

Woody had a repertoire of almost six-hundred country western songs under his belt, and maybe another couple of hundred of the more mainstream easy rock stuff, but he was bored with every damn one of them. In fact, Woody was beginning to think this line of work wasn't exactly a manly sort of business to be in. There is a certain panache to being a *recording* star, someone with an honest-to-God contract with a legitimate industry label, but to just flit around from one town to the next, following his agent's leads, singing for a bunch of drunken cowboy wannabe's in their too tight Levi jeans and overblown cowboy hats, which they only drag out of the closets on Saturday night, with their bleached blonde girlfriends hanging worshipfully on their arms like Cissy Spacek in *Coal Miner's Daughter* being dragged around by Tommy Lee Jones, just seemed a little—well—*demeaning*.

But Woody loved to sing. That was the problem. When he sang he did it for himself, not the audience. He could lose himself in the lyrics of a song sometimes, and when he did, those were the moments he most cherished, closing his eyes to the crowd and letting the words and the music carry him to a place where he didn't have to think of anything at all. A place where he could lose all sense of self completely. The meth had helped carry him to that place too, but at the same time, he knew, it was killing him. On meth he could sometimes lose himself so completely inside a song it was hard to let it end. He would find himself repeating verses over and over until the audience started wondering what the hell was going on. Finally, to bring him out of it, his band would play the closing bars right over him, just to get him to shut up.

It had seemed kind of funny at the time, but looking back on it now, he realized it wasn't funny at all. The euphoric high that kicked in when he snorted that expensive white powder might be making him happy, or at least making him *think* he was happy, but it was dragging the band down behind him like an anchor tossed over the side of a ship, sinking farther and farther into the depths until it hit the ocean floor with a resounding *clunk*. Fact was, they were losing gigs. Word got around. Club owners didn't want to risk their business to a drugged-out singer who might or might not show up for work, a singer who wore Band-Aids across the end of every finger because he had played them down to the bone the night before while on a high that numbed everything from fingertips to brain.

Another problem with meth was that he smoked constantly while on it. It had affected his voice. Did a real number on it, in fact. An occasional cigarette cough in the middle of a lyric was one thing, but when you started bending over the microphone, gagging and spitting and hacking up a lung, the audience tended to notice.

So Woody gave the drugs up for Lent, metaphorically speaking, and he was glad now he had. For one thing, he was still alive. That was a plus. For another thing, as his body gradually tuned itself up again like an engine coughing out the last drops of water from the gas tank, he found he could still, once in a while, find that euphoric state where he lost himself inside the music. It didn't happen as often now, but it happened.

And it was a blessed relief when it did.

Woody regretfully stubbed out his second Pall Mall—the one habit he could *not* break, no matter how many times he tried—drained the last drops of beer from his glass, and did a couple of flaps to his trouser leg, trying to speed up the drying process from the beer the dizzy broad had spilt there earlier. Then, after looking down at himself to make sure everything was properly in place, zipper closed, shirt tucked in, no hawks of phlegm on his boot tops, he headed back inside the bar.

Oakland. There seemed to be a whole lot of cowboy wannabe's in Oakland. Looking out across the dimly lit club was like looking at a Stetson store closing up for the night. Hats everywhere. The name of the club was Diablo's. He had worked it once, a year or so back. It wasn't a bad gig. The owner was a decent enough guy who paid nightly without a fuss, and the clientele, although pretty well sloshed at this late hour on Saturday night, were reasonably well behaved. He hadn't had to duck any flying beer bottles or watch from the stage as the patrons disassembled the place in a drunken brawl, clutching his beloved Gibson to his chest to keep it out of harm's way as the furniture went sailing past his head, which had happened more than once in other drinking establishments he had been employed in. So on the whole, it had been a good night. A good run.

In a couple of hours, he would crank up the old Chevy Suburban and head south. Maybe stop somewhere along the way to cop a few zees at the side of the road. Find a Laundromat, do his laundry. Pig out on fast food as he drove along, watching the California countryside unfurl before him, carrying him back to the place he was born, the place he had sworn he would never go back to.

He thought of that place now as he climbed the black wooden steps to the stage and settled himself on the barstool behind the two microphones, one for voice and one for guitar. He heard the noise in the crowded bar lower itself by maybe a decibel and a half as the audience turned their faces to him behind the spotlight that always looked, to Woody, like the critical eye of God, appraising him as he worked. There were drunken faces in the audience now, faces a little like his own but still receptive, once again wanting to be taken to that same place Woody always longed for, that place inside the song where mundane reality fell away and euphoria took over.

It was a nice place to be. A nice place to return to. That place inside the song was always safe. Always free from fear.

Unlike home. Unlike San Diego.

Sipping occasionally at another beer, Woody dutifully played his songs and waited for the night to end, dreading the day ahead.

Dreading the trip south.

THE HOUSE Woody grew up in still sat at the end of a dead-end street in an older section of San Diego known as Park Canyon. The area was aptly named, with one great canyon and multiple small ones slashing through the neighborhood, dividing streets, separating one house number from the next by sometimes as much as a mile. The catchphrase in Park Canyon was "never expect hot pizza," meaning most delivery drivers found themselves lost four or five times, on the average, before they accidentally stumbled on the destination they were shooting for, if they stumbled on it at all. The "under thirty minutes or your pizza is free" rule was automatically cancelled when the phone-in order came from Park Canyon.

Woody had been paying taxes and utility bills on the house for the past ten years, ever since the stabbing deaths of his mother and father in what the police had called a "robbery attempt" of the mom-and-pop store they had owned and managed since before Woody was born. His parents' murderer had never been found, and this constantly tortured Woody, sometimes causing him to erupt into such impotent bursts of rage it was all he could do to hold onto his reason. But the thought of selling the house he was raised in, the house his parents loved so much, the house he himself had loved so deeply during the years he grew up there, troubled Woody even more. He had no siblings to fight over the property, so the choice he made to do nothing at all about the house after his parents died was an easy one to make. He had sold the store, of course, and that had given him a few grand to get his life rolling, but the house he had left exactly as it was. A time capsule, holding all his memories. Both the good and the bad. But it was the good ones he wished to protect. The bad ones he could live without.

Woody's grip tightened on the Suburban's steering wheel at the first sight of the battered Dead End sign perched up ahead at the end of the street. That sign had been there for as long as Woody could remember. His was the last house on the right. Cut into the hillside, it looked like a one-story Craftsman from the street, but at the back, hidden from view by towering plumes of flowering bougainvillea that climbed into the trees and hung heavy from the eaves, the house was two-story. Back there, in an area passersby never saw, was a small lawn bordered by jade plants and roses, and beyond the border the ground plummeted away into the largest of the many canyons that intersected the area. That canyon had been Woody's playground until his thirteenth year. After that, he never entered it again.

The house on Highview Lane was surrounded by others like it. Built back in the forties, the homes were a little worse for wear but maintained as well as could be expected, considering the fact that most of the people living on the street were older now. Looking at it as he drove up, Woody could see no signs of children anywhere. No bicycles or skateboards dropped carelessly on lawns. No tires hanging from tree limbs like the ones that were popular when he was a kid. No tree houses, no sound of children's laughter rising up from the canyon beside the house where Woody and his friends had played that summer so long ago, back when Woody's body was beginning to change, when manhood was a concept he was just beginning to understand. It was during the summer of Woody's thirteenth year when the horror actually raised its head from the canyon for the first time. It screamed out its fury at the young interlopers who were trespassing on its territory, disturbing its sleep, causing it to waken, causing it to unsheathe its claws and reach out with gnarled, grasping fingers, and in doing so, giving Woody, and maybe his friends too, something to trouble their dreams for a lifetime to come.

Woody wondered, not for the first time, what had become of those friends he had been so close to that long-ago summer. Cathy. Jeremy. Chuck. And Bobby, of course. Just names now. The faces he remembered would not be the faces they wore today. Except for Bobby, they would be all grown up now, like him. All grown up and probably as far away from this place as their adult lives could carry them. Only he would be dumb enough to return here after everything that had happened, he thought. Jeez, he must be nuts.

Woody parked his Suburban on the macadam driveway and stared at the house for the first time in a decade. It didn't look too bad, actually. The two ancient palm trees, one at either side of the front porch, were still there, reminding Woody, as they had when he was a child, of towering masts flanking a sail-less ship. The yard had been kept up by a gardener Woody paid once a month by mail, and if the windows were dirty and the paint on the stucco had faded to a rather bilious olive color, which wasn't at all the cheerful seafoam green he remembered, at least the place was standing. Familiar curtains still hung in the windows, limp now with age, deceiving strangers as to the house's vacancy, and neighbors had kept a continual eye on the place for him without his requesting them to. His parents had been very popular in the neighborhood, probably because of their willingness to extend credit to those finding themselves a little short in the purse when it came time to buy family groceries at the end of every working month. Upon their deaths, many of those neighbors had come forward at the funeral to press an envelope of money into Woody's hands, paying as much as they could on their outstanding debt to help the boy, not yet twenty, through his grieving period and give him a better start on his own life, a start which his parents were no longer there to help him with.

Woody could have given that start a considerable boost by selling the property his parents maintained with such love through all the years of his growing up, but he could never quite bring himself to do it. It was not a matter of thinking he might one day return here to live in the house. That was something he never intended to do. Ever. For with all the wonderful memories still living like silent tenants inside the house, it also harbored other memories, memories he spent every waking hour of his adult life trying to forget. It was not so much the house that bore these memories to Woody, but the neighborhood. The sloping hills. The sage- and juniper-padded canyons.

He climbed from the Suburban and walked to the front porch, where he paused to take in the view to the south: the Mexican hills surrounding Tijuana, hazy in the distance. Memories flooded through him as he stood there, looking out across the sun-drenched vista spread out before him. It was a vista he remembered so well as seen through much younger eyes than the ones he looked through now.

God, Woody was suddenly so inundated with memories he could barely contain them all. He had always tried to keep those memories buried, hidden away from himself, stashed away in the darkest cellars of his mind, where he hoped they would languish, forgotten, never to see the light of day again. But he could feel them now, trying to claw their way out of the shadows—trying to gain a foothold on his consciousness. If those fears were allowed to show themselves, Woody knew, they would unleash a flood of terror he had spent a lifetime trying to lose inside his music.

Simply looking at the house now forced the truth to well up in Woody's mind. His fears were not buried at all. They never had been. They were still waiting for him, right here where he'd left them. On Highview Lane. House number 3436. The house of his childhood. The place where he had once learned what fear was all about, and the place he had been running from ever since. Until today.

He slipped the long-unused key into the front door and entered a different world. Stepping from sunlight into shadow, he could almost smell his mother's bread pudding bubbling in the oven. Could almost hear Lucy and Ricky going at it in reruns on the old RCA TV in the living room. Could almost hear his father calling out from the back bedroom, wondering where the hell his clean socks were. Could almost see his mother coming out to greet a thirteen-year-old Woody as he plodded in from school, his book bag dangling from one arm and his battered skateboard tucked under the other. Giving him a gentle peck on the cheek, ruffling his hair, telling him he needed a haircut, telling him to go wash up, dinner would be ready soon. Asking him how his day went. Making him feel loved and safe and home. Like she did every day of her life.

Woody propped his Gibson inside the front door. He would bring in the rest of his stuff later. For the moment, he stood in the doorway and breathed in the smell of the house. It smelled just as he remembered it. The air was a little staler perhaps, the place having been shut up for so long, but the aromas inside the house were even now, after all these years, as familiar to him as the scent of his own skin.

Everything had been left in situ, as archaeologists were fond of saying. The furniture still placed exactly as he remembered it. The long sofa against the far wall, his father's brown recliner set at an angle at the end of it. His mother's piano parked in the corner by the picture window where she would sometimes look out on the street as she played. The old spinet still sprouted a growth of framed snapshots across the top, like those pictures you used to see of some homesteader's shelter in the Old West, built into a prairie hillside with maybe a garden or a few stalks of corn shooting up from the roof. The fireplace, long bereft of fire, looked dusty and forlorn, desperately in need of a good cleaning. In fact, the whole house needed a good cleaning. Dust was everywhere, sprinkled across the furniture like powdered sugar on a baker's tray of goodies. His mother would have had a conniption fit if she saw the house looking this way.

In her day it had been kept spotless. Squeaky clean. The windows gleaming. The furniture polished. The carpets vacuumed daily. Everything in the exact same place it had been the day, the week, the year before.

A surge of sadness threatened to bring tears to Woody's eyes, thinking of his mother slaving away inside this house for the better part of her adult life. But she had enjoyed it, that was the funny thing. Go figure. Woody never quite understood it. It was like she was born to clean and loved every minute she spent with a rag in one hand and a bottle of 409 in the other, cleaning everything that didn't clean her first, as his father used to say.

What the hell was he doing here anyway, Woody thought, clearing the emotion from his throat. He could stay in a motel somewhere. He had money. Not a lot, but enough for that. Seemed kind of silly, though, wasting money on a motel when he had free lodgings right here at his fingertips. He didn't have to start the gig until tomorrow night, and he supposed he'd be spending every minute of his time between now and then making the house livable. He wasn't a clean freak like his mother, but he sure couldn't live in the place the way it was.

He took a peek down the long, dimly lit hallway and could almost hear Willie Nelson moaning out the lyrics of one of his old tunes from the Motorola radio that used to sit in Woody's old room, the nasal twang of Willie's voice echoing sweetly through the shadows of time and memory. "Turn that blasted thing down," Woody's mother used to rail. "I can't hear myself think!" But he never did, and she never seemed to mind.

Woody approached his room now, wondering if it would look the way he remembered it. The Batman bedspread. Posters of X-Men on the wall. Storm was his favorite. She was hot, with her snow-white hair and a body to die for. Woody used to wonder why real women never looked like that. He made the mistake of asking Cathy once, and he could still remember her rolling her eyes like he was a first class nimrod and telling him real women weren't "*drawn,* stupid."

Good old Cathy. He wondered where she was now. Wondered, too, if she still wore those heavy red pigtails dangling off either side of her head. Probably not. Now she probably had a spiky new do with a few streaks of blonde scattered through it like every other young woman on the planet. Too bad. He used to like watching those pigtails swing around her head when she spun quickly, or bounce up and down like Slinkys when she was pedaling her Sting-ray bike, trying, as always, to keep up with the guys, or better yet, outdo them completely.

She *was* one of the guys, actually. As tough as a cob, and if mad, as apt to swing a left hook as the rest of them. Until the summer of her thirteenth year, at least. After that, she wasn't quite as tough. Or as fearless. None of them were. That summer changed them all one way or another. Things were never the same after that.

Woody peered around the doorway of his old bedroom and couldn't believe his eyes. Everything was exactly the way he had left it. NASCAR, he remembered now, had replaced Batman on the bedspread along about his fifteenth year, and there it still was, a little faded, a little musty smelling, but still the same old red NASCAR spread he had conned his mother into buying for him after explaining to her that he was almost a *man* now, for God's sake, and Batman was for *kids*. "God help us when you get your driver's license," his mother had said, but she bought him the bedspread anyway. And curtains to match. They still hung on the windows overlooking the canyon.

Woody stepped to the window and gazed out. The backyard looked just as he remembered it. The grass had been recently mown. The roses on the verge of the canyon were properly manicured, adding a riotous touch of color to the landscape. The flagstone path that meandered through the lawn was neatly swept. His old swing still hung from the jacaranda tree in the corner, but the bare patch of earth under the swing, scraped raw over the years by sliding tennis shoes, had been gradually filled in by the encroaching grass until now the lawn beneath it looked as pristine as it had the day the swing was strung up by his father. It was as if nature had erased all memory of the time Woody had spent there, contentedly swinging back and forth, dragging his feet across the ground, chewing Baby Ruths and contemplating his young existence.

Before his eyes could be drawn farther out, past the lawn toward the depths of the canyon, he turned away from the window and, as an afterthought, drew the curtains closed behind him. Still, in a corner of his mind, deep down in a place where nature had *not* encroached, he heard the voices of the twins, Jeremy and Chuck, yelling out to him yet again from the stand of willow trees deep in the canyon, their voices practically squeaking with fear. "Jesus, Woody, look at the blood! It's everywhere!"

Then he heard another voice. A voice from the darkness of a summer night long ago. A voice he had once heard in this very room. A calmer voice. A whisper so filled with longing that even now, it tore at his heart like a knife. "Touch me, Woody. Touch me like I'm touching you."

Woody closed his eyes to that memory. Trying to squeeze those voices, those echoes, from his mind was like squeezing pus from a wound. But even as they faded in the distance, he knew they were not really gone. They would be back. They *always* came back. Closing a curtain wouldn't keep those voices out. And closing his eyes only made the voices louder. The trick was to concentrate on something else. Like cleaning. How many hours had he spent polishing his Gibson, or scrubbing the Suburban, or straightening motel rooms before the maid got there, in his attempt to make those voices, those memories, go away? How many times had he stood in front of a mirror and cut his own hair, usually botching it up pretty good in the process, just to have something to do to tear his mind away from the past?

For the first time, standing in his old room, standing in this place he thought he would never see again, he wondered if maybe that was why his mother would lose herself so completely in the job of keeping this house spotless. Was she trying to escape memories of her own? Did she have fears, or regrets, or true terrors of her own that only the reek of Pine-Sol could wash from her mind? Did her cleaning truly make her happy, or like himself, did it merely keep her sane? Had she known of the horrors surrounding this house, this neighborhood? Surely not. If she had, she would never have let her young son set a foot outside the door.

Shaking his head, trying to clear his mind like an Etch-a-Sketch, he strode purposely from his childhood room and headed for the door that led from the kitchen to the garage. The cleaning supplies were there, or had been once. Maybe they still were. Time to get the house in order. He was here. He might as well stay. He would clean away the cobwebs and the dust and open the windows to air out the miasma of all the empty years, and then he would go to the old market and pick up some groceries and beer. He wondered if Mr. Mendoza still owned the place. Woody remembered how the man had come to his door on the morning after his parents' funeral, hat in hand, offering condolences, and offering money too. Money for the business. Money that Woody had pretty well gone through by now, but money that, at the time, had been sorely needed. Woody had named a price, and the old Mexican gentleman had whipped out a checkbook and paid him in full. And just like that, a part of Woody's past had been no longer his own.

Amid the solid clatter of his boot heels on the three concrete steps that led from the kitchen to the garage, worn smooth by a million footsteps over the years, Woody all but clutched his chest and gasped at the sight of his father's old Fairlane sitting there. God, he had forgotten the car was still here. Old, even when Woody was young, the car had survived the ages almost unscathed thanks to Woody's dad's tender care. Woody had not sold the car after the funerals, thinking, he supposed, it might come in handy at some time or other. And here it still sat. Woody tested the driver's side door to see if it was locked, but of course it wasn't. He eased himself onto the wide bench seat and saw the keys still hanging in the ignition, right where he had left them after driving the car from the store that day after the police had gone. With a hand that seemed to be trembling, Woody turned the key and was met with total silence. The battery was as dead as Caesar, and why wouldn't it be? He sat there for a moment in the silence and ran his fingers over the dashboard, thinking of the many times his father had driven him and his friends to the library, to the movies, to the park where they would play until dark, until he returned, hours later, cheerfully blasting his horn, to pick them up.

Woody thought of the way his father sometimes, if the traffic was light, let him snuggle up beside him and steer the monstrous Fairlane down the city streets while his dad worked the pedals. He could still remember the feel of his small hands on the wheel and the car's rumbling power beneath them. Remembered craning his neck to see above the dashboard while his father draped one arm across his shoulders and let the other rest, bent, in the open window beside him. Remembered, too, the comforting smell of his father's warm body so close to his, the homey mixture of spearmint gum, tobacco, and Old Spice cologne. Scents that would forever remind Woody of the man who raised him with such love. With such gentle kindness.

It was his father, he remembered now, who had bought him his first guitar. His mother had spent hours with him as Woody sat nailed in misery and guilt to the bench beside her, trying to teach him piano, but much to her disappointment, his heart was never in it. His father had seen the boy's anguish, taken pity on him, and bought him the guitar instead. He had taken to it like a duck takes to water, his father always said, and even his mother had to agree. They paid for lessons from a man down the street, and Woody had gone faithfully to those lessons every Saturday afternoon for more than two years, until the day the man, Mr. Peters his name was, told him there was nothing more he could teach him. The man had taken the last payment of five dollars from Woody's hand, wished the boy a terse "good day," closed his front door behind him, and Woody never saw Mr. Peters again. He found out later the man had died shortly after that. Cancer, his mother said. He had been sick a long time. Woody still wondered if the lessons had stopped because the man wasn't up to teaching him anymore, or if he truly had learned everything the man had known about guitar. It was one of those questions in life that would never be answered.

Now, approaching thirty, Woody had begun to realize that life dealt out a lot of unanswered questions. Questions that simply would *never* be answered, no matter how much you fumed and fussed and fretted over them.

Woody stepped from the car, ran a hand lovingly along the sill of the door, and heard the solid, satisfying *clunk* of it slamming shut. Maybe while he was here he would get the Fairlane running again. Take it out for a spin around the neighborhood. Burn out the kinks. His father would like that, if he was still looking down from whichever celestial plane his murderer had sent him to.

The garage was stifling hot on this summer day and stuffy from being closed up so long. Woody released the simple hook and eye that held the garage door closed and peeled it up into the ceiling, creaking and groaning, to let the air and sunlight stream in for the first time in a decade, replacing the past with the present. Airing out the memories. Shedding light on the darkness of old hurts.

Illuminating Eagle, leaning against the wall in the corner.

His old bike. Woody stood there in the breeze blowing up from the canyon, staring at it with a smile creeping across his face. How many hours had he spent perched high on Eagle's seat, feeling the wind in his hair and the sun at his back, as his bike carried him to all the places his childhood led him? It had been a damn good bike. A Cannondale. His father and mother had bought it for him on his ninth birthday. It had taken a couple of years for his body to grow into the 26-inch racer, but when it did, he and the bike became inseparable. He had named her Eagle because she could *fly, dammit!* She could really *fly!* Cherry red and as sleek as a bird of prey, she had sped him down these neighborhood streets like a steed carrying its warring master into battle. Always faithful. Always there. Always ready for the next adventure.

She had even saved his life once. And not only his life, but Chuck's too, back on the day when the evil in the canyon had reached out to snatch them both from this world, as Woody's father had been snatched from it years later. He still remembered Chuck's arms around his waist, holding on for dear life, practically squeezing Woody's guts up into his throat. Remembered Chuck screaming into his ear, into the wind, "Faster! Go faster!" as desperate, running footsteps rattled the gravel behind them and cruel fingers strove to reach out to pull them from their seats and tear their young bodies to shreds.

The evil had taken human form that day, if you wanted to call it human. Jesus, he and Chuck were both screaming their heads off by the time the Cannondale bounced out of the canyon and onto Juniper Street. But they had made it. The evil did not leave the canyon, and they had known somehow it wouldn't. When they realized they were safe, that scrabbling fingers and slavering fangs were no longer reaching out behind them, groping and snapping, eager to rip them off the bike and snatch their lives away, they had howled with joy. Their victorious young voices rang bright in the summer twilight, echoing off the houses, sailing down the street. The sound of simple childish laughter that had only moments before been screams of horror.

They had turned then, with Woody still pumping the pedals like a madman and Chuck still all but strangling him, trying to hang on, as the summer-hot asphalt hummed beneath their wheels. Still screaming, in jubilation now instead of fear, they yelled taunts at the terror that no longer pursued them. And in the distance on that day, from somewhere among the sage and juniper and willow trees that stood like proud sentinels at the base of the canyon, they had heard laughter. A wicked gurgle of sound that once again burned fear into their hearts. But for the moment, they knew they were safe.

Chuck and Woody had gone to their separate homes that night, watched TV with their parents as if nothing strange had happened during the course of the day, and later they had climbed into their beds alone, far away from the comfort of each other, and only then did the terror once again raise its head to bring the darkness crashing down around them like cold black water settling over a drowning man.

Woody wondered now why neither he nor his friends had ever gone to their parents with the news that an evil presence stalked the neighborhood; that a demon lurked in the canyon, waiting to pounce from the underbrush and drag their screaming bodies into oblivion. None of their parents would have believed them, of course, because somehow Woody and his pals knew, as well as they knew their times tables, that the horror was never meant to be seen by adult eyes, was never meant to be grasped by adult minds. The terror was real enough, no two ways around that. But it was real only to them. Which didn't mean it couldn't still kill you deader than snake shit. It wasn't *their* fault there was too much reality in an adult mind to see it, that something about mortgages and paychecks and the rote of daily grown-up living could block out childish visions. And it sure as hell brought Woody and his friends closer together, knowing the danger was directed toward them alone. In battling their fear, they had no one to turn to but each other, and this made them a unit.

One.

Never again would Woody be as close to anyone as he had been to his friends on that hot, hot summer of his thirteenth year when all hell broke loose and fear was no longer something you caught a glimpse of on a movie screen, but a real live rampaging beast, all fangs and snapping jaws and a mind gnawed by malice and madness that was just as goddamn real as you were.

Poor Eagle. She was looking fairly pathetic these days. Her tires were flat, one of her spokes had popped out of the rim, and she was covered with the same patina of grimy dust as everything in the house. A clothespin was still clamped to the frame beside the back wheel but the Bicycle playing card it once held against the spokes had at some time during the course of the ensuing years drifted to the floor. It had all been illusion, of course, but that playing card had given a pretty good semblance of motorized speed when it *bbrapped* against the spokes, especially when Eagle was fairly flying beneath him. Woody picked the card up now and looked at it. The ace of spades.

Shit. That wasn't a good sign.

He let it fall from his fingers and, pushing all thoughts of Eagle and that long-ago summer from his mind, continued his search for cleaning supplies, occasionally turning a leery eye to that ace of spades lying on the garage floor.

He found everything he needed, and after peeling off his sweat-stained shirt and tossing it into a corner, Woody walked back through the kitchen door and set about the awesome task of making the house livable.

As always, the act of cleaning cleared his mind. By the time he finished three hours later, he was surprised to hear himself humming. There might even have been a smile on his face as he looked around at the place, freed now from the residue of ten empty years. Once again, the furniture shone. With all the windows open, the stale air had been swept away, leaving behind only the comforting smells of Lemon Pledge and Comet and the sweet scent of roses wafting in through the back bedroom window, as it had in the days of his childhood.

In his parents' bedroom, he even imagined a whiff of his mother's favorite perfume, White Shoulders, reaching out across the years to comfort him. But it was just his imagination, of course. It had to be. There was nothing left of his mother inside this house now but her memory.

Yet somehow, at the moment, memory seemed to be enough.

AT SOME point between then and now, while Woody's youthful dreams were settling into stark realities, his father's old store had undergone a change of its own. STILES MARKET was no longer painted on the wall above the front door. Now, high above the street, in Day-Glo neon, it proclaimed itself to be JAYCEES. Woody didn't know what the hell "Jaycees" was supposed to mean, but it certainly wasn't the store he remembered. As much as he hated to admit it, the place looked considerably better than it had when his father ran it. It even boasted a butcher shop now, according to the sign, something his father had often talked about but never seemed to find the time or money to initiate.

Woody wasn't more than two steps inside the front door when Mr. Mendoza, considerably heavier now than he was ten years ago, as if maybe he had been hanging around the potato chip aisle too long, came out of nowhere and started pumping Woody's hand up and down for all of two full minutes while, in his melodic Hispanic accent, he welcomed Woody back to the neighborhood. He dragged Woody through the store, proudly pointing out all the changes he had made over the years. He had added not only a butcher shop, but also beer and wine and a separate little pharmacy area, and the back of the store had been extended out another ten feet. While Mr. Mendoza was obviously proud of the improvements, Woody thought something had been lost in the renovation. It took him a moment to put his finger on what it was, exactly, that was lost, but when he did, he summed it up in one word. Heart.

Jaycee's was no longer a simple mom-and-pop store, where people could come not only to shop, but to chat. To visit. To show off their kids and gab about the weather. Now, between the electronic scanners at the checkout counters, the sterile, air-conditioned air, and the efficiently laid out aisles, there was only a sense of commerce. All personality had been swept away. Now the place felt like every other supermarket Woody had ever walked through. Cold, impersonal, and slightly desperate in its desire to lure every shopping dollar from the pocket of every patron that was sucked through the automatic front doors. Woody couldn't imagine any one of these check-out girls in their crisp yellow uniforms reaching out to the customer with a comforting hand and saying, as he once heard his father say, "That's okay, Mrs. Chen. Pay me when you can. I'll not go out of business over a pound of bacon and a dozen eggs."

Mr. Mendoza seemed to sense Woody's disappointment.

"Times change, hey, son? The days of the little store are over. Now we have to compete with the big boys up the street. If your papa was still here, he would understand."

And Woody supposed he would. Business was business.

Too bad.

With a final handshake, Mr. Mendoza scurried off to the front of the store, where one of the clerks was screaming over the screeching intercom for a price check on disposable diapers, and Woody set off in search of what he needed. He gathered up enough food to last a few days, grabbed a 12-pack of beer from the massive cooler on the back wall, and after paying for his purchases with a MasterCard, he headed back out into the California twilight.

Away from the store, away from a past that had already left him far behind, Woody steered the Suburban along the old neighborhood streets, and here, in the growing darkness of evening, he felt more at peace. On the surface, the neighborhood hadn't changed that much. Every house was still familiar to Woody. Even the faces of some of the people he saw meandering along the sidewalks tugged at his memory. They were older faces now, but, like the houses, still familiar. He knew if he put his mind to it he would be able to add a few names to those faces, but he didn't really try. It was enough to know *everything* hadn't changed while he had been away.

As he drove down Juniper Street, approaching his turnoff on Highview Lane, he pointed out to himself every house where his friends had lived that summer. The twins, Chuck and Jeremy, in that white monstrosity on the corner. Cathy in the house right next to it with the three lean cypress trees towering at the edge of the lawn. Those trees always seemed to be swaying, whether there was a breeze or not, as if trying to keep their precarious balance on the planet. And on Highview after he made the turn, only two blocks down from his own, was Bobby's house.

Good old Bobby. He had been battling his own demons back then. With alcoholic parents who seemed to be at each other's throats from the moment they woke up in the morning, day after day after day, Bobby had spent as many nights in Woody's house as he had ever spent in his own. They were almost brothers, him and Bobby. Even Woody's mother had said so. She would have been shocked out of her socks to learn that he and Bobby had become considerably *more* than brothers during that summer of their thirteenth year, when puberty raised its ugly head and brought them closer together than they could ever have imagined. Woody still wondered at times, when sadness and memory combined to take him to that place he was always trying to escape, if he and Bobby would still be together today in the way they had been that long-ago summer.

The summer Bobby would not survive.

That summer, awakening manhood and all the rampaging desires that came with it were suddenly replaced by grief and outrage and a sense of loss so stunning it all but swept Woody away in its wake.

Woody's parents had tried to comfort him through the aftermath of Bobby's death, explaining to him that sometimes the world was a cruel place to live, where death sometimes reached out and snatched away even the youngest, the most promising. But there was no way for them to know it was not only the loss of friendship Woody mourned that summer, but the loss of so much more. Woody and Bobby had stirred truths in each other that transcended friendship. Love had been born that summer, and as quickly taken away. And Woody still, sixteen years later, ached with the loss of it.

By the time Woody was once again parked outside his parents' house—he would never think of it as his own, only theirs—his sadness had crashed down around him like a pall. Again and again he was forced to swallow the emotion that threatened to spill out of him, blinking back tears as he stowed the groceries in the kitchen. A weariness of body unlike any he had ever known made him long for sleep, but he knew mere sleep wouldn't be enough to still the memories. It never was.

He popped a beer and carried it through the darkening house, sipping as he went, surveying all the work he had done during the afternoon, trying to think of himself as the sole proprietor of this fairly expensive piece of California real estate, this house that after only a few hours of cleaning was once again as he remembered it. But in every room, through every shadowed doorway, the sound of his parents' absence rang out like an empty echo.

This was no longer his home. He was an interloper, trespassing on the past, intruding into a place that was no longer meant to feel his presence.

And as he sat in the darkness in his father's recliner, drinking his second, and then third, beer, he felt the deepening night outside pressing against the walls, weighing heavily on the roof over his head, gnawing away at the stucco and tile. In his imagination, he could feel the darkness trying to worm its way into his very heart, bringing with it all the memories he had desperately tried to keep at bay for so many years.

But with the fourth beer, Woody's memories abated. His fear, and much of his sadness, left him. Alcohol, like music, could sometimes take him to a place where old hurts couldn't enter, and he was grateful for the comforting emptiness it brought him once again.

A full moon now softened the darkness inside the house with tinges of blue. Through the windows, that big fat moon watched Woody roam from room to room, following along behind him like a trailing spotlight, illuminating his footsteps, dispelling the shadows that, without the beer inside him, might have sent him running from the house forever.

Woody stepped through the back door and felt the night breeze on his face. He could hear soft wind rustling the willows down in the canyon, stirring up the smell of sage and honeysuckle and flowering cactus as well. Scents Woody remembered clearly from his youth. How many times had he stood here with his father, watching the sun set and the moon rise, both at the same time? An anomaly of nature, his father once told him, that some people in other parts of the world never got a chance to witness.

Woody awkwardly slipped his adult body into his childhood swing beneath the jacaranda tree. He could smell its blossoms overhead. In daylight those blossoms were a beautiful blue, as deep as an evening sky. In darkness they were only a scent, invisible to the eye, lost in the evening shadows. The swing creaked beneath his weight. What should have been smooth earth beneath him, but was now grass regrown after his years of absence, felt strange and out of place under his feet.

He pushed himself into a lazy arc, gently swinging back and forth in the darkness. The weight and motion of his body brought a gentle fall of jacaranda blossoms raining down around him as his hands clutched the rusted chains that held him in place.

Woody closed his eyes and, as he had as a child, imagined himself in flight. He was a hawk, soaring high above the canyon, looking down on the world splayed out beneath him, surveying this dominion that was his and his alone.

The wind on his face blew away the years, the soothing motions of the swing rocked away his fears, and once again he was thirteen, with Keds on his feet and patches his mother had sewn on the knees of his jeans. It was the beginning of summer vacation. With nothing but freedom staring him in the face for the next three months, Woody thought of all the ways he and his friends would spend their time. Movies. Bike rides. Days at the park, wandering through the museums, exploring the zoo. The possibilities were endless. With no schoolwork to worry about, his days would be filled with only laughter and adventure and the comfort of good friends.

In the moonlight now, years away from that last remarkable summer, a smile lit Woody's face as he sat swinging in the cool night air. The beer inside him smoothed out the rough edges of memory he didn't wish to see.

But the other memories, the *good* memories, were scooped up in his hawk's talons and carried to that private place where he always kept them neatly laid out, on display, ready to be sorted through and savored whenever the mood took him, like favorite pieces of art or well-loved books.

Jacaranda blossoms continued to drift down around him, shaken from the tree by the weight of his swinging body. They brushed his face in the darkness with the softness of butterfly wings as his mind carried him back to his thirteenth summer.

The summer of best friends and days that never lasted quite long enough. Days when laughter rang through these canyons like crystal bells, until the terror started. When even the nights in the midst of that terror were filled with wonders that pushed the horror of the Willow Man away, at least for a little while.

Nights with Bobby.

They had come together so slowly, he and Bobby. He wondered now how it had all begun. And then he remembered. It was the first week of vacation. Summer lay before them all like an endless, unknown road, waiting to be explored. Cathy, Chuck and Jeremy, and he and Bobby had all stepped fearlessly onto that road and been swept away to a destination that, but for the innocence of youth, might have destroyed them all.

As it was, it destroyed only one. But that came later.

It was the beginning of their journey together that Woody remembered now. Not just him and Bobby, but all of them. It began with the bones Cathy found among the willows. Human bones. Woody still remembered how they shone like porcelain in the sunlight.

They were almost… beautiful.

CHAPTER TWO

CHUCK AND Jeremy weren't exactly *twin* twins. Jeremy had a little birthmark under his left eye, almost in the shape of a teardrop, so if you were looking at the boys head-on it was easy to tell them apart. Except now. Now, the two were covered with so much gunk and crap, as they all were, that they might not even be twins at all, or even the same species. Who the hell could tell?

"Which of you is which?" Cathy asked. "I'm getting a headache trying to figure it out."

"Who the hell are *you*?" Bobby asked, referring to the fact that Cathy was just as filthy as the twins, and if it wasn't for her long hair, not red now but pretty much the color of mud and hanging off her head like dirty seaweed, she might have been Woody or Bobby or *anybody*. Of course, Bobby wasn't in a position to be throwing stones either, since he was as crudded up as everybody else.

Chuck's mouth opened up in a parody of a scream. "My God, she's a *girl*! Look at those little tits poking up through the crap on her shirt!"

Everybody howled with laughter. Everybody but Cathy. She seemed to find her burgeoning breasts, not yet much more than a couple of gentle swells with pencil erasers at the end but promising to be a whole lot more one of these days, a matter for intense embarrassment. It was hard to be one of the guys when your tits were growing *out* quicker than you were growing *up*.

She reached out a finger and wiped a smear of mud from beneath her tormentor's eye, and seeing no birthmark there, said, "Fuck you, Chuck."

Chuck gave her a leering wink, the effect of which was pretty much lost in the sea of mud from which it came, and said. "Okay, Toots. Spread 'em."

Cathy rolled her eyes. "Oh, please. I prefer taller men. You barely come up to my—"

"Tits?" Bobby offered, grinning.

And in truth, Chuck and Jeremy were both a head shorter than Cathy, than *any* of them. While the others were growing taller almost daily, the twins' pubescent growth spurts seemed to be stuck in a holding pattern. It didn't mean they couldn't talk a good game, though.

Cathy settled back in a casual stance, arms folded across her muddy chest—and maybe hiding it as well—studying the twins like one of their teachers at Cedars Junior High looking down on a couple of rather slow and particularly ugly students.

"Do either of you even *have* pubic hair yet, or are you going to be bald down there forever?"

"Maybe we shave it. Ever think of that? Maybe we shave it to make our dicks look longer." That was Jeremy. He was just as embarrassed about his lack of pubic hair as Cathy was about her growing tits, and Cathy and everybody else knew it.

"Yeah, right," Cathy said. "If your dicks were any shorter, you'd be peeing down the back of your legs. Hair has nothing to do with it."

"Yeah, well, if your tits were any bigger, you'd fall flat on your face."

"If your dicks were any shorter, they'd be pimples on your asses."

"If your tits were any bigger, they'd have their own zip code."

Bobby groaned. "And if any of youse guys's mouths were any bigger, we'd all be in the dark right now." Then he turned to Chuck and said, "Why do you need to make your dick look longer? Good Lord, son, how teeny *is* it?"

"Oh, would everybody please shut up!" Cathy said. "Let's finish this and go home. I've got mud creeping up the crack of my ass, and it's not a good feeling. I need a bath."

"You *always* need a bath."

"*Shut the hell up.*"

Woody plopped himself down on the trunk of a fallen tree that had been lying at the bottom of the canyon for as long as he could remember and surveyed the work they had done so far. It was not an encouraging sight.

Taking their cue from the Watusi tribe, or so Chuck had said, they were trying to erect a mud hut at the base of the canyon where they could go to have a little privacy. Sort of a clubhouse, if you will. Why they needed privacy, they weren't quite sure, but it sounded like a good idea at the time.

With old latticework they had swiped from a neighbor's backyard, and fence posts they had glommed from Home Depot because they were as crooked as a dog's hind leg and therefore unfit to be sold to the credit-card-carrying public, they had built a framework for their mud hut, which, in its skeletal phase, didn't look too bad really. It was the mud part that was giving them problems. The Watusis just sort of patted it on, Chuck had explained. Of course, they had cow shit to add to the mixture, so maybe that gave it a better consistency. Who the heck knew? It wasn't until Bobby thought of adding grass to the recipe, smooshing it all together with his hands like Woody's mom mixing a meat loaf, that they finally got the crap to stick to the latticework.

What they finally ended up with was the ugliest fucking structure Woody had ever seen in his life. It listed to one side because of the damn crooked fence posts at the corners, and it looked like it was growing hair, something the twins might have been envious of if you could see their faces through the muck they were plastered with, which you couldn't.

"It looks like it's covered with some sort of fungus," Jeremy noted. "We've got an aunt with a big mole on her face with all these little black hairs sticking out of it that looks exactly like this clubhouse. Except Aunt Gertrude's mole is bigger."

"Maybe it won't look so bad when it dries."

"Maybe it'll look worse."

"What are we supposed to use for a roof?"

All eyes turned to Chuck, the resident architect.

"Thatching," he said. "The Watusis use thatching."

"Great."

"No, it'll be the easiest part. We just tie bunches of long grass together with string, and then sort of lay them in a circular pattern across the top. No problem."

"No problem, he says. This whole project has been a problem from the very beginning."

"No, really. Watch."

Chuck gathered together an armful of reeds sticking out of the drying mud at the base of the canyon, the mud being left over from the last good rain they'd had, which probably wouldn't be repeated for the next six months, and tried to pull them from the ground. They wouldn't budge. Their roots must have gone all the way to Taipei. So Woody pulled out his trusty pocketknife and proceeded to saw off the reeds at ground level, laying them in Chuck's outstretched arms. When Chuck had a good-sized bundle, Jeremy pulled a Duncan yo-yo from his pocket and chewed off the string like a beaver gnawing through a tree limb, then handed the string to Woody, who handed it to Chuck. Chuck laid the reeds on the ground and tied them in two places, after gnawing the string in two again. The whole process took a good ten minutes.

When he finished, Chuck looked down proudly at the bundle of what was now a reasonably good replica of thatching lying at his feet.

"See?" he said.

Cathy rolled her eyes. "Jesus, Chuck, we're going to need about a hundred of those. Anybody got another hundred yo-yos and a couple of years to kill?"

Chuck eyed her with a withering glare. "The yo-yo was a matter of expediency, cupcake. Somebody must have a roll of string lying around."

"Don't call me cupcake."

"I do," Bobby said.

"I hate it when you call me cupcake."

"Yeah. Me, too," Woody said.

"Good," Chuck said, ignoring Cathy completely. "Your house is closest, Woody. Go get it."

Woody looked down at himself and saw nothing but mud from his clavicle to his Keds. "Like this? My mom would shoot me dead for walking into the house like this."

"Well, shit. Okay. I'll tell you what. We'll cut down all the reeds we need to thatch the roof and lay them on the ground until we get the string. The mud needs to dry before we thatch the thing anyway. Maybe the reeds need to dry, too. Who the hell knows? We'll finish it up tomorrow after Miss Prissypants brings the fucking string."

"For somebody with a teensy weensy pecker you sure talk about fucking a lot," Cathy noted.

Chuck's eyes narrowed to two muddy slits. "Shut up and cut the grass."

"Gotcha."

An hour later, they had maybe enough reeds in a pile to thatch not only the clubhouse, but a goodly section of Baja as well. They were just about to call it quits, thankfully, since every one of them was about as tired as they had ever been in their lives, when Cathy screamed from the bushes about a hundred yards up the canyon.

"Oh, crap, a rattlesnake," Woody mumbled to the others. He had seen a rattler here a couple of years back, and to this day, he still watched where he was stepping.

But it wasn't a rattlesnake.

"Look," Cathy said, pointing to the ground after the others ran up beside her. "Bones."

"What died?" Bobby asked, moving closer to get a better look. "A coyote?"

"Not unless it was wearing a wristwatch," Cathy said, as calmly as could be expected under the circumstances.

"Holy shit, it's an arm!"

And it was. A human arm with a human hand, or the bones of one, sticking off the end of it. Where the hand bones met the arm bone, a Timex circled what once would have been a wrist.

"Jeez Louise, is it still ticking?"

Bobby gave a nervous little laugh that seemed to fall dead in the silent air. "I think you're missing the big picture here, Chuck. That's a human arm laying there. Who gives a shit if the watch is still ticking?"

"Well, they're supposed to take a licking and keep on tick—"

"*Shut the hell up!*"

They all stood in silence, staring down at the pathetic arm, which was really no longer an arm at all, poking out of the bushes. On closer inspection it was determined the wristwatch was as dead as the arm, tickless and silent, and somehow this made the sight of the fleshless arm even sadder.

Jeremy cleared his throat. "You don't suppose the rest of the body is in those weeds, do you?"

"Go see," Cathy said. "I'll just wait right here."

"I'd rather not."

"Me either."

"Oh, for Christ's sake," Bobby said. "Scootch over."

And after taking in a lungful of oxygen to give himself courage, he poked his head through the tall bushes and took a gander inside. Woody could see Bobby's shoulders tensing up like maybe he was about to puke or something, and then he withdrew his head from the reeds.

"Well? What did you see?" they all asked.

Bobby was looking a little pale under the mud on his face, or Woody imagined he was. "Yep. He's all there. Or most of him is."

"What do you mean, 'most of him' is?"

"His head is missing."

Jeremy, always clinical, asked, "How do you know it's a man?"

Bobby shook his head and pointed to the Timex. "Man's watch."

"Could be a lezbo," Chuck said. "They wear men's watches."

"Brilliant, Holmes," Woody said. "So it's not a man, it's a lesbian. Who the hell *cares*? It's still a *body*! The question is, what are we going to do about it? We can't just leave it there. We'll be tripping over the damn thing for the rest of the summer."

It was Jeremy who stated the obvious. "I guess we'd better call the cops."

"Shouldn't we tell my mom first?" Woody asked.

"Why?" Cathy asked. "You think she killed him? Or her?"

"No, but—"

"Yes," Bobby said. "Tell your mom. Let her call the cops. This'll probably ruin her whole day, you know. It'll interrupt her cleaning."

There were a few nervous giggles. Everybody knew of Woody's mom's passion for housework and constantly ragged him about it. The thought of someone actually *enjoying* cleaning was not something any of them could ever quite get their heads around.

"Maybe we'd better hose ourselves off before we do anything drastic," Cathy said. "I don't want to be seen on the five o'clock news looking like this."

"Wow. You think we'll be on the news?"

"Who the heck knows? Maybe we'll be heroes. Maybe that's somebody famous laying there."

"Famous people don't wear Timexes."

"Famous people don't usually die behind my house either," Woody said. "Come on, let's get the heck out of here."

In single file, with a few uneasy glances back at the bones they were leaving behind, they scrambled up the steep canyon wall to the roses that bordered Woody's backyard. Once there, Woody lined his friends up like a bunch of suspects on *Dragnet* and hosed them down with the sweeping action of a fireman spraying water on a burning building, squirting the water back and forth with the garden hose until the lawn was muddy and everybody was screaming at him through chattering teeth to knock it the hell off, they were clean *enough* already!

Turnabout was fair play, so they all took turns spraying Woody next, and having so much fun doing it they almost forgot about the dead body lying back there in the bushes. Almost.

Cleaned up, everybody looked a little better, although the shock on their faces from finding a human skeleton in what they considered to be their own private playground was considerably more noticeable with the mud washed off. It had crept back at about the same time Woody turned off the hose. Every pair of young eyes now looked, once again, a bit stunned by the immensity of the whole thing. People found dead bodies all the time on TV and seemed to take it in stride. Real troopers. In real life it was a trifle more disconcerting. Damned upsetting, actually. Creepy.

Woody studied his friends standing before him. They were all the same age as Woody, but the twins, as noted, were small for their age, and even Cathy sometimes admitted they were as cute as buttons— which they hated to hear, and which was probably why she said it. Pale and tow-headed with slender frames, they stood there now dripping water and looking positively charming doing it. A couple of cherubs. Each had about a pound of wire inside his mouth. Their father was a dentist and had a thing for straight teeth, which the twins apparently were not born with but he was determined to give them anyway. Lightning was a rarity in southern California, but when it did come, the twins scattered like rabbits for the nearest shelter, figuring, maybe rightly, that with all the metal in their heads, they were little more than a pair of blond lightning rods waiting for God to incinerate their asses the first chance He got. Like maybe He was up there skeet shooting or something, and they were targets too enticing to ignore.

Cathy, also dripping wet at the moment, had a sprinkling of freckles across the bridge of her nose to go with her red hair. Woody had a sneaking suspicion one day he was going to blink and the next thing he knew Cathy would be standing there in front of them all looking absolutely beautiful. Even now she cleaned up pretty good, as his mother always said about people she found attractive. Through her wet shirt, the nubs on her chest were really poking up, probably from the icy water, and Woody looked away, embarrassed. He thought about playing the true gentleman and offering her his own shirt to cover herself with, but he figured this would only embarrass her more, so he did nothing. Embarrassing Cathy could be a dangerous endeavor. She was as apt to knock your lights out as she was to give you a sisterly peck on the cheek and say thank you. The dangerous part was not knowing which it would be, and either option—being kissed by a girl you thought of as one of the guys or having your brains scrambled by a girl who shouldn't be able to beat you up, but could—was equally humiliating.

Bobby's was the one calm face in the bunch. Nothing much rattled Bobby. He had seen so much warfare in his own household, with his mom and dad drinking themselves into oblivion six nights out of the week and usually beating the crap out of each other in the process, that nothing much fazed him anymore. He was staring at Woody now with those calm brown eyes of his, and just looking at them made Woody calm as well. With his clothes dripping around him, Woody could see Bobby's body had changed in the past few months. He was no longer a boy. He was a man. Or pretty darn close to one. His shoulders were broadening, his legs lengthening. The contours of his face, with the healthy dark complexion that came from having a mother who was Mexican, had sharpened lately, but not in a bad way. Of course, none of this was exactly an epiphany for Woody. Bobby spent more nights in Woody's bed than he did in his own. Being 13-year-old boys, with a healthy new interest in all things sexual, they had even whacked off together a few times, so it wasn't like they hadn't seen each other's bodies before.

Woody's feelings for Bobby were complex and growing more so as time went on. Their friendship was as solid as a friendship could be, but there was another layer to it Woody hadn't yet been able to put his finger on, and that other layer was pretty confusing at times. It continually reared up out of nowhere and filled Woody's mind with so many conflicting emotions he couldn't begin to sort them out. He suspected Bobby sometimes felt the same confusion he did, but they never seemed to get around to talking about it. Or maybe they were just afraid to. The confusion usually came about late at night when they were alone in Woody's bed, and sometimes Woody was glad for the darkness of his room. That darkness kept a lot of things hidden from them both, things safer to contemplate in the shadows.

On the surface however, in daylight as they were now, things were less complicated. Yet even in the sunlight, longings sometimes found their way to the surface. Longings Woody didn't understand and didn't want to. But they were, for the most part, easily hidden within the camaraderie among friends. The banter, the joking, the chaotic exuberance of youth, all were a welcome shield for Woody. And maybe for Bobby as well. It made them normal. It gave them time to postpone the confrontation of their awakening feelings for one more hour, one more day. Putting off the inevitable, maybe, but putting it off nevertheless. In a group, with Cathy and the twins running interference, their lives were as simple as any other kid's on the planet. And Woody liked it that way. Or thought he did.

Woody's mother was forever calling Bobby's mother and making arrangements for Bobby to stay over. She knew what Bobby's home life was like, and she tried to spare him as much of it as she could. Woody figured his folks would probably adopt Bobby if somebody actually drew up adoption papers, but no one ever did, so Bobby remained a frequent, damned near permanent, houseguest.

Bobby smiled at Woody now, and something in the way Bobby was staring at him made Woody stop what he was doing and stare back for about five seconds. Their eyes couldn't have been locked any tighter if someone had sewn them together with thread. The connection was broken when Bobby gave him a little wink, as if to say "Well hell, let's get this show on the road."

So Woody girded his proverbial loins and headed for the back door. He still wasn't crazy enough to walk dripping wet onto his mother's sparkling kitchen floor, so he politely knocked at the screen door like a vacuum cleaner salesman instead of the kid who actually lived here. A kid with reddish hair and his own spray of freckles, but a soft stubble, too, beginning to blossom on his face as manhood crept ever nearer. His shoulders, like Bobby's, had broadened, and his body was leaner now than it had been only a few months before. He was growing up, and he was growing up handsome. Everybody said so. Even Bobby. And when those words came from Bobby's mouth, Woody wasn't embarrassed by it at all, like he was when his mother said it. He *wanted* Bobby to think he was handsome. Just as he thought Bobby was handsome. Somehow that was important. It meant something. He wasn't sure why, but it meant a great deal.

The look on his mother's face when she pushed the door open and gazed down at them all standing there in front of her was everything Woody had expected it would be. First came shock, then came a sort of weary resignation.

She held her hand out as if checking for rain, and when she didn't feel any, a wry grin twisted her face.

"Fall in the ocean?" she asked, looking at each of their dripping faces in turn. "Or are you all just perspiring heavily?"

This was his mother's way of being funny. Sometimes it worked. This time it didn't. She seemed to sense this quickly, and the grin fell from her face like the last dead leaf of autumn dropping from a tree.

"What's wrong?" she asked. "What have you kids been up to?"

The day pretty much went downhill from there.

THE POLICE were there for hours, questioning each of them in turn, poking through the underbrush, trying to calm Woody's mother, who was having some sort of emotional episode over the whole thing, as if she actually knew the dead guy and had been wondering for years where the heck he had gone to. Woody's father even closed up the store and came rushing home to get in on the excitement, although most of his time was spent trying to calm his wife, which he did so sweetly and with such patience that Woody felt a bursting renewal of love for the man.

A van from the coroner's office carted the bones away along about sunset. They never did find the skull. Woody supposed he'd be stumbling over it one of these days, and he wasn't much looking forward to *that*.

A news truck did show up, and a woman with a notepad asked the cops a few questions, but she never approached Woody or his friends and they were a little offended by the slight. Jesus, where was the cameraman? Where was the hoopla? Dead bodies didn't turn up every day of the week, did they? It seemed their fifteen minutes of fame, which Andy Warhol said everybody enjoyed once in their life, would have to be postponed for another day. The high point of the afternoon came when the news lady was driving away and Chuck gave her the finger from the driveway. She smiled sweetly at him through the car window and gave him the finger in return, and that pretty well summed up the media's reaction to the whole thing. The next day there was a two-inch blurb in the *San Diego Union-Tribune* about human remains being found in Park Canyon, but no names were mentioned, and that was it. That night on the local evening news they saw a story about a dog who had found its way home from three hundred miles away when the dog's owner stupidly drove off, leaving it stranded in the desert, but nary a mention was made of the skeleton in the canyon. Good grief, what did it take to get a little airtime? Woody and his friends figured the media should get its priorities in order, and until they did, they swore never to watch the news again.

Of course, Woody didn't know it at the time, but it wouldn't be until later that night, under the cover of darkness and his Batman bedspread, that the real news story would be written. A scoop to beat all scoops, and one Woody hadn't been expecting at all.

Or maybe he had. Maybe he had been waiting his whole life for it, but simply wouldn't admit it.

Anyway, when it came, he accepted it as easily as he had ever accepted anything in all his thirteen years of living.

Love, it seemed, had a way of making itself accepted, whether you really wanted it to or not.

WOODY'S MOM, with the help of three glasses of wine forced on her by Woody's father, had calmed down considerably by the time ten o'clock rolled around. When she spoke, her words had the least little slur to them, which made Woody and Bobby grin at each other from where they were lying in the middle of the living room floor watching the closing credits of *Star Trek*. Since school was now officially over for the summer, they were enjoying their extra hour of TV time in the evening.

"You boys get to bed now," Woody's mom said. "It's been a long day. And try not to find any more dead bodies as you wend your way down the hall." Woody's dad chuckled at that. "And don't forget to brush your teeth," she added, as if even in the midst of skeletons and death, oral hygiene was the thing you really had to watch out for.

As the boys started to leave the room, she reached out and took Bobby's hand. "I called your mom, Bobby. She's not feeling well so I told her you could stay here for a few days. She said she'd put some clothes for you in a bag and leave it on the front porch. I guess maybe she doesn't want you to see her in the shape she's in."

"Okay," Bobby said. "Thanks, Mrs. Stiles."

"You boys sleep tight," Woody's father said from his recliner, laying his paper in his lap and looking at them over his reading glasses. "Good night."

"Night, sir."

"Night, Dad. Night, Mom."

Woody had his own bathroom. After peeling off their clothes, he and Bobby stood there in their white BVDs, taking turns spitting toothpaste into the sink and gargling in unison to the tune of "Jingle Bell Rock." They weren't sure why. It sure as hell wasn't Christmas. They had showered earlier because Woody's mom wouldn't let them within five feet of the dinner table until they did, figuring maybe dead bodies were simply seething *cauldrons* of germs and creeping bacteria that could hurl them all into the very arms of death from some sort of pestilence or other. Even she had taken a long hot shower, and she hadn't come within three hundred yards of the dead guy.

As usual, you could barely breathe in Woody's bathroom. It reeked of bleach. Woody's mom had a thing about bleach. Thought it could kill just about anything. Woody figured she was probably right, since it was damn near killing him and Bobby. He stared at their reflections in the mirror over the sink through fume-induced tears and wished for about the thousandth time his bathroom had a window they could open up and air the place out.

They got out of there as quickly as they could and closed the bedroom door behind them, sealing themselves in for the night.

Woody dragged a few horror comics off his nightstand, thinking maybe they could read them together, but he quickly slapped them back down. They had *real* horrors to discuss now. They didn't need to read about them.

Woody swept his bedspread from the bed and they climbed in side by side, just as they always did. Woody propped his head on his hand and looked over at Bobby lying next to him. Bobby had his hands behind his head, staring up at the ceiling. Woody thought the hair in Bobby's armpits was looking pretty lush these days. As was his own. Only his was a lighter color. He could even see a little trail of dark hair curling up from the waistband of Bobby's BVDs toward his belly button. He supposed they really were growing up. Next year they'd be in high school. Jesus, who would have thunk it could happen so quickly? Their lives were practically *over* already, and it seemed like they had just gotten started.

Through the bedroom wall, they could hear Woody's parents getting ready for bed, so when they spoke, their voices were lowered accordingly.

"Who do you suppose he was?" Bobby asked, still staring straight up, lost in thought.

"The dead guy?"

"Yeah. The dead guy."

Woody sighed. "You heard the cops. It was probably some homeless man who wondered into the canyon and just died there. Maybe he was sick."

"Then where was his head?"

"Maybe it got washed away in the winter rains. The bottom of that canyon is like a river when it rains hard. That head could have rolled all the way to the ocean like a bowling ball, swept along in the water. It could be lying on a beach in Mexico by now. Maybe a bunch of Mexican kids are playing volleyball with it. Who the hell knows? Poor guy."

"I don't think he was sick," Bobby said, rolling to his side and looking into Woody's face from a distance of about six inches. He was so close Woody could smell his breath. Smelled like toothpaste. Something stirred in Woody at the nearness of Bobby, but the stirring was lost in more immediate mysteries.

"You don't?"

"Naw. I think he was murdered."

"You mean you think somebody *sawed* off his head?"

"Yeah. That's exactly what I think."

"Jeez. That's creepy."

"No shit."

Woody thought about this for a minute. "So what do you suppose happened to the murderer?" he finally asked.

Bobby blinked. "That's the other creepy thing. Maybe he's still out there."

Woody grinned. "The guy's been dead for years. What makes you think the murderer's still hanging around? And if he is, don't you think we would have seen him by now?"

"Not necessarily. We didn't find the body until today, did we? He could have been watching us from the bushes. Maybe he was about to saw *Cathy's* head off when she screamed. Maybe her scream scared him away."

"Cathy would have beat the crap out of him. His murdering days would be over real quick if he tried to mess with Cathy."

"Yeah. She'd saw *his* head off."

"Then cram it up his ass."

They both laughed.

"Look," Bobby said, brushing his hand across Woody's chest. "You're getting some little hairs there."

Woody looked down at himself. Bobby's hand felt warm against his skin. Felt good. "I know. My dad has a hairy chest. Maybe I will too."

Bobby let his hand rest on Woody's chest for a second, then pulled it away and tucked it under the side of his face. "You think we'll always be friends?" he asked. "I mean, do you think that when we grow up, we'll move away from each other and maybe never see each other again?"

"Not if we don't want to. We'll be grown-ups. We can go anywhere we want. We could even get an apartment together if we wanted. Who's going to stop us?"

"What if we got married?"

"Is this a proposal?"

Bobby laughed. "No. I mean what if we married girls someday. Then we couldn't be together, could we?"

"I suppose not."

"I wouldn't like that," Bobby said.

Woody smiled at him. "No. I guess I wouldn't like it much either."

Bobby smiled back. "Good. Then we won't."

A comfortable silence settled over them. In the next room, they could hear the squeak of bedsprings. A lot of squeaks. A veritable *ocean* of squeaks.

Woody grinned. "They're at it again." Woody couldn't even count the times he and Bobby had lain there in his bed listening to his parents getting it on in the other room. His folks tried to be quiet about it, he supposed, but those damn squeaking bedsprings always gave them away.

Oddly, the sound of Woody's parents making love in the next room always seemed to sadden Bobby. Usually Bobby's parents were too mad to make love. Or too busy screaming at each other. Or too drunk.

"Your parents love each other, don't they?" Bobby asked.

Woody smirked. For some reason he was always a little embarrassed by those nightly sounds coming from the other room. "Either that or they just like to screw."

This time Bobby didn't smile back. "Don't make fun of it. I think it's beautiful."

"Well, yeah. I guess maybe I do too."

"Ever wonder what it's like? Making love to another person?"

"You mean instead of just whacking off?"

"Yeah."

Woody rolled over onto his back and tucked his hands behind his head like Bobby had earlier. He stared up at the ceiling, thinking about it.

When he spoke his voice was hushed. He sure didn't want anybody but Bobby hearing what he was about to say. Least of all his parents. Talking about love always made him feel a little—goofy.

"If you marry somebody, I guess you *want* to make love to them all the time. That's part of being married."

Woody turned his head to see Bobby's eyes burrowing into his. Bobby's words were spoken so low Woody could barely hear them. So low—and so sad. "You're lucky."

"Yeah, I guess I am."

"Your parents are lucky, too. Lucky to be so happy together. My folks hate each other."

"Then why do they stay together?"

"Too lazy to split up, I guess. Or too bombed all the time to get around to it."

"I'm sorry."

"I know."

Bobby reached out and once again laid his hand on Woody's chest. This time he left it there.

"I feel more at home here," Bobby said, "than I do in my own house. When I'm there it's like they can't wait for me to leave. And when I'm here it's like I never *want* to leave."

"My folks like having you here, you know. They'd let you stay here all the time if you didn't have parents of your own."

"Would they?"

"Yeah. They figure we're brothers now, I guess. And maybe we are."

"Is that what you want?" Bobby asked. "To be brothers?"

Woody looked away from Bobby's face and back at the ceiling, embarrassed a little by the sadness in Bobby's eyes. The sadness—and something else. It was the "something else" that troubled him.

"I don't know. I think maybe we're *more* than brothers." They were words Woody had wanted to say for a long time, and suddenly there they were, out in the open. He forced himself to turn again and gaze at Bobby. "Do you ever feel like that?"

The sadness never left Bobby's face, even when a gentle smile appeared. "I *always* feel like that."

Bobby's hand was moving now in a gentle, circular motion over Woody's chest. A calming motion. Woody couldn't even tell if Bobby knew he was doing it. But *Woody* knew he was doing it. He could feel his pecker give a little lurch inside his shorts, like maybe his pecker knew Bobby was doing it, too.

"Uh—"

"You're more than a brother to me, Woody," Bobby said. "You know that, right?"

And looking over, Woody was surprised to see tears standing in Bobby's eyes.

"I don't want you to hate me," Bobby said.

Woody wrapped an arm across Bobby's shoulders and pulled him close, so close that Bobby's cheek rested alongside his hand on Woody's chest. Woody could feel Bobby's breath tickling his skin as Bobby's hand slid a little farther south toward his navel to make room for his head.

"I'll never hate you, Bobby. Why would I?"

"I don't know."

Woody could feel his penis lengthening inside his shorts, stretching the fabric, raising its head with excruciating slowness that in a couple of seconds would be impossible to hide, especially with Bobby's head lying so close to it.

He reached up and flicked off the light to hide it.

"Go to sleep," he said, as darkness settled over the room. He kept his hand buried in Bobby's hair, comforting him as best he could. And comforting himself as well.

Bobby's fingers were gently kneading the skin of Woody's stomach. Idly, again, like maybe he didn't even know he was doing it. Woody realized he was trembling and wondered where it came from.

Bobby felt it, too. "You're shaking," he said.

"I know."

Bobby's head shifted, and Woody felt Bobby's lips against his chest. When Bobby spoke, his lips moved against Woody's skin with a softness that was almost painful.

"You smell clean," Bobby said. He was trembling now too.

"Irish Spring. Good soap."

Bobby laughed. His fingers slid a millimeter beneath the waistband of Woody's BVDs, and Woody closed his eyes at the sensation. His boner now was poking up like a goddamn tent pole, and he had a sneaking suspicion even darkness wouldn't hide it much longer.

He was right.

Bobby freed it with a tug of Woody's shorts and then pulled Woody's underwear down his legs and tossed them to the floor at the foot of the bed. Woody lay still, torn between shock and… something else.

Again, Bobby laid his head on Woody's chest, and in the moonlight Woody could see Bobby's hand encircle him. His penis bucked in Bobby's grip, and Woody closed his eyes, stunned by the sensation.

"Don't hate me," Bobby said again, and before Woody could answer, before Woody could do anything, Bobby slid his warm, soft face along the length of Woody's torso until his breath brushed the head of Woody's dick. Without waiting for a response, Bobby pressed his lips to it and slid it into his mouth.

"Don't," Woody almost said, but then he didn't. Instead, he gripped Bobby's head and held it still. His heart was bucking and pounding, and he thought maybe he was having a heart attack or something. Only heart attacks, he figured, didn't feel this good.

God, Bobby's mouth was like hot velvet. Bobby held his head still like Woody wanted him to, but his tongue was moving around in there like it was mapping out and memorizing the lay of the terrain. Above the sound of his own heart, Woody could hear, and feel, Bobby's heart pounding, too.

When Bobby's hand cupped his balls, Woody did gasp, and before he could stop it, he pushed himself deeper into Bobby's mouth and shot his young sperm into that heavenly warm cavern.

His first orgasm at the lips of another human being was so powerful it almost rocked his universe. Woody thought maybe the house was falling in, or the top of his head flying off, or maybe his teeth were exploding in his mouth, one after the other, like popcorn. Jesus, it was like every nerve ending in his body had been ripped right out of its socket. It took all the willpower he had not to yell out.

Bobby held him firmly in his mouth. Woody could hear Bobby's throat working as he swallowed what Woody had given him, swallowed it right down like ice cream. The knowledge Bobby had done that sent another tremor through Woody's body. He could feel Bobby's hands on his legs now, softly stroking the hair there, kneading the flesh as if he enjoyed the feel of it.

The knotted muscles in Woody's neck finally relaxed, and he dropped his head back to the pillow, still holding Bobby in place, his hands clamped tightly in Bobby's hair. Woody could feel himself softening in Bobby's mouth until finally, his penis slid free.

They lay there for a long time, with Bobby's head resting on Woody's stomach, Woody's penis still inches from Bobby's mouth.

Woody found himself wanting Bobby to do it again. Right now. And then he thought maybe he didn't.

He grasped Bobby's shoulders and pulled him up, tucking him into his arms as he had earlier. In the darkness, he could feel Bobby's shoulders heaving, like maybe he was crying. But when Bobby pushed his face into Woody's chest, Woody felt something he didn't expect. A smile.

Christ. Bobby was smiling.

"Thank you," Bobby said.

Woody figured maybe he was the one who should be saying thank you, and when that thought struck him, he found himself smiling too.

"That was intense," he said. "I didn't know you were going to do that."

"Neither did I."

"Then why did you?"

"Don't know," Bobby said. "Seemed like the right thing to do. I love you, you know. What's wrong with trying to make the person you love happy?"

"Bobby—"

"I'll never do it again if you don't want me to. I swear I won't. But I had to do it once. Just once." He looked up into Woody's face. "You liked it, didn't you?"

Woody grinned. "God yes, I liked it. I thought my head was going to blow off."

"Maybe that's what happened to the dead guy," Bobby said, and then they were both laughing like idiots, lying there in the darkness holding on to each other for dear life.

Soon, Bobby fell asleep in Woody's arms. Woody lay there naked beside him, wide-awake. And later, in the wee hours of the morning, when an approaching dawn began turning the room from black to gray, Woody pressed his lips to Bobby's mouth and Bobby opened his eyes.

"My turn," Woody whispered. Sliding down in the bed, he took Bobby's dick into his mouth, just as Bobby had done to him. He smiled as Bobby immediately hardened inside him.

And in a matter of seconds, Bobby stifled a cry and spilled his seed across Woody's lips. It was at that precise moment that Woody began to understand the joy to be found on the other side of the equation—not just the joy of taking, but the joy of giving as well. He closed his eyes to savor the taste of Bobby's come, all the while suppressing an ecstatic tremble. He knew who he truly was now. Bobby had just proven it to him.

After caressing the warmth of Bobby's thigh with his cheek, and running his fingers over the length of Bobby's long legs relishing the feel of them, Woody lifted his chin and gazed into Bobby's eyes.

"I love you too," he said softly.

"I know," Bobby whispered back. "We've always loved each other. We just weren't old enough to know it."

"Now we are," Woody said.

Bobby nodded, stroking the soft skin at the nape of Woody's neck. "Now we are."

They slept then, peacefully, in the scent of their lovemaking, reveling in this new journey, this brave new world they had discovered in each other's arms.

Being only thirteen, they could not know some things that are meant to be, and actually come to pass, are not always destined to stay that way. They could not know that even the most promising of journeys can be interrupted.

Sometimes the *beginning* of happiness, the *beginning* of the journey, is as far as some people ever get.

CHAPTER THREE

SWINGING GENTLY in the old swing beneath the jacaranda tree, Woody remembered every moment of that night and morning as if he had experienced it only hours before. He could still feel Bobby's smooth skin. Could still feel the silky heat of the boy. Still feel Bobby's fingers in his hair. Still taste Bobby's passion flying into him as they both gasped in amazement at the force of his climax. And the joy it all gave Woody was as strong today as it had been sixteen years ago. His time with Bobby that night, and all the other nights that followed, was an awakening like none Woody would ever experience again. His destiny to lead the life of a gay man was born in those few hours of darkness between that one long-ago day and the next. Finding that destiny in the arms of his best friend, in the arms of someone who felt the very same way he did, made the acceptance of it easy. Because of Bobby's courage that night in making the first move, Woody's life was irrevocably changed, and happily so, for his sexuality was no longer a mystery.

Bobby did not cause Woody's gayness, but Bobby gave it a voice. Bobby gave it a reason to speak and a safe venue in which to first be heard. For Woody, sex with Bobby was not only a release for himself. It was a shared journey. A wondrous tandem discovery. Only in pleasing each other did they please themselves. Together, holding each other in the darkness on those summer nights when puberty was still so new they sometimes didn't know what to do, although their bodies always did, they became a unit. One body. One mind. One great, interminable longing.

In all the days since, for Woody, for the man Woody would become, to be gay was to never feel quite comfortable in his own skin. He was a recipe with a missing ingredient. A wall with a missing brick. Like that wall, there was a hole in Woody he could never quite fill. He knew what caused it, that hole. Bobby caused it. Or rather, the *absence* of Bobby caused it.

Woody closed his eyes, absorbing that aching absence yet again as the evening air blew his long hair across his eyes, as the old swing squeaked beneath his weight, as he felt the empty beer can warming in his hand. He could smell the scent of his mother's roses surrounding him in the darkness. Funny they should still be here when his mother was not. Funny his mother would be little more than dust now, but those roses were still pliant and vibrant and as sweetly scented as they ever were. She had planted them with her own hands, watered them, nurtured them, then left them to the whims of fate, and still they throve. Yet of his mother, only memory remained.

As he had so many times as a child, Woody scraped his feet across the ground to slow the swing's momentum. He eased himself out of it and stepped to the edge of the lawn where the roses stood guard. The lighter colored ones glowed in the moonlight, and Woody bent to smell them. He thought he could detect a different scent to different colored blooms, but he wasn't sure. Maybe they all smelled the same, no matter what hue they took. Maybe he wanted them to smell different, like the scent of different men Woody had bedded over the years.

There weren't many of those. Not really. He had always kept his sexual preferences to himself. Only the direst need drove him to seek out other men. His band had not known, nor had his parents when they were alive. It was not morals, or even prudishness, that kept his conquests to a minimum. It was the knowledge that none of those men whom he met in shadowed bars, or plucked from audiences, would ever fill the void Bobby had left inside him. In Woody's mind, sex was a poor substitute for love. It always had been and always would be.

Woody looked out past the rosebushes to the canyon. Vaguely, in the light of the newly risen moon climbing up the eastern sky, he could see the willow trees down in the lowest depths of the canyon, swaying gently in the night breeze. He could hear the soft rustle of their long, slender leaves. In the moonlight, those rustling leaves, as thick as hair upon a human head, but flowing, like mercury, shifted continually from black to silver. Black to silver.

It was beneath those trees the bones had been found. And later, it was there, in that very spot, where the Willow Man first came to them.

Willow Man.

It was Chuck who had seen him first. Woody could still hear the kid screaming like a banshee as they flew out of the canyon on that hot July morning. Eagle had sprouted wings that day. God, she had really flown. Both of them, Woody and Chuck, had been crying so hard as Eagle carried them down the hill, with Chuck holding on for dear life and Woody pumping the pedals for all he was worth, that tears and snot, and blood too, had dribbled down the front of their shirts and whipped back around their ears in the slipstream of their panicked flight. Chuck's eyes had been so wild that day, so crazy mad with fear, they weren't Chuck's eyes at all. They were the eyes of a hunted rabbit. Or a fox, captured in a steel trap. They were the eyes of an animal that knew death was a mere two steps behind and about to make the grab. There was a hopelessness in Chuck's eyes that day, as if he *knew* they wouldn't make it. As if he *knew* their lives would be over with their next heartbeats.

But they *had* made it. They had *all* made it. All but one. But *that* day, Woody wouldn't think about right now. He pushed it away from his mind like a recovering alcoholic pushing away a badly needed, yet unwanted, drink. Woody knew one sip of that memory would lead him to a place he didn't want to go.

"Fuck you, Willow Man," Woody muttered into the darkness and threw his empty beer can as far as he could. He watched it shimmer for a second in the moonlight as it arced across the sky, then it simply disappeared, silently swallowed up in the shadows below.

OLD HURTS have a way of foraging through the mind even in sleep. As tired and emotionally drained as Woody was—thanks to the deluge of memories that had swamped his thoughts ever since entering the house again after his long absence—still, when sleep found him, it did not let him rest.

Instead of hitting him one at a time, as they did when he was awake, those memories swept through his sleeping mind like a movie played at fast-forward. One scene crashing into the next. Chaotic. Image after image bumping heads with each other until they were all a blur. Had he been awake to analyze it, it would have felt like he was back on speed.

The images that assailed him were both good and bad. Both reassuring and terrifying.

—the sound of Bobby's breath, gentle and comforting, in sleep beside him. The scent of Bobby's skin permeating the bed. The feel of Bobby's hand, sleep-warm, resting on his arm.

—the Coroner's van hauling away a bag of bones as Woody stood watching, all alone on a hillside, wondering where his friends had gone, wondering where *everybody* had gone.

—Woody's mother, screaming over the body of her dying husband, before the blood-drenched knife that killed him was pulled from his chest and plunged into her as well, blending her fluids with his one last time, not in passion this time, but in a final excruciating blast of pain.

—soup cans in Aisle 4, clattering to the floor and rolling through a pool of gore, leaving trails of blood in their wake.

—Bobby's lips coaxing him to climax yet again as Woody writhed beneath this boy who first became friend, then became lover. Who would *always* be his lover, even after death.

—the Willow Man, reaching out his hand from the brambles, hungrily groping through the darkness for young flesh to rend and tear and feed upon.

—Woody and his friends sitting by a campfire among the willow and pepper trees in the canyon, roasting marshmallows and hot dogs on long sticks and talking about death in hushed voices, feeling the darkness closing in around them, held at bay only by the flames.

The images kept coming. An avalanche of bliss and misery. But always in the background Woody seemed to hear the quiet voice of his mother, urging him to wake, urging him to follow her, taking his hand, even as he slept, to lead him away. Through the door. Away from this house. Away from his memories. Back into a world where he was safe from the evil that had taken residence on Highview Lane. The evil he and his friends would awaken in the summer of their thirteenth year. The evil that was still there. Even now. Still waiting. Still hungry.

And in the darkness of his old room, as his adult body lay dreaming these dreams on his childhood bed, Woody suddenly awoke with a cry. Before his mind could register where he was, his hand reached out from memory to the light switch on the wall by his head and drove away the darkness. He saw the NASCAR curtains fluttering at the open window. Smelled the roses and the pepper trees outside. Saw his beloved Gibson propped in the corner. Lonely. Silent. Yearning to be played.

As his thoughts began to calm, as the images from his dream began to recede from his waking mind, both the horror they brought and the solace they offered receded with them. And just as Woody came fully awake, he saw and heard movement at the doorway. A wisp of white. The faintest rustle of cloth. His heart gave one gigantic thud inside his chest, and he sprang from the bed.

"Who's there?" he yelled, standing at the edge of the bed, knees weak with fear, voice hoarse from sleep. He cast his eyes around the room for a weapon and saw his old Louisville Slugger leaning against the wall beside the closet door. He grabbed the bat in both hands as if he were standing in the box and waiting for the next pitch. Teeth clenched, he eased himself into the hallway.

The house was dark and silent around him. At the end of the hall, where it led to the living room, he saw another glimpse of white before it disappeared around the corner, a hint of some gossamer floating fabric, like a ghostly trail of ectoplasm bleeding away into the shadows.

He took a firmer grip on the bat, choking up good and tight with both hands as his father had taught him to do. Since he was wearing only briefs, the night air wafting through the windows was cool on his skin. Still, he felt a bead of sweat trickle down his ribcage, and he thought maybe his knees were going to give way any second. "And why the hell shouldn't they?" he asked himself, taking a deep breath and forcing himself to move down the hall toward that last glimpse of white, which he could no longer see but somehow knew was still there. It was there, and it was luring him forward. Beckoning to him. "Follow me," a voice said inside his head.

And Woody followed.

Somewhere at the back of his mind, Woody wondered if this was all another segment of his disjointed dream. But of course he knew it was not. At this moment he was as wide-awake as he had ever been in his life. Wide-awake and scared poopless, as good old Bobby used to say.

Woody wished Bobby were here with him now. He suddenly realized he was wishing a lot of things. He wished he had a gun. He wished he wasn't so damned scared. He wished he could whip out the old Johnson and take a long, soul-satisfying pee, and *that* was one thing he wasn't wishing off the top of his head. He *really* had to pee. He wondered why fear always seemed to cause that reaction. As love supposedly resides in the human heart, did fear reside in the bladder? And where did anger reside? In the adenoids? Jesus, that was a stupid thought.

Woody gripped the ash handle so tightly his fingers began to ache. Bat held high, he peeked around the doorway into the living room.

There was no one there.

Again, he remembered his mother's voice in the dream, and turning toward the kitchen, he saw her standing there at the sink with her back to him. She was rinsing her hands under the faucet, frantically, as if trying to wash away a burning acid eating into her skin. But it wasn't acid she was rinsing from her hands. It was blood. Even in the moonlight, Woody could see it splattering against the porcelain, splashing onto the window above the sink, dappling the voluminous white nightgown she wore. And as she furiously wrung her hands, over and over, in the spray of water, Woody could hear her sobbing out her anguish at the feel of it. The *uncleanliness* of it.

When she turned to look at him, the bat tumbled from Woody's hands, and his own tears rose up to join hers.

She looked just as she had the last time he'd seen her. Not the last time he had seen her alive, but the last, and only, time he saw her dead. It had been a glance, really. A mere handful of seconds out of the millions, perhaps *billions* of seconds of his lifetime. Enough time to identify her body and his father's for the police, but it was more than enough time to scar his heart, to mark Woody's existence indelibly.

The knife Woody had seen piercing his mother's chest that day as she lay, silent and unmoving beside his equally bloodied and equally silent father, was gone now. But the wounds were still there.

Every one of them. Both his mother and father had been stabbed and slashed so many times that perhaps only Woody could have recognized them for who they were. But even he couldn't recognize them by their faces. Their faces were far too torn and mangled. No, he could only identify them through inanimate objects that lay glistening in the blood around them. His father's watch, the crystal shattered now from his fall to the floor (but the second hand still sweeping round and round in a silent dance). His father's reading glasses, the metal earpieces bent and twisted, lying in the blood beside him. His father's Marlboros, too, the red and white pack poking up from his bloodied shirt pocket. His mother's earrings. Her favorite pair. Little silver starbursts Woody had seen a thousand times, screwed tightly onto her lobes. The cameo she had inherited from her grandmother, nestling in the hollow of her torn throat where, deep down where the killer had slashed so deeply, Woody could see the glimmer of bone.

Now, in the darkness of the silent house, Woody took a step toward her, or toward what was *once* her, but she held out a hand to stop him. He could see her try to work a smile to her lips with the torn muscles the killer had left her with, but the effect of it was not a smile at all. It was a grimace. And to Woody, it was a heartbreak.

"Mother—" he said.

Her voice, when she spoke, was unlike any voice he had ever heard. It didn't belong to his mother. It couldn't belong to anyone alive. There was a coldness in the timbre of it when she formed her words, and as she did so a mist of vapor flowed from her lips. Winter vapor. Meat locker vapor. Icy and translucent. Woody could feel the chill of it from across the room.

"You're so handsome," she said, and when her mouth moved to speak, Woody could see blood still weeping from the wounds on her face. "How did you get to be so handsome?"

Woody tried to smile at her words, but his attempt to bring a smile to his lips was no more successful than hers. He tried to hide his horror from her, tried to hide his fear from her, too, but they were there, blatantly scrawled across his face. *This is my mother. She will not harm me.*

And she read his thoughts as easily as she had when he was a child.

"No, Woody, I won't harm you. I'm not the one you need to be afraid of."

"Who, then?" Woody asked, surprised to hear his own voice booming out of him as strong as ever. "*Who* should I be afraid of?"

Again she tried to smile, and a rivulet of blood swept down her chin to splash her breast.

"Him," she whispered, looking worried now. Looking frightened. "The man in the canyon. You know who I mean. He came to us, Woody. He came to us in the store. He was looking for you, I think, but he found us instead." She held her hands out to her sides and looked down at herself. "Look what he did to me, Woody. Look what he did to your father."

And feeling a cold wind brush his back, Woody spun to see his father standing behind him, only an arm's length away. He too was covered in the blood of the day when his life had ended. But unlike his mother, Woody's father didn't try to smile. He merely looked at him with a sadness so profound Woody felt his breath catch at the misery in it.

Woody reached his hand out to him, but before the movement was complete, his father disappeared back into the shadows. Only a tiny wisp of vapor remained behind, and in a moment, that too was gone.

"You have to leave this place," his mother said. "You aren't safe here. He'll kill you, Woody. He'll kill you just like he killed us. Don't let him do it. Get as far away from this place as you can. Forget about us. Forget about everything. Forget about me."

"The Willow Man—" Woody muttered, tasting his tears on his tongue as he said it. "*He* did this?"

His mother silently stood there, watching him. He could see her hands working at her sides, clenching and unclenching, as if still uncomfortable at the feel of blood on her skin.

He took another step toward her, but again she held a hand out, warning him to come no closer. "Don't look at me again," she said, turning away, shielding her face from his eyes with a bleeding hand. "Once was enough. Once was more than enough."

Woody saw her then begin to fade. Slowly she turned to mist, melding back into the shadows as his father had done.

Before she could leave him, before she could disappear forever, Woody reached out, pleading for her to wait. "Where's Bobby?" he asked through a sob. "Is Bobby here with you?"

But his mother had already gone.

Woody was standing alone in the darkness.

WOODY FUMBLED with the lock on the door and stumbled out onto the front porch, breathing in great gulps of night air, trying to calm himself, trying to clear the stench of blood from his nostrils. It had smelled so real, that blood. It couldn't be just a memory. It couldn't be a figment of scent dredged out of the past, safely locked away until tonight, archived in some sensory circuit of his brain until the sight of his parents heralded it back. No, the blood had been real. Or had it? Unreasonably, the vision he had seen of his parents' mangled bodies standing before him and his mother's strangely timbred voice actually *speaking* to him took secondary importance to whether the blood he had smelled, the blood he *still* smelled, was real.

He stepped back into the house, closing and locking the door behind him and trying to ignore his fear. He walked with determined strides to the kitchen, where he flicked on the light.

Woody swayed on his feet. Blood was everywhere. On the window. On the curtains. Splattered across the floor. Dripping down the sides of the sink. He realized suddenly that the faucet was still on, and he reached out with a trembling hand to turn it off.

She had been here. His father too. This was no dream. Woody stared at a smear of blood on the countertop for a long time. Finally, the urge to urinate drove him to the bathroom, where he relieved himself, and when that mundane task was finished, he pulled on a pair of sweat pants and returned to the kitchen, rag in one hand, bottle of 409 in the other, and proceeded to clean up the mess.

He cleaned and scrubbed like a man with a mission, and when the kitchen was spotless, he wiped it all down again. He removed the curtain rods from the wall, slid the curtains off, and carried them to the washer in the garage. He set the washer for the maximum time, adjusted the water to the maximum temperature, and poured in enough soap and bleach to kill every germ known to man. With the comforting sound of water spilling into the machine, he closed the lid and returned to the kitchen.

Checking the clock on the kitchen wall, he saw it was almost three in the morning. He readied the coffeepot and plugged it in, went to the bathroom to shave and floss and brush his teeth, then stood beneath a hot shower until the mirrors in the tiny bathroom were dripping with moisture. When *that* mundane task was finished, he redonned his sweat pants, knotting the drawstring tight around his slim waist, and returned to the kitchen.

The coffee was ready. He filled a cup from the cupboard, stirred in sugar and powdered creamer, and sat down at the kitchen table, cradling the coffee cup under his chin. He stared past the uncurtained window to the darkness outside, and only then did he begin to cry.

God, he had spent his whole life trying to forget the day his parents died, but now he let the memory of it return to him, *begged* it to return to him. And it did. The coffee cooled in his cup, forgotten, as the memory swept over him, carrying him back in time...

IT WAS his second summer out of high school. He was working on a fishing trawler, trying to decide what to do with his life. He had spent most of the summer repairing nets and swabbing fish guts off the deck, but now the boat was in dry dock having repairs done to the keel and screws, and Woody spent most of his days painting and chipping away at the rust that was the bane of every ship, large or small, that plied the seas. He was as brown as a hazelnut from working shirtless in the hot summer sun. His hair, always long, had streaked to a pale, pale blond, shades lighter than it usually was. He had recently taken a small studio apartment not far from the bay, and sometimes he walked to the pier where the boat was dry-docked rather than hassling with trying to find a place to park his car.

Overall it had been a pretty good summer. He enjoyed working in the ocean air. He enjoyed the sun burning into his back. And he enjoyed his nights too. Nights with the band, perfecting the music, testing the limits of his voice, his skill with the guitar. They had even had a couple of gigs. Private parties, mostly. Those jobs didn't pay much, sometimes nothing more than the beer they could drink, but it was a thrill to stand away from the crowd and see the effect of their music on strangers' faces.

Woody had a good ear. He knew when they played well, and he knew when they didn't. The other guys in the band—keyboard, drums, bass, and electric guitar—were pretty good at what they did. They were committed. And the more they played, the better they became. Suddenly, the dream of playing their music for a living seemed less a dream and more an actual possibility. They had scraped enough money together to make a demo record and shopped it around to recording companies in San Diego and L.A., and even to a couple of agents. So far they had heard nothing back, but maybe one day....

A uniformed policeman came to Woody on the deck of the boat that day. Woody knew something was wrong immediately by the look of misery on the policeman's face. "Come with me, son," the cop had kindly said, and Woody did as he was asked, snagging his shirt off the ship's rail and slipping it on as he followed the man to the patrol car parked on the pier.

In the car, as they drove through the familiar streets, Woody learned what had happened. A robbery, perhaps, although nothing seemed to be missing from the store's till. Fear for his father made him lean forward to grip the dashboard as they neared the store, but it was not until he stepped inside to find a dozen other cops and crime techs quietly surveying the scene that Woody learned his mother had also worked in the store that day. One of the girls was sick, he later learned, and his mother had filled in for her.

Their bodies were sprawled side by side in Aisle 4. A display of soups had crashed to the floor around them, the cans rolling all over the place, leaving snail trails of blood wherever they went. How many times had Woody stacked those cans for his father? How many times, when he was younger, had he earned a few extra bucks by buffing this floor to a shine with the big electric buffer, which almost always got away from him? How many times had he bagged groceries and priced items and mopped up messes and cleaned the fingerprints from the front door just to earn a little spending money?

Woody knew this store with the same intimacy with which he knew the house he lived in. He knew it as well as he knew himself, as well as he knew his parents.

But these people he saw now on the floor in Aisle 4, Woody did not know at all. They were strangers to him. The store seemed suddenly to be a place he had never been before. He didn't know these policemen in their tight blue uniforms and polished boots, standing around talking in hushed voices. He didn't know the young man crouched on the floor attempting to lift fingerprints from the handle of the long kitchen knife protruding from his mother's chest. He didn't recognize the feel of the man's hand, the man in the crisp brown suit who said he was a detective, as it rested on his shoulder, trying to give the boy a glimmer of comfort as he asked softly, "Are these your parents, son? Can you identify these people as your parents?"

In answer to the question, Woody had simply nodded, too numb to speak. Too numb to *think*. And the detective, understanding, waved over one of the uniformed cops to lead Woody outside. Before he left, the detective said, "I'm sorry, son. I'm sorry for your loss." And then Woody was outside the store, once again watching the sun set and the moon rise, both at the same time, and feeling for the first time in his life—truly alone.

Not knowing what else to do, he had driven his father's Fairlane home, parking it in the garage where it would sit for the next ten years. The house had seemed so quiet in those first hours after his parents' deaths. As quiet as it felt now. He had not returned to his apartment that night. He had sat alone in his parents' house, letting the darkness gather around him. He listened to the phone ring, again and again and again, as neighbors called to offer their condolences, but Woody just let it ring. He didn't grieve for his parents as he sat there in the dark. Their death was too near for him. Too incomprehensible. Grief would come later. No, for the moment all he could do was try to squeeze the image of those blood-soaked bodies from his mind. He didn't think of the anguish they must have suffered during the course of their deaths. That too would come later.

WOODY TOOK a sip from the coffee cup he still held beneath his chin and was surprised to find it cold. How long had he been sitting here at the kitchen table? He glanced at the clock and saw only twenty minutes had passed. Twenty minutes of his life had swept past him, and he hadn't even seen it go.

The sky outside the kitchen window, so bare without the familiar curtains hanging around it, was still black with night. The kitchen reeked of Pine-Sol and Windex and 409 from where he had cleaned up the blood. His mother's blood. And now Woody remembered the words his mother had spoken to him. "He came to us, Woody. He came to us in the store. He was looking for you, I think, but he found us instead."

"The man in the canyon," she had said, although she had not given him the name Woody and his friends had given him on that long-ago summer day when he first made his presence known.

Cathy had been the one who named him.

Willow Man, Cathy had called him. "Fucking old Willow Man," she had said with her little-girl voice that could spout obscenities like the crustiest of sailors.

Before that summer was over, Willow Man would take Bobby from him. From all of them. But not until tonight had Woody known it was Willow Man who had also taken his parents.

Why would he do that? "He was looking for you, I think," his mother had said in the darkness as the blood dripped from the cuts in her face. Cuts that had been made more than a decade before. Yet his mother was still here. And his father. If they were still here, then Bobby must be here too.

Maybe Willow Man was still here as well. His mother said he was. Maybe death didn't really exist at all. Hatred did, certainly. Hatred was burning in Woody's chest right now. And maybe there was some fear mixed up with it too. But overriding both the hatred and the fear was a growing, seething anger. Woody could feel it welling up in him as he sipped his cold coffee and waited for the sun to rise.

"Come on, then," he said, listening to his own words, his own voice, as it echoed through the silent house. "Come and get me, you miserable piece of shit. I'm right here."

Woody rested his head on his arms and closed his eyes, willing his childhood terror to come and snatch him away as it had snatched away everyone he had ever loved. He was here. Unarmed. All too eager to let death come and find him. Maybe in death he would see

Bobby again. Maybe Bobby would be waiting for him there, somewhere in the shadows on the other side of life.

But Willow Man did not come. Not yet.

Soon, Woody dozed. Remembering.

CHAPTER FOUR

THE MORNING after Woody and his friends had found the bones in the canyon, Woody and Bobby came to breakfast in such a lighthearted mood Woody's mother didn't quite know what to make of it. How could these two kids not be affected by the horror they had stumbled on the day before? Was it strength or innocence that left them so completely unsullied by their first exposure to death? She sat across the table from them, sipping her morning coffee while they gobbled down Post Toasties and Pop-Tarts (she wasn't in a mood to cook). More than anything, she wished she could share a little of their exuberance.

She had been fielding phone calls from the neighbors all morning. The finding of a dead body in what was practically her backyard might not have been deemed newsworthy by the media, but in the neighborhood it was a blockbuster. After about the tenth call, Woody's mom had left the phone off the hook, and when the electronic wail of an interrupted connection began to grate on her nerves, she had slipped the receiver into a drawer to deaden the sound.

After Woody and Bobby finished eating, she slid a large Tupperware container across the table and said, "Take this with you when you pick up your clothes, Bobby. It's potato salad. Your mom probably isn't well enough to be cooking right now."

Bobby looked stricken by her kindness. It was the first flash of anything other than happiness she had seen on his face all morning.

"She isn't sick," he said, his voice sullen. "She's drunk."

"Well, take it anyway," she said gently. "Please."

"Okay." And after a moment, he grudgingly added, "Thank you."

Woody shifted his chair a little closer to Bobby's, and the happiness in Bobby's eyes returned as quickly as it had left. Woody's mom wondered at the transformation on Bobby's face but racked it up to the ability of a thirteen-year-old to take the worst of what life has to offer and absorb it like a pinprick, whereas an adult would have had to tie a tourniquet around his feelings, around his heart, to stop the pain. There was a lot to be said for being a kid. Every time she looked at these two, she found herself longing for the simplicity of her own childhood. Life might pummel you when you're thirteen, but it didn't beat you to death like it did when you were grown. There was a lot of talk about the resilience of youth, and Woody's mom figured truer words were never spoken. Her own resilience had wandered off years ago. Slipped out the door, never to be seen again. Maybe that's why she cleaned, she thought, wearing herself out day after day, doing the same chores over and over again, seeking out every little imperfection in her universe. Maybe she was trying to find that old resilience again beneath the dust and the grout and all the other detritus of everyday life that continually accumulated in the corners of her existence. Maybe one day it would show up again, that resilience, crawl out from beneath her sponge and fly right back into her like it had never been gone.

Fat chance.

"I want you boys to stay out of the canyon."

Woody grinned and said, "Sure, Mom. Whatever you say," and she was instantly suspicious of his easy acceptance. But she let it go because sometimes all you could do was hope for the best. She had the sudden sense her young son was growing up. Perhaps he was already beyond the safety net she had thrown over him in infancy. Perhaps now was the time when he must begin to battle the vagaries of life on his own. While the thought terrified her, all she could do was let him go. Let him be.

"Thanks for breakfast," Bobby said, echoing Woody's grin.

And then they were gone, scraping chairs, banging doors, taking the potato salad with them. Woody's mom sighed, gathered up their dirty dishes, and began another day of cleaning.

Like yesterday. Like the day before.

THE BOYS decided to walk to Bobby's house. It would have been too hard juggling a gallon of potato salad on their bikes. They found Bobby's bag of clothing on the front porch, right where they were told it would be, and left the potato salad in its place. They did this all as quietly as they could, for inside the house with the green shutters that needed painting and the grass that needed cutting, they heard Bobby's parents revving up for another battle, screaming obscenities at each other, their voices muted by the walls that held them captive inside their own private war zone.

"They don't even know I'm gone," Bobby said quietly. "They don't even know I live here. And I don't. I've never lived here."

Woody stepped closer and pressed his shoulder to Bobby's to offer his strength. "Then fuck 'em," Woody said, making Bobby giggle.

Five minutes after tossing the bag of clothes onto Woody's back steps, the boys were back in the canyon, scrutinizing their clubhouse.

It didn't look much better than it had the day before. They grinned at each other, shaking their heads.

"Ugly."

"*Butt* ugly."

They stood shoulder to shoulder, distance being something Woody didn't want to feel right now. And as other thoughts began to intrude, thoughts that had nothing to do with clubhouses or potato salad or parents and everything to do with touch and taste and simple human desire, Woody began to reach out to maybe sample those things once again, sensing Bobby's willing response, but then they heard a voice calling out behind them.

"Is it still standing?"

Both boys jumped and spun to see Cathy slipping and sliding down the side of the canyon toward them. She wore faded jeans, cut off at the knees, a white T-shirt, and tennies with no socks. The mud from the day before had been scrubbed from her hair, and pulled back now in a ponytail, it shone in the morning sunlight like red fire.

"Barely!" Bobby yelled back.

"Find any more dead guys?" she asked, sidling up beside them. "And don't look so guilty."

"Not yet," Woody said. "And who's looking guilty?"

"You are. You guys been up to something you shouldn't have? Jesus!" Cathy croaked, suddenly eyeing the mud monstrosity that sat looming there in front of her. "It looks like a big, square, fungus-covered turd. Only Chuck would think up something like this."

"It's called genius," a voice said, and they all turned to see the twins coming up behind them, looking as innocent and cherubic as ever. Beneath the rays of a wakening sun, their white-blond hair glowed like halos around their heads, and when they grinned, the sun glinted off the metal wire strapped to their teeth with little sparks of light. They looked electric. A couple of short circuits walking around in dirty tennis shoes and baggy shorts and matching yellow T-shirts. One of those T-shirts said "I'm With Stupid" and the other one said "Me Too." Chuck was the "Me Too."

"So what are we doing?" Jeremy asked. "Slinging mud again?"

Cathy groaned. "God forbid."

"Roofing?" Chuck asked, eyeing the reeds laid out around them, drying in the sun.

"Hell no," Bobby said, looking again at the lopsided structure. "I wouldn't crawl inside that thing even if it *had* a roof. It looks like something a proctologist would drag out of Godzilla's asshole."

Cathy snickered. "God, I love a man with a good vocabulary who isn't afraid to use it."

"So do I," Woody said, with a secretive grin on his face he knew only Bobby understood for what it was. Bobby grinned back, and Woody could almost see him thinking of the night behind them, but thinking of the night ahead as well.

"So what *are* we going to do?" Jeremy asked again.

Woody knew what Bobby was going to say before he said it. "We're going to find that fucking head."

Cathy groaned. "I was afraid somebody was gonna suggest that. Couldn't we just roof this turdhouse and pretend like yesterday never happened?"

"We've been thinking," Jeremy said. The twins never said "I" anything, it was always "we," as if their neurons had been spliced together at birth. Two minds incapable of producing anything other than one single thought at a time. Oddly, though their minds often headed off on similar tangents, they could never really seem to *agree* on anything once they got there.

Woody rolled his eyes at Bobby. "Oh God. They've been thinking. That can't be good."

Bobby agreed. "Never is."

"No, really," Jeremy plowed ahead. "We've been wondering. Why wasn't the guy wearing any clothes? No matter how long he's been dead, don't you think there should have been a few rags left on the bones from the clothes he was wearing when he died?"

"Maybe they just rotted away," Cathy said.

"Maybe he didn't have any to begin with," Chuck suggested. "And if he didn't, why the hell was that?"

"Maybe he was a nudist," Bobby suggested. "A homeless nudist. Naked and proud and starving to death with nary a shred of raiment to shield him from the cold, cruel world. Maybe it was like a Zen thing. Poor misguided bastard."

"Very funny."

Chuck was looking serious now, like maybe he had been thinking about this a long time. "I suppose a coyote might have dragged the clothes away. Heck, maybe a coyote dragged the *head* away. You know. To eat the tongue and lick the eyeballs out and gnaw on the skullcap until the brains spilled out like goose liver pate." Chuck always got carried away when his mouth kicked into gear, and somehow his metaphors always related to food.

Cathy groaned. "There's a lovely image."

Bobby laughed.

But Woody was looking thoughtful. "The moron has a point. Where *were* the guy's clothes? If a coyote took them, the bones would have been scattered to hell and back, but they weren't. They were pretty much still all hooked together. Except for the head."

Cathy was beginning to look annoyed. "Can't we just forget about the damned head? What are we going to do if we find it? Call the cops again? They didn't much give a shit the *last* time we called them."

"We have a theory," Jeremy said.

"Oh, great. Now they have a theory."

Only Woody seemed interested in hearing what it was. "Well?"

Chuck and Jeremy glanced at each other and smirked. They looked like a couple of cats who had just snagged a goldfish from the bowl.

"It's our dad's theory, really. Him and Mom were talking about it last night at dinner." Chuck's eyes brightened. "We had meatloaf."

Jeremy interrupted his brother. "They don't care what we had for dinner. Get to the point, jackass."

"Right." Chuck gazed at each of them in turn. "Dad thinks the body came from the plane crash."

This announcement was met with total silence. Woody glanced up at the sky, while Bobby looked off into the trees at the base of the canyon. Cathy just said, "Hmm."

Chuck was trembling like a tuning fork, waiting for some sort of response. "Well? Don't you think it's possible?"

They all knew about the crash of Flight 182 in the very neighborhood where they now stood. It had taken place more than a decade earlier, but their parents still spoke of it now and then, and when they spoke of it, they almost always did so in hushed voices, like they were in church or something. Their hushed voices were meant to convey the awe and gratitude they had felt at the time, and *still* felt years later, for the fact that they themselves had not been swept along in the carnage. Sometimes, for the residents of Park Canyon, all it took to revive memories of that day was an inbound plane coming in a little lower than usual as it made its final approach to Lindberg Field, the airport situated by the bay on the other side of downtown, less than four miles away. Living under a flight path was a risky business at best, but for most of the residents, it was a danger they'd simply learned to live with. Only when the roar of an incoming jet was louder than the one preceding it, for the airliners swept across the sky in a continual procession, one after the other, day after day after day, did the people of Park Canyon look skyward and give a silent little prayer. Most of the time those screaming jet engines were little more than background noise, but once in a while one grabbed their attention, and when it did, more than one person in Park Canyon held his breath until it had safely passed.

One hundred and forty-four people had died that day, most of them mutilated beyond any resemblance to human bodies at all. When the commercial 727 airliner collided with a light plane over

Park Canyon on that warm September morning, back when Woody and his friends were still toddlers barely out of diapers, bodies had spilled out of the torn fuselage even before the stricken aircraft hit the ground. Bodies were strewn from one end of Park Canyon to the other. All during the course of the day, screams could be heard as new victims were discovered. Bloody chunks of meat lay on the city streets and rooftops and lawns like Specials of the Week offered up in a butcher shop window.

Woody's mom had been standing at the kitchen sink washing dishes when the plane went down. She said the house trembled around her as the 727, already dying, floundered overhead, spewing smoke and flames and bodies. Woody's father had rushed home from the store, guided by a horrific column of black smoke that soared straight up into the sky on that windless day, all but blocking out the sun entirely. He expected to find his home and family consumed by the fires he could see scattered throughout the area, but the plane, thank God, had crashed into the homes on the other side of their canyon. Perhaps the pilot had been aiming for the canyon, *their* canyon, hoping to take as few lives as possible from the ground, but he overshot it and hit a residential street less than half a mile away.

Most of the people who died that September morning were passengers, but a handful were not. Those were the ones who were going about their everyday concerns, safely tucked away in their houses, or so they thought, getting dressed for work, watching TV, idly sipping their coffee and reading the morning paper, until tons of burning metal and bleeding flesh came crashing down on them from the crystal blue California sky overhead.

Woody and his friends had all heard the stories. A woman screamed and went bugshit crazy when a body flew through her bedroom window, drenching her in blood. A man, weeks later, found a human hand while he was trimming his shrubbery and damned near whacked a finger off it with his clippers. It was a woman's hand. A couple who had moved away shortly after the disaster did so because they found their dog, Fluffy, gnawing the meat from a human arm it had dragged from the bushes. The dog was euthanized. Woody and his friends weren't sure why. Were the authorities afraid Fluffy would become a man-eater after tasting human flesh? It seemed a bit unlikely. "How many man-eating poodles have *you* ever seen?" they had often asked themselves?

And Woody knew, as all of them did, that every body found had been stripped of clothing by the explosions, or the fires, or the wind, or the tree limbs. Stripped clean, right down to the skin. And sometimes right down to the *bone*. Most were torn to pieces, but a few remained intact. Some were still strapped to their seats and found hundreds of yards from the body of the plane.

The sky had rained death that day. It surely had. Maybe their headless skeleton *had* been part of the downpour. In the silence following Chuck's question, Woody looked at his friends and saw they were all considering what Chuck had said. If it made sense to Chuck and made sense to Jeremy, Woody figured it would soon be making sense to the others too.

He was right.

"Weren't all the bodies accounted for?" Cathy asked.

"Who the hell knows?" Jeremy shrugged. "They were gumbo. They could have DNA tested every scrap of meat they found, but that doesn't mean they didn't miss a few. Shit, there were fingers and assholes from here to Juniper Street. Maybe even farther. Bodies were sucked out as soon as the airliner hit the little plane, and that happened a mile south of here. Face it, guys. Pop is right. What we found yesterday is the last remaining survivor—well, no, I guess he's not a *survivor*—but the last remaining *victim* of Flight 182. Cool, huh?"

Cathy looked appalled. "Jesus, Jeremy? Where's your sense of compassion? Where's your respect for the dead? Where's your—?"

"Oh, shut up, Catherine. You think it's just as cool as I do, and you know it. Don't be so fucking Julie Andrews."

"Eat me."

Chuck slapped his cheeks in horror. "Oh, Julie. The nuns in the abbey will have your ass for talking like that. It simply isn't *devout*. They'll nail your tits to the chapel wall. They'll spread your legs so wide your toes will be in your ears, and then they'll—"

"Would everybody please shut up for a minute." It was Woody. "I hate to admit it, but I think maybe the dentist has a point. It makes sense, doesn't it?"

"Makes sense to me," Bobby said.

"Us too," the twins said in unison.

"So he wasn't a homeless guy after all," Cathy said, mulling it over as if even she was beginning to come around.

"Hell," Woody said, getting excited now. "The guy could have been anybody. A stockbroker. Or a preacher. Or a pickpocket. Hell, maybe he was even the pilot."

"Or a murderer," Bobby said.

"Yeah, right. Murderers always fly when they travel. I think they get a discount. Well, whoever he is, or *was*, he's fucking headless now. Maybe his head is hanging in a tree somewhere like a big papaya."

"I hate papaya," Cathy said, apropos of nothing, "and I am sure as hell not going to waste my day looking for some guy's head, which won't be nothing much but a skinless skull now anyway. What's the point of looking for it? What are you going to do if you find it? Stick it on a pole to ward off other plane crash victims?"

"You think we should call the police and tell them?" Bobby asked, looking at Woody. "Maybe they haven't figured it out yet. Maybe we're smarter than they are."

"Screw the police," Woody said, and that seemed to pretty well put that suggestion on hold permanently.

Cathy was all but hopping up and down with frustration. "But what's the point of *looking* for it? If it's here, it'll turn up sooner or later. I just hope to hell I'm not the one who stumbles over it like I was the last time."

"You don't like head?" Chuck asked with a leer.

"I do." Jeremy said, with the exact same leer thanks to all those mutual chromosomes he shared with his brother.

"Me too," Bobby said, gazing at Woody.

Woody only smiled.

Cathy shooed a fly off her nose. "None of you idiots would know head even if you actually got some, which seems unlikely. You two," she said, looking at the twins, "don't even have pubic hair yet." Turning to Woody and Bobby, she said, "And you two are just too fucking ugly."

"Thanks a lot, bitch."

"Don't mention it."

Woody couldn't help wondering what his friends would say if they could have been in the bedroom with him and Bobby last night. But the more he thought about it, the gladder he was they weren't. He imagined they would be having a completely different discussion right now.

Bobby seemed to read his thoughts.

Looking at him, Woody felt a tightening in the front of his jeans and, embarrassed, turned away from the others, studying the canyon sprawled out peacefully around them. Hard to imagine the way it must have looked ten years earlier, with the sun blocked out by thick black smoke and body parts tumbling into the willows and pepper trees from the crippled, screaming airliner as the earth rose up to meet it.

Woody wondered who their skeleton really belonged to. What was his name? What did he look like, back when he had meat on his bones? Was he skinny? Fat? Short? Tall? What were the last thoughts that ran through his mind as he watched the airliner disintegrate around him? Was he a nice person? Did he open doors for women, or was he the type to snicker lewd comments behind their backs? Was he as sweet as pie or a total asshole? Would the world be a sadder place without him, or would it be better off having him gone?

Woody supposed he'd never know. Not really.

In that, he was emphatically wrong.

"He's here. I know he is."

Chuck sounded so convinced of his own words they all looked around with a certain amount of trepidation. All but Cathy.

"Oh, do shut up," she said. "You don't even know where *you* are half the time. How can you know where *he* is? Besides, we're not looking for a *he*, we're looking for a *head*."

Chuck twisted an invisible moustache, like the villain in one of those old silent movies where the actors always wore too much makeup and some poor dame was always tied to a railroad track, waiting for the train to come along and slice her into lunchmeat. "I know we're in Death Central. Can't you feel it? If you close your eyes, you can still hear people screaming."

And Woody almost thought he did.

They had been at it for a couple of hours now, searching through the underbrush among the willows and pepper trees at the very bottom of the canyon, seeking out another glimmer of bone. Or a shred of clothing. Or a piece of the aircraft. All they had actually found was a metal rod about three feet long that could as easily have come off a '53 Buick as a Boeing 727.

The sun had risen in the sky, and it was hotter than hell down among the bushes where the wind didn't reach. Even the shade beneath the trees didn't offer much protection from the heat. But they were used to heat. They had grown up in Southern California, after all. It was the smell that really bothered them.

"What the hell *is* that *stench*?" Bobby asked for the tenth time.

They had worked their way several hundred yards down the canyon, far away from Woody's backyard, in the belief that if the head was going to migrate, it would migrate downhill. The undergrowth was thicker here, and they had to fight their way through it half the time. A machete would have been useful. Or a Bush Hog. Or a flamethrower. It didn't take too much of a stretch of the imagination to feel they were the only people since the Indians who had ever ventured into this place.

And for good reason. The place smelled like a toilet.

"Something's rotten in Denmark," Jeremy muttered, holding the tail of his T-shirt over his nose.

"Maybe it's a broken sewer pipe."

"No," Bobby said. "It smells like rotten meat."

"Well, our guy died ten years ago. If it's his head, it wouldn't have any meat left on it, would it? The rest of him sure as hell didn't."

Cathy untangled her ponytail from a tree limb. Her face was as red as a Christmas ornament, and she wasn't looking particularly amused. Her shirt was soaked in sweat, but her nipples were nowhere in evidence. Woody wondered if she was wearing a bra. That would be a first. For reasons of self-preservation, he decided not to ask.

"The smell is getting stronger," Bobby said. And it was. The farther they followed the canyon down the hillside, away from the houses, away from the neighborhood, the stronger the odor became.

It seemed to be almost visible now before their eyes, like a layer of quivering air, sodden with bacteria, filled with stench, packed with corruption.

They left the shelter of the trees, and Jeremy was leading them now, single file through head-high sage and scrub, slipping now and then down the steep decline, causing little avalanches of rock to skitter off ahead of them.

Jeremy stopped so quickly, Woody almost plowed right into him. Jeremy pointed to the ground ahead.

"I think I'm going to puke."

Everybody snuggled up close behind him and gazed over his shoulders. "What is it?"

"Death," he said.

And sure enough, that's exactly what it was.

"Holy shit!" Chuck cried out, causing Cathy to jump. "It's Wilbur!"

"What? It can't be. My God, it is."

Wilbur was Woody's neighbor's dog. A Pomeranian Woody had known and put up with his whole life. The little yappy bastard was known for practically going into cardiac seizure every time anybody came within twenty yards of his mistress's yard. Old Miss Timken, a spinster who was about a thousand years old and looked it, loved the dog like she loved nothing else, and she had been frantically searching for it for the past week. Woody had seen her standing at her back fence only the day before, tears running down her wrinkled old cheeks, calling out Wilbur's name over and over, holding a dog biscuit pathetically in her withered hand, like maybe that would do the trick.

Looking at the carcass, Woody figured Wilbur's yapping days were over. The mailman would probably throw a party.

Chuck whistled. "Holy crap. The old lady's going to have a heart attack. What happened to him, do you think?"

They all moved closer, more than one of their noses now covered by a shirttail. They could hear flies swarming over the dog, and stepping closer, they could see the maggots those flies had spawned on the putrefying flesh of poor old Wilbur. His mouth was open, like maybe he was still yipping and yapping in whatever afterlife Pomeranians are headed for when they give up the mortal vale. Of course, Wilbur's mortal vale hadn't just been given up; it had been yanked out from under his four little feet like a rug.

There was a wooden stake poking up out of his rib cage, securely planted, nailing him to the ground like a butterfly in a bug collector's display cabinet.

"Well, *there's* something you don't see every day," Woody said. He felt guilty about it the minute the words popped out of his mouth. No creature, no matter how noisy and annoying they were in life, deserved to end up like this.

"Somebody killed him," Bobby said.

"Gee, you think?" Chuck asked.

Cathy gave the back of Chuck's head a slap that sounded like it hurt. "Are you blind? Of course, somebody killed him. Don't you see the stake sticking out of his ribs? He didn't commit suicide, for Christ's sake. He didn't crawl down here and commit hari-kari. He's not Japanese. He's a Pomeranian. Somebody stabbed him."

"Why would they *do* that?" Jeremy asked. His voice was hushed. Somehow the sight of this poor butchered Pomeranian disturbed him more than the human skeleton they had found the day before. Maybe because this one had a face. Something the other had thankfully lacked.

"Should we take him back to the old lady? She might want to give him a proper burial."

Cathy considered this. "I think maybe we should bury him ourselves and leave her out of it. What's the point of letting her know somebody killed her dog? Just let her continue to think he ran off. She'll eventually get over that. *This* she'll *never* recover from."

Woody nodded. "I think you're right."

"Poor little guy," Chuck said, still rubbing the back of his head where Cathy had whapped him.

"Poor old lady," Jeremy countered.

Woody suddenly realized Bobby was giving him one of those "I told you so" looks. It looked more at home on his mother's face than it did on Bobby's, but Bobby's was a pretty good replica.

"What?" Woody asked.

"He's still here."

Chuck piped in. "*Who's* still here?"

"The murderer," Bobby said, still staring at Woody like maybe Woody at least knew what he was talking about, even if no one else did.

"*What* murderer?" Cathy railed. "What the hell are you talking about?"

Woody almost lost all sense of where he was and what he was doing staring into Bobby's brown eyes. They were so soft, so beautiful. He remembered the feel of Bobby's warm stomach against his cheek the night before. The feel of Bobby's strong legs beneath his hands, quivering as he spilled his seed in Woody's mouth. The taste of his come. Woody's dick twitched when *that* memory popped into his head. He almost forgot he was standing in the middle of what was practically a jungle, smelling death, staring down at the bloated body of poor old Wilbur lying there in front of them with a stake poking out of his chest. The sound of a million flies swarming over the carcass brought him back.

"The dentist isn't the only one with a theory," Woody said quietly, shaking himself back to the present. He still stared into Bobby's eyes, still held his shirttail over his nose to filter out the reek of Wilbur's rotting corpse. "Bobby's got a theory too. And I think maybe I'm starting to believe it."

Cathy looked like she was about to pass out from the smell. "That's dandy, Woodrow. Another theory is just what we need. And I for one am eager to hear it, but let's do it somewhere else, okay? Please? I'm going to be barfing my Eggos up any minute now if we don't get away from this goddamn dead dog. We'll come back later and bury him. I promise. But right now, let's just go."

"We're with you," Chuck said, nodding, and Jeremy nodded with him, just like those bobble-head dolls you see in back car windows.

Woody glanced at them and almost laughed. Chuck and Jeremy had both stuffed twisted Kleenex up their noses and the white ropes of paper were hanging down from all four nostrils. They looked like a couple of little blond walruses.

"You're right," Woody said. "We'll need to get a shovel anyway. Let's go."

That was all the encouragement anyone needed. This time with Cathy leading the way, they tripped and stumbled up the steep embankment toward more familiar territory. By the time they reached the top and were moving through the pepper and willow trees toward the part of the canyon that abutted Woody's backyard, they were all sweating bullets. Woody's legs were trembling with the exertion, and his shirt felt like it was glued to his back.

"The turdhouse at last," Cathy said, giving a feeble cheer from her position of authority up ahead at the sight of their miserable construction project. "Thank God we're home."

They plopped themselves down on the fallen tree trunk and wiped the sweat from their eyes.

"Okay," Cathy said, breathing hard and gazing over at Woody. "What's this theory of yours?"

"Not mine," Woody said. "Bobby's."

All eyes turned to Bobby, but before he could speak, Jeremy raised his hand to silence him. "Wait a minute. I still smell it."

"Smell what?"

"Wilbur. I still smell Wilbur."

"It's just your imagination," Cathy said. "We're too far away to—"

Bobby stood and looked around. "I smell it, too."

Chuck took a whiff of his shirt. "Maybe the smell got on our clothes. It'll go away in a minute."

"No, it won't. Listen," Bobby said, uneasy, looking for all the world like a U-Boat commander who suspects depth charges are about to drift down through the ocean current and blast him out of the water.

"Listen to what?" Woody asked.

"Flies."

Then they all heard it. The droning hum of about a gazillion insects, just like the ones who were feeding on poor old Wilbur six hundred yards down the slope. But these were close.

Cathy pointed. "It's coming from in there."

And all eyes turned to the turdhouse.

"Oh, shit," Chuck said.

They moved en masse, shoulder to shoulder, toward the back of the clubhouse where they had placed the hole in the wall that would serve as a door. The smell was stronger here. And so was the noise.

"Maybe it's a swarm of bees," Jeremy whispered, breathless.

"Bees don't stink," Cathy said, equally breathless, equally hushed. Once again, she had pressed her shirt to her face, filtering out the stink. "Nimrod," she muttered through the fabric.

As always, when times were most dire and dangers were nearest, Bobby led the way. He peeked through the doorway, and Woody heard him gasp. Without turning, Bobby reached behind him and stuck a hand under Woody's belt buckle, pulling him closer. Bobby dragged him forward, and Woody had no choice but to look through the doorway over Bobby's shoulder.

Being roofless, the inside of the clubhouse was as sunlit as the outside. There were no shadows to make Woody think maybe he was seeing something that wasn't really there. And the muddied walls with the dying grass sticking out like diseased hair, were as butt ugly in here as they were out there. Uglier, in fact, because now those walls were covered in blood. Blood and flies.

But even the walls were not nearly as ugly as what lay on the floor between them. Surrounded by a squirming mass of maggots, Wilbur, still impaled by his ghastly wooden stake, and still just as dead as he had been when they'd discovered his carcass six hundred yards down the canyon not fifteen minutes before, looked up at Woody through eyes that had stopped seeing long ago.

As Woody stared into those dead white eyes, Wilbur blinked one of them, for all the world like he was sharing a joke with the two of them.

Bobby gasped again. "Did you see that?"

"No," Woody lied. "I didn't see anything."

Then Chuck was there, leaning over him, digging his chin into Woody's shoulder, trying to get a better look. Woody felt him tense when he saw what they were looking at.

"This is impossible," he whispered, his breath ruffling the hair on Woody's head. "Look at the blood. It's everywhere. But how did he get here?"

And after a pause, while Jeremy was saying, "Oh, crap, oh, crap, oh crap," over and over again like a mantra, and Cathy was using considerably stronger words to display her amazement, Chuck turned to Bobby and said, "I think we'd better hear about this theory of yours."

But Bobby only said, "Let's get that shovel first."

THEY BURIED Wilbur as deep as they could, but that wasn't very deep. The ground, even down at the base of the canyon where it was softer thanks to the winter runoff, was so interwoven with roots that it took forever to chop and hack their way through them. They scooped the body up with the shovel and dumped it in a garbage bag to lessen the stink while they worked.

Rather than pull the stake out of Wilbur's chest, they left it there, burying poor old Wilbur flat on his back with his stiff little paws sticking straight up so the stake wouldn't poke up through the shallow grave.

Before covering him with dirt, Jeremy said, "He looks like he's playing rollover."

"This dog's playing days are over," Cathy said, looking bug-eyed from the smell. "Let's just cover him up, okay?"

Since Bobby was the one holding the shovel, they gave him the honors. He filled in the grave as quickly as he could, and when he was finished, he slapped it a few times with the shovel blade to pack in the dirt. Then they pried a large stone out of the hillside and rolled it onto the grave, sealing Wilbur in forever and assuring that no critters would come along during the night and try to dig him up. The last thing they wanted to do was come down here tomorrow and see this goddamn dog staring them in the face again. They had seen more than enough of Wilbur to last them a lifetime.

With the burial finished to their satisfaction, they scrambled up the side of the canyon and plopped themselves down on the grass in Woody's backyard after first quenching their thirst with the garden hose. Grave digging was thirsty work. Looking at each of his friends in turn, Woody saw they weren't quite as filthy as they had been the day before, but they weren't exactly ready for high tea either.

"Let's hear it," Jeremy said, wiping the sweat from his eyes with his shirttail, which at this point was no longer yellow. More of a mocha brown. I'M WITH STUPID was barely legible.

"Wait for Chuck," Bobby said.

Unconvinced there weren't *two* dead Pomeranians rotting in the canyon, Chuck had trundled back down the hillside to where they had found the first dead Wilbur, just to see if he was still there.

They all knew he wasn't, even Chuck pretty well knew it, but he had to see it with his own two eyes before he would admit the fact.

A few minutes later, they heard Chuck scrambling up the scree on the canyon bank, and when his head came into view, they could all see by the look of confusion on his face that the damned dead dog had indeed beaten them up the hillside earlier.

Chuck went for the garden hose and drank about a gallon of water before saying anything. Then he dropped to the grass beside the rest of them and sat there staring at his filthy shoe tops.

"*Well?*" Cathy finally asked, exasperated by his silence. "Was he *there?*"

Chuck's face was two-toned. The lower half washed clean by the spray of the hose, the top half just as cruddy as his shoes. He twisted the clean half into a lopsided grin and said, "Nope. He's gone."

Cathy wasn't buying it. "How can that be? Even if somebody lugged that dead mutt up the hill and beat us to the top, how could they have gotten past us without us seeing them? This isn't making any sense at all."

"The man brought him," Bobby said quietly.

"*What* man?"

"The man who murdered the guy without a head."

"Oh, please."

Woody watched Jeremy scoot a little closer to his brother and cast a nervous glance past the roses at the edge of the yard to the canyon below. Jeremy was looking none too happy at the moment, and Woody wondered if he was going to start screaming like a madman or what. Chuck seemed to sense his twin's fear and gave him a little comforting nudge with his shoulder as if to say, "Cool it. Everything will be just fine."

And at that moment Woody saw what he had always known but never really understood. Chuck was the stronger of the two. The twins might look alike, but it was Chuck who kept them going when things got rough.

Before realizing he had done it, Woody found that he had scooted a little closer to Bobby. They had the same synergy going as the twins, he supposed. One the stronger and one the weaker. Leader and follower. It didn't take a brain surgeon to figure out which was which.

Woody had always followed Bobby's lead. Even last night in the darkness of his room, it was Bobby who had dredged up the courage to lead them to the place they had always been headed. It was through Bobby's courage, not his own, that their relationship had taken one quantum leap forward to the place where it had always been destined to go. Bobby had known Woody's needs were the same as his own, even if Woody had not, and he had acted on that knowledge. Fearless, as always. And Woody had followed. Happily. Just as he was still following.

"Tell them," Woody said, nudging Bobby with his elbow.

And Bobby did. With a minimum of drama, like he was reciting a shopping list or something, Bobby laid out his theory that the body of the man they had found the day before had not died in a plane crash more than ten years earlier. He had been murdered. And the murderer was still here. Wilbur proved it.

Whether the murderer was alive or dead was another question.

While Bobby talked, Woody studied the faces of his friends. All eyes were nailed to Bobby. All ears were absorbing Bobby's every word. If there was any disbelief in what they were hearing, it didn't show on any of their faces. Maybe only thirteen-year-old minds would so easily accept the impossible as fact, but accept it they did. Woody could see it in their eyes. Even Cathy seemed at a loss for words to argue the point Bobby was making.

When Bobby finished talking, they all sat there in silence. Pondering.

It was Chuck who finally raised the inescapable question. "So what do we do about it?" he asked.

"We stay the hell out of the canyon," Cathy said. "That's what we do about it."

To Woody's surprise, it was Jeremy who spoke the words that would outline future events. He looked frightened as he said them, but he looked determined too.

"Bullshit. That's *our* canyon. Maybe it's haunted, maybe it ain't. So what if there's a dead psychopath wandering around in the underbrush? It's still *our* underbrush. I say we run the fucker off and reclaim it for ourselves."

Maybe Chuck wasn't the only twin with balls after all, Woody thought. Hairless though they may be.

Cathy looked at Jeremy in the same way she had looked at Wilbur earlier. With disgust. "Are you nuts? If there's a murdering ghost down there, and I'm not saying there is, what makes you think he won't come after us? If he's strong enough to poke a stick through a dog, what makes you think he can't do the same to us?"

Bobby answered before Jeremy had a chance to. "Wilbur didn't have his friends with him to watch his back. Wilbur was all alone and weighing all of, what, ten pounds? We've got each other. Wilbur was just a little Pomeranian. We're an army. And we've got *right* on our side."

Cathy groaned. "Nice pep talk, shitwad. For the sake of argument, let's say we decide to do what you're suggesting we do. Enlighten me. How the hell do you go about killing a ghost?"

Bobby grinned. "Beats me. It'll be fun trying, though, don't you think?"

"Oh, yeah. A barrel of laughs. A chuckle a minute."

Woody could sense a plan unfolding in Bobby's mind even before he spoke. "We'll meet him on his own turf. And we'll meet him in the dark. Tonight."

"Oh, shit."

"And then," Bobby finished up, "we'll kill him."

No one commented on the holes in Bobby's plan. Like how were they all going to sneak out of their houses in the middle of the night without their parents knowing about it, and even if they did, how were they going to kill something that was already dead? And what if this ghost of Bobby's didn't *want* to be killed? Did anybody think of *that?* Maybe it *liked* being dead. And maybe it wasn't exactly averse to making *them* dead, too. By the look of determination on Bobby's face, Woody supposed these were all minor glitches to be ironed out later.

NONE OF them could have known as they sat there in the grass on Woody's backyard on that summer morning, with the jacaranda blossoms occasionally drifting down on their heads, wondering each in their own way what adventures the night ahead would bring, that Bobby's theory was all wrong.

The twins' father had almost nailed it. But even he didn't have all the pieces of the puzzle necessary to make his theory ironclad.

You had to combine the two theories, Bobby's and the dentist's, to really get at the truth.

And even then, there was one major flaw in all their suppositions. The ghost in the canyon might exist, but aside from poking a stick through poor old Wilbur, he was not a murderer.

Not yet.

CHAPTER FIVE

WOODY AWOKE with a kink in his neck from sleeping with his head on the kitchen table. He took another hot shower, which pretty well solved the problem (if only the rest of his troubles could be so easily dealt with), then set out to begin the day. He wasn't scheduled to go on stage until eight o'clock that evening, so he had a whole long day ahead of him to prepare.

As always, Woody kept the angst of opening a new show at bay by following a standard routine, one he had worked out over the years. First, he ironed his denims and polished his cowboy boots. Then he sorted through his vast array of shirts, all western cut and tailored to within an inch of their lives, and finally settled on two. One with big black and white checks and another sewn in the pattern of the American flag. They weren't shirts he would ever wear on the street, but under a spotlight they looked pretty good. Gaudy as hell, but effective. He ironed those too, using just enough spray starch to make them crisp but not uncomfortable, and hung them over the jeans. Most country western singers sported cowboy hats, but Woody had never worn a cowboy hat in his life. He looked stupid in hats. He figured his shoulder length hair was all the decoration his head needed, and if his audiences didn't agree with him, they could go screw themselves.

When his clothes were ready and hanging neatly on the bedroom doorknob, he dropped two extra guitar picks in each shirt pocket for backup, in case one flew out of his hand in the middle of a number, and sat down on the edge of his bed to tune the Gibson. The E string was sounding a little flat, so he replaced it with a new one. He did a couple of runs to see if his fingers still worked, then sang a verse or two of an old George Strait tune to see if he still had a voice. Somehow, he always expected his talent to leave him during the night, so every morning he tested it, and every morning, wonder of wonders, it was still there. Woody wasn't sure why, but this always surprised him.

As he did his prep work for the show, he tried not to think of his dead mother standing at the kitchen sink washing the blood of her own death from her hands. Tried not to think of that grimacing smile she had given him through the wounds on her face. Tried not to think of the words she had spoken in the darkness. But it was the thought of his father standing silently in the shadows that troubled him most. He had seemed so—beaten down. So lost. In life he had been a happy guy. Always smiling. Always taking things as they came. Rattling off at the mouth every chance he got, telling jokes, making people smile. But last night there had been no happiness left in him. Only a bone-chilling sadness. Woody's heart ached at the memory of him silently stepping backward to hide in the shadows, away from sight, as if ashamed of what he had become.

Woody wondered. Had his parents never left this house? Had they been here through all the empty years while Woody was away? Had they been roaming through the vacant rooms, listening for the sound of footsteps on the porch, the turning of the doorknob, hoping to see their only son walk through that doorway as he had done so many times before, back before the world took him away, before he was *driven* away by everything that had happened?

Did they suffer through all those silent years alone, or did they find comfort in each other's company? Did they pass each other in the darkness, never knowing the other was there? If they could sense each other's presence, did they speak together of the day they died, did they remember it at all, or did their deaths rob them of even that?

As the sound of a perfectly tuned C major chord echoed away to silence, Woody felt the crush of the house settling over him. Too many memories. Too much pain. He needed air. He grabbed the house keys and stepped through the front door, facing what promised to be another scorching hot Southern California day, just like those of his childhood.

He needed to move, get the blood pumping, stretch his legs. Needed to get some fresh air into his lungs and maybe drive away the smell of the house, of the past. He needed to drive away the memory of last night too. Of his mother's savaged face. His father's shame.

Needed to wash away all those flashbacks of his childhood, which he had been bombarded with ever since he stepped back in time to this place where he grew up, where he was once happy, but where he no longer seemed to quite fit in. Even the good memories, the memories of Bobby, had left him with a sadness that was almost debilitating. How could a love affair that took place when he was thirteen years old—damn near two decades earlier—have left him so emotionally fucked up? What the hell was wrong with him?

Woody plastered a smile on his face as he stepped through the front door. The smile felt as out of place as he did as he set out to walk those streets again after all the years he had been away. Every house, every tree was still familiar to him, but even so he felt like a stranger dropped without warning into new surroundings. He felt *alien.* Like he didn't belong. But even that feeling was familiar to him. After that summer, he never felt like he belonged *anywhere*. Never had. Probably never would.

Jesus, he was fucked up.

There used to be a small diner on Thirtieth Street, a few blocks from the house, so Woody headed in that direction. Maybe some breakfast would make him feel better. He had to eat sometime. Might as well be now. For one brief moment, he longed for a teeny line of crystal meth to ease himself out of the funk he had fallen into, but he pushed that thought away before it had a chance to really settle in. Going back to drugs was something he swore he would never do, although sometimes, just *sometimes*, one little snort of burning crystalline powder shooting up his nostrils was all it took to make him feel like he had a nice firm hold on his life. Of course, it was all illusion. He had never had a *weaker* grip on his own existence than he did when he was snorting meth. Half the time he hadn't even known what he was doing. But even *not* knowing was sometimes better than knowing. There was a certain peace and contentment to be found in oblivion.

Still, a promise was a promise, even if it was only made to oneself. A return to drugs would get him nowhere but dead, or worse, unemployed. So eggs and bacon would have to do.

Leaving his old street, he suddenly found himself in unfamiliar territory. What used to be a small, rundown enclave of dusty Laundromats and thrift shops packed to the ceiling with nothing anybody with any brains would ever want to buy, along with a couple of neighborhood beer bars with names like Spanky's and The DewDrop Inn, or some such silliness, was now a jazzy little maze of bookstores, ice cream parlors, holistic health food shops, and high-end restaurants with flashy menus posted in the windows, touting everything from prawns to sushi to crepes. What was once the diner—Mabel's Diner, it used to be called—was now a Yoga Center with a big fat Buddha sitting smugly in the window and the heavy odor of incense wafting through the open doorway. So much for eggs and bacon.

Two doors up he found a small coffee shop with a massive brass espresso machine standing in the window, looking like something NASA might have engineered for a lunar mission, or maybe a jog around Neptune, and which must have set the proprietors back a few thousand bucks. There, after snagging a morning paper from the kiosk on the corner, he settled into a sidewalk table and ordered a mocha cappuccino with fresh croissants and a little dish of hand-churned butter on the side.

When the waiter brought his order, Woody was surprised to hear him say, "Good morning, Mr. Stiles. Welcome back."

Woody didn't know the guy from Adam. He laid his paper aside and asked, "Have we met before?"

The waiter, who was obviously gay and obviously not afraid to show it, smiled sweetly as he arranged Woody's order neatly in front of him and said, "No, but I recognized your picture from the paper."

"The paper…?"

"Page six. The Entertainment section." Then the waiter wagged a friendly finger in his face and added, "Some friends and I are coming to see you tonight, so put on a good show, okay?"

"You must be a bowler," Woody said, but the waiter only laughed and walked away, leaving him in peace to enjoy his breakfast.

Woody thumbed through the newspaper until he found the Entertainment section, and sure enough, there he was, splattered across page six in a quarter-page ad that must have cost Strikers a goodly number of dollars. It was an old publicity shot he remembered posing for a couple of years back. Backlit by phony stage lights, he was standing with his guitar strapped across his chest, his long jeans-clad legs rooted firmly beneath him, his ever-present cowboy boots poking out below, obviously singing his heart out to what only he knew had been a nonexistent audience. He remembered how stupid he had felt, standing in the studio posing for the shot, but now he had to admit he looked pretty good. Looked like an honest-to-God entertainer, he did, with his long hair and lean hips and a promising bulge that offered all sorts of good things to come, and not just music either, my friends, pushing up against the fly of his faded Levi's.

Woody almost laughed.

He read the come-on line at the top of the ad. "Strikers is proud to present—blah blah blah—the incomparable Woody Stiles—In Person—for two weeks only—blah blah blah blah blah—bring a friend and spend the night with San Diego's very own Woody Stiles—blah blah blah—cover charge $30.00 per person."

Thirty dollars? Jesus, Woody thought, how had his agent pulled that one off? He thought he was playing a bowling alley, for God's sake.

Woody felt his toes begin to tingle inside his boots. The first sign of stage fright and he hadn't even seen the club yet. Oh, well, stage fright was just one ailment in a long list of miseries he had learned to live with during his years in show business, and he knew it always came *before* the show, not *during*, so he didn't worry about it too much. What worried him was that $30.00 cover charge. Good Lord, aside from his nelly waiter and what was undoubtedly his waiter's coterie of nelly friends, God love 'em, would anybody else show up at all?

Woody had a sudden urge to see the club he was playing tonight, check it out, and maybe find the moron who decided to post that cover charge on the night's entertainment. Maybe Woody could get it reduced or, with luck, done away with completely. There was nothing more depressing than playing to an empty house. Woody doubted if *he* would pay thirty bucks to watch himself perform, so what made them think anyone else would?

He wolfed down his croissants, drained the coffee from his cup, and since the waiter was so seemingly enamored of his talents (or maybe the bulge in his jeans in that publicity shot), he left a sizable tip on the table (didn't want the guy to think he was one of those shitheel performers who treated their fans like a pestilence) and, tucking the paper under his arm, headed back to the house.

Once there, Woody grabbed his clothes from the doorknob, gathered up his guitar and play sheets, and dumped it all in the Suburban. It was still only noon; he had eight long hours of worrying to endure before curtain time if he didn't act now. Best to find out quickly what sort of place Strikers really was.

Woody had played more than his share of dumps in his day. There had been a few where he wouldn't even touch a beer glass unless it came with a saucer of antibiotics on the side. Never knowing what sort of environment his agent had booked him into, Woody carried with him everything he needed to put on a decent show. Amplifiers. Mikes. Even his own lighting system. More than once, he had practically been forced to build a stage to stand on.

After taking a couple of wrong freeway exits, he found Strikers at last, nestled on the coastline between Sea World and the San Diego Hilton. Not exactly a crummy section of town. What he had been told was a mere bowling alley turned out to be an entertainment park with everything from bumper cars to batting cages to a driving range for practicing golfers. It even boasted a gigantic Ferris wheel, spinning high overhead. Walking beneath a neon archway that said "Funworld," Woody discovered arcades, clothing and souvenir shops, a McDonald's, and, at the very end of the promenade, a gigantic bowling alley where he could hear the rumble of bowling balls from half a city block away. He doubted if even his own sound system could compete with that racket.

Through another archway up ahead, he could see a marina where dozens of boats were moored, and there, facing the water, comfortably far from the noise of the bowling alley, was Strikers. Woody wasn't certain what he had expected to find, but it certainly wasn't this. The place was massive.

Laid out like an amphitheater. Stepping through the open doors, he saw tiered tables surrounding a center stage floored in gleaming oak. An ornate mahogany bar as long as a tractor trailer was sprawled across the back wall, and even at this early hour of the day, there were a fair number of patrons perched on barstools, sipping beers and highballs. Parents, maybe, waiting for their kids to run out of quarters back at the arcade.

The place was as clean as his mother's kitchen after a day of scrubbing. Mirrors sparkled. Wood glistened. Chairs were neatly upended across the tabletops as a team of workers ran vacuum cleaners across a couple of acres of red carpeting that looked as pristine as if it might have been laid down only the day before.

At the edge of the stage was every electronic device known to man. Vast speakers. An electronic keyboard. Microphones and a tangle of spots and strobes hung down from the ceiling. A dozen instruments—electric guitars, steel guitars, a bass fiddle, and even a mandolin—stood propped on stands waiting for talented hands to bring them to life. A drum set stood in the corner like a growth of mushrooms. A ring of colored spotlights circled the stage, all off now, but promising a damn good light show when they were all switched on and the room was darkened around them.

At the moment, a technician was rigging what Woody saw was a setup for him. A barstool. Double mikes. A little table off to the side to hold his beer, if he decided to sip on one during his performance, which he knew immediately he wouldn't. Not here. This wasn't a corner dive where you could get as shitfaced as the clientele and no one would know the difference. This had all the makings of an honest-to-God *concert*, and Woody felt a smile creeping across his face at the prospect. Jeez, maybe he wasn't quite as unknown as he thought he was.

Another technician was standing where Woody would later stand, testing the mikes, while the first techie dragged the cords across the stage and out of the way so they would be as inconspicuous as possible under the spotlights. Woody jotted down a mental note and thumbtacked it to the bulletin board inside his head, reminding himself to remember where those electric cords were placed. No sense tripping over one of them and making an ass of himself even before the show began.

As the technician spoke into the voice mike, "One, two, three, testing. One, two, three—" Woody heard the man's voice booming out from every side of the room, clear of static and electronic squeals. And mellow. Damned mellow.

"It's perfect!" Woody yelled out, and both technicians stopped what they were doing to look in his direction.

Woody strode down the sloping walkway between the tiers of tables and climbed the steps to the stage. Sticking out his hand, he introduced himself. The techies introduced themselves in return. One was Manny. The other Jack.

Manny looked back at the voice mike with a doubtful expression on his face. "You sure? Sounds a little tinny."

"No," Woody said. "It's great. Don't change a thing."

"What about the lights?" Jack asked. "How do you want us to run it? Simple spot?"

"That's fine," Woody said. "I'm not picky. Just so they can see me."

"We'll need your playlist," Jack said, "for the light cues, if you have any."

"Sure. I've got it in the car."

"We thought about running some colored spots around the room while you're playing. Would that be all right?"

"Sure, guys. Whatever you think. You know the layout better than I do."

Woody looked around the place for the first time from the vantage point of the stage. "What the hell is the seating capacity in this joint, anyway?"

"Six hundred. Couple hundred more if we pack 'em in."

Woody laughed. "You gotta be kidding." He had never played a joint this big in his life. "Think anybody'll actually show up?"

Both technicians looked at him like he had just fallen from the rafters. "What?" Manny asked. "You kidding? Look over there."

Woody let his eyes follow to where the guy was pointing and saw a life-size poster of the same picture that was in the paper that morning placed in a marquee by the front door. Angled across the top of it were the words TONIGHT'S PERFORMANCE SOLD OUT. And in smaller letters below that, it said, "Limited Tickets For Future Performances Still Available Through Ticketmaster Or At The Box Office On The Plaza."

"Jesus!" Woody said.

Manny grinned at the look of stunned disbelief on Woody's face. "Come on," he said, "I'll show you where your dressing room is."

"I have a dressing room?" Usually he had a toilet stall.

Manny shrugged. "This is the big time, kid. You know who played here last week?"

"God?" Woody asked.

Manny laughed. "Almost. Stevie Nicks."

"No shit?"

"No shit."

For lack of anything better to do, Woody reached out and raised the voice mike to the proper height. "I think I need a drink," he said, and was more than a little embarrassed to hear his words boom out from the speakers circling the stage. A few heads at the bar swiveled around to see what was going on, then just as quickly swiveled back. Cows at a trough.

"No problem," Jack said. "For the next two weeks this place is yours. Enjoy it."

"Thanks," Woody said, honestly humbled by the kindness he saw in the technician's eyes. "Thanks a lot."

WOODY'S AFTERNOON was filled with surprises. Thankfully, these surprises were considerably less traumatic to contemplate than those of the night before.

His dressing room was just what he had always imagined a dressing room to be. Rows of lights around a wall of mirrors. Sofa in the corner. A Coke machine just outside the door. There was even a closed-circuit TV, and when Woody switched it on, he saw a flurry of activity on the empty stage. The technicians were in the process of removing all the extraneous equipment, musical instruments mostly, that had been scattered across it earlier. Pretty soon there would be nothing on that stage but himself, his guitar, and a couple of mikes cranked up to amplify every fuck-up he made during the course of his performance. And beyond the spotlights, there would be six hundred plus people either enjoying the hell out of his music or throwing tomatoes at this inept nitwit who thought he was of a class worthy to follow the incomparable Stevie Nicks.

Oh, well. Come what may, Woody was determined to enjoy the evening. Even if this turned out to be his first and last shot at the big time, he intended to make it memorable, for himself if no one else.

He was a bit amazed to find he was actually looking forward to the show. His toes weren't tingling at all. If there was any unease in Woody, it came from the horrors he had witnessed the night before as he stood in his mother's kitchen, not from what was happening now.

His preshow jitters were nowhere in evidence, thanks to the friendliness of the technicians and the jovial welcome he had received from the club's owner, who came knocking at his dressing room door shortly after Woody arrived, shaking his hand for a full two minutes, telling him how glad he was to have Woody performing at his club, and, before leaving, pointing to a phone on the dressing table and telling Woody if he needed anything, anything at all, pick up that phone and one of the waitresses would bring it. Food, drinks, whatever he wanted. And with a parting, "Have a great show!" the owner left, leaving Woody stunned by his generosity.

Just when Woody was beginning to think nothing else could happen to make him feel any more content with the way things were turning out, his agent came walking through the dressing room door with a Cheshire cat grin on his face and told him a couple of recording executives were coming to the performance tonight to watch the show with an eye to maybe giving Woody a shot at a recording contract. If Woody played his cards and his music right, this could be the break they had both been waiting for.

With everything else that had happened in the last twenty-four hours, Woody couldn't quite wrap his head around *that* bit of news. He was too flabbergasted to even try.

"What the hell are you doing here?" Woody asked. Noah's talent agency was in L.A. During all the years they had been together as agent and client, Woody had never seen the guy anywhere but there, sitting behind his cluttered desk, smoking one cigar after the other until you could barely see the other side of the room through the haze.

Noah Taylor was at the wrong end of his sixties, with a paunch that grew annually and a hairline that receded at about the same clip. Usually Noah was a saturnine sort of guy, more at home with a scowl on his face than a smile, the kind of old fart who lives his life in a perpetual state of crankiness. No one would ever suspect he made his living in the entertainment business. But Noah wasn't looking cranky now. Now he was looking pretty darned pleased with himself.

"The club owner's an old friend of mine," he told Woody conspiratorially. "I've been trying to get you booked in here for months. I figure you've paid your dues by playing all the shitholes I've thrown at you over the years, and not once did you ever let me down. You got yourself off the drugs, and I'm damned proud of you for that.

Your voice is stronger than it's ever been, and with two weeks at Strikers on your resume, it'll be easier to book you some good venues in the future. If these record guys like you, Woody, we'll be on our way to the top. I'm happy for you. Hell, I'm happy for *me*! So what do you think? Think you can pull it off tonight?"

Woody blinked. "Well—sure. I'm ready. At least I think I am. Hell, I *know* I am. I've been ready for ten years." It was true. Woody knew it with as much certainty as he knew his own name. The rest of his life might be a clusterfuck, but this one small part of it, the part comprised of music and spotlights and lonely hours behind the mike, was the one part he had no doubts about whatsoever.

Before he could stop himself, Woody wrapped his arms around Noah, kissed the stubble on the guy's cheek, and gave him a bear hug that would have paralyzed a real bear. Then, for the hell of it, Woody kissed Noah's other cheek.

Noah looked a little embarrassed by the display of affection, but he looked pretty pleased by it, too. "Geez, kid, you don't have to suck my dick or anything." Then he laughed. "We're going to the top like a bullet, you and me, just wait and see if we don't." He pushed Woody away and studied his face. "You're not going to become one of those prima donnas that starts demanding a big bowl of M&M's before the show with all the green ones plucked out, or starts shopping around for an agent with more clout and a fancier office, or forgets who made him who he is, are you? I mean, you're not going to turn into an *asshole* or anything, are you?"

There was a grin on Noah's face when he said it, but Woody thought he detected a hint of desperation in his words too. And that, more than anything, made Woody suddenly take his words about the recording execs seriously. Jesus, maybe he really did have a shot at the brass ring. And maybe, just maybe, it would happen this very night.

He cupped Noah's jowls in his hands like he would cradle a plum pudding and, grinning right back, said, "It's not the green ones I hate, it's the red ones. But I'll pick those out myself. I promise."

"Oh, good."

"And trust me, Noah, as long as I'm working, I'll be working for you. If you make this happen, I'll even forgive you for booking me into that dive in Tucson where I damn near got my balls shot off by the drunk with the Winchester who thought he was Billy the Kid."

Noah chuckled. "Last I heard, the guy was still doing some serious time over that little escapade."

"Thank God," Woody said, and meant it.

Noah shrugged. "Yeah, well, you know, everybody's a critic."

Woody grinned. "True. But most of them don't back it up with artillery fire."

THEY HAD a good long laugh over that, and then Noah left to let Woody prepare for the show in his own way. Noah understood performers. Once, a lifetime earlier, he had been one himself. But not a very good one, he had finally decided. Or maybe he hadn't wanted success enough to make it happen. Woody wanted it. Woody was hungry for it. And Woody was special. Noah had sensed it the first time he heard him sing. They had been through a lot during the years Noah had represented Woody, and as he had told Woody earlier, the kid had not once let him down. If anybody deserved a break, Noah figured it was Woody Stiles. And he was determined to be the one to give it to him. It wouldn't hurt his own pocketbook either, he thought, and this brought another grin to Noah's weathered old face as he closed the dressing room door behind him, popped his reeking cigar back in his mouth, and headed for the bar.

WOODY WAS glad to be away from the house, away from the memories of childhood. Glad to be back in the world he knew. The world of music. It was the one place where he felt, if not totally at home, at least not totally out of his element, either. He belonged here. He always had.

As the afternoon wore on, Woody introduced himself to the waitresses who were just starting their shifts and the bartenders who were working the day crowd. He had a beer at the bar with Noah, made nice with a couple of customers who said they had tickets for the show later in the week, and since there was nothing left to do between then and show time, he made one final check of the microphones onstage before the audience started drifting in. Then he wandered outside to get a little fresh air and check out the view from the landing.

There wasn't much to see, really. Any view of the bay he might have had was pretty much obliterated by the forest of masts and superstructures on the scores of sailboats and pleasure crafts that were lashed to the piers in front of him. But the ocean air smelled clean and fresh and redolent with life, reminding him of his days working the fishing boat back at a time when his parents' death hadn't knocked him for a loop yet. Well, maybe that loop had finally come full circle. Maybe things would start looking up after tonight.

The boardwalk was packed with people. Families mostly, with lots of kids running around, begging quarters from their folks for the arcade, slurping ice cream cones, packing stuffed animals they had managed to snag from a bank of claw machines Woody had spotted earlier.

He lit a cigarette and watched the smoke drift out across the bay. While gazing down over the railing at the steep jumble of rocks that had been dumped there to abut the boardwalk and hold the Pacific in its proper place, as if the powers-that-be were afraid the ocean wouldn't have enough sense to do that on its own, Woody saw a man standing at the edge of the water, looking up at him.

The guy was a mess. In his fifties, Woody guessed, with a bald head surrounded by a strip of long wispy hair, mostly gray, that covered his ears and stuck out on either side like a clown's. There was a patch of crusty skin on the dome of his head, like lichen, the man dug at constantly, as if it itched. His clothes were little more than rags, and his feet were bare. Not bare like somebody taking a casual stroll along the beach, but bare like somebody who didn't own any shoes. His toenails were black and grungy, and looking closer, Woody saw the man's fingernails were infected with a fungus that had all but obliterated his nails. The ends of his fingers looked like they had been dipped in oatmeal. Woody shivered.

The man continued to stare up at Woody, and he did it like someone with a few cracks in the old engine block. His jaw was slack, and a rope of drool dangled off his chin. The front of his shirt, which wouldn't have qualified as one of Woody's mother's cleaning rags, was stained with slobber from collar to hem. Woody began to back away, feeling suddenly uncomfortable under the guy's vacant, disconcerting stare, but before he could back off completely, the man opened his mouth and called out in a loud friendly voice like a carnival barker enticing a crowd to step right up and for two bits take a gander at the one and only Alligator Boy.

"Hello there, Woody. How's tricks?"

Woody halted his retreat like somebody had nailed his feet to the pier. He mentally pried them loose and approached the railing again to study the man below.

"Do I know you?" he asked.

"Maybe you do and maybe you don't," the man said. He shoved one of his fungus-coated fingertips into a nostril, digging around for all he was worth, doing a little mining for gold before he pulled it out again and wiped it on his filthy shirt. Woody almost puked.

"How's the folks?"

"What folks?" Woody asked, honestly confused.

The man's eyes narrowed, and a sneer twisted his mouth. His voice didn't sound so friendly all of a sudden. "Your *parents*, dumbass. How are your *parents*? Saw them recently, didn't you? Popped in for a little surprise visit, I hear. That must have made your butt pucker."

Woody figured his own mouth was probably now hanging open like a trap door, making him look every bit as stupid as the homeless guy, if he *was* homeless. He was certainly crazy enough to be.

"What the hell are you talking about? Look, if you want some money, I'll—"

"She was sucking his dick, you know."

"What?"

"Yeah, right there in the soup aisle. Ain't *that* a kick in the head? They had the front door locked, of course, but that didn't stop me."

Woody was getting angry now. Angry and maybe a little scared. This wasn't making any sense at all. "Are you talking about my—"

"Your mom, yeah. She was down on her knees gobbling away at your old man's cock, just slobbering all over it like a kid with a Popsicle. Spit shining the old knob for all she was worth. It was pretty funny to watch. She looked like such a lady, you know? And your old man was really getting into it, too. Knees shaking, holding onto her head while he drove the old salami through those innocent looking lips. Over and over and over. His balls slapping her chin. His hairy naked ass hanging.out by the Campbell's Cream of Chicken. It was a sight to see. It surely was."

Woody's own knees were beginning to tremble now.

"Look, you son of a bitch, I don't know who the fuck you are or what you're playing at, but—"

"If you interrupt me one more time, I'm going to climb up there and stick my salami down *your* throat, you little shit. But then, you'd like that, wouldn't you? I mean, you like sucking dicks, too, I hear. Just like your mama. Golly, who'd ever think something like that would be hereditary? I always sort of figured being a cocksucker was an acquired taste, you know? But hell, maybe it's in the genes." He spit up a cackling laugh that made the little hairs on Woody's neck stand up. "Get it? *In—the—jeans?* What d'ya think? Speak up, Woodrow. Let's get a conversation going here. I seem to be the only one doing any talking. Conversation's like head, you know. It's always more enjoyable if you get a little back now and then."

"Who—who are you? What do you—?"

"How about some drugs, Woodrow? I've got some good shit here." He pulled out a plastic baggie and dangled it in the air, giving Woody a wink when he did. "Crystal meth, kid, just the way you like it, made from the finest household chemicals known to man. Guaranteed to get your ass *moving*."

Woody's mind was spinning. His cigarette, forgotten in his hand, suddenly burned his fingers and he let out a yip, flinging it away. He looked around and saw there was no one on the pier but him. Not a soul. Where was everybody? Where had they all gone, all those families with their screaming kids? What was happening here?

The man still stood below him at the edge of the water, looking up expectantly, like maybe he was waiting for Woody to climb over the rail and join him by the water. As if that was ever going to happen.

As confused and angry and *shocked* as Woody was by everything the bum had said to him, he also felt safe. He was well out of reach from the fucker. There was nothing the man could do to harm him. But still—why had this guy said the things he said? *Who was he?*

Woody placed his hands firmly on the rail and dredged up the courage to speak. "How do you know what my parents were doing that day in the store? Were you there? Did you see the murderer?"

The man coughed up another chuckle. He flung the plastic baggie back over his shoulder like a man tossing away trash, and Woody watched it sail out onto the water, where it landed with a teeny splash and drifted there until the current slowly dragged it away. Although

Woody knew he wouldn't have touched anything this man offered him, he still felt heartsore to see that bag of crystal meth drifting out to sea. *Jesus, who's the crazier person here,* Woody asked himself, *this miserable fucker or me?*

The man was now gazing up at Woody with a smirk, as if he knew exactly what Woody was thinking. Woody saw for the first time there was a scar around the man's neck. Not an old scar, but one that looked pretty darned fresh. Like maybe he had been choked with a rope and was somehow lucky enough to have survived. Woody could see a clear fluid oozing out of the wound as the man continued to stare up at him with his mouth stupidly gaping open. But there was nothing stupid in the guy's eyes. The eyes were cunning. Like the eyes of a leopard stalking its prey.

"You should have seen your old man jump, Woody, when I popped up in front of him. Pulled his pants up so fast he damn near tore your old lady's chin off with his belt buckle. Knocked over a whole shitload of soup cans. They were rolling all over the place. That was pretty funny, too. Jeez, it was just a fun day all around."

Woody had finally had enough. "Who are you, dammit? If you saw what happened that day you should have gone to the police! Maybe they could have caught the guy!"

"What guy?" the man asked, all innocent and wide-eyed.

"The man who killed my parents!" Woody screamed out the words with such force that a couple of seagulls took off from the boardwalk a hundred yards away, flapping and *yawking* as if someone had chucked a rock at them.

The man stared up at Woody for a couple of beats with a look of bemusement, like maybe he couldn't believe what he had just heard. "Good Lord, son, I think all those drugs you used to snort must have killed a few brain cells. You're not making any sense at all. *I* killed them. Did you think I was in there to pick up some Hot Pockets and a Diet Coke? I *went* there to kill them. Sort of a day trip. An outing. Golly, I sure did have fun that morning. I can leave the canyon anytime I want, you see. One of the perks of being a free spirit, I guess. No pun intended." He spread his arms wide and took in the view. "I can even spend a day at the beach if I want. How much fun is *that?*"

Woody could barely hear his own voice for the blood rushing through his head. "The—the canyon?"

"I was hungry that day. I wanted the twins. They were so delectable when they were young. But just like you, they had grown up and moved away. No one ever came into my little canyon anymore. I should have killed you all when I had the chance, but, well, I've always been something of a procrastinator. Fiddling around, missing one opportunity after the other. Been that way my whole life, back when I had a life, that is. Yeah, I should have killed you all years ago. Back when you were ripe for the picking. Should have known when I took Bobby, the rest of you would skedaddle like frightened chickens. Never saw any of you again after that. Bad planning all around. That's why I killed your folks, Woody. Thought maybe it would bring you back. You and all your friends. And who knows? Maybe it's finally happening. At least *you're* here. You took your sweet-ass time about it, but at least it's a start."

Woody could feel his heart flailing away inside his chest. A trickle of sweat (or was it a tear?) slid down his cheek, and he angrily brushed it away. Suddenly, everything the man had said to him began to make sense.

"*You* killed Bobby."

The man yawned. "I killed them all, kid. I had to. I was bored."

Businesslike, the man brought his wrist up to his face and stared at it like he was checking the time on the wristwatch that wasn't there. "Holy cow, son. Look at the time. Gotta run. I can't spend all eternity standing around shooting the shit with you. I've got things to do. And unless I'm mistaken, so do you. This is a big night for you, Woodrow. Wouldn't want you to blow it by showing up late, or worse yet, not showing up at all."

Woody was trembling so badly that if it wasn't for the railing he was holding on to, he would have toppled over like a tree. "Wait!"

The man grinned, showing green, fuzzy teeth. "Don't worry, kid. We'll meet again." And with a jaunty salute, he added, "Later, dude."

And then he was gone. Simply gone.

"Wait!" Woody screamed again. "Who are you? Where did you come from? *Why did you kill Bobby?*"

Hearing footsteps behind him, Woody spun around so fast he almost stumbled. A woman walking a child along the boardwalk looked over at him, at the terror on his face, and steered her child away as quickly as she could. She hurried off, dragging the kid behind her, losing herself quickly in the crowd of adults that had suddenly reappeared from nowhere. Once again there were people all over the place, strolling along the boardwalk, eating cotton candy, drinking Cokes, enjoying the evening, while their kids ran around like a panicked herd of gazelle, screaming, laughing, making a racket.

Woody gazed back over the railing to the rocks below, but there was no one there.

Maybe there never had been. Maybe everything that had just happened was simply the product of an overly active imagination. Maybe the stress of returning home after all these years, and the stress, too, of seeing what he thought he had seen last night in the darkness, maybe it had all been too much for his little pea brain to absorb. Maybe he was going shithouse crazy, and wouldn't it be just like him to do it on the day recording execs were coming to catch the show?

With trembling hands, he shook out a Pall Mall from the pack in his shirt pocket, and as he held the lighter's flame to the tip of it, drawing a satisfying cloud of deadly carcinogens deep into his lungs, he stared into the lighter's flame long enough to lose himself yet again in the past that seemed to always be reaching out for him, snatching him up at the most unlikely of times. Like now.

Darkness fell around him, or he imagined it did, as he was drawn into that tiny flame he held in his hand. Drawn into it, nearer and nearer, until he could feel the heat of it on his skin, hear the flame snapping and crackling and popping like a bowl of Rice Krispies, eating at the wick, lapping at the tobacco… drawing Woody in… drawing Woody back…

HIS EYES saw only red flame now, streaked with yellow. He could hear the dried wood sucking in the heat. He could taste the ashes on his tongue that came from eating the hot dog that tumbled into the embers after it fell off the stick. He saw the stars overhead, pinpricks of light in the night's mantle, like maybe God was up there on the other side with a knitting needle, poking holes in the evening sky. Woody felt the night breeze on his face, so cool after the red-hot heat of the day.

Smiling, he saw Bobby sitting on the other side of the fire, the *camp*fire, watching him. Waiting for him. Wondering, like Woody, where the others were, but like Woody, not really caring either.

As usual, it was enough that Woody and Bobby were together. Hell, it was *more* than enough. As long as they had each other, the rest of the world, including their friends, could go pound sand.

As always, they needed nothing but themselves.

And at the moment, after last night's adventures in Woody's bedroom, you can bet they had only one thing on their minds.

CHAPTER SIX

"THINK THEY'LL show up?" Bobby asked.

Woody didn't care if they showed up or not. In fact, he sort of hoped they wouldn't. He would much rather spend some quality time alone with Bobby than shoot the bull with all the rest of his friends. There were things he could do with Bobby that beat the holy bejesus out of jabbering away all night with Cathy and the twins. His first taste of sex the night before had given Woody such a hunger for more it was all he could think about. Even now, he was sitting on the edge of this campfire with a boner creeping down his pant leg he was *dying* to set loose on the world. He couldn't take his eyes off Bobby's face, hovering there in front of him in the firelight. Woody began to tremble, thinking of all the things they had done to each other, *with* each other, the night before.

Bobby grinned at him from the other side of the fire.

"You cold?" he asked, but Woody knew he was kidding. Bobby knew what Woody was thinking as well as Woody did. Knew why he was trembling, too.

"Maybe we shouldn't have camped out tonight," Bobby said. "Maybe we should have stayed in your room."

"I know it," Woody said, and he said it with more conviction than he had ever said anything in his young life.

He wasn't really sure why they had decided to spend tonight bonding with nature down in this damn canyon when there were so many other natural wonders they could be discovering back inside the house. Woody supposed there were a couple of mysteries taking place here. The mystery of the murdered dog (which was tied in with the mystery of the headless skeleton, natch), and the mystery of two young men, still boys really, finding love and desire during what should have been just another summer vacation from school. And there was a third mystery too. The mystery of why they had been so stupid as to even *suggest* camping out tonight. Behind Woody's locked bedroom door, they would have had far more freedom to let themselves go than they did out here in the open canyon with the campfire illuminating their every move.

It had taken Woody a solid hour to convince his mother to let them sleep in the canyon, and even then it was only his father's intervention that made it happen.

"Let them go," Woody heard his dad telling her in the other room while he and Bobby sipped Cokes in the kitchen. "You don't want the boy to grow up being afraid, do you? Afraid of the dark. Afraid of death. Afraid of all the crap that life throws at you when you're not looking. He's a kid, for God's sake, and he won't be a kid forever. Let him have some fun now while he still can. Pretty soon he'll be punching a time clock and dragging his ass to work every morning, just like the rest of us. Let him be, Sue. Cut the boy some slack. There's nothing dangerous about camping out, and he'll be less than fifty yards from the back door. What could possibly happen to him?"

"But those bones…," Woody heard his mother say. He could tell by her voice she was weakening, and he and Bobby grinned at each other over their Cokes.

"Don't worry," his dad said. "You can hose them down with Lysol when they get back."

And that was pretty much the end of the conversation.

So there they were, sitting on their sleeping bags by a campfire in the canyon behind the house, waiting for their friends, who might or might not show up, and wishing they were back in Woody's bed where they really belonged. Sometimes maybe they were too clever for their own good.

The campfire was ringed with stones ("Try not to burn down the neighborhood," Woody's father had said), and it wasn't really a big roaring bonfire like they wanted, just a tiny little pile of sticks, enough to roast a hot dog and give them some light. But it was burning cheerfully enough, and it made them feel adventurous and daring, facing the elements with nothing but their libidos to sully the contentment of the moment.

Woody listened to a night bird chortling somewhere up in the pepper trees. It was a happy sound, but kind of spooky too.

"You saw it too, didn't you?" Woody asked, dragging his mind away from sex and back to more practical matters. His voice sounded unusually loud in the stillness of the canyon, where darkness hemmed them in around the glow of their little campfire. They were like a tiny island of light in a vast, black sea. Even the rustling of willow and pepper branches moving in the gentle breeze that crept down from the hillside above sounded a little like waves brushing a nonexistent shore.

"Yeah," Bobby said. "I saw it."

"He winked at us. Wilbur winked at us."

"I know he did. Creepy, huh?"

"Major league creepy."

Bobby poked at the fire with a stick, causing sparks to fly up. "Wasn't really Wilbur, though. It was the murderer."

"I sort of figured that."

"He's playing with us," Bobby said. "Hauling Wilbur's body up the hill so we'd find it a second time. Winking at us with a dead dog's eyes. I used to think the murderer was alive, you know. Hanging around, waiting for another victim to diddle ass along, but now I think he's just as dead as the headless guy. Just as dead as Wilbur. And maybe he's not just a ghost either. Maybe he's more like a poltergeist, you know? A ghost that plays pranks on people? Maybe he's trying to spook us."

Woody gave a theatrical groan, emoting like crazy. "Well, he's doing a pretty darn good job."

Bobby stared into the fire like he had never seen one before. What he said next sounded like something he had been wanting to say all night. "Nobody saw it but us, though. Did you notice? Nobody saw that dead-ass dog blink his eye but me and you."

Woody *hadn't* noticed, not until Bobby said it. "Good thing. The twins wouldn't have stopped running until they hit the state line, and Cathy would have probably thrown one of her hissy fits and stomped the whole lot of us into the dirt. I don't think she was too amused by the whole thing anyway. She would have been even less amused if she had seen old Wilbur winking at her."

From across the fire, Bobby patted the ground beside him. "Come over here," he said. "Sit beside me."

Woody smiled. "You scared?"

Bobby smiled back. "No. Just want you closer."

When Woody had shuffled around to the other side of the fire, dragging his sleeping bag along with him, and was sitting cross-legged next to Bobby, their knees touching, their arms brushing together as the fire warmed their fronts and the cool night air chilled their backs, Woody's mind once again, for the millionth time, traveled back to the night before.

"Do you think what we did last night was wrong?" he asked.

"No," Bobby said. "I think it was exactly right. Don't you?"

"I guess so. I know I always wanted it to happen, but I was just too dumb to know I knew it. You know?"

Bobby grinned, reaching out to take Woody's hand. "Nice sentence structure."

Woody saw Bobby's grin, but somehow he could not dredge one up in return. "I guess that makes us queer, then."

Bobby's grin died as quickly as it had come. He released Woody's hand and his sneaker-clad foot jerked outward and gave the fire a little kick. The burning branches settled in on themselves with another flurry of sparks. "It makes us happy, is what it makes us. The way we feel about each other doesn't have to have a name, does it? I don't care what other people call it. You shouldn't either. I'm not ashamed of anything we did last night. In fact, all I can think about is doing it again. When two people love each other, it isn't something that should have a nasty label stuck on it."

He reached out again for Woody's hand, staring down at his strong brown fingers intertwined among Woody's paler ones. He brushed his fingers across the hair on the back of Woody's hand almost worshipfully, and Woody noticed how golden it looked in the firelight. Is that how it looked to Bobby, he wondered? Woody felt the heat from the fire and the heat where his body pressed against Bobby's as well. Felt the life there. It was all he could do not to quiver when Bobby brought Woody's hand up to his face and pressed his lips to it.

"We shouldn't let the world make fun of how we feel about each other," Bobby said. "It's nobody's business but our own. Loving each other should be enough. Loving each other should be *more* than enough. Fuck the world. We don't need anybody but each other. We shouldn't be ashamed of anything we've done."

"I'm not ashamed." And Woody knew it was true.

Woody raised Bobby's hand and brushed it along his cheek. Other hands had touched his face before. His mother's. His father's. A sundry assortment of relatives. None of those other hands had caused such a stirring in Woody as Bobby's did. The feel of Bobby's skin against his own was—magic. A burst of light. A sensory avalanche. A jolt of electricity shooting straight into his heart. If the rest of the world had a derogatory name for it, for this feeling he was feeling right now at this very moment, then that name had nothing to do with them. What they had was beyond what the world could understand. If everybody else in the world wanted to laugh at him and Bobby for feeling about each other the way they did, then let them.

Woody knew he could endure anything the world threw at them as long as he had Bobby there beside him to remind him what was truly important. Happiness was important. And Bobby's love for him was important too. And his love for Bobby. That was all that mattered. Together they were whole. Apart they were nothing. In Woody's thirteen-year-old mind it all made perfect sense. The innocence of his body might have fallen away from him with his first taste of sex, but the innocence in his mind was as yet unspoiled. It would take a few more years of living for Woody to learn that the world *could* harm a person. The opinions of others *could* bring hurt, sorrow, and a crushing sense of shame. Difference *could* be looked upon as a sickness by those who didn't or wouldn't understand it. But at this moment, at this precise point of time in his young life, Woody could ignore what the world might think of him. He didn't understand yet, not really, that he still had to live in that world.

Nor did he understand yet that Bobby might not always be there to help him through it. When he learned that one lesson, when he learned of the impermanence of loved ones, how they could sometimes simply drift away and at other times be torn away in the blink of an eye, then Woody would become a man. But that time had not yet come. Now his mind was filled with definites. Love was a definite. As was fear. Love for the boy beside him. Fear of the darkness surrounding him. Sadness, that which came with learning the truths of the world he lived in, was an indefinite. Inexplicable even to the wisest. Men, after living long lives consumed with sadness, have died of old age never understanding it. Love and fear they understood with the first beatings of their infant hearts.

And Woody's heart was still young. And in love.

"What if the others find out?" he asked.

Bobby shrugged. "If they're really our friends, they'll understand. If they don't, they're not." Again, he pressed his lips to Woody's hand, tasting the flesh with his tongue, sending a shiver up both their spines. "I only care what you think."

Woody, while filled with love as Bobby was, still took a more judicious approach to the matter. "No one can find out," he said. "Not yet. Not until we're older. If my folks get wind of it, they might keep us apart. Your folks too."

Bobby spat into the flames. "My folks don't even know I exist. They only give a shit about where their next bottle is coming from. I could be sucking donkey dicks in Tijuana, and they wouldn't care."

Woody laughed. Bobby seemed surprised to hear him doing it then, as if realizing what he had just said, he giggled too. Their voices rang out happily through the darkness, traveling into the trees, beyond the reach of the campfire's light. They lay back on the ground side by side, nudging each other and laughing up at the sky like a couple of idiots.

As their laughter died away, fading into the distance, Woody looked over at Bobby lying beside him and said, "I think maybe we deserve each other."

Bobby grinned. "Sort of looks that way, don't it?"

And then they were laughing again. And as Woody began to reach out, to lay his hand across Bobby's chest to feel the warmth of the boy beside him, and perhaps to absorb a little of Bobby's spirit into himself, or maybe just to feel the comfort of touching the person who meant so much to him, their laughter was cut short by a voice speaking softly from the shadows behind them.

"Cocksuckers."

Both boys leapt to their feet and spun to face the sound. The voice that had spoken had not been the voice of a child. It was a grown-up voice. Filled with malice. Seething with ridicule. There was a cold, taunting scorn in the voice that neither boy had ever heard uttered by human lips. And it was directed at them.

"Who's there?" Bobby called out, his voice tense with fear. And anger too. Anger at the mockery in the bodiless, guttural voice spitting out that one vicious word from the darkness.

Woody thought maybe every hair on his head was sticking straight up as he tried to pierce the darkness with his eyes, taking every shadow as a human form, hearing every rustling branch shifting in the wind as a spiteful voice spewing out further words of hate. Of contempt. He sidled closer to Bobby, needing Bobby's strength to see him through whatever this was that was happening, and deep down, for the first time, he caught a glimmer of guilt trying to burst into flame inside himself. Guilt for everything he and Bobby had done, everything he and Bobby had spoken about. That one word uttered with such ridicule and contempt from the shadows had brought it all crashing down on him.

And the guilt, more than anything, angered him.

"Show yourself, you shit stain!" he yelled into the trees. He thought he heard the sound of faint laughter off to the right. Bobby must have heard it too, for they both looked in that direction at the same time. They heard then the sound of another night bird, high in the branches, awoken perhaps by their yells, disturbed from sleep, crying out in offended tones at the unholy racket taking place down below in the world of humans.

The sound of laughter the boys heard might have been imagined, but the sudden clatter of scattering stones and solid footfalls behind them certainly was not. They spun yet again to look out across the campfire in the opposite direction.

In the distance, almost but not quite buried in the darkness, they saw bodies moving toward them.

Woody's heart was hammering so hard he thought it might just explode out of his chest like a rocket taking off from its underground silo in one of those end-of-the-world nuclear war movies he loved so much. He could imagine it soaring skyward as his body, suddenly heartless, slumped to the ground below, a worthless husk of flesh without the all-important pump keeping things chugging along like a finely tuned V-8 engine.

He was about to reach out for Bobby's hand to steady himself when he heard a familiar voice singing out from one of those approaching bodies.

It was Cathy's voice, and there was no small amount of humor in it. "Shit stain? Is that the best you could come up with? My God, boys, even I can cuss better than that."

Chuck chimed in with, "Who the hell were you yelling at, anyway? If it was us, you were aimed in the wrong direction."

Bobby whispered to Woody, his voice still tense. But there was relief in it too, relief that they were no longer alone. "It wasn't them."

"I know," Woody whispered back.

Cathy and the twins moved into the light like conquering heroes swaggering home from the war. They had sleeping bags draped over their shoulders and grocery bags in their hands. They plopped down beside the fire after spreading their sleeping bags on the ground and began unpacking everything they had brought with them. Woody was sorry he had eaten the ash-covered hot dog, for now they had more food than they knew what to do with, and better stuff too. Cathy was toting a pound of ham and a loaf of Wonder Bread. Chuck had chips, peanuts, and a bag of miniature Snickers, and Jeremy had two six packs of soda, one 7UP and one Coke.

"I guess we won't starve," Bobby said. Woody could see him trying to get into a party mood even while still casting a few uneasy glances at the darkness surrounding them. By unspoken understanding, both boys knew not to mention the voice they had heard only moments before. Maybe they would have told the others about it if the disembodied voice in the shadows had said anything other than what it had. But being called "cocksuckers" by a ghost, or what they perceived to be a ghost, required way more explanation than what they were prepared to dish out at that moment, even to their friends.

Cathy was rattling on. "My folks think I'm staying over at Patty's house. Didn't figure they would be too attuned to the idea of me sleeping out in the woods with a bunch of boys." Here she cast an eye at the twins. "Even if half those boys haven't sprouted pubic hair yet."

"Jesus," Jeremy said, looking crushed. "Let it go, will ya?"

Cathy giggled.

Chuck was eyeing Woody and Bobby. "Who the hell were you yelling at?" he asked again. "Did you hear something in the trees?"

Bobby unwrapped a miniature Snickers and popped it in his mouth. "Just you guys, I guess. Woody here was a little spooked by all the noise you made coming down the hill. Thought maybe it was Wilbur coming back for an encore, dragging his stake along behind him."

"Pussy," Cathy said.

Woody sighed, suddenly glad to have the rest of his friends with them, even though it cut into his and Bobby's private time. "How many times do I have to tell you, skirt? You're the pussy, we're the dicks."

"Got that right."

Jeremy was building a ham and potato chip sandwich in his lap. "So now that we're here, what the heck are we going to do? Me and Chuck just laid our lives on the line, sneaking out the bedroom window like we did. I'd like to think it was for a good reason." He slapped frantically at a moth the size of a helicopter that suddenly loomed up in front of his face and in doing so scattered potato chips all over his sleeping bag.

Chuck leaned over and scooped them up, one after the other, stuffing them in his mouth as he went along. He was eyeing the darkness around him as he did it. "Fuck reason." Then, less philosophically, he said, "It's kind of spooky out here, ain't it? Hope our dead guy's head isn't propped up in one of those tree limbs looking down at us. Maybe his mouth is working up and down like he's trying to say something, but since he doesn't have his voice box, no sound is coming out. Maybe there's worms and shit crawling out of his mouth when he opens it." After a moment, he added, "Jeez, I'm kinda sorry I said that." He looked like he meant it.

Cathy popped the tab on a soda can, and everybody jumped. She found this intensely amusing.

"Good Lord, you boys are just a bundle of nerves. Well, don't worry. You have me to protect you from all the ghosties and goblins lingering out there in the shadows waiting to snatch you away from the fire and rip your bloody guts out. And even if you do get your guts ripped out, I promise I'll avenge your miserable deaths. Doesn't that make you feel better?"

"Oh, yeah. Lots."

Chuck pulled a small bottle from his hip pocket. "Anybody care for a drink?"

"Say what?"

Jeremy leapt to his feet, scattering even more potato chips across his sleeping bag than he had a minute before. "Is that Dad's? It is! My God, he'll nail our balls to the wall for taking that. He'll unscrew our braces from our mouths and cram them up our asses with a plunger handle. He'll poke his dental drill up our noses and scramble our brains like mashed potatoes. He'll saw our heads off with dental floss. What the hell is wrong with you?"

Chuck blithely said, "I figure we need it more than he does. What do dentists have to be afraid of?"

"Cavities?" Bobby grinned.

"Bad breath?" Woody asked, grinning back at him.

"Gingivitis?" Cathy chimed in.

"Thieving children?" Chuck offered up, "and I'm afraid that really is a problem. Look how *I've* turned out."

Jeremy was standing with his hands on his hips, and as everyone looked up at him glaring down at his brother, wondering what he was going to say next, the ham slid out of his sandwich and landed on his foot. Twenty seconds later, Woody was still laughing so hard he thought he was going to pee in his pants.

When everyone's laughter had trailed away (everyone but Jeremy's, who hadn't laughed at all, and *still* wasn't, and wasn't really sure why everybody *else* was since he hadn't noticed his slice of ham making a run for it), Cathy pointed to the bottle and asked, "What *is* that stuff?"

Chuck leaned a little closer to the firelight to look at the label. "Peach brandy." He tsk-ed. "Dad always was an effeminate drinker."

"Jeez, what self-respecting dentist would drink peach brandy? If I was digging around in people's diseased mouths all day long, I'd want something a little stronger." Woody made a face. "Like hemlock."

"I'm not having anything to do with this," Jeremy said, watching as everyone held out a soda can to Chuck, who was doing the honors of pouring a generous dollop of booze into each one. Bobby didn't seem too thrilled about it either, but he held his Coke can out like the others. Only Jeremy refused.

"Tastes like cat piss anyway," Jeremy grumbled, lowering himself back down onto his sleeping bag and looking at his sandwich, suddenly wondering where the meat had gone. When he saw it slathered across his filthy shoe top, he merely peeled it off and primly tucked it back inside the bread.

Then he held out his Coke can. "Okay. What the hell? Pour me a shot. We're as good as dead anyway."

While everyone else took an exploratory sip of the liquor, making faces as they did so, Cathy threw out the opening pitch. "I've been thinking, guys."

"Uh-oh," Chuck said.

Cathy ignored him. "The way I see it, we got ourselves a ghost. And it's not the headless guy. It's the guy that killed him. Old headless guy didn't die in the plane crash. He was murdered. And the guy that murdered him is still hanging around."

"Well, duh," Woody said.

Bobby added, "I think we already figured that out, dear."

"Don't call me dear. And since you've already figured it out, what are we going to do about it?"

"Why should we do anything at all?" Jeremy asked. "I sorta like the idea of a ghost haunting our canyon. It's kind of exciting."

Cathy looked at him like she might have looked at a two-headed chicken at the county fair. "Well, he's already killed a dog. What makes you think he won't come after one of us next?"

"Why would he?"

"Because he *can*, shithead. What else has he got to do to amuse himself? He's dead. He can't just go shopping at the mall for a few hours to kill the rest of the eternity he's stuck in. They probably canceled his credit cards when he kicked the bucket. If I was a ghost, *I'd* want to kill something. You know. Jealousy. Revenge. *Payback*. It must irk the crap out of him to see us sitting here in the blossom of youth, sipping peach brandy and eating Snickers while he's forever stuck in the netherworld between life and death and wondering what the fuck he did to deserve to be there. Poor unfortunate asshole."

As always, Woody found himself admiring Cathy's ability to swear like a brain-damaged heathen and still look so pretty and virginal while she did it. He giggled. "The blossom of youth?"

Cathy shrugged. "Or whatever you want to call it."

"Who do you think he is?" Jeremy asked. "How do you suppose he got here? And why didn't he just go to heaven or hell like most people do when they die? Why the heck is he still hanging around our canyon?"

"Don't know," Cathy said, sipping her drink for the first time and making a face like the others when she did. She looked at her Coke can like she thought it might be about to explode, then shrugged and took another sip. "Maybe we should try to talk to him and find out. He's probably lonely. Maybe he just needs a friend."

Chuck coughed up an uncharitable chuckle. "Well, he could have had a pet dog if he hadn't killed the poor thing by cramming a stake through its heart. Does that seem like the act of a man who wants to make friends?"

"That dog was more annoying than you are, Chuck. I wouldn't have wanted to be his friend either. Willow Man probably got sick of all the yapping and decided to shut him up. Perfectly understandable."

"Willow Man?" Bobby asked.

Cathy calmly shook a few peanuts from a can of Planters and popped them into her mouth one at a time, chewing thoughtfully as she spoke. "Well, we have to call him *something*. Murdering Dickwad doesn't sound too nice. We don't want to offend him."

Jeremy's eyes were rolling around inside his head like a couple of marbles in a soup can. "Offend *him*? The guy's a homicidal maniac, for Christ's sake. He killed a dog. He murdered some poor homeless guy and chopped off his head, and now you're worried about offending his delicate sensibilities?" He gazed at Cathy like he had never seen her before, and now that he was seeing her, he wasn't sure he liked what he was seeing. "Who are you, Mary Fucking Martin?"

Jeremy loved musicals.

Cathy didn't. "Mary *who*?"

"Never mind."

"So how do we contact a ghost?" Bobby asked.

Cathy shrugged. "Hell, *I* don't know. Just concentrate real hard on him showing up, I guess. It always seems to work in the movies."

Woody reached out and plucked the bottle of peach brandy from its resting place between Chuck's legs. He unscrewed the cap and poured a generous portion of it straight down his throat.

After the convulsions stopped, and after he wiped away the tears that had popped into his eyes after the alcohol burned a fiery path all the way from his tongue to his belly and maybe down to his toes as well, he said, "Okay, so what do we do first?"

"WHAT TIME is it?" Bobby asked.

Cathy checked her wristwatch in the firelight. "Darn. It stopped."

Jeremy checked his. "That's weird. So did mine."

No one else was wearing one, so they racked it up to coincidence and thought nothing more about it.

Woody looked up at the moon shining high above their heads and took an educated guess. "It's probably about midnight. I don't think we're getting anywhere. Want to give it up?"

"Not yet," Chuck said. "Give it five more minutes."

Woody figured they had been holding hands in a circle around the campfire and concentrating with all their might on having their resident spook give them a sign he actually existed for about twenty minutes now. So far their spur-of-the-moment séance had been a big bust. Aside from his ass going numb from sitting on the hard ground, nothing had happened yet, and Woody was beginning to think nothing would. He hadn't quite decided whether he was disappointed by that fact, or happy as hell.

Actually, he was just going through the motions now. Woody's mind had wandered away from their ghost about ten minutes ago, and all his thoughts were now centered on the feel of Bobby's hand in his. He had another boner, and he was hoping he wouldn't have to stand up anytime in the near future, or his friends would have something more than ghosts to think about. Bobby's finger slid along his palm, and Woody's hard-on gave a lurch beneath the fabric of his jeans. He could sense Bobby grinning beside him.

"Concentrate!" Cathy demanded. "Stop dicking around!"

Woody almost laughed. Bobby did.

"What the hell is *that*?" Jeremy asked.

For one horrifying moment, Woody thought maybe Jeremy was talking about his upright pecker, but when he opened his eyes, he saw everyone looking off into the shadows surrounding them, as tense and rigid as fence posts. Then he heard what sounded like the flapping of wings. A lot of wings. It was coming from every direction and growing louder as the seconds passed. A moment later the night was thrumming with the sound of it.

When a burning branch burst open from the heat of the campfire and sparks shot out of it like shotgun pellets, peppering them all with little dots of flame, everybody jumped up, cussing and bellowing, desperately brushing away the sparks from their clothing and hair.

And just as Woody was about to say, "I think I'm having a heart attack," which he wasn't so sure he wasn't, the darkness came alive around them. What had been empty shadow only moments before was now a flurry of velvet wings and screeching, high-pitched cries that beat around their heads with a cacophony of sound and movement that almost blinded them in panic.

Bats! There must have been a thousand of them. And they were big suckers, too.

Cathy screamed and took off running like a marathoner when the opening gun goes off. She ran straight through the campfire as if it wasn't there, scattering even more sparks in her wake. As Woody swatted at the cloud of bats suddenly flapping around him, he caught a glimpse of Cathy pulling one from her hair before she disappeared into the darkness beneath the trees, still screaming like a banshee, her arms windmilling around her head, her feet going a mile a minute.

The horrible sound of all those bats screeching in their ears was almost drowned out by Jeremy's screams. Woody saw Chuck run to him and fling a sleeping bag over his head. Then Chuck ducked under it too, and they hunkered down on the ground, pulling the sleeping bag tight around them, apparently hoping to ride out the storm that way.

For the first time in his life, Woody saw panic in Bobby's eyes too. The kid who was so adept at absorbing life's minor setbacks, as well as its major fucking miseries, with what appeared to be very little effort or damage to his psyche, wasn't exactly acting lackadaisical at the moment. He was digging around inside his shirt, hopping up and down as he did it, and Woody was horrified to see him pull out a bat the size of a puppy and fling it into the fire, where, with a scream like fingernails on a blackboard, the beast shriveled up in the flames and finally stopped flapping around in the embers long enough to die.

Woody had just enough time to register the smell of burning flesh and smoldering hair before another flock of bats swooped down on them.

"Where the hell are they coming from!" Bobby screamed, pulling another off his back and hurling it into the night like a football.

Woody was too busy to answer. He had about a dozen bats hanging off the front of his shirt. He scraped them off and started stomping them into the dirt, all the while letting loose with a string of obscenities that at any other time he might have been rather proud of. He could feel fat bodies squooshing beneath his sneakers, hear little bones snapping like party poppers as he tap-danced over them, and in the light of the campfire, he could see bat guts scattered everywhere. He also had one or two lucid nanoseconds where he had time to notice his hard-on had gone the way of the dinosaur. Extinct. And apt to stay that way for a while. He had other things besides sex to occupy his mind right then.

He yelped in pain when tiny incisors, sharp as needles, pierced his ear. He swatted at his head and saw another bat tumble into the fire with a tiny desperate scream of its own.

"Ha!" Woody yelled. "Take that, you little fucker!"

Chuck and Jeremy were still huddled beneath the sleeping bag. At the moment they were also rolling around like a couple of pigs in a sack. Apparently a few bats had taken refuge under there with them. Woody could hear them yelling and swearing and screaming as they carried on their own little battle under the bag.

Woody snatched up his own sleeping bag and ducked under it, dragging Bobby in with him. Holding onto each other, they made as small a bundle as they could, all the while tucking the corners of the sleeping bag around them, desperately trying to keep out the swarming bats that were now pummeling them from the outside, trying to get in.

"Jesus!" Bobby said, his lips against Woody's cheek, his body trembling in Woody's arms. "What the hell is going on? What happened to Cathy?"

"She took off running," Woody said. "She could be in L.A. by now."

"Not funny," Bobby said. "We have to find her."

"Maybe she got away from the bats. I don't hear her screaming."

"I don't care. She shouldn't be out there all by herself. It isn't safe. He could be out there with her."

"He who?"

"Willow Man. Maybe he brought the bats down on us to drive us apart so he could pick us off one at a time."

"Oh shit, Bobby. It's just a bunch of bats. Probably doesn't have anything to do with him."

"Yeah, right. When was the last time you saw about a million bats flying around this canyon?"

"Well—"

Woody interrupted the conversation long enough to smash his hand down on the head of a bat that was trying to crawl beneath the edge of the sleeping bag, and he was heartened to hear its little neck snap like a matchstick.

"You stay here," Bobby said. "I'm gonna go find her."

"Fuck that," Woody said. "We'll go together."

"Good. Let's go."

They each took a deep breath and flung the sleeping bag away. Woody couldn't even see the moon, the swarm of bats was so thick. They swirled across the sky like an eddy of black water. Grabbing Bobby's hand and yanking him along for the ride, Woody took off running in the direction they had seen Cathy go only minutes before. In two seconds they were in the darkness beneath the trees, getting whapped in the face with branches and tripping over sage brush and stumbling over roots and rocks. Woody spotted a fat bat clinging to Bobby's back, so he pulled it off and slammed it against a passing tree trunk with a satisfying *splat*. He could feel a little trail of blood creeping down his neck where tiny teeth had pierced his ear earlier.

"Cathy!" Bobby yelled out ahead of him.

Woody noticed a sudden silence and grabbed Bobby by the shirt collar and dragged him to a stop. "The bats are gone," he said. "They didn't follow us."

Bobby stood stock-still for about two seconds, as if testing the truth of Woody's words. It didn't take him long to realize Woody was right. The bats were gone.

"Thank Christ," he said. He turned to Woody in the shadows. "You all right?"

Woody looked down at himself. All his parts seemed to be intact. "Yeah. I guess so. Could use another drink, though."

"No kidding. I hate bats. Little vermin fuckers."

"Those weren't so little."

"I know. I don't think they were real."

Woody wasn't buying it. "Seemed real enough to me." He touched his bloody ear. "Their teeth were sure as hell real."

Bobby reached out and took Woody's hand. "Come on. We have to find Cathy."

They took off deeper into the trees, brushing willow branches away from their faces as they walked. Their knees were still shaking, but they were calmer now the bats were no longer dive-bombing their heads and screeching little bat screeches into their ears. Even in the distance, the sound of bats was gone. Suddenly, they noticed Chuck and Jeremy were silent too, no longer screaming like maniacs. Maybe the bats had left the campfire, going back to wherever they had come from before they decided to wage their little rodent war on the five of them. Or maybe this was just a lull between attacks, like when the Indians gave the mangy white men a few minutes to relax and lower their defenses and maybe take a dump before the braves swept in and cut them all to ribbons.

Here in the shadows beneath the pepper and willow trees at the bottom of the canyon, the darkness was so intense Woody couldn't see Bobby walking two feet in front of him. And the silence was as absolute as the darkness. There were no crickets chirruping away like usual, no sound of night birds, no wind tossing branches overhead, nothing. The canyon was as silent as an empty cathedral. The sound of their footsteps fell dead on the air.

Woody tripped over a stone embedded in the ground and fell hard to his knees. A hand, Bobby's, came out of the darkness to help him up.

"You okay?"

"Yeah," Woody whispered, rubbing his knees. Felt like he'd lost a little skin there. "Notice how quiet it is?"

Bobby's voice was a whisper, too. The silence seemed to demand it. "Yeah, the bugs are laying low. They probably know that bats eat bugs. They're not stupid."

Bobby laid his hand across the back of Woody's neck, and they stood there like that for a minute, listening. Woody couldn't see it, but he imagined Bobby cocking his head to the side.

"Maybe she ran all the way home," Woody said.

Bobby's fingers kneaded Woody's neck as he spoke. "Not in this direction she didn't. The only way out of this canyon is back the way we came. Come on. Let's go a little farther."

Bobby relinquished his gentle hold on Woody's neck and took his hand instead. Together, they moved deeper into the trees, walking slower now over the uneven ground, wondering where Cathy could have gone, wondering what was happening with the twins back at the camp, and wondering most of all what the hell they were getting themselves into, stumbling around in the dark with a murdering ghost lingering out there somewhere in the shadows.

Woody was about to say, "She's gotta be here somewhere," when they heard a twig snap up ahead.

Bobby called out in a frantic whisper, "Cathy? That you?"

The boys froze at the sound of weeping coming from the shadows. A high-pitched murmur of sound sent shivers shooting up Woody's back and made Bobby's grip tighten around his hand.

"It's her," Bobby said. "Come on."

And suddenly they were running through the brambles. The darkness was Stygian. Since they couldn't see shit, they were getting whapped in the face every second or two by invisible low-hanging branches. Bobby pulled Woody along behind him like a kid with a pull toy, and Woody had all he could do to stay on his feet as they tore through the brush, stopping every few seconds to get a new bearing on the sound of crying up ahead and adjust their course accordingly.

Woody's blood was ice water in his veins. The sound of Cathy crying was enough to freeze anyone's heart. Usually she was more apt to be cussing and swearing and throwing things like a mad woman rather than sobbing like a little girl, even though technically she still was one. Woody figured it would take more than a few bats to make her cry like that, and he wasn't particularly looking forward to finding out what it was. Couldn't be anything good, he knew that much.

The boys stumbled out of the trees into the clearing where they had found Wilbur that morning. The *first* time they had found Wilbur.

Away from the trees, the moonlight cast a bluish glow over the landscape. At least they were no longer steering blind. Above the pungent stench of sagebrush, Woody thought he still caught a whiff now and then of Wilbur's decomposing body, even though it was now buried under a foot of earth six hundred yards up the hillside.

Sitting on the ground in the middle of the path made by the spring run-off, they saw Cathy, huddled into a ball like one of those starving kids you see in pictures of some famine-stricken African shithole. She didn't look up at the sound of their footsteps. Her face was buried beneath her arms as she wept into the ground. Woody could see her bare shoulders heaving as she cried.

"My God," Bobby mumbled. "Where's her shirt?"

Only then did Woody realize she was naked from the waist up. Her blouse had been torn away. And moving closer, he saw scratches across her pale back, *deep* scratches, as if some sort of wild animal had tried to take her down.

The boys rushed to her side and dropped to their knees next to her.

Cathy screamed so loudly Woody almost passed out from the shock of it. Then he heard Bobby talking to her in a low voice, telling her it was only them, asking her what had happened.

Cathy raised her tear-streaked face from under her arms and looked at them as if she couldn't believe they had actually found her. When the realization hit her it was her friends kneeling beside her, she grabbed them both and buried herself in their arms, sobbing so hard she couldn't speak.

Only after Woody peeled off his shirt and draped it around her, did she look up into their faces.

In a little girl voice Woody would never have guessed could come from her if he hadn't been staring at her face when she spoke, she said, "He tried to rape me, I think. He—he tried to tear my clothes off. He got my shirt, and then I took off running."

"Who?" Bobby asked. "*Who* tried to rape you?"

Cathy's breath came in short gasps as her adrenaline level began to drop. Having her friends beside her once again was turning her fear into something else. Anger maybe. With an impatient swipe, which seemed more like the old Cathy Woody knew, she brushed the tears from her face, and said, "Willow Man. He was waiting for me under the trees. I saw him, at least I think I did. It was so damned dark." She looked up at the sky, and her voice was filled with wonder when she said, "The bats are gone."

"Yeah," Bobby said. "They're gone."

Cathy sighed. "He brought them. He told me so, just before he started tearing my clothes off."

"What happened to him?" Bobby asked. "Where did he go?"

"I don't know. He took off when he realized it was me. I don't think I was the one he wanted. I think he was expecting one of you. I think—"

"Think what, Cathy? *What* do you think?" Woody's words were gentle. Consoling. Patient.

She reached out and laid a trembling hand on each of their cheeks. In the moonlight, drying tears sparkled her face like party glitter.

"I think—he wanted a boy," she said, and then the tears started up again.

Chapter Seven

WOODY SAT in the dressing room, staring at the stage monitor. The stage was empty at the moment, but in a few minutes, he would be out there doing his thing, and hopefully doing it well, laying his life and career on the line like he never had before. Whatever happened tonight would be a culmination of all his years of hard work, and he wasn't ready for it by any stretch of the imagination. The show he was about to do, the show he had done a thousand times before by rote, now seemed like an impossible obstacle lying in his path. Tonight of all nights, record execs would be appraising his performance, and for the first time since his days of taking drugs, Woody wasn't sure if he could go on at all. His future depended on what happened in the next couple of hours, and all Woody could think about was trying to get through it, putting it behind him. Or avoiding it altogether. Getting away from this bar, away from these people, and finding some secluded corner to sit and think about what had happened out there on the pier.

He could see people now, milling around the edge of the stage, finding their seats, heading to the bar for preshow drinks, laughing and cutting up and acting like this was the biggest night of their lives. Jesus! The place was packed. Woody watched them on the monitor, listened to them through the closed dressing room door, and all the while his hands were shaking so badly he almost spilled the Coke he was trying to drink. He couldn't remember one lyric. Not one. He didn't know what his first number was supposed to be. He didn't know if he still had a voice or if it too had gone, like his boner on that night in the canyon so long ago, the way of the dinosaur.

All he could think about was the man standing by the water. The way he looked. The things he said. It was Willow Man who had confronted him only minutes before. It had to be. How else could he know the things he knew? Woody knew now it was Willow Man who had murdered his parents, cutting them to ribbons in the little store they loved so much. Laughing at their misery. Taking their lives as easily as some asshole snatching candy from a baby. He remembered his mother's voice the night before, saying, "He came for us, Woody. He came for us in the store," as if even now, after all these years, she still couldn't believe it. He remembered again his father's silence, his father's shame as he backed away from Woody, disappearing into the shadows like some unclean creature. Seeking the darkness. Not wishing to be seen. Not wanting to frighten his son any more than he was already.

A tear slid down Woody's cheek even as a knock came at the dressing room door and a voice said, "Five minutes, Mr. Stiles."

Woody sighed a sigh that only through sheer willpower didn't become a sob.

"Thank you," he called out in a voice he had never heard before. It wasn't him speaking those words; it was someone else. A stranger. For a moment, he longed for drugs—to ease the angst, to take him away from everything that was happening. Then, from somewhere deep inside himself, he plucked a thread of strength. Holding on to that tiny thread for dear life, he stood and draped the guitar strap across his shoulders. He took comfort in the Gibson's familiar touch and weight. He began to feel the music waiting to be drawn from the Gibson like water from a well. Even if his career was about to crash and burn, he was determined not to see it go up in smoke without a fight. People were counting on him. His agent. All those people out there who had paid thirty bucks a pop for a little entertainment. And most of all, himself. Everything else happening in his life could be put on hold for a couple of hours. It had to be. He had bigger fish to fry at the moment. Everything else, Willow Man included, would simply have to wait.

He could almost hear Bobby speaking to him from the shadows of his past. He could almost feel Bobby's strong hands at the back of his neck, kneading, encouraging. "The show must go on, dipshit," Bobby seemed to be whispering in his ear. "Old show biz adage, you know. I'll be waiting for you when you're done. We'll deal with Willow Man then."

Deal with Willow Man. Yeah, right.

Woody took a great gulp of air and walked to the dressing room door. The raucous roar of the crowd greeted him as he pulled it open and stood in the shadows, out of sight. He tried to absorb some of the energy in the auditorium into himself. He could hear some resident comic walking among the tables, warming up the crowd. He hadn't even known they *had* a comic. Hadn't even known he *had* an opening act. Jeez, wonders never seemed to cease in this town.

On legs made of Jell-O, Woody walked down a long hallway lined with beer and liquor cases. Peeking through the doorway by the bar, he saw the crowd, hooting and stomping, laughing at the comic's jokes; saw the waitresses flitting around in their tiny short skirts, delivering drinks, slyly smiling at the hungry looks they got from every guy they passed. Woody watched it all, feeling the thrill that can only come from an opening night, wondering what would happen when he stepped up on that stage. None of it seemed to have anything to do with him, yet it had *everything* to do with him.

How could he feel so disconnected from it all on what might very well prove to be the most important night of his life? *Christ, Woody, pull yourself together. Get some adrenaline going. This is your big chance.*

Suddenly Noah was standing beside him, patting him on the back, whispering words of encouragement in his ear. Over the roar of the waiting crowd, Woody couldn't hear a single one of those encouraging words, but he got the general gist of what Noah was trying to tell him.

"Give 'em hell, kid. Prove to these people that my faith in you all these years has been well placed. Sing your little peckerhead heart out, and when you walk off that stage tonight, we'll be headed for the big time. Bigger shows. Bigger bucks. Bigger everything." Even though he couldn't really hear the words, Woody found himself grinning at Noah's enthusiasm. Felt his heart lighten, all thoughts of everything that had happened to him since he returned to San Diego sliding away from him like rain sluicing off a canted roof. Felt the guitar against his chest like the reassuring hug of an old friend and the pick in his hand like an extension of himself, eager for the feel of the strings. Eager to make some music. Eager to be *heard*.

Woody plucked the beer from Noah's hand and downed it in one long, satisfying gulp, and when he heard the comic speaking his name out there onstage, he knew the time had come.

"Show 'em what you can do, kid," Noah said, and Woody boldly stepped through the doorway and entered that magical place he knew he was always destined to be. He waved at the crowd as he raced up onto the stage, feeling every eye on him, hearing every hoot and holler of greeting, and at the first touch of pick to string, at the first sound of his own voice booming out into that netherworld of darkness behind the spotlights, he found himself feeling right at home. No stage fright. No jitters. The grin he felt spreading across his face wasn't a trick of showmanship; it was real.

"Hello, San Diego!" he cried out, jubilant for the first time in years. All thoughts of his mother bleeding at the kitchen sink, of his father hiding his misery in the shadows of a darkened, empty house, of the man at the pier who spoke so uncaringly of murdering them both, left him. It was all lost somewhere in the staccato pounding of his own heart, in the electric thrum of six hundred people cheering and hollering, vibrating the floor beneath his feet, making the auditorium *hum* as if it too were part of the show.

Woody accepted the adulation of the crowd as if he knew he deserved it, and when his music began, when his voice reached out to everyone there, starting up on its own as if it were something beyond his control, he let it come. And as he sang, as his music filled the room, the crowd quieted; he could feel their acceptance of him as he had felt his acceptance of *them*. He and the audience became one at the moment his crystal clear voice soared out beyond the footlights. He gave a silent prayer of thanks to find his voice still with him, and after that, he let the music take over, drawing him into that special place where the music sometimes took him.

Until that moment, Woody had not known what a great audience could give to a performer. They fed him. They led him on from one song to the next, never tiring, never letting their enthusiasm seep away. They were here for Woody Stiles, and they intended to get everything they could from him. And Woody was more than happy to oblige.

Thirty minutes into the show, Woody could feel the audience's love for him still pulsating through the room. He soaked their love up like a sponge, relishing every second of it. Even if nothing bigger came of this night, even if those recording executives hidden somewhere among the crowd out beyond the footlights decided not to give him a shot at a recording contract, Woody knew this night would still be one of the best he would ever know. Noah was right. He truly was at his peak. He sang each song as if it was the last time he would ever sing it, and his voice, echoing in his ears through the incredible sound system, sometimes amazed even him.

At the end of his first set, the house lights came up, and Woody watched in amazement as the crowd rose to their feet, applauding his music, applauding *him*. He tucked his guitar behind his back and bowed beneath the wave of acceptance that poured over him. And looking up through misting eyes, truly humbled by the response of the audience, his eyes came to rest on a woman and two men standing behind a table in the front tier, clapping and hooting like all the rest. But whereas everyone else in this room was a stranger to Woody, these three rang a memory bell somewhere in the back of his head.

The woman was beautiful, with long flowing red hair that framed her face. She stood between the men, both taller than her and both with thinning blond hair that looked like it might be gone altogether in another five years. The men were twins. Woody could see it at a glance. And as he stared at them, wondering why they seemed so familiar to him, one of the blond men, seeing Woody's eyes on him, raised his hand in the air and gave Woody the finger, grinning. The man was so close Woody could see a small birthmark, shaped like a teardrop, beneath his left eye.

It was Jeremy.

As the realization hit Woody like a two-by-four to the back of the head, the woman, giggling, slapped Jeremy's finger away and aimed an apologetic hands-up gesture in Woody's direction.

Cathy was just as beautiful as Woody had once suspected she would become. The other twin, Chuck, held a couple of fingers behind Cathy's head like two horns, and Woody found himself laughing like an idiot, even while the rest of the audience continued to clap and hoot and wonder, maybe, what the hell the entertainer was laughing about.

And as he stared across the footlights at his three old friends, cutting up in front of him just as they had when they were thirteen years old, Woody watched another person rise up from the crowd behind them.

It was Willow Man, dressed in faded denims, with a ridiculously huge cowboy hat perched atop his head and a belt buckle the size of a small pizza strapped across his stomach. He was eyeing Woody over Cathy's shoulder. Like some weird-ass Marlboro Man, he plucked a small pouch from his back pocket, pulled the drawstring open with his teeth, deftly sprinkled tobacco into a cigarette paper cupped between his thumb and forefinger, and proceeded to roll a smoke between his fungus-tipped fingers like Rowdy Yates on *Rawhide*. Willow Man licked the paper with an obscenely long tongue, sealing the cigarette together, then popped it into his mouth with a flick of the wrist and lit it with a kitchen match he pulled from somewhere, all the while staring intently at Woody.

With the cigarette dangling from the corner of his mouth and the smoke billowing up around him, Willow Man slowly drew a finger across his throat, leering madly at the three in front of him.

Woody blinked, and when he opened his eyes, Willow Man was gone. Just like that. Only a cloud of cigarette smoke remained where he had been standing.

Chuck yelled out above the slowly diminishing applause, unaware of what had just transpired behind him, "We'll meet you after the show, Woody." He pointed to the doorway. "Out by the pier. Be there or be square!"

And then the house and stage lights dimmed, and Woody was hustled away by one of the stagehands, who was there to prevent him from breaking his neck in the dark as he led Woody back to his dressing room to prepare for the second half of the show.

Noah greeted him backstage with a grin that pretty well obliterated his entire face. "Jesus, kid, even *I* didn't know you were *that* good!" He leaned over, only half-joking, to gaze deeper into Woody's eyes. "You're not on drugs again, are you?"

"Fuck you, Noah."

"After tonight, son, you can fuck me six ways to Sunday and I won't say a word. Might even squeal with delight, I might. Being fucked by a rising star has that effect on some people, you know. Saw some old friends in the audience, huh? I thought you might."

"Yeah, I did," Woody said, peeling his sweat-soaked shirt off and dropping it at his feet. He accepted the beer Noah offered and drank it down in ten seconds flat. He stared at himself in the mirror. His hair was damp with perspiration, and there was a glimmer in his eyes he hadn't seen there for a very long time. *Triumph,* he thought. *I'm looking at triumph.* But there was fear there too. Not fear of anything in *this* world, but fear of something from the other world. Even after everything that had happened since he returned to this goddamn town, he knew he had still harbored hopes of it all being a figment of childhood imagination. But unless he was stark raving nuts, what he had seen on the pier that afternoon and in the audience tonight as he'd looked out from the stage was anything *but* imagination. And what he had seen at the house the night before went so far beyond imagination Woody couldn't begin to know how to classify it.

Jesus. Willow Man had been standing right there in a crowd of hundreds of people, and no one but Woody had seen him. How could that be? He thought of the way Willow Man had drawn his finger menacingly across his throat like a knife and wondered what it meant. He had been looking at Woody's friends when he did it. Did he mean to go after them next, or was he just adding more torment to Woody's already tormented existence?

Woody let these thoughts stampede through his mind even as he went through his usual routine of preparing for the second half of the show, all the while sipping a lukewarm Coke, the best medicine he had ever found for soothing a tired voice, with Noah all the while rattling off in his ear about what a success the first half had been. Woody had never seen the guy so happy.

Noah was practically tap dancing with enthusiasm.

"Christ, Woody, the record execs are probably out there right now with dollar signs flashing before their eyes, drawing up the mother of all contracts. How in the hell could they not be after watching you on that stage tonight? Jeez, you had me sobbing like an old lady with that one ballad you sang. And the upbeat songs were even better. Did you see that couple dancing in the aisle?"

"Shut up, Noah," Woody said, toweling off and drying his hair with a blow dryer before pulling on the second shirt he had brought with him. Giving a cursory glance to himself in the mirror, he sat down on the edge of the dressing table and tweaked the tuning on his guitar before setting it aside.

Glancing at the stage monitor, he saw his friends at their table in the front row at the verge of where the camera panned. They were sipping their drinks and looking around with a proprietary air as if they owned the place. Woody knew the proud smiles on their faces were due to the reception he had received from this crowd, who even now seemed keyed up and ready to party. Tonight had nothing to do with Chuck or Jeremy or Cathy, and they knew it. It had everything to do with Woody Stiles alone, and they were happy for Woody's success, just as real friends should be.

Woody experienced a pang of guilt in knowing he might have finished his two week run here in town without making so much as a perfunctory attempt at locating them. Well, apparently they had had no such compunctions of their own. Hell, to cop those front row seats on opening night, they must have been ready to pounce the moment his tickets went on sale. What had he ever done to deserve such loyalty?

He found his heart swelling with affection for those three people sitting out there in the crowded auditorium. He realized suddenly how much it meant to him to have his old friends here to witness his success.

If only Bobby could have been here too.

As he stared at the monitor, a hand suddenly filled the screen, blocking out his view of the auditorium. As the hand slid away, a face appeared, so close to the camera he could see the veins in the eyes, the hair in the nostrils.

It was Willow Man. When he grinned, Woody saw chunks of flesh dangling from his yellow teeth. Could almost smell the stench of putrid meat and rancid breath.

Woody gasped.

"So sorry," Willow Man said. "Your old cocksucking buddy couldn't make it. He was a tasty morsel, though. Yes indeedy do, he certainly was. Such lovely flesh. Such succulent tasty meat. Wish you could have been there when I unzipped his guts. But that was long ago, wasn't it? Maybe later tonight I'll show you exactly how I did it. Would you like that?"

Woody stood frozen, staring at the horrific face on the monitor.

"Noah," he managed to utter, pointing at the screen. "Do you see that?"

Noah stopped whatever the hell he was doing and glanced at the monitor. "Yeah," he said. "The audience is still primed up. Looks like the second half of the show might even be better than the first."

"No," Woody said. "The face. Don't you see the face?"

Noah peered closer at the monitor, and Woody could see now that Willow Man was gone.

"Which face you talking about, boy? Those are your fans out there. Having a good time too, by the looks of them. You about ready to do your magic one more time?"

Woody shook off the fear, shook away the words Willow Man had said about Bobby, and tried to drag himself back to the reality of the moment. He wondered if he would have to put up with this shit every night for the next two weeks. If he did, he doubted he would have much sanity left by the end of it.

Noah was giving him that funny look again, like maybe even now he was wondering if there were drugs rooting around in Woody's system, so Woody dragged up a smile from somewhere and stuck it on his face for the man's benefit.

"Don't worry, Noah. I'm clean."

Noah looked guilt stricken by his own suspicions. "I know, son. I know. Sorry. Old habits die hard. Mine, I mean," he added hastily. "Not yours."

"It's okay," Woody said, trying to laugh it off. "And don't worry. The second half of the show will be even better than the first. I promise."

Ninety minutes later, after his final song was sung, after the applause died away and the adrenaline began to ebb, Woody's and everyone else's, Woody knew he had kept that promise.

Just as Noah had asked him to do, he had sung his little peckerhead heart out, and while Noah went to meet with one of the recording execs, who had sent a note backstage requesting an audience with Woody's representative, Woody snuck out the side door and headed for the pier where his friends were waiting.

WOODY SPOTTED them leaning on the rail at the edge of the boardwalk, talking quietly and staring out at the boats bobbing in the moonlight. The years had done quite a number on everyone, himself not excluded, Woody supposed. They were four entirely different people now. Four different people from the ones who had camped out that night in the canyon. Four different people from the ones who stood by the graveside at Cedar Lawns Memorial Park, uncomfortably decked out in their Sunday best, watching Bobby's white casket, the casket Woody's folks had picked out and paid for because Bobby's parents were too drunk and too broke to do either, slowly sink into the ground on a sultry afternoon in the summer of their thirteenth year. The four of them had drifted apart after that, never really coming together again until tonight. If their fates had been left up to him, Woody knew, they would have remained apart. Funny that his old friends should feel the need to reunite at a time when Woody needed them most, whether Woody was aware of it or not. It was almost as if they knew the time for them to lead separate lives had now ended.

Friendship was like a song that way, Woody thought. You could set it aside for years, never thinking about it, never feeling a need for it, and then one day you simply longed to sing it again. And like a trusty old dog, or a trusty old friend, it was still there waiting for you, right where you left it, bearing no grudges for being ignored so long, feeling no need to retaliate for imagined or unimagined slights. Friendship wasn't diminished by time or distance. It was not weakened by the passing years as people were. Like music, friendship lived a life of its own, safe and strong in its own little cocoon of perpetuity.

And thank God it did. For the umpteenth time since returning to his hometown, Woody found himself choking down a confusing mass of emotions. Aside from his music, and aside from Bobby, Woody had always been unsure of what he wanted. The only thing he had ever been sure about was that *whatever* it turned out to be, it wouldn't be enough.

Well, maybe *this* was what he had really wanted all along. Maybe *this* was finally enough. Having his friends here beside him again, nonjudgmental as always, accepting him for who he truly was, not expecting any great shakes, just happy to have him around, happy to be along for the ride. If they were impressed by the way he had presided over that stage tonight, it would be only because they had expected nothing less. And if he had fallen flat on his face, they would still be loving him the same as they did now. They weren't here because of what he could do; they were here because of who he was. Woody Stiles from Highview Lane. The kid who once shared the most important summer of their lives. The kid who had faced their fears with them and, by the simple act of remaining steadfastly at their side during that long, deadly summer, had given them the strength to face their own fears as well.

Woody was feeling so humbled by their need to seek him out on this night that meant so much to him in so many different ways, he couldn't begin to express it to himself in adult terms. He was so happy not to be alone anymore, he found himself opening his mouth and speaking in the argot of sixteen years ago, as if he were still a kid on the verge of manhood, as if they had all resumed their standings in the pack, as if not one minute of the years that had fallen behind them had ever actually passed. Woody felt like a kid again, and somewhat to his own horror, he found his vocabulary and communication skills following right along in the wake of that feeling.

"Hello, pea brains," he said. "How the fuck's it hanging?"

All three of them turned at the sound of his voice. The twins stepped forward, and Woody stuck his hand out for a shake, but they scooped him into their arms, both at the same time, and gave him a bear hug that all but drove the air from his lungs. Woody was amazed to find they were both taller than him now. Considerably taller. It seemed the growth slump they had experienced at thirteen had at some point finally come to an end. During the time he had been away, they had grown into strong, handsome men, California tanned, as lean as athletes. Their hair, although thinning, was just as blond as it had been when they were children. Blonder, maybe. Pale from the sun. Woody figured they must spend a lot of time at the beach. Their skin radiated a healthy golden glow. As they wrapped their arms around him, he saw that the hair on their tightly muscled forearms was as pale as the hair on their heads. One or maybe both of them smelled faintly of Polo aftershave. Jeremy's birthmark had deepened in color since Woody had seen him last. A perfect teardrop beneath his left eye. To a stranger, Woody thought, it might appear to be an inmate's prison tattoo. A teardrop meant to symbolize suffering. But to Woody's eyes, it was a teardrop of laughter. Like a beacon, it stood out on Jeremy's beaming face, and he thought he detected real teardrops glistening in Jeremy's eyes as he looked upon his old childhood friend.

And staring now into Jeremy's beautiful blue eyes for the first time in a decade and a half, Woody felt his heart give a quiet thud inside his chest. *My God, the guy is gorgeous. Chuck too, of course. But Jeremy. Wow.* Woody closed his eyes for a moment at the feel of Jeremy's strong arms wrapped around him, savoring the heat of the man. The strength. Feeling Jeremy's heart beating against his own chest, Jeremy's long thighs pressed against his.

Cathy leaned back against the railing and watched their reunion, a gentle smile spreading across her face, enjoying the moment.

When the twins were finished mauling him, and Woody was finally forced to relinquish Jeremy from his clutches—not an easy task—Cathy came to him. She laid a cool hand to his cheek and kissed his forehead like a blessing. "You were wonderful tonight, Woody. We're all duly impressed."

Woody grinned, not knowing what to say, still fairly amazed that these old friends' feelings for him had not changed one iota in all the years that had fallen between them. He could see it in their eyes. He knew the same look was flowing from his eyes, and he could tell the exact moment when the realization struck Cathy as well. Her smile broadened, as if maybe she had been a little unsure of the reception they would get, but now she knew everything was all right. Everything was the same as it always had been.

Woody cast one more quick, appraising glance in Jeremy's direction. Well, maybe not *exactly* the same as it always had been.

In a heartbeat, Cathy resumed her own standing in the pack, transforming herself from the beautiful woman she had become into the young girl with freckles on her nose who once fought like a boy and cussed like a sailor and didn't give a shit about anyone or anything.

Flipping her long red hair away from her face like Rita Hayworth, she said, "As you can see, Woody, some things have changed while you were away. My tits got bigger. Nice, huh? And the twins finally got pubic hair, although now their heads are pretty much bald. But at least the braces on their teeth are gone. Can't say they improved their appearance much."

Chuck and Jeremy laughed, and Woody saw their teeth were as straight and white as boards in a picket fence.

"Very nice," he said. "No more running from electrical storms."

"Or picking food out of our teeth with a screwdriver," Jeremy chuckled.

"Or blinding people when we smile," Chuck added. "Now we blind them with our personalities."

Woody was stunned to see Chuck's arm reach out to enfold Cathy's waist. She sidled closer to him, eyeing Woody as she did so as if waiting for a comment from the peanut gallery.

She didn't wait for it long. Grinning at the look of surprise on Woody's face, she said, "Another benefit of losing the braces is that now when Chuck goes down on me, I don't have to worry about an unintentional clitoridectomy. Having my private parts shredded by metal isn't my idea of foreplay. I don't imagine it's *anybody's* idea of foreplay. What's the matter, Woody? Cat got your tongue?"

"Nope," Woody grinned. "Just pondering." Pondering indeed.

"Well, ponder this," Jeremy said. Obviously the stunning realization that Chuck and Cathy were an item was old news to him. "Every one of us in the past two weeks has had a visit from our old friend Willow Man. He seems to be revving himself up for a coup. He actually told us you were coming to town, Woody. That's why we knew about the show. That's why we bought tickets."

"I think we were the *first* to buy tickets," Chuck said. "And thank God we did. You really were great tonight. Although I wouldn't have pegged you for the county western type. How did that come about? You weren't exactly raised in Appalachia, you know." He was rattling on as if he didn't want to talk about Willow Man. As if he'd rather talk about *anything* other than Willow Man.

Woody ignored the question, kindly he hoped, as his eyes burrowed yet again into Jeremy's.

"I saw Willow Man too. Twice. Once right here on the pier, and later he was standing directly behind you guys during the show, all decked out in cowboy gear like some half-assed Clint Eastwood. I think he means to come after us. I think he intends to do to us what he did to Bobby. What he did to my folks."

It was Cathy's turn to look surprised. "Your folks?"

Woody stepped to the railing and looked out at the water. "I saw *them*, too," Woody said, sadly, gazing out past the bobbing boats to the whitecaps in the distance. "He killed them. My mother told me so. *He* told me so too, right here by the water not more than four hours ago. He—he thought it was funny."

"Christ," Jeremy said, his eyes as big as baseballs. "We didn't know. About your parents, I mean. We knew they were murdered, of course, but—"

"Nobody knew." The words fell from Woody's lips with such sorrow that Cathy came and wrapped her arms around him for the second time. Then Chuck's and Jeremy's arms were around him too, and the four of them stood there in the moonlight for a couple of beats, holding onto each other, listening to the waves lap at the pier. Were they, Woody wondered, each thinking their own separate thoughts of Willow Man, as he was? Of that goddamn long-ago summer, of death and murder and a small grave dug into a hillside with their friend lying inside. Were they worrying where it would all end this time? Wondering what they were getting themselves into? Or, like Woody, were they mostly speculating whether the courage they had had at thirteen was still with them, or if adulthood had leached it out of them?

It was Jeremy who answered Woody's unspoken question as they remained huddled together. "I'm not sure I'm up to this. We aren't kids anymore. There was something fearless about us back then. We're still friends, but do we see things the same now as we did then? I've spent my whole life thinking the things that happened back then were part fantasy, part imagination. A child's game we all played together. None of it really real."

"Bobby's death was real enough," Woody said, his face next to Jeremy's, feeling the smooth skin of Jeremy's cheek against his own. He whispered softly into Jeremy's ear. "My parents' death was real, too. It was all real. And the fucker who caused it all is still here. I guess he wants to finish it now. And I think maybe I'm willing to let him try. Maybe we'll have a few surprises for him this time around. Maybe he's not as strong as he thinks he is."

"But what if he is?" Jeremy asked. "What if he kills us all?"

"Then we go down fighting," Chuck said, all bravado, just like when he was thirteen. He pulled himself out of the huddle and placed both hands on Woody's shoulders. "Don't listen to my brother. Gay people are always a little angst-ridden. Must be in their genes."

"Gay people?" Woody asked, looking at Chuck, then turning his eyes to Jeremy, who gave him a little hands-up shrug. Not exactly apologetic. More resigned. There was a hint of laughter in his eyes. And maybe a shred of defiance.

"Well, I'll be damned," Woody said.

Cathy giggled. "We'll probably all be damned. Well, now that we have the unfortunate truth about Jeremy's sexual orientation out of the way, what do you say we all go somewhere and have a drink? We have a lot of years to catch up on. And apparently a battle strategy to lay out. Jeez, I feel like a kid again." There was a smile on her face when she said it. As gutsy as ever, Woody thought. The scrappy young girl had turned into a formidable woman. Why was he not surprised?

Woody continued to stare into Jeremy's eyes as he heard himself say, "Let's go to my place. That's where it all started. Maybe that's where it needs to end."

Woody slid an arm across Jeremy's shoulders and pulled him into a neck lock, dragging him along the pier toward their cars. "Now then, son, what's this I hear about you being gay?"

"Why?" Jeremy asked, ignoring the giggles from Cathy and his brother as they trailed along behind, hand in hand. "Find that a bit exciting, do you? Find it a bit *erotic?*"

Woody gave up a chuckle of his own. "Mayhaps I do. As one gay man to another."

He was amused to hear a little gasp pop out of the two behind them. Jeremy, too, looked properly amazed.

Woody heard Cathy whisper to Chuck, "Well, this is certainly turning out to be a night of surprises."

"No shit," Chuck said, a grin in his voice. "Who'da thunk Woody could sing?"

Cathy laughed, and the sound of it carried out across the water, losing itself on the distant waves.

"Yeah," she said. "There's that too, I suppose."

Chapter Eight

CATHY GAZED around the living room. "It looks like your mother just cleaned."

"Nope," Woody said, "I did."

"Holy Moly, it's *another* miracle," Jeremy said. "This night is just spitting out one bombshell after another."

Chuck schlepped the case of beer they had picked up at Jaycee's into the kitchen and stuffed it into the fridge. Then he extracted bottles for each of them and dealt them out like cards. He laid a hand atop Jeremy's head, and grinning, gave it a ferocious little rub like he would a favorite pet. "I think maybe my brother the fruit cup is right. I'm not ready for all this amazement."

Woody eyed them warmly, but there was a tinge of dread in his voice as well. "Well, Chuck, I think you'd better *get* ready. Willow Man is here somewhere. No doubt waiting for the most opportune time to pop out and scare the pants off us like he did when we were kids. Maybe this time we'll be ready for him when he does." He didn't feel particularly ready. He wondered if any of the others did.

"Not me," Jeremy said, twisting the cap off his Budweiser. "I'll *never* be ready."

"Me either," Cathy agreed, taking a dainty sip from her own, then tilting the bottle back and downing half of it while Woody looked on, impressed.

Chuck spat up a derisive chuckle, but there was a glimmer of real fear in his eyes when he said, "Well, I guess we're all agreed on *that* point."

Cathy continued to look about the room, studying the pictures on the walls as if remembering them from years past, casting leery glances at the darkness outside the windows. "What do you suppose he wants? What's his motivation?"

Jeremy shrugged, his eyes on Woody. "Spooks don't need motivation. They just do what they do. They're like pit bulls that way, I guess. Only crazier."

Chuck pulled Cathy down onto Woody's father's recliner, and the two of them snuggled in together. Jeremy plopped down on the sofa, and Woody joined him there. Sitting close, but not too close, but still close enough to cause Cathy and Chuck to share an amused glance. Woody fought the urge to reach out and lay a hand on Jeremy's leg. Christ, even in the midst of wonders, his libido had somehow managed to kick in. To waylay it, Woody turned his thoughts to Chuck and Cathy.

"So how the heck did you two end up together? I thought Cathy would be president of the local chapter of Dykes on Bikes by now. There was certainly nothing feminine about her as a kid."

Chuck nuzzled his face into Cathy's neck like a hog rooting for truffles. "Now she simply *exudes* femininity." He glanced at Woody with a lascivious look in his eyes. "Some men are drawn to that sort of thing."

"And some men aren't," Jeremy said, so matter-of-factly that Woody laughed.

Jeremy turned to Woody. "So let me get this straight, if you'll pardon the expression. Are you just having us all on, or are you truly gay? I need to know how to be acting right now. Usually when I'm with Chuck and the bimbo and their little coterie of friends, I'm the only one who favors opera over hog calling, crepes over deep-fried Twinkies, and a delicately scented styling mist over axle grease and a pound of lard. Makes me somewhat of an individual."

"Makes you a fruit cup," Chuck said.

Cathy gave him a gentle slap on the arm. "There's nothing wrong with liking men. *I* like men. Of course, lately I seemed to have settled for Chuck instead."

"Thanks, babe. That little comment should improve my sexual prowess. Nothing like instilling confidence in the man you love. Really gets the testosterone flowing."

Jeremy sighed, still gazing at Woody. Still waiting for an answer. "Well?"

For the first time since his thirteenth summer, lying in the darkness with Bobby, Woody found himself holding nothing back about himself. He had never been ashamed of his homosexuality. He just never figured it was really anyone's business but his own. But these were his friends, and if anyone was more apt to accept him for who he was, he didn't know who it would be.

"Yep," he said. "Queer as a three dollar bill. If that bothers anyone here, you know what you can do about it."

"Nicely put," Jeremy said.

Chuck turned to Cathy. "God, gay people are always so damned *militant*. You'd think they were the ones who were normal and the rest of us were degenerates. I'm appalled at their lackadaisical attitude toward morality. I truly am. They should carry their difference like a cross across their backs, don't you think? Humbled. Ashamed. Mortified. But no, they just go their merry ways, plodding gaily through life, seducing a shoe salesman here, a 7-Eleven clerk there, usually getting more sex than any three straight people put together. Gee, now that I think about it, maybe I should be batting for the other team too. I like sex as much as the next guy. Maybe not *with* the next guy, of course. Don't much care where I get it either, or who with, as long as I get it and as long as there are tits involved."

Cathy rolled her eyes. "Golly. You really know how to cement a relationship."

Chuck batted his eyelashes and feigned a blush. "Why, thank you."

Jeremy ignored them. His eyes still rested on Woody. There was a sadness in Jeremy's eyes now that spoke of more than old friends spilling their guts.

"It was Bobby, wasn't it?" he asked, his eyes delving into Woody's. "You guys loved each other. Am I right?"

"Yes," Woody said. "We loved each other. Bobby taught me about myself. He opened up the world for me. If he still lived in this world, I think maybe we would be together even now. I've never found anyone since who could make me feel the way Bobby did. Maybe I never will."

The room had grown silent as all eyes studied Woody. Cathy snuggled closer to Chuck and rested her head on his chest, the beer forgotten in her hand.

"I think about him every day," Woody went on. "Sometimes I go for weeks without remembering my parents, how they lived, how they died, but the memories I have of Bobby never seem to leave me. I guess maybe his death tore a hole in me I've never been able to fill. I've never loved anyone since. I've never *wanted* to love anyone since. I guess that's why I turned to music. Music takes me away from it all. The memories. The pain. Sometimes the music plugs that hole in my heart, at least for a little while."

He seemed to realize suddenly he was dragging the room down into sadness. "Anyway, now I've got you guys to plug the hole."

Chuck groaned. "We *are* speaking metaphorically, right?"

Cathy bopped him on the head as if he were one of those mechanical gophers that pop out of holes at the arcade. Then she turned to Woody and asked the question they were all dying to ask but didn't quite have the nerve to.

"Did the two of you have sex? You and Bobby? Is this really a *physical* love you're talking about or just, you know, *emotional*."

Woody smiled when he felt Jeremy's hand reach over and cover his own. He glanced at Jeremy for a moment, then turned to Cathy. "We had the most incredible sex I've ever experienced. Because of the love, maybe. Or maybe because we were only thirteen and our hormones were raging and it was all so new to us. Or maybe just because we belonged together. We always did, you know. Belong together. There was never any doubt about that. We both knew it."

"Good Lord," Chuck said. "I was still playing with toy trucks at thirteen. I thought an erection was a stately building. Jeremy and I didn't hit puberty until more than a year later. If I had known you and Bobby were bonking each other every time our backs were turned, I would have probably paid to watch, just to see what it was all about."

"You're such a nimrod," Cathy said. "I knew something was going on. Jeremy did too. We talked about it once." She turned to Jeremy. "Remember?"

Jeremy nodded. "Yeah, I remember. I guess subconsciously I was jealous. I might not have hit puberty yet, but I still knew where my preferences lay. At least I thought I did." He gazed at Woody with such depth of emotion Woody was a little taken aback. "I had a crush on you back then. Never knew that, did you?"

Jeremy's hand felt warm and comforting lying atop his own. Woody almost expected the tear-shaped birthmark to slide down Jeremy's cheek and spill over onto his collar, but of course it didn't.

"No," he said. "I never knew. I'm sorry."

"Christ, I never knew that either." Chuck gazed around the room as if he had forgotten where he parked his car. "Why do I keep expecting Jerry Springer to pop out of the woodwork?"

"Oh, do shut up," Cathy said. "This is beautiful."

"It's disconcerting, is what it is, and I for one need another drink to cope with it." He squirmed out from beneath Cathy and made his way to the kitchen, kicking off his shoes as he went. "Anybody else up for seconds?"

Everybody was. Cathy might look like a lady, but she could drink with the best of them, Woody saw. He wondered how many other surprises would be popping up tonight. He was also beginning to enjoy the heat of Jeremy's hand—the way it felt atop his own, so strong and all-encompassing—and wondering where that simple touch of friendship might one day lead them if they didn't watch their step. He was only mildly amazed to realize Bobby's face was fading from his mind a bit. He was seeing Jeremy there now. What the hell did that mean? A tremor of guilt echoed through his heart.

Cathy took his mind away from it by asking, "When did it begin? You and Bobby. When did you first realize you loved each other?"

Woody thought back, remembering all the horrors of that summer, but remembering the beauties of it too.

"It was the day you found the skeleton in the bushes. That night, in my bed, one thing just led to another. Before the sun came up the next morning, we knew where our destinies would lead. Or at least we thought we did," he added.

Doling out beers, Chuck thought back, remembering that summer as well. "But Bobby died less than three weeks after that. You didn't have much time together."

"No," Woody said, turning the beer bottle in his hand, staring at it, feeling the coldness of it. "No, we didn't."

"I remember the funeral," Jeremy said, watching the sadness in Woody's eyes. "You didn't shed a tear. None of us did. Remember that? It was like we were too young to grasp what was going on. Or too shocked. Our folks were blubbering all over the place, but we just stood there at the edge of the grave like rocks. Stony eyed. Sober as judges."

"That was the first time I ever saw Bobby's parents," Cathy said. "Remember how Bobby never spoke of them? I suppose they weren't the best parents in the world, but maybe they had their own demons to contend with. They died a few years ago, you know. A murder-suicide. Maybe they never got over Bobby's loss either."

"I didn't know that," Woody said, wondering suddenly if Willow Man had played a part in those deaths as well. He could find no pity in his heart for them, however. Not an ounce. They had made Bobby's life a living hell back then, but he supposed he should feel at least a little gratitude toward them, since it was their indifference to their son that had driven Bobby to him. He found himself hoping wherever death had taken Bobby, his parents had not joined him there.

Chuck's eyes kept wandering to the darkened hallway that led from the living room to the rest of the house, as if expecting a face from the past to suddenly materialize there. Woody's mother in gossamer robes, maybe. Or Woody's father, grinning that sappy grin of his, not much more than a big kid himself. Or Bobby, so young and handsome, on the verge of a manhood he would never reach, and apparently harboring secrets that Chuck had known nothing about at the time.

"Why do I get the feeling we're not alone?" he finally asked.

Woody, too, turned his eyes to the darkened hallway. "I know my parents are here. I saw them. My mother spoke to me. I know it sounds crazy, but it's true. We're *not* alone. I keep hoping that Bobby is here, too. I'd love to see him again. Even if it's just, you know, his—spirit."

"I wouldn't be wrapping my head around any of this if I hadn't seen Willow Man with my own eyes just a few days ago," Jeremy said matter-of-factly, as if he was rattling off insurance quotes. "He's put us on some sort of journey, I think. We were meant to be together again, and he's orchestrating the whole thing."

"Where did you see him?" Woody asked.

Jeremy squeezed his eyes shut, as if even the memory of it still pained him. "I was shaving, and suddenly there he was, looking out at me from the mirror. He was shaving, too. Had himself all lathered up with shaving cream, scraping away at his face with a big old Bowie knife like Daniel Boone. I was so startled I damn near cut my nose off. I may never use that bathroom again. I'll have to start pissing in the backyard."

"I saw him at work," Cathy said. "He was all decked out in a UPS uniform, like an honest-to-God human. Afterward, I learned that no one else saw him. Only me. He delivered a package to me. Even had one of those electronic boxes where the recipient signs his name."

"What was in the package?" Woody asked.

Cathy retrieved her purse from the floor and dug around in it until she extracted a folded sheet of paper. She handed it to Woody without a word.

Woody unfolded it to see a picture of himself, guitar in hand, seemingly singing his heart out. It was the studio snapshot taken so long ago. The one in the ad for the San Diego show. The one on the poster at Strikers. Scrawled across the top of it in red ink, or blood, were the words, "Be there or be square. And bring your little friends. It'll be a hoot."

"Jesus," Woody said. He turned to Chuck. "What about you?"

"I didn't really see him," Chuck said, looking uncomfortable, looking as if he'd rather be talking about anything else. But when he started speaking, he couldn't seem to stop. He closed his eyes and let the words pour out. "It was just a dream, I guess, but it didn't feel like one. He was leading me by the hand through the canyon. He led me past that butt-ugly clubhouse we built, past the place where we buried Wilbur. Remember that? He was holding my hand so tight my knuckles were popping. In the dream I was just a kid again. I was crying. I was afraid. He was taking me somewhere to kill me. I knew that. But still I couldn't get away. 'This is where you belong,' he kept saying to me. 'This is where you all belong. Here with me. Forever.' And then beneath the willow trees where it was so dark you couldn't see your hand in front of your face, I felt his lips suddenly all over me. Kissing me. Licking me. His breath smelled like rotten meat. He tore at my clothes and pushed me to the ground. He rolled me over like a rag doll and pulled my pants down around my ankles. I was screaming and—and that's when I woke up."

"I *woke* him up," Cathy said. "He was yelling and crying in his sleep, drenched in sweat. I knew what he was dreaming. I could sense it. It was almost as if I could see everything that was happening to him. I still get goose bumps thinking about it."

"He was going to rape me," Chuck said. "He was going to drive himself into me, and afterward he was going to kill me. I can still feel his hands on my naked flesh. His fingers probing at me. Spreading me apart." He shuddered. "It was two days before I dared to go to sleep again."

"He was walking around like some sort of zombie," Cathy said. "I finally had to give him something to knock him out."

"So you see," Jeremy said, still holding Woody's hand, still bestowing comfort with it, and maybe absorbing comfort from it as well, "there was never any question about us coming to your show. We would have been there anyway if we had known about it, but maybe without Willow Man intervening, we wouldn't have known about it at all. He made sure we were there. He made sure we would all come together again, just like he wanted. Now, I suppose, all we need to do is wait and find out why."

"I'm glad you're here," Woody said. "Glad for me, at any rate. But sorry for you, I guess."

"Don't be," Cathy said. "Willow Man might be a first class putz and a raging asshole, but he's right about one thing. We do belong together. If something's going to happen, we need to be here for each other when it does. Our destinies are just as intertwined as yours and Bobby's were. Maybe they always will be."

Woody suddenly recalled the voice he imagined to be Bobby's, whispering in his ear before he went out onstage tonight. Telling him the show must go on. Telling him, too, that he would be waiting for him when the show was over. They would deal with Willow Man then, Bobby had said.

Maybe that voice wasn't imaginary after all.

"Bobby's here," Woody said, suddenly believing it beyond all doubt. He didn't care if his friends believed it. He didn't care if they thought he was as mad as a shithouse rat for believing it. A smile crept over his face as he looked at each of them in turn. "He spoke to me before the show, you know. Bobby, I mean. With everything else that has happened, I guess I just sort of forgot about it until now. How could I forget something like that? Are we all crazy, or is it just me?

Are we so used to weird crap happening to us that nothing much impresses us anymore?"

"Oh, *I'm* impressed." Chuck said.

"Me, too," Cathy echoed. "Impressed and scared poopless."

The timid one in childhood, Jeremy appeared the epitome of strength now. He had a mellow timbre in his voice that seemed to radiate a quiet stoicism, a calm efficiency. His strong, warm hand still covered Woody's, their fingers comfortingly intertwined.

"Bobby was alone when he died. None of us were with him. I think if we stay together, we'll be okay. Willow Man can't harm us if we put up a concerted front. I would just like to know what the hell it is he wants. Did we anger him so much when we were kids that he's still holding some wild-ass grudge? I guess what I'm asking is, what exactly did we do to piss him off?"

"We left," Woody said. "That's what we did. We left. After Bobby's funeral, we never went into the canyon again. With Bobby's death he was just getting warmed up. I think he meant to kill us all that summer. When we didn't return, he wasn't allowed to finish his little game. I don't know what his motivations are, but I know what he is. He's a killer. Maybe it's only me he wants. Maybe that's why he went after my parents. And Bobby too. Maybe he knew that would hurt me most. Or maybe he's just jealous that we are alive and he isn't. Who the hell knows? The big question we have to ask ourselves is how do we stop him? He's not limited to the canyon now. Maybe he never was. He can go anywhere he wants. He told me so, and we all know it's true. But how do you go about killing something that's already dead?"

No one answered. It was the same question they had asked themselves as children, and the answer was no clearer to them now than it was then.

Chuck pushed himself up from the recliner. Leaving Cathy sitting there alone, he headed for the kitchen. They all heard the clink of beer bottles as Chuck returned with another round for everyone.

"Let's get drunk," he said. "I'm braver when I'm drunk."

Jeremy laughed. "You're an *idiot* when you're drunk."

Cathy rolled her eyes. "A *horny* idiot."

Chuck didn't disagree. "Yeah, but idiots don't sense fear. Idiots just go happily assholing through life without a care in the world. That's how I want to be right now. I don't want to be thinking about dead people trying to kill me or the fact that I'm going bald at thirty or the astounding revelation that Woody is just as queerly oriented as my brother. I just want to drink. I want to get so happily shitfaced that even ghosts can't penetrate the haze. For tonight at least, I just want to be an idiot."

Woody smiled up at Chuck standing in front of them. Chuck was still wearing that earnest pleading expression on his face that Woody remembered so well from childhood. "I think you've already succeeded," Woody said. "And I for one would be happy to join you. No, I'd be *honored*."

"Fine then," Cathy said. "Let's all get drunk. Far be it from me to stem the tide of idiocy."

Jeremy nudged himself a little closer to Woody's side and rested his head on Woody's shoulder. "I get horny when I'm drunk too," he said in a little boy voice, as innocent as a cherub.

Woody grinned. "Imagine that."

THE CASE of beer they had picked up after the show was long gone, and they were making inroads into what was left of the twelve-pack Woody had picked up that afternoon. None of them were feeling any pain, and in the happy reunion atmosphere, Willow Man seemed almost forgotten. Chuck and Cathy were sprawled out with the recliner at full tilt, and Woody was sitting on the floor at Jeremy's feet. Jeremy's fingers were idly twining a strand of Woody's hair. His strong knees were pressed into Woody's shoulders. When Woody tilted his head back for a second, enjoying the feel of Jeremy's hands in his hair, the back of his head bumped against something pretty darn substantial in the crotch of Jeremy's slacks. It was all Woody could do not to turn around and go prospecting. He could feel his own dick lengthening at the thought. Lord, this evening wasn't turning out the way he thought it would at all.

"You should call your agent," Jeremy said, acting like he didn't know what Woody was thinking, but of course he did. Or Woody *hoped* he did. "Maybe you got that recording contract. I can't imagine why you wouldn't. As you know, I'm a little more into opera than country western, but I have to admit you blew my socks off tonight."

"Is that like a *homosexual innuendo?*" Chuck asked, his words slightly fuzzy around the edges from all the beer he had consumed.

Cathy gave him a sharp elbow to the ribs.

"Ouch," he said.

Woody hooked a thumb in Chuck's direction and twisted his head around to look up into Jeremy's face. He took the opportunity to bump Jeremy's crotch again, this time with his chin. Innocently, of course, or so he hoped it appeared. That *really* made his dick twitch. He was pretty sure it made Jeremy's dick give a lurch too.

"Is Chuck always like this when he drinks?"

There was a sparkle in Jeremy's eyes that couldn't be entirely attributed to giving his brother a hard time. He knew exactly what Woody was doing. "Oh, no. He's usually much worse. When the beer is gone, he'll probably get into the cough medicine, or anything else you've got lying around with any alcohol content, and then we'll all be in trouble. He doesn't just *strive* for idiocy when he drinks, he reaches its full potential and then improves on it. It's like a gift."

"You're talking about the man I love," Cathy said with a wistful look in her eye. She wasn't feeling much pain, either. "And God, how I wish you weren't."

"Thanks ever so," Chuck said. "I love you, too, pumpkin puss."

Cathy rolled her eyes. "Christ."

"How *did* you two get together?" Woody asked again, repositioning himself properly between Jeremy's legs, facing out, trying to ignore the ever-growing urge to do a Greg Louganis double backflip into the crotch behind him. Even so, he wasn't just making conversation. He really wanted to know. Cathy and Chuck seemed to fit so well together. Like two pillows from the same bed. It amused him they still ragged on each other like they had when they were kids, but now there was an underlying thread, a history behind the ragging that complemented them. It filled them out. Made them a unit. They truly appeared to belong together. Comfortable in their love for each other even while they spouted insults back and forth.

Cathy laughed while Chuck groaned. "God, I hate this story," he said.

Cathy's face beamed. Woody was struck once more by how beautiful she had become.

"You haven't been around for a while," she said, "so maybe you don't know just how mechanically challenged Chuck turned out to be in adulthood." Here she cast a fond eye on the man beside her and added, "If you want to call this adulthood. He can only change a light bulb if there is someone there to spin the ladder."

Woody laughed, enjoying the happy lilt in Cathy's voice, enjoying the feel of Jeremy's fingers still twining through his hair. Even enjoying the look of patient forbearance on Chuck's face as he listened to Cathy tell the story.

"He called me up one day out of the blue. I hadn't seen him or Jeremy for maybe five or six years, and even then we only occasionally bumped into each other at the mall or something. None of us ever seemed to want to rehash the time we spent together as kids, so those meetings were always a little uncomfortable. A little awkward. Then suddenly I hear Chuck's voice on the phone asking me how I'm doing, what's been happening with my life, do I have any kids, am I married, and by the way, how does one go about fixing a vacuum cleaner that only blows instead of sucks and while we're on the subject, how about dinner?"

"The vacuum cleaner was a ruse," Chuck interjected.

"Ruse, my ass," Cathy laughed. "I went to his apartment and walked into what looked like Oklahoma during the Dust Bowl. The vacuum cleaner was sitting in the middle of the floor screaming like a wounded moose, blowing crap from one end of the apartment to the other. Chuck was standing there looking at it like it was some unwanted relative named Hoover who had suddenly plopped himself down in the middle of his life and was making a mess and he didn't quite know how to get rid of him. Chuck didn't even have the brains to unplug the damn thing. He just stood there glaring at it, looking all hurt and offended. Totally helpless."

"Another ruse," Chuck said, grinning now. Like Woody. Like Jeremy.

"You wouldn't know a ruse if it popped up and bit you on the chin," Cathy said. "You're not that subtle."

"Ooh," Chuck said. "*That* hurt."

"Anyway, I don't know what he had done to the poor thing, but the vacuum cleaner was totaled. Never worked right again."

"Faulty merchandise," Chuck giggled.

"In the hands of a moron, yes," Cathy agreed. "So after the two of us spent most of the afternoon cleaning dust balls off the furniture and spraying everything down with Windex and Lysol like your mother would have done, we went out for cheeseburgers and Cokes and a little fresh air, and before the day was over, things took a disastrous turn when I found my hormones kicking in. I must be attracted to helpless men and didn't know it. Or maybe I had just never met one who was capable of elevating helplessness to an art form."

"It's part of my charm," Chuck said.

Cathy patted him sweetly on the head. "Oh, yeah. Well, thank God, I soon learned there were a *few* things he knew how to do, if you know what I mean, and we've been together ever since. I know now that I would have been smarter to set my sights on Jeremy, but unfortunately he doesn't seem to find me all that attractive. I like to be worshipped in a relationship. Hard to do that with a man who'd rather be shtupping the plumber instead of you."

"That depends on the plumber," Jeremy said. He opened his mouth to say something else, when suddenly he leapt to his feet, taking several strands of Woody's hair with him.

"Y-y-ouch!" Woody rubbed his head and looked up to see Jeremy standing over him, staring at the picture window beside the piano. There was such a look of astonishment on his face that they all turned too, to stare at the window, at the darkness outside.

At the face staring in at them.

Cathy screamed. It wasn't one of those ladylike little eeks you might hear from some pampered, swooning Southern belle in the movies with crinoline petticoats and a corset pushing her boobs up to her chin. It was a full-blown scream of horror that seemed to shake the walls and sent the hair on the back of Woody's neck into tap-dancing mode and shriveled his skin up like a prune by the mere forcefulness of the damn thing. Cathy had a set of lungs on her. No two ways around that.

With his heart thumping wildly inside his chest, Woody stared at the face looking in at them through the glass.

Then he laughed.

"It's Noah," he said. "What's he doing here?"

Chuck sounded considerably more sober than he had only a few seconds earlier. Maybe Cathy's scream had knocked the beer right out of him. "Who the hell is Noah?"

"My agent."

Cathy was holding her chest like maybe she was having a coronary or something. "Good God, does he always pop up like that? Hasn't he ever heard of a doorbell? And what the hell is he doing?"

Noah had his nose smashed up against the windowpane with a finger in each ear. His remaining fingers were doing a little finger wave at the sides of his head like some kid giving the raspberry to a street cop who had just told him to stop riding his bike on the sidewalk, for Christ's sake. Noah's hair was sticking up at all angles from the bushes he had waded through to get to the window. He looked truly deranged. And happy.

"I think maybe I got the contract," Woody said, heading for the front door.

Jeremy's voice trailed along behind him. "*This* is the man you allow to guide your career? Gads, I think you'd be better off with Clarabelle the Clown."

"Ugly fucker, isn't he?" Chuck asked, studying the face for a second longer before heading for the kitchen. "I think I need another drink."

"Bring me a tranquilizer," Cathy called out after him. "In fact, make it two. And another beer. And anything else you can find with drugs or alcohol in it. And a psychiatrist if you see one hanging around."

Jeremy grinned at her. "Tense?"

"You bet."

By the time Woody got to the door, Noah was on the doorstep waiting for him, looking just as happily deranged as he had at the window. He made a little salami-salami-boloney bow when Woody opened the door, then held out a piece of paper and a pen and said, "Autograph, please."

"Say what?"

Noah's goofy smile reached from ear to ear, all but slicing his head in half. "I'm a celebrity stalker. I collect autographs. I just *love* recording artists, don't you? But of course you do, since you are one."

"Am I?" Woody asked, feeling his own smile beginning to widen now. Feeling that old tom-tom once again pounding away inside his chest, but not from fear this time. From something else. Excitement, maybe. And disbelief. "What are you saying, Noah? Spit it out."

"They've agreed to produce three albums over a two year period."

"Who?"

"Sun Records."

"My God."

"You don't have to go that far," Noah said. "Just call me Noah." Then he held up a fifth of Chivas and said, "How about a celebratory drink? Or several?"

Without waiting for a response, Noah barged through the doorway, and two seconds later he was introducing himself to everyone in the room. Jeremy and Cathy were thrilled by the news of Woody's contract, while Chuck seemed more centered on the bottle of Chivas in Noah's hand. He offered to make drinks.

While Chuck rattled around in the kitchen with glasses and ice, humming to himself one of the songs Woody had sung during the show, Noah looked around, scoping out the house, studying the effect of his news on Woody's face, sizing up Woody's friends as well.

"Guess I interrupted a reunion. Sorry about that." With that formality out of the way, he turned his full attention to Woody. "So what do you think? Am I the man, or what?"

He looked so proud of himself Woody had to laugh. You'd think Noah was the one up on that stage tonight.

"You are definitely the man," Woody said. "So how much money are we talking about? Round it out to the nearest million."

Noah chucked him on the arm, looking a little uncomfortable as he did it. "You know it doesn't work like that, kid. Everything hinges on the first album. If that does well, we go on to the second. If the second album does well, they want the third to be a Christmas album. Apparently those always sell like hotcakes. You don't have a problem with that, do you? I mean, you're not an atheist or anything, are you?"

"Who cares?" Woody asked, already thinking of which tracks he wanted to put on the first album. "Hell, I'll sing Gregorian chants, call hogs, and yodel if that's what they want. As long as the money is there, I'm putty in their hands."

Chuck called out from the kitchen. "Atta boy, Woody! Hold onto those artistic freedoms! Let them know who's boss!"

"Fuck artistic freedom!" Woody yelled back. "I just want the money!"

"Spoken like a true celebrity," Cathy said, laughing. "Integrity be damned."

"Hell, yes," Jeremy chimed in. "Make the bucks and run like a rabbit."

Chuck was muttering something about what a greedy bunch of shitheels his friends were when he stepped through the kitchen doorway with a handful of drinks. He doled them out like a proper cocktail waitress and pulled Cathy back down onto the recliner beside him, sipping his drink before his ass ever hit the chair.

Noah squeezed in between Woody and Jeremy, causing them both to scootch over to make room for him. He took a long pull from his drink, totally oblivious to the fact he was de-splicing a burgeoning relationship. He gazed around like a real estate agent on the make.

"Christ, kid, if I had known you were a property owner, I'd have been a little greedier with my commissions. This house is nicer than mine."

"It was my parents' house," Woody said. Then a sudden thought struck him. "How did you find it, anyway? I never told you where I was staying."

"Will told me."

"Who the hell is Will?"

Noah shrugged. "Never caught his last name. He popped into the dressing room after you left. I assumed he was an old friend of yours. Gave me the bottle of Chivas and told me to congratulate you on a job well done. Meaning the show, I guess."

"What'd he look like?" Woody asked, confused.

Noah laughed. "Looked like Tex Ritter. All decked out in cowboy gear. A little lax in his ablutions, I think. Smelled like a pound of bad hamburger. Had some sort of fungus on the end of his fingers. Pretty darn disgusting. Now that you're on the road to stardom, you might want to consider being a bit more discerning in your friendships. Present company excluded, of course," he added quickly, looking around at the others.

Woody stared down at the drink in his hand, and leaning forward, sat it carefully on the coffee table as if afraid it might explode.

Jeremy watched him. "What? What's the matter?"

"Will, my ass," Woody said. "That was Willow Man."

Cathy's eyes opened wide, and she, too, leaned over the arm of the recliner and placed her glass on the floor. Jeremy followed suit. Chuck leaned over and poured the contents of his glass into an empty urn sitting on the end table.

Noah watched this all as if he suddenly suspected he was the only sane person in the room.

Woody plucked the glass from Noah's hand and carried it into the kitchen where he poured it down the sink.

"Are you people nuts? That's perfectly good booze!"

"No, Noah," Woody said, dropping the half-empty bottle of Chivas into the wastebasket and stepping back into the living room. "That's a recipe for disaster."

"What the hell are you talking about? Who the hell was that guy? An enemy of yours or something?"

Woody gave his manager a weary smile and said, "You might call him that. He's had it in for me, had it in for all of us, for a very long time. Stay away from him, Noah. If you see him again, just stay as far away from him as you can get. He's—crazy."

Noah was looking more confused by the second. "You mean he's like a stalker? Like an actual *stalker*? Geez, who would stalk *you*? It's not like you're famous or anything. Not yet, anyway."

Woody wasn't about to explain Willow Man to anyone, least of all his agent. Noah would probably drop him like a hot potato, or worse, think he was back on drugs.

As nicely as he could, he steered Noah toward the door, thanking him profusely for everything he had done, and eased him out onto the front porch, telling him to go home, get a good night's sleep, and leave the matter of old Will to himself and his friends.

Noah left, but not happily, and when Woody heard his car start up outside, he turned to his friends and said, "Let's take a walk."

"Into the canyon?" Cathy asked.

"Yeah," Woody said, ignoring the look of horror on Chuck's now sober face, and ignoring Jeremy's quizzical expression as well. "Into the canyon."

CHAPTER NINE

THE SCRATCHES on Cathy's back weren't as deep as Woody had originally thought, but they were deep enough. Five perfect claw marks running diagonally from shoulder to ribs. He swabbed at them lightly with a T-shirt soaked in drinking water from a bottle Bobby had brought with him for the camp-out. He could feel Cathy shiver and cringe away beneath his gentle prodding, but she didn't cry out. She was too mad for that.

"I guess even ghosts don't see very well in the dark. Stupid bastards." She glanced over at Bobby, who was watching her, his face molded into a rictus of concern, illuminated by the firelight in front of him. Cathy hugged her sleeping bag to her naked chest with one arm, covering her budding breasts, a graceful, womanly gesture totally out of sync with the look of fury and the aftermath of fear on her face and the smear of dirt on her freckled cheek. She had a stick poking out of her hair too, like some half-ass geisha, but so far no one had found the courage to reach up and pluck it out. Chuck seemed the only one mesmerized by the fact that Cathy was sitting among them half-naked. He tried to look everywhere else, but his eyes were constantly drawn back to those perfect bare shoulders and what was hidden so carefully beneath them.

Cathy hissed in pain when Woody's fingers delved a little too harshly into her wounds as he tried to remove the grit and dirt from her torn flesh, but still she didn't cry out. Woody figured he would be howling like a baby by now if someone was digging at him like he was digging at her, and when that realization struck him, his respect for Cathy, already great to begin with, took another leap skyward. She had guts. No doubt about it. Thank Christ those guts weren't scattered all over the canyon at this very moment, considering who she had run into out there in the darkness.

Apparently she was having the same thought. "Thank God I'm a girl," she said, still staring into Bobby's composed face; the calmness she saw there in front of her was helping her cope with what Woody was doing behind her back. She didn't look at the twins at all, but focused all her attention on Bobby, like a marooned sailor, gazing off to the horizon at the glimmer of a white sail in the distance, promising rescue, promising salvation. Gazing into Bobby's tranquil face gave her hope that maybe tonight would end some way other than how she had thought it would for a while there. It wouldn't end with her lying dead in the bushes, at least. She knew that now. Bobby's caring eyes told her that much. She felt safe under his gaze. Safe and protected.

But still pretty damn scared.

At the periphery of her awareness, across the campfire, she noted Jeremy's worried expression, and she noted Chuck's sidelong glances at her bare shoulders, too, but she didn't let that bother her. She was too mad at what had risen up out of the canyon tonight to be angry at anything or anyone else. A matter of priorities, she supposed. And maybe she even enjoyed the wide-eyed look of longing on Chuck's cherubic little face as he gazed at her bare flesh in the firelight. Made her feel like a woman somehow. Maybe even a desirable woman. Or the makings of one. She needed that feeling right now. Needed it badly. Maybe someday, if Chuck ever hit puberty, she might even find herself looking back.

But it wouldn't be tonight. Tonight her attentions were focused elsewhere, so she pushed all thoughts of Chuck's interest in her body away from her and latched onto that sea of calmness and caring that floated so peacefully there in Bobby's liquid brown eyes. She needed Bobby's calmness now, needed it more than she needed Chuck's longing.

"It was *you* he wanted, I think." She spoke the words softly to Bobby, but they carried with them an awful importance. To her way of thinking, at least. "Either you or Woody. He spoke your names when he was talking to me. Spoke your names as if in the darkness, he couldn't tell it was really me, but thought it was one of you. His fingers on my skin didn't feel like fingers. They were so rough. Like concrete. Hard. You know? Like they were coated with something."

"Is that how he scratched your back?" Bobby asked. Bobby's voice was hushed too, as if he thought maybe Willow Man was out there in the shadows, listening to every word they were saying. And how the hell did they know he wasn't?

"Yeah," she said. "He was scraping at me. Peeling my shirt off like you'd peel off a sock. I fell backward trying to get away from the son of a bitch. He had my blouse off before I even knew what the hell was going on. One minute I was swatting at bats, and the next minute Willow Man was all over me. I don't know where he came from. Suddenly the bats were gone and he was just there. Groping at me. Tearing at my clothes. I could smell him. He smelled like Wilbur. Like he was rotting. His breath made me want to puke.

"But it was those hands that scared me most. They were so strong. So—*rough*. He pawed and dug at me with those rock-hard fingers like he wanted to pull my guts out through my skin. He didn't care if he hurt me. He just wanted to get *at* me. Get *into* me. Like a boll weevil burrowing into a boll of cotton. Yeah," she said, thinking about it. "*Just* like that. Like a bug. Like a fucking *parasite*."

She cringed away from Woody's fingers and turned her head to peer over her shoulder at him. "Jesus, aren't you done yet? You're worse than he was."

Woody stuck his hand on his hip and glared at her. He was sweating bullets. He didn't like what he was doing any more than she did. "You've got dirt and stuff in there. You don't want it to get infected, do you? Cut me some slack. I'm doing the best I can. Takes time is all."

She grunted impatiently, but leaned forward again to let him finish.

Jeremy held out the bottle of peach brandy, offering it to Woody. "Pour this shit on the scratches," he said. "Maybe it'll kill the germs. Or get them drunk enough to fall off."

Woody snickered but took the bottle. Sounded like a good idea to him. There sure as hell wasn't any peroxide lying around. He splashed some brandy onto the cloth and pressed it to the deepest scratch. Cathy's reaction was all and more than he expected it to be.

She sucked in enough air to fill a dirigible and started spouting obscenities in a long continuous stream, with nary a comma, semicolon, or period stuck in anywhere to interrupt the flow. In the cursing department, she had finally managed to outdo even herself.

"Shit fuck damn snot dickheaded cocksucking motherfucking shiteating *hornytoads!* Why don't you just set me on fire and get it over with!"

"Stop whining," Woody said, impressed once again by Cathy's flare for expletive, as his father had once called it (yes, even *he* had seemed impressed after overhearing Cathy go off on one of her verbal rampages). Sometimes Woody wished he had a pencil and paper handy to write Cathy's rantings down, that's how educational they were. Like a really fucked-up form of poetry. "This'll *help*," he cooed, blotting more gently with the brandy-soaked T-shirt, hoping she wouldn't start swinging her fists and knocking his lights out as she was sometimes prone to do when things didn't go the way she wanted them to.

"Yeah, right," Cathy groused, but then she settled down and let him continue, soaking up the pain like a woman in childbirth, knowing it would soon be over, knowing the result would eventually be worth the effort. Hopefully. Woody figured God probably knew what He was doing when He gave women the job of bearing children. They could handle pain a hell of a lot better than men. Men were babies. Women were rocks. Cathy was living proof of that. Going through what she was enduring, Woody would have been a whimpering pool of whining misery by now, dribbling tears and snot, screaming his fool head off, pooping his pants, and more than likely running off into the brush like a fucking antelope.

Chuck looked more appalled by Cathy's pain than she did. "Think of it as perfume," he said in a wheedling tone. Almost pleading. "The brandy, I mean. Think of it as peach perfume. You'll smell all peachy when Woody's done."

"Piss off, Chuck. And stick a peach up your ass while you're doing it."

Poor Chuck looked like he'd been kicked in the nuts. "Right." He withdrew to a neutral corner, resuming his perusal of those bare, beautiful shoulders, envying Woody his nearness to them, wishing he were the one to be swabbing at her wounds. Touching her. Making her feel better. Making himself feel better.

"So what happened then?" Bobby asked. "After he tore your shirt off." And without thinking, he reached up and pulled the stick from her hair, tossing it into the darkness.

Cathy didn't notice. She seemed mesmerized by Bobby's strong young hands. So finely formed. So adept at whatever he seemed to be doing at any given moment. A shiver of desire swept through her, which she mistook for pain, her mind too young to understand what desire truly was, too innocent to understand that one was sometimes very much like the other.

As always, her innocence did not extend to her vocabulary, but while the words were harsh, there was an emotion behind them that transcended anger. There was sorrow there somewhere. Sorrow and shame.

"If he wasn't already dead, the stinky fucker should have his balls cut off. He had my shirt up over my head, and he was working my shorts down around my ass. Then his hand touched me down there, and he suddenly pulled back. Guess he found something he didn't expect to find."

"What was that?" Chuck asked, his eyes wide and bright in the firelight.

Cathy's hand lashed out so quickly Chuck didn't have time to flinch. She whapped him such a good one across the chops that Woody heard the kid's teeth rattle. Chuck gasped, more from the shock of it than the pain, and then his shock was compounded even further when Cathy began to cry.

"My pussy, you nimrod. He *touched* me down there. Don't you get it? He *touched* me down *there*!" Tears welled up in her eyes and spilled out over her lashes, sparkling in the firelight. "He touched me, and feeling what he felt down there, he pushed me away. He called me—he called me—" But this thought was too much for her. She buried her face in her hands and wept. Woody had to stop working on her scratches because her back was heaving so much with her sobs he was afraid he might really hurt her.

Bobby reached out and laid his hand across her arm, stroking it gently, trying to calm her, trying to ease the pain she was feeling, whatever that pain really was. It wasn't fear. That much he knew. She had gone beyond fear. She had gone somewhere inside herself, he suspected. Deep inside herself where something other than fear resided. Maybe it was always there. Maybe what had just happened to her had brought it out.

"*What* did he call you?" Bobby asked, so softly that Jeremy, sitting on the other side of the fire, could not hear his words.

Cathy lowered her hands from her face, trying to get some of her old anger back. Trying not to feel the disgust she felt. Trying to will the tears to stop flowing from her eyes, the pain to stop digging at her heart. Wanting to reach out and tell Chuck she was sorry she slapped him but knowing she never would.

"He called me—a fucking cunt. He said I was unclean. An—an abomination. Like some twisted little sideshow freak."

"Cathy." Bobby spoke her name in pity. Trying to soothe. Trying to calm. His heart going out to her. Sensing her shame. And suddenly sensing something else. An uncertainty, maybe. An uncertainty of worth. Something so out of whack with the Cathy he thought he knew, he found himself somewhat speechless at the revelation of it. Was this what it was like to be a girl? Did they always feel so—incomplete? So—unfinished? Or was this just part of her own battle with puberty? Like Bobby's battle. And Woody's. And the twins too, if they ever got there.

Except for Woody, Cathy was the most complete person Bobby knew. He admired her "take no prisoners" attitude, and he sometimes envied her ability to spout obscenities with such effortless ease, shooting out words that could curdle a jug of milk and stop a parent's heart dead in its tracks if a parent ever heard them. Bobby felt no longing for Cathy as Chuck did. His longings were directed to no one but Woody, but that did not diminish his love for her. She was his friend, just as the twins were, and he sensed her anguish, although he didn't understand it.

He searched for words to comfort her, but Jeremy found them first. From across the campfire, he said, "I think we've got ourselves a queer ghost," he said to them all. And to Cathy alone, he said, "The only reason he didn't want you was because you don't have a pecker. That's all it is. Don't feel bad about it, Cath. Just be glad he didn't grab one of us instead. If he had, he might not have stopped when he did."

Cathy stared into Jeremy's face through the flames of the campfire, still blinking back tears. A dawning light of understanding blossomed across her face as she soaked in Jeremy's words.

"My God," she finally said. "I think you're right. The fucker's a faggot."

Woody cringed. The word rolled so easily off Cathy's tongue, bringing him his own stab of shame in the sound of it. He looked at Bobby, but Bobby's eyes were still centered on Cathy alone. If that word caused any shame in Bobby, then Bobby was keeping it well hidden.

"Cocksuckers," Willow Man had said earlier from the shadows as he watched Woody and Bobby lying side by side next to the fire, as he watched them reach out to each other, touch each other, long for each other and maybe begin to do something about that longing before Cathy and the twins came along to kill the moment. Was there simply hatred and disgust in the way Willow Man had said it, or was there envy there too? Was he appalled by the feelings Woody shared with Bobby, thinking them an abomination, a sin, or did he long to experience those feelings again himself? Was he a pedophile? Was it the fact that they were children that fed his longing, or was he simply missing the life of a gay man he had once led? Was he a predator, or was he simply lonely?

Woody thought about it as he dabbed carefully at the scratches on Cathy's back. Whatever Willow Man felt, there was no question he had powers. Powers Woody didn't understand. He had summoned the bats. He said so. And he had probably killed Wilbur too. Who else would have done it? Whatever his motives were, Woody figured, they were driven by evil. Evil and the will to inflict pain. Would he murder one of them if he got the chance? Were their lives in danger at this very moment? Woody didn't doubt it for a minute.

They would have to be careful. They would have to be on their guard.

And they would have to destroy him. Otherwise they would never be safe again.

"We have to kill him," Woody said out loud before he even knew the words were coming. "We have to kill him and take back our canyon. We can't let him hurt one of us again."

The others, even Cathy, turned to stare at him as if he had just sprouted horns and a tail.

But it was Bobby who finally spoke.

"My God, Woody," he said, in a breathless whisper. "You're absolutely right. We have to kill *him* before he kills *us*."

CATHY LAY on her sleeping bag, wearing Woody's shirt. She didn't know what had happened to hers. They hadn't been able to find it in the darkness. She hoped when the sun came up the damn thing would turn up, otherwise there would be some massive explaining to do when she got home. She was weary all the way down to the bone. She had had a close call tonight. Willow Man had got to her even with her friends around, and that frightened her. And the fact that it wasn't her he wanted, but one of them, frightened her even more.

The scratches on her back were still stinging from the brandy, but she supposed it was a smart thing to do, cleaning them the way Woody had. An infection could kill a person as easily as Willow Man could. Just might take longer, is all. And with considerably less drama. And it wasn't only the grit and dirt Cathy worried about, but the memory of how Willow Man's fingers had felt on her skin. There was something wrong with those fingers. They didn't feel like flesh. God knows what sort of germs they had all over them, what sort of germs he had transferred onto her. She was sort of glad her wounds were on her back where she didn't have to look at them, otherwise she'd probably be obsessing over the whole thing, like Woody's mom persistently digging away at a spot of grout, imagining it seething and teeming with every bacterium known to man. Out of sight, out of mind, Cathy figured. Of course, it wasn't out of her mind at all, not really. Just because she couldn't see her wounds didn't mean she didn't know they were there. She could feel the tightness of her torn flesh with every breath she took, but she could feel the alcohol in the brandy working at it too, cleansing, sanitizing, healing, and she relished the pain of it stinging away back there, knowing it was for her own good, knowing it was obliterating anything Willow Man might have left behind on her skin.

She rested her head on her arm and stared into the dwindling flames of the campfire. It was late. Maybe two in the morning. The air had turned cool about an hour ago, and now she welcomed the warmth of the sleeping bag snugly wrapped around her, neatly tucked under her chin. She welcomed the fire too. It created a welcome haven of light and warmth there in the darkness. She felt safe with her friends around her, felt comforted by the unfamiliar feel and smell of Woody's shirt across her breasts, but still she longed to be home in her own bed, with her parents down the hall, the familiar smells of the old house she grew up in lulling her to sleep as they did every night of her life.

She glanced over at the twins, who were sound asleep, side by side in separate but matching sleeping bags. Chuck was snoring a little bit. They both looked so innocent lying there, she thought. Like a couple of angels stuck up on the ceiling of the Sistine Chapel. Mirror images of each other physically, but so different in temperament they might not have been related at all.

Bobby and Woody were talking quietly on the other side of the fire, sitting so close together their knees and shoulders touched, seemingly more in tune with each other than even the twins could ever be. Cathy didn't try to hear the words they were speaking. She was too tired to care. She was just happy to know they were there. Happy to know they were awake and on guard. She knew she could close her eyes now and sleep until morning, and when she opened her eyes to the rising sun, her two friends would still be sitting there, keeping her safe from whatever dangers might be lurking in the shadows. She loved them for that.

And her love for them was the last awareness she felt before sleep overtook her.

As she slept, the campfire warmed her face, and all thoughts of Willow Man were lost in that dreamless place her mind had gone to. Yet somewhere in the pleasing darkness of it, she remembered the feel of Bobby's strong hand on her arm, comforting.

And the softer touch of Woody's fingers on her back. Easing her pain. Soothing her wounds.

Making her feel wanted. Making her feel protected.

But mostly she remembered Chuck, staring at her naked shoulders with a gentle hunger, his eyes as bright as diamonds in the firelight.

Making her feel like maybe being a woman wasn't such a bad thing after all.

JEREMY LAY with his eyes squinted into a semblance of sleep, but he was not asleep. He was wide-awake. He watched Woody and Bobby whispering softly to each other on the other side of the fire, sometimes catching words here and there, but mostly not. They were talking about Willow Man. He knew that much. And sometimes, when Bobby's hand came out to lay itself across Woody's shoulder, or to touch Woody's knee, Jeremy would shudder inside his sleeping bag.

His two friends shared a closeness Jeremy envied every day of his life. It was not an envy made of greed or jealousy Jeremy felt, for he was truly glad Woody and Bobby were as close as they were. They fit together so well, those two. It was like they *belonged* together. The rest of their little group, himself included, were auxiliary moons orbiting around Woody and Bobby's gravitational pull, continually circling the edge of their solar system but never quite touching the core of it, never quite veering inward enough to become a part of the integral whole.

The role of auxiliary moon was one Jeremy was happy to play, for he had not yet decided what his true role should be. For the present, he was content to hover there in his moonlike orbit, along with Chuck and Cathy, and wait. And envy. Endlessly circling. Watching Woody. Watching Bobby. And sometimes, as he did so, feeling his heart ache like a broken tooth, but not really understanding why.

What Jeremy envied most about Woody and Bobby were the looks that sometimes passed between the two. The casual touching that came so easily and unashamedly to them. And he envied, too, the way their bodies had changed over the past few months. Especially Woody, who had become so beautiful, so sweetly handsome during the course of the past year, it sometimes took Jeremy's breath away. The broadening shoulders. The lengthening legs. The clean lines of sinew at the sides of his sun-browned neck. These were all things Jeremy's thoughts continually wandered back to when he was not occupied with other endeavors.

He sometimes looked down at his own body, so pale and small, and wondered if he would ever become what Woody was becoming right then before his very eyes. A man. Was he destined to be a kid for the rest of his life? Or would his body, like theirs, one day grind itself into the proper gear and bring about wonders of its own? Cathy's, too. Adulthood was reaching out to her as well. Jeremy could see it in the swell of her young breasts, and the new narrowness of her face. The childish plumpness of her cheeks had been chiseled away, leaving in its wake a strong jaw, a clean graceful line from brow to chin that promised beauty one day soon if it had not attained it already. There was a fearlessness, a pride of self, in Cathy's silhouette that spoke of strength and honor and reliability.

Perhaps that was what made what happened to her tonight, and the effect it had had on her, so frightening to Jeremy. In one fell swoop, Willow Man had burrowed past Cathy's defenses and released the little girl still cowering inside, unleashing once again all the fears, the self-loathing, and the feelings of inadequacy that maybe her burgeoning womanhood had, for a short time, hidden from her.

Jeremy gave her a concerned glance as she lay snuggled there in her sleeping bag, her breath soft, her body composed now in sleep. Reassured, he aimed his attention once again to Woody and Bobby.

But to Woody most of all. Jeremy's feelings about Woody were more than confusing. To him, they were a mystery beyond solution. He continually felt he should be reaching out for something, but if he grasped it, he would be unable to hold it. It was not sex that entered his mind at such times, merely a disconcerting emptiness. An incompleteness. Only later, months from this night, when sex *did* enter his mind (and he was nearer to it now than he might ever have suspected) would he understand what that incompleteness truly meant.

He knew he looked at Woody the same way Chuck looked at Cathy. There was a hunger in both brothers' eyes at such times, but Jeremy was not sure yet what either of them hungered for. Chuck, he knew, although his brother never spoke of it, had had a crush on Cathy for as long as either of them could remember. And Jeremy, as confusing as it sometimes was to him, suspected his feelings for Woody were much the same. That it made him different from Chuck did not enter Jeremy's mind. And if he didn't speak of his feelings for Woody, it was only for the same reason Chuck didn't speak of his feelings for Cathy. For Jeremy, there was no shame involved in it. It was simply the way things were. He did not sit himself down and analyze his longings. He did not put a name to them. He did not say, "Yes, I am gay, or I will be when I become a man." His mind could not truly encompass the idea of sex yet, and even if it could, his body wouldn't have been ready for it. In another year, it would be a totally different story, but on this night, as the campfire lit Woody's face and Jeremy feigned sleep, staring through his pale lashes, he merely knew that if he could be anywhere in this whole wide world right now it would be there, where Bobby was sitting at this very moment, next to Woody.

He didn't know his friends had opened a new door on their relationship the night before, but if he had known, he would have understood. How could two such perfect specimens be anything other than everything they could be to each other? They were both so beautiful. They were both so perfect.

Jeremy touched himself beneath the sleeping bag and found his little penis as hard as a rock.

He supposed he had to pee, although he didn't really feel like he did.

Funny that.

Still feigning sleep and staring at Woody through his blond lashes, with his movements hidden by the sleeping bag that covered him, he wrapped his hand around the hardness until other feelings, other sensations, began to intrude upon his mind. Willow Man was all but forgotten as he stroked himself, sliding the flesh along the shaft of his penis, which was not so little anymore. As he stared into Woody's sweet face on the other side of the fire, his body bucked once and a searing pain tore through his groin. A pain at once devastating and glorious. Later, he would come to realize this pain was a precursor to ejaculation, an ejaculation his not-quite-pubescent body was as yet unable to supply. But one day it would. One day *soon*, in fact. But on this night, as Jeremy's very first sexual awakening rippled through his body with a pain both seemingly fatal and life-giving, he would forever connect those feelings of arousal and desire with the dear face he stared at now through the flames of the campfire.

Woody would forever be Jeremy's fantasy of choice as moments came in his adult life when he needed a little boost in the arousal department. It would be Woody's face Jeremy conjured up to add a bit of spice to whatever loveless pairing he was striving to bring to fruition, with whatever nameless person he had found intriguing enough, at least fleetingly, to take to his bed.

Woody's face would carry Jeremy toward a thousand ejaculations over the years, and while the face of the nameless stranger in front of him at those times might be forgotten before the sweat dried from their bodies, Woody's face, as it looked this night in the firelight, as it lived inside his head from this night forward, would be with Jeremy always.

The boy slept then, his hand still securely wrapped around himself, with feelings that would carry him forward into adulthood firmly etched into his subconscious mind. Jeremy's love for Woody would hibernate in the shadowy corners of his heart until a night came, years away from this night, when he would face Woody again, here in this very canyon. On that night, years in the future yet, with the scents of sagebrush and rosebuds wafting through the darkness as they did tonight, Jeremy would find the love he had always hoped to find.

And it would be Bobby, long dead but not forgotten, who would make it happen.

Had Jeremy known these things on this night in his thirteenth summer, he might never have slept again. But he didn't know them.

So his sleep was as deep and dark as Bobby's grave would one day be, covering him like warm earth, wrapping itself around him like a mother's arms. Safe. Secure. Mindless. The only sensation to penetrate the depth of Jeremy's sleep was the heat of the campfire on his face.

He did not dream of Willow Man.

Those dreams would come later. Years later.

BOBBY LISTENED to a night bird kicking up a fuss in the branches above his head. Perhaps the fire disturbed its sleep. But for the bird, the only sounds Bobby heard in this little world of flickering light that the campfire afforded him and Woody, was the peaceful breathing of his sleeping friends. They were safely tucked into their sleeping bags with the horror of the bats forgotten for the moment, thank God. They did not hear the vague rustle of willow branches swaying softly in the gentle night breeze. Neither did Bobby, but he knew its story nonetheless. That breeze wafted down through the canyon, wending its way toward the ocean, where it would travel on to unknown destinations, to faraway places Bobby could only imagine. The air that rustled the willows here and stirred the scent of sage might one day sway the palms in Honolulu, or ripple green rice paddies in Cambodia, or whip red flags of power atop a building in Beijing. It might one day lift the hair on the back of a tawny tiger creeping through a dappled sea of bamboo somewhere in the jungles of India as the great cat silently stalked some unsuspecting native who was about to become dinner. And even in the aftermath of the terrors this night had brought to him and his friends, that thought made Bobby smile. Not for the fate of the poor unwary native, but for the beauty of the thought. The whimsy of the notion.

Did he envy the wind and all the wondrous things it would see? No. Bobby was content to be exactly where he was. Next to Woody. Feeling Woody's leg against his own. Feeling the heat of Woody's body mixing with the heat of the fire, making him feel all toasty and warm and hungry for more of the boy next to him. Making him feel safe.

A feeling he suspected was about as far from the truth as it could be. There was no safety for any of them here in this canyon. Not tonight. Maybe not ever. Perhaps only the wind could move safely through this place. Perhaps only air was beyond the powers of Willow Man to harm.

Woody was speaking softly to him of the injuries on Cathy's back. He seemed to feel the need to rehash the whole episode over and over again, as if only in that way could he come to grips with what it all meant. Bobby let him talk, offering himself up as a comforting presence, nothing more, and while Woody rambled quietly on, trying not to disturb the others but needing to get the words out, Bobby felt his mind being carried off into the trees, into the very shadows where all the terror was waiting.

Waiting for him. Waiting for Woody. He knew now it waited for no one else. It *hungered* for no one else. Bobby didn't know why the creature, whatever it was, had centered its malevolence on the two of them, him and Woody, but something in the touch of the wind on his face and the feel of the cold hard ground beneath his butt told him this was true. The whole canyon seemed to know it. Maybe even the birds in the pepper trees were watching from their shadowy perches, waiting for the moment when Willow Man would reach his foul arms into the circle of firelight and snatch the two of them from life as easily as a farmer plucks two weeds from a garden. Maybe that's what they were to this creature. A couple of weeds, cluttering up his canyon, lowering the property value, making Willow Man's deathly retreat less than the perfect haven he had hoped it to be.

Another smile crossed Bobby's face at this thought, but there was a hardness now in the boy's eyes the firelight had not captured before. A cool, steely look of determination shone from the boy's perfect young face.

He leaned his head closer to Woody, listening to each word Woody spoke as if more important words had never been said, but not really hearing those words either, not individually, not collectively. It was more the sonorous sound of Woody's whispered voice Bobby heard, enjoyed listening to. He draped his arm across Woody's shoulder and, uncaring of his friends sleeping there so close to the fire beside them, nuzzled his face into Woody's neck, kissing the smooth skin beneath the ear, once again feeling the heat of Woody's body, and feeling now the stirring of desire in his own. *I won't let anything happen to you,* Bobby said into the silence of his own head. *I'll let Willow Man take me before he takes you. I swear I will.*

Woody leaned his head into Bobby's kiss even as his eyes scanned the faces of his friends, lying there before him, lit by the fire. All eyes were closed but his and Bobby's. None were on them. He let himself be drawn into Bobby's embrace for a moment longer, then gently pushed himself away. The fear of his friends seeing them was, at the moment, greater than his pleasure at the feel of Bobby's lips against his skin.

Woody didn't know the words Bobby had spoken in thought, but he sensed Bobby's need for him, and he sensed, too, Bobby's determination to protect him from the harm that hovered out there somewhere in the darkness, waiting, biding its time.

BOBBY COULD not have known the creature waiting and watching from the shadows sensed these things as well. It did not once enter Bobby's head that the creature in the shadows might have heard the words he spoke to himself in the secluded corridors of his mind—the secluded corridors from which words and thoughts supposedly could not escape.

But the creature *had* heard. Oh, yes.

A guttural laugh that sounded like the chirrup of some night creature, a possum maybe, or a raccoon, talking to itself as it made its weary nocturnal rounds, caught Bobby's ear, and Woody too seemed to have heard it.

They both turned from the firelight to stare into the shadows, but there was no fear on their young faces. Not now. The fear had faded hours ago.

Willow Man smiled from the darkness, his body a trembling cauldron of evil and longing, overflowing into the night air around him, bubbling with hunger and spite and a craving need to rend flesh. As he watched the two beautiful boys before him in the firelight, a gleam of malice lit his eyes, like burning embers. His body, formless now that no eyes were upon him, shuddered with a desire that swept away all other emotions. He spoke words to himself in that soft chirruping sound he had learned could be heard by the living, but not feared by them, as his own voice would be. The boys heard the sound of it as they sat by the fire before him. He knew this by the sudden turnings of their heads, the immediate tenseness in their shoulders, the abatement of their sweet breath, the scent of which Willow Man longed to breathe into the foul, misshapen body that was now his lot to bear.

He imagined his hands on the warm, sweet flesh of the two before him, the boys he had watched for so many years now, watched and wanted, coveted, and finally decided to make his own. He had followed them and their friends through the canyon for a long time, watching them grow, watching their bodies awaken and blossom. He had seen the games they played when they were younger, and he had watched as their games, like their bodies, changed with the years. He sensed the one boy's longing for the girl, and he sensed that boy's twin's longing for these boys before him now. Especially his longing for the fair-haired one. The one they called Woody. The one who lived in the house at the top of the canyon. The one the creature himself most craved. And as the years passed and time awoke their desires, turning these innocent children into sexual beings themselves, the creature's own desires were rekindled. They were the same desires that had ruled over every moment he had once spent in his years among the living; the same desires that had made him a hunted man in life, despised and hounded, until his own death freed him from the chase.

And, oh, the memories, the sensory echoes, these two had reawakened inside him!

Only the night before, he had watched through the window, and later had stood in the shadows at the very foot of the bed, unseen by either of these two children, as they discovered each other's bodies for the first time. He had heard their gasps of pleasure, their pleadings. He had watched as their seed spilled from them in torrents, and he had smelled their fresh young semen in the night air. The scent of it had whipped him into a hunger he had not felt for many long years. Not since death had seemingly taken all hunger from him had he known such desire. Such need.

And now, as he cowered in the bushes like an animal and loathed himself for being forced to do so, as he gnawed at himself in the shadows like the basest of creatures, tearing with his teeth at the fungal growth that had invaded his fingertips and constantly pained him, he heard the words the darker boy had spoken to himself, even if the beautiful blond boy had not.

The creature's lips spread wide in a malicious grin that freed the smell of corruption from his decaying lungs, sending it wafting about his head like a cloud of filth, a stinking mist even he could barely stand. He spoke words to himself from the darkness that the boys by the campfire could only just hear, but not quite comprehend.

"And I *will* take you," the creature said to no one but himself. The words were aimed at the dark-skinned boy, who even now pressed his lips into the other boy's neck as he silently promised protection he would ultimately be unable to give. That kiss, that unspoken promise, was so intent with love and longing Willow Man had to close his eyes for a moment to absorb the pain it caused him.

Willow Man, as the children had come to call him, closed his eyes, absorbing the darkness into his corrupted body, and imagined the moment when death would bring this boy into his world, and as he did so, he asked himself, "How much pain can one body accept before death becomes a blessing?"

One day soon, he decided, he would simply have to find out.

And after death, of course, the dark-skinned boy would be his.

Forever.

Only then would he go for the other. The fair-haired one. The child he truly craved.

Willow Man, as he was *not* called on the day long past when death overtook him, had not known his fate would bring him here. He had not known his death would be only the beginning.

That was a waker-upper, no doubt about it.

His foul smile grew ever wider as he crouched there in the darkness, letting his new-found hunger burrow through him, enjoying the sensation of it—and fearing it a little too as he watched the boys and gnawed and tore at the dead, hardened flesh of his fingertips.

His mind carried him back, as it had so many times before, to the day his own death awakened him. He could see it and smell it and *live* it now as clearly as he had lived it then. More clearly, in fact. For now he saw it all, every aspect, every moment, and as he always did when memories of that day retook him, he reveled in the seeing. He didn't know at the time it would be a beginning, thought in fact it would be the ending of all things.

And it was. For so many. But not for him...

IT WAS a beautiful day to fly. If circumstances had been other than they were, he most certainly would have enjoyed the journey. As it was, however, his enjoyment level was pretty much on the bleaker side of the happiness meter. The chuckle factor, to tell the truth, was just about nonexistent.

The man sitting beside him on Flight 182—destination San Diego on this perfect fall morning—smelled of rank cigars and sweat, and there were what looked like cat hairs sprinkled across his cheap, wrinkled suit. Every time the man reached out to the seatback tray in front of him and raised the plastic cup of coffee to his lips, Willow Man (as he would later come to be called) had to follow the movement with his own arm, manacled as it was to the wrist of the man beside him, and he was getting pretty damned tired of it. It never seemed to occur to the detective that he could as easily lift the goddamn cup to his mouth with his other hand, thus sparing his ward, his *prisoner*, the discomfort of mimicking every move he made and being dragged along in his wake like Mortimer Snerd in the jet trails of Edgar Bergen.

Occasionally, between sips, the detective would taunt him with little witticisms he seemed to find highly amusing. "Your ass belongs to the state of California now, boy." Or "You should try getting your rocks off with an adult some time, asshole. At least it's legal." Another time it was "You guys never learn. You think you can just pecker along through life doing anything you want, breaking all the rules, preying on *kids*, for Christ's sake. What the hell is wrong with you? Is your dick the size of an eight-year-old's? Is that the problem?"

Willow Man sat scrunched between the window alongside Seat 12A and the fat fuck squeezed up against him on the other side, and stoically ignored every comment. He was more concerned, perhaps, by the woman sitting across from them and a row ahead in the aisle seat, 11D, watching him out of the corner of her eye every time she got a chance, like maybe she had never seen a real live pervert before and found the sight rather intriguing. Willow Man supposed she didn't really know what the hell he had been arrested for; it wasn't posted on his forehead or anything. The broad was probably just drawn to the sight and sound of those metal handcuffs clinking and clanking every time the goddamn detective took another sip of his fucking complimentary airline coffee. Coffee which, by the way, he had refused to let his prisoner partake of on the grounds that carting a child molester across country was demeaning enough. He wasn't about to have the perv turn hyper on him from an infusion of caffeine. "And besides," the detective had said, "this isn't a pleasure jaunt. Get your coffee with the rest of the scum when we arrive at detention in San Diego."

"They just *love* child molesters in prison, you know," the detective was saying now. "They won't even *stoop* to plowing your ass like they do with all the other newbies. Wouldn't want to soil themselves, you know. Besides, you're too fucking ugly. No, they'll just be happy beating the shit out of you ten times a day. You think you're pond scum now, wait'll you get *there*."

"They've got no case against me, and you know it," Willow Man muttered, figuring it was pointless to speak the words, but feeling the need to say them anyway.

The detective brayed a jackass laugh, sounding like Frances the Talking Mule from one of those old Donald O'Connor movies back in the forties. "They've got enough shit on you to bury you behind bars for the rest of your life, don't think they don't. Juries and judges hate child molesters just about as much as other prisoners do, maybe even more, so don't expect any pity when you get to trial. They've got your cameras and boxes of photographs in an evidence locker in San Diego, and from what I hear, there are pictures in there that would curl the hair of every parent from here to Jersey. You are one sick, twisted fuck, you know that?"

"Bite me," Willow Man said.

The detective laughed again, pretty much inhaling a doughnut while he did it. Willow Man hoped the bastard would choke to death on it, but of course he didn't. More's the pity. Some days *nothing* went the way you wished it would.

An electronic beep rang through the cabin and the seat belt sign went on as Willow Man felt the familiar sinking feeling that indicated the plane was losing altitude, homing in on Lindberg Field after skimming past the mountains at the edge of the city. He stared disconsolately at the robin's egg blue sky outside the window and wondered if he would ever see such a perfect sky again. Wondered, in fact, if he would ever see *any* sky again. For the detective was right about one thing. They did have enough evidence to put him away forever, and that was the sorry, pathetic truth of it. He had been a fool to keep the pictures. And even now, the thought of those photographs, so carefully posed, caused a tightening in the dungaree trousers he had been forced to wear on the trip, his own clothes having been seized at the time of his arrest for the purpose of DNA testing. He closed his eyes at the sensation of his cock hardening against the seat belt binding him to his seat.

As he shifted his hips to ease the rather enjoyable pain of it a moment later, he opened his eyes and saw a tiny plane hover into view at the edge of his vision. He leaned closer to the window and stared at it. Jesus, the damn thing was awfully close. Before he could open his mouth to mention it to the fat fuck beside him, the long chrome wing poking out from his side of the jet like a knife blade tore a hole in the fuselage of the smaller plane, and as Willow Man watched through the window, a body went somersaulting through the morning air, spat out of the tiny plane like a spitball from a kid's mouth. The body hadn't yet disappeared from sight when a portion of the little plane's wing, torn off by the collision, bounced off the larger wing that had struck it and pierced the roof of the 727 like a shiv.

The noise of the piercing was deafening. A sharp boom ricocheted through the shuddering aircraft, and the sudden screams of his fellow passengers were even louder than the blast of the collision. Wails of fear and horror mingled with the scream of outrushing air and tearing metal. A chorus of voices cried out as one to coalesce into a keening wail so sharp, so acute, so *deathly terrified,* that the passenger in 12A, soon to be Willow Man, had to swallow the urge to join right in.

A stewardess, in the act of scooping up coffee cups and other litter and dumping it all in a trash bag she was dragging down the aisle for that purpose, was lifted out of her shoes and sucked through the tear in the roof. As she sailed out of sight with a look of intense surprise registering on her face—and why the hell wouldn't there be?—she was still clutching a cup in one hand and the green bag of crap in the other, as if determined to take them with her to the afterlife.

Along with the unfortunate stewardess, the oxygen was quickly and thoroughly sucked out of the passenger cabin. Willow Man glanced at the bastard beside him and almost laughed at the look of shock on his face. As the detective opened his mouth to scream, doughnut crumbs dribbled out and were sucked toward the opening in the ceiling like tiny components of a bursting nova sailing through the heavens toward a black hole. Willow Man, securely belted into his seat, watched amused as the fat fuck frantically tried to buckle his own with trembling fingers. The fear on the face of the drooling, horrified detective was such a wonderful sight Willow Man's own fear was almost forgotten in the pleasure of witnessing it.

But that didn't last long.

The young pilot of the Cessna and the stewardess with the garbage bag in one hand and a coffee cup in the other were only the first to feel the sun-drenched air on their flesh over San Diego that day. Many others quickly followed.

Simultaneous with the rending of the fuselage and the plummeting of cabin pressure, the stricken wing outside Willow Man's window burst into yellow flames. The Boeing 727 canted to the left like a breaching whale, slamming Willow Man against the bulkhead even as the outrushing air pulled him in the opposite direction. The great body of the jet rolled over, offering its belly to the morning sun, dying even then, still half a mile above the earth. It nosed downward, and with a wail of tortured metal, the wound in the torn fuselage opened a little wider, spilling out another dozen passengers. Some watched silently as their lives ended, too stunned to believe it was happening even as the rush of air ripped the clothes from their bodies and sent them sailing into death as unclad and unfettered as the moment they had entered life. Others screamed, and their dying wails of dismay were reminiscent of that first great intake of breath as life begins and the long slow process of dying commences. Willow Man thought, for the briefest of moments, how odd that life and death should both arrive with a scream of such fear and outrage.

Only then did he come to realize it wasn't merely the deaths of two hundred strangers he was talking about here, people he didn't care two hoots about except for the entertainment value of watching them die, but his own death as well. And it was then, at the very moment of *this* realization, that Willow Man felt the first stirrings of anger well up inside himself. No longer just a spectator to everything that was happening, he abruptly found himself a *participant.* Suddenly, it was his own beloved flesh at risk, and this pissed him off mightily.

Willow Man watched with a mixture of horror and amusement as the detective was pulled from his seat by the force of the decompression and the rolling motion of the plane. What had been a hole in the ceiling was quickly becoming a hole in the *floor* as the plane continued to cant to the left, not quite upside down yet, but striving for it. It was gravity now, more than decompression that tried to pull the detective out of his seat. As he clawed blindly at the seatback in front of him, holding on for dear life, the handcuffs binding the two men, detective and prisoner, together pulled at Willow Man's arm like a child's fingers plucking the wings from a fly. Willow Man cried out with the agony of it, and with his other hand, he struck out at the horrified face of the detective. Both men were now screaming in pain, spitting out expletives that could not be heard over the rushing wind and the cacophony of screams surrounding them as they fought for their very survival in a battle that, had they taken the time to admit it, was already lost.

Finally, in desperation, Willow Man clutched the detective's shoulder and tried to hold him in place, not to save him, but to stop the pain in his own arm, to ease the pressure of the handcuff against his own wrist. From the corner of his eye, he caught a glimpse through the smoke and flames on the burning wing of the earth hurtling upward toward them.

The plane was going down. There was nothing he could do but wait for death. Just like all the others, his life was over. There could be no other outcome.

The detective frantically pawed at him with groping fingers, panic so embedded on his face he was almost unrecognizable. As his hands sought the neck of his prisoner, not to maim, but merely to save himself from that horrible gaping maw, which even now was opening wider behind him with a screech of tearing metal, the prisoner, seeing the fear in the man's eyes, smiled.

And at that moment, as the eyes of detective and prisoner burrowed into the other, as filled with hate and loathing for each other as they were filled with fear for themselves, the Boeing 727 gave a great shudder and opened up like a flower. Still hundreds of yards above the earth, she spat humanity out into the morning sunlight like a regurgitating condor feeding her featherless nestlings. Rows of seats peeled away from the floor, each and every one containing a screaming entity, and were sucked out into the morning light, where they simply disappeared.

The window next to Willow Man's head exploded in a spray of plastic shards after being struck by a somersaulting body outside. Sharp blades of plastic flew through the air like darts and pierced his neck. Screaming in pain, he reached up to pull them out, but before he could tear his hands away from the detective who was still scratching and clawing at him in his desperate attempt to save himself, the flaming wing doubled back on itself and crashed against the side of the fuselage, peeling the metal bulkhead away like the skin of a fruit. Willow Man watched in horror as the sky opened up beside him. He felt the sunlight and the air suddenly beat against his skin, and a moment later the skin of his hand was peeled away like the skin of the plane by the sharp metal edges of the handcuffs as the detective was finally yanked away and thrown into that screaming windswept vortex he had been fighting against for so long. With a dwindling scream, the detective was swallowed by sunlight. The prisoner opened his mouth to scream at the unimaginable agony of his hand being unsheathed of flesh, but his scream was cut short when he saw a band of metal suddenly spring from the shattered fuselage, as keen and narrow as a ninja's blade.

The quivering band of metal, as if directed by some malevolent presence, peeled away from the inside cabin wall, and as it grew in length, it sawed away at everything in its path. Biting and tearing, it wended its way along the side of the plane, opening up the Boeing like a zipper.

The prisoner screamed in terror as the edge of jagged metal tore at the seat in front of him, ripping through it as easily as a child's hands slicing through a ball of mud. His own seat began to tremble and screech beneath him as it was torn slowly from the floor; the band of metal approached his face without a moment of hesitation. He watched it come. Knew where it was destined. He was not surprised, only saddened, when he felt it saw into the soft meat of his throat, then through the tougher tendons and bones, to remove his head as easily as snipping the bloom from a sunflower.

And before the earth could rise up to meet the dying plane, to catch it, to cradle it in its waiting hands and render it a twisted pile of fiery refuse from the impact, Willow Man's headless body sailed out into the morning light and fell, spiraling downward almost gracefully toward a line of trees far below. Willow trees, he would have thought, had he been alive to watch them rise up to meet him.

But as it was, he thought no such thing.

THOUGHT WOULD not find the creature again for several years. And even then, perhaps not surprisingly, it would be the laughter of living children that brought it rushing back.

Along with memory. Along with desire.

God, even in death its body hungered for the touch of living flesh. And as time passed, as awareness of a sort slowly came to dwell once again inside its vile mind, it watched the children who came down into the canyon, the four boys and the girl. It watched their bodies turn ripe, ready for plucking. It slowly came to realize its hunger could be fed. It could reach out and touch the living if it wished. It just took practice. Small animals fell prey to its scrabbling hands as it reached out from the shadows to pluck them from the night. Cats no longer meowed at familiar windows. Neighborhood dogs no longer returned home from evening wanderings. Instead, they lay rotting in the underbrush, torn to shreds by vicious, maniacal hands that no longer resembled human hands at all.

But for the laughter of the children, the canyon, *its* canyon, grew quiet, especially at night. The animals that still remained refused to roam far from their nests for fear they too would find themselves snatched into the shadows and never seen again by mate or litter. They hunkered down, the animals, and waited for the unnamed terror to pass. And later, somehow, they came to understand it was no longer *their* lives in jeopardy, it was no longer *their* flesh the terror hunted, but those of the humans, the small ones. And for the human children, the animals felt no pity. They felt only renewed hope, at last, for their own survival.

That, after all, is nature's way. It does not matter how survival comes to pass. It only matters that it comes. The hunter in the shadows had trained its eyes elsewhere now, away from them, and the small animals of the canyon were glad it was so. They breathed easier, resumed their nightly searching for food and mate, and all the while they watched, and waited, for the death of the human children.

What the small creatures could not understand, however, was that the creature that stalked the canyon now, did not do so for its own survival. It did it for the joy of the hunt. The pleasure of the kill.

Fear, after all, was the true prize. And it shone in the eyes of a child as it did in no other.

One night, as the creature stalked the shadows of the canyon, it came upon the bones of a human. Headless. It sat on putrid haunches for long hours, studying the still bones, prodding them occasionally as if willing them to move. There were bits of flesh and tendon attached to the bones, for they had not yet fully rotted away, and as the creature stared at them, memories came flooding through its mind. Memories of capture. Memories of flight. And at long last, memories of its own death.

The bones, it realized, were once its own.

Inexplicably, in this death it now found itself existing in, its body was whole. It could be formed into whatever shape it wished to assume. If it did not wish to be seen, it was not. If it did not wish to be heard in its true voice, it learned to mimic the sounds of the small animals that lay cowering from it in the brambles.

The bones it discovered, the bones that were the creature's in life, made all things clear to it at last. It understood now its hunger for living flesh. It was a hunger that had taunted the creature in life, and now the same hunger tortured it in death.

On that night, as the creature sat fingering the bones of its past life and all the memories came flooding back for the very first time, it raised its treacherous voice to the heavens and roared out its pleasure in the knowing.

It was then that Willow Man was truly born. And the joyous hunt for Woody and his friends began in earnest.

CHAPTER TEN

AFTER THE night of the bats, Woody knew battle lines had been indelibly and inescapably drawn. Cathy's injuries infuriated them all, but to Bobby and Woody, it was that one demeaning word spat at them from the shadows that preyed heaviest on their minds.

"Cocksuckers."

The two boys sat down one afternoon when the others were nowhere around and dissected the word, breaking it down into meaningless syllables that in and of themselves meant nothing. Even the word as a whole didn't truly bother them, for if you parsed it out, it was a factual enough description of what had taken place on the night the bones were found, on the night when they first truly came to understand how they felt about each other.

They finally had to admit it was not the word itself that disturbed them, but the way it had been spoken. Any word, no matter how benign, could become, as this one had, an implement of hurt if delivered with the proper inflection.

But even this didn't disturb them as much as the realization that, by the uttering of that one hateful word, the creature had shown a knowledge of what was happening in their lives, and an *intelligence* concerning their activities, that was truly frightening. This was no mindless animal they were dealing with. It was a creature of cunning and spite, and its attack on Cathy showed a willingness, an *eagerness,* to inflict real physical damage. And although a creature it might be, there was human thinking behind it. It did not act from instinct alone. It acted from hatred and malevolence and a gleeful desire to instill terror.

These were not traits found in the world of animals. They were solely human.

The creature had a power, too, that neither boy understood, but that had to be taken into consideration as well. If it could control the movement of bats, what other powers might it hold in those diseased fingertips Cathy had described? What other dangers, what other perils, might it invoke in the war it had apparently decided to wage against them?

The most frightening aspect of the whole thing to Woody was the fact that Bobby seemed to think the creature had set his sights on the two of them, above all others. Bobby began to speak of death. Not just the creature's, but also his own. And when he spoke of it, it was in a manner that said to Woody that Bobby considered it a fate already sealed. Bobby seemed to have accepted his own death, even as he railed against the thought of Woody falling victim to the creature.

"I will not let it harm you," Bobby said over and over, when the boys were alone. But not once did he say, "I will not let it harm me." To Bobby, it sometimes seemed, his death at the hands of Willow Man was a foregone conclusion. A contract already drawn. Why Bobby should feel this way, Woody could not understand.

But even the creature, even the unending talk of death, could not fill the boys' minds exclusively, for love had entered into their lives that summer, and they found many opportunities to express that love. Their bodies might be young, barely past puberty, but their passions were as strong as any. Stronger perhaps. For when love and passion are mixed, they bring with them a power beyond either. Many times, their lovemaking left them awestruck by the sheer breathless *need* of it. And the pleasure they found in the joining of their bodies, in the simple touch of each other's skin and the taste of each other's seed, was beyond anything either boy could express in words.

It was not only their love for each other that grew during the long days and nights of that unfolding summer, but their friendship as well. They became closer than brothers. Closer than lovers. They became almost a single entity.

Cathy watched as the synergy of Woody's and Bobby's relationship began to change during those first days after the campout. Being the wisest of the group, as women often are, Cathy began to suspect what it was that brought about the change. It did not trouble her to think the two boys might be doing things some people would consider wrong, for the happiness she watched blossom on their faces as the days of June rolled into July told her that *whatever* it was they were doing was not wrong at all. Not for them.

She was, after all, a child of the city, where homosexuality was not something to be whispered about behind closed doors. Hell, she told herself, homosexuals had an annual parade, with floats and everything. Marched themselves right through the middle of town like Irishmen on St. Patrick's Day, for God's sake. Cathy was not totally naïve about the workings of the world. Homosexuality was looked down upon, she knew, in some parts of the country. She knew this because she read the newspaper every morning of her life, a habit she'd picked up from her father. Even so, she herself could see nothing inherently wrong in the concept of two people of the same sex loving each other. The logistics of it might still be a bit confusing to her at thirteen, what body parts went where, what you did with them when they got there, and what the hell you did with them afterward, but to Cathy, love was love. It didn't matter who was feeling it. As long as love went both ways, flowing back and forth between two consenting people, she figured it was a good thing. There was enough hatred in the world. How could a little more love hurt?

Jeremy, too, saw the changes in Woody and Bobby, for in truth, there was nothing about the two he didn't notice. His gaze, it seemed, was always cast in their direction, but at Woody's face especially, for it was there Jeremy found his own love battling inside him. To him, that war was a battle of one, for he had no one to confide it to, and even if he had, he would not have known the words to express it.

Chuck alone didn't see the changes taking place with his two best friends, for he was too wrapped up in his infatuation with Cathy to even watch where he was walking sometimes, let alone seeing anything of consequence in anyone else.

And it was Chuck, with Woody at his side, who next came face to face with the creature Cathy named Willow Man.

Chuck sought Woody out that day for the sole purpose of unburdening his heavy heart. His unrequited love affair with Cathy, a one-way deal all around that was forever chomping away at his innards like a determined and rather nasty beaver gnawing down a sycamore, had reached critical mass, and if he didn't talk about it to *someone* sometime soon he was going to blow an O-ring. Since Woody was the undisputed leader of their group, and since even the *thought* of discussing affairs of the heart with the dentist (his dad) or the dentist's wife (his mom) gave Chuck a killer case of heartburn only about two pangs away from a full-fledged coronary infarction, he turned to Woody for the honors.

On a Tuesday afternoon with the neighborhood drowsily roasting beneath a blistering California sun, when even the sound of insects was stilled by the heat and neighborhood dogs lay panting in the shade, too weary and too hot to bark at passing children, Chuck wended his way around to Woody's backyard, where he found his friend sitting cross-legged in the shade of the jacaranda tree, applying a fresh coat of oil to the bearings in Eagle's rear tire.

"Squeaks," Woody said in greeting.

"*Life* squeaks," Chuck replied, plopping his ass down in the grass and staring disconsolately past the roses at the edge of the yard to the canyon below, silent now, unthreatening in the light of day. Somnolent in the heat.

Woody poised the oilcan in midair and looked at him. "What the hell does that mean?"

"Means life squeaks," Chuck replied. "It's imperfect. There's always some sort of shit clogging up the mechanism."

Woody laughed. He couldn't have expressed it better himself. "So what seems to be clogging up your mechanism today?"

"Life."

"Yeah, you said that."

"Love."

"Uh-oh."

"Heartache."

"Jesus, Chuck, try to be a little more depressing, will you? I can't stand all this cheerful bantering. Gives me a headache."

Chuck dredged up a self-deprecating chuckle from somewhere and reached out to give Eagle's back tire a spin.

"Squeak's gone," he said.

"Yours?"

"No. Eagle's."

Woody stared at him for a moment. "So are you going to tell me what's wrong, or do I have to beat it out of you? I don't mind, you know. At the moment, beating the crap out of you seems like a pretty good idea."

Chuck sighed. "I'm in love with Cathy."

"Now *there's* a news flash."

"You mean you know?"

"Hell, everyone knows."

"Even Cathy?"

"She's not stupid, Chuck. She sees you staring at her all the time. Maybe she's the one you should be talking to."

"Great. Then *she'd* be the one beating the crap out of me."

"At least you'd have some physical contact going."

"True. Until I passed out from blood loss or internal hemorrhaging or concussive bruising." Sometimes Chuck talked like his dad. Having a medical practitioner in *any* family seemed to bring that about, his father had once told him, and Chuck believed it right down to his tarsal ligaments. Jeremy's opinion would have seconded his own had his brother been around to ask.

"So what happens if you *don't* tell her?" Woody asked. "You go right on being miserable, embarrassing yourself, embarrassing everybody else, and driving Cathy nuts the way you stare at her all the time."

"I'm not embarrassed."

"Yeah, right."

"I'm suffering. There's a difference."

"Not to me."

"And I kinda think Cathy likes it when I stare at her."

"You're not only suffering, you're insane. She *hates* it when you stare at her." In this, Woody was wrong, but the ways of women were as alien to him as the ways of Mao. "What you need to do is just sit her down and tell her how you feel. It's not like she has anything to worry about. You haven't hit puberty yet, have you?"

"Working up to it."

"Not the same."

Chuck gave a long, deep sigh like Mt. St. Helens coughing up a cloud of ash. "Love sucks."

A secretive smile passed over Woody's lips. Not to him, he wanted to say but didn't. To him, love didn't suck at all. Not in the *emotional* sense, at least. That thought brought forth another smile, but it wasn't something he was about to share.

Instead, he gave his friend a cheering chuck on the chin and said, "Come on. Let's go flying."

"Where *is* everybody?" Chuck asked, looking around.

"Bobby had an appointment with your old man to get his choppers cleaned, and Cathy's doing some errands for her mom. Where's Jeremy?"

"Getting a haircut."

"Then it's just the two of us, my friend," Woody said, giving Eagle's kickstand a whack with the heel of his tennis shoe. He took a moment to survey the sky, not unlike a wizened old Indian chief prepping himself for battle against the great white oppressor. "It's a good day to die," he sagely added. "Climb on."

"I don't like the sound of that," Chuck mumbled as he straddled the passenger seat and settled his feet on the protruding axle bolts. "Where we going?"

"Down," Woody said, and he awkwardly straddle-walked Eagle forward before hopping onto the seat in front of Chuck with a grunt, and with Woody's legs pumping a mile a minute to pick up some speed, Eagle was soon sailing over the lawn, past the roses, and down the steep incline toward the canyon. Chuck found himself holding on for dear life, clutching Woody's waist like one of those poor Jewish kids in the war documentaries hanging on to their parents for all they were worth before being sorted out and dragged off to separate holding pens at Dachau. Eagle bounced and rattled over the rough ground, gathering speed at an alarming rate. The Bicycle card clothespinned to Eagle's frame *brrapped* against the spokes on the freshly oiled rear tire, sounding like the world's biggest bumblebee homing in for the kill. Just as the wind was beginning to make both boys' eyes water, they hit the base of the canyon with a solid *whump!* that almost drove their splintered testicles up into their throats. They sailed past the unfortunate clubhouse, which still looked like a piece of unfinished crap and was pretty much apt to stay that way, and suddenly they were flying down the trail leading into the farthest depths of the canyon.

Chuck's eyes opened wide against the rushing air, and he cried out in a voice staccatoed by the bumpy terrain, "What the hell are you doing? Willow Man's down here!"

"Think he's fast enough to catch us?" Woody yelled back. He stood on the pedals now, urging Eagle faster, letting the slope of the hillside and the strength of his young legs urge her to a speed she had never before reached. Tree limbs whapped them in the face, and a sudden pothole almost unseated them before they reached a smooth stretch where the winter rains had swept the earth clean of debris. Here Eagle hunkered down, spread her wings, and *soared*, the Bicycle card wailing a solid note of speed in her wake.

The hillside in this part of the canyon was a twenty-degree slope—straight down into the jaws of hell, Chuck might have added if he wasn't too busy hanging on. He figured Woody must have been struck by some sort of temporary insanity to bring them down here, but there wasn't much he could do about it at the moment. Just hold on and pray for rain, as his grandfather always said, which made about as much sense to Chuck as what Woody was doing now.

He tried again. "Where we going, for Christ's sake?"

The sound of Woody's voice whipped past his ears like autumn leaves swept along in a windstorm. "I want to see him! I want to know what he looks like! I want to know what it is we're up against!"

"We're up against the *wall*, you nimrod! That's what we're up against! You're going to get our asses killed!"

"I don't think so!"

A small washout suddenly opened up in front of them and when they hit it, Eagle bounced high and came back down with a bone-jarring shudder, and it took every ounce of determination they had for both boy's to keep their seats. The landing dislodged the Bicycle card, and the sudden silence, broken now only by the sound of tires on dirt, their gasping breaths, and Chuck's frantic cursing, settled over them like a fog.

Woody squeezed the hand brakes a smidgeon too hard, and the whole lot of them, Eagle and the two boys, damn near went ass over teakettle with the suddenness of the stop. Only by the grace of a benevolent God, and blind stupid luck, did they come to rest in an upright position with all four feet and both wheels safely on the ground.

In a cloud of dust, Chuck took soundings and decided he was still alive.

"Holy shit, Woodrow! Give a little warning next time!"

Woody turned his grinning face to Chuck and spat out a bug. "Was that intense, or what?"

Chuck eased his aching nuts off the metal seat and stood on wobbly legs. "Yeah," he said. "Intense pretty well covers it." He looked back up the long slope behind them, wondering how long it was going to take them to push Eagle back to the top.

Before he had time to make an educated guess, a rock came out of nowhere and ricocheted off his elbow, sending him into a frenzied howl, hopping up and down as he clutched his throbbing arm. A direct funny bone hit.

"Jesus H. Christmas! What the fuck was that!"

"It's him!" Woody yelled. "It's Willow Man!"

"Bullshit! It's some kid!"

"Wanna bet?" Woody sounded almost triumphant in his certainty.

Another rock whistled past Chuck's head and clanged hard against Eagle's rear fender. This rock came from a totally different direction than the first. And as Eagle slowly keeled over like a vaudeville comic doing a slow-motion, stiff-bodied pratfall, crashing to the ground with a clatter of metal and a puff of dust, her handlebars poking up like a dead moose's antlers on the opening day of hunting season, Chuck watched Woody pick up a handful of rocks and start pelting them into the underbrush, all the while screaming, "Come on, asshole, we're not afraid of you! Show us your ugly face! Show us what you're made of! No girls here now for you to pick on! Just us men!"

"*What* men?" Chuck yelled right back at him. "You're not talking about *us*, are you?"

Both boys heard a soft chuckle coming from the bushes to their right, and a moment later, they heard the same sound coming from their left. Then it came from behind them.

And suddenly the air was filled with stones, large and small, flying in from every direction, kicking up dirt on the ground, banging against Eagle's metal frame, and a few of them making even more personal contact. Woody was stunned into silence for a good five seconds when a fair-sized rock bounced off the top of his head with a hollow bonking sound that would have been pretty damn funny if it hadn't hurt so much. Chuck howled again when two rocks, one right after the other, caught him on the knee and shoulder, making him so mad he lost all sense of fear. Scooping up some rocks of his own, he started returning fire, although he didn't have the vaguest idea what the hell he was supposed to be aiming at.

He glanced over to notice a trickle of blood seeping off Woody's chin where a stone had split his lip, and this more than anything convinced Chuck it was time to get the hell out of there.

He tugged at Woody's sleeve, dragging him toward Eagle, but Woody pulled away and started throwing rocks so fast Chuck could hardly see the movement of his arm.

"Come on, motherfucker! Show yourself!" Woody screamed, tears of either anger or pain or both streaming down his face to mix with the blood on his chin. A glob of snot hung off his nose and his body was trembling like he had malaria or something. For one horrible moment, the thought crossed Chuck's mind that his friend had gone stark raving nuts. Chuck's own anger, which had flared so brightly only seconds before, had now receded into the woodwork of his mind, replaced in the blink of an eye with pure unadulterated fear. He wanted out of here, and he wanted out of here *now*.

But he couldn't leave Woody behind. Woody was his friend. Plus Woody had the wheels.

He opened his mouth to plead with Woody to please, let's just go, but before the words were out, the incoming rocks stopped flying and a weird silence settled over the canyon.

Chuck watched as the stones fell from Woody's hands, and he followed Woody's gaze to face the pepper and willow trees bordering the north side of the washout. There, where sunlight ended and the shadows beneath the trees began, they saw movement, but what it was they were seeing they couldn't tell.

Woody raised a trembling hand to shield his eyes from the glare of the sun. "What the hell *is* that?" he asked in a voice trembling as hard as the rest of him. "What the hell am I looking at?"

Chuck sidled closer to Woody, needing the comfort of closeness but needing a better line of sight as well. He too raised his hand to shield the glare of sunlight from his eyes.

"I don't see *anything*," he started to say, but the words never made it to his lips, for suddenly he *did* see something. Movement. A gliding shadow. Two glints of red, low to the ground, like the burning eyes of a stalking animal, moving through the dappled darkness beneath the trees. In the sudden silence, he could hear, too, what sounded like claws scraping at the earth, digging in, maybe, preparing to pounce.

"Oh, shit, Woody, this ain't good," he whispered.

"Don't be afraid," Woody said, his voice so calm Chuck wondered yet again if his friend had lost his reason.

Chuck figured this was no time for humoring Woody, and certainly no time for piddling around with a soothing bedside manner. If Woody wanted to be calm, that was his problem. Chuck wasn't about to join in. He took a careful step backward, grabbing Woody's shirttail and dragging him back too. Away from the trees. Away from whatever it was crouched there in the shadows studying them.

To Chuck's great relief, Woody allowed himself to be pulled away, even as he continued to stare out beneath his trembling hand at the vague outline of a creature, or a man, or *something* that seemed to be staring right back at him from that place where the sunlight couldn't reach.

The back of Chuck's foot touched Eagle's rear wheel, and ever so slowly, he bent to haul Eagle upright, trying to be quiet about it, although he wasn't sure why, and trying not to make any sudden moves, like maybe a jerky movement would cause the creature to attack.

"Let's go," he said so softly his voice might have been mistaken for a breeze in the treetops if there had *been* a breeze up there, which there wasn't. The canyon was as silent as a tomb, dead in the heat. His own heartbeat was the only sound Chuck truly registered in his own ears. And that was a mighty pounding. He was scared shitless.

Thank Christ, Woody finally seemed to be in accord with Chuck's desire to get the heck out of there. "Get on," Woody whispered, and, grateful for small favors, Chuck flung his leg over the passenger seat in slow motion while Woody raised his long leg to straddle the bike, and with Chuck's fingers digging into Woody's ribcage like those claws he had heard digging in the dirt behind them, Woody eased Eagle forward until the slope of the hill and the pressure of his strong young legs urged her into a little forward momentum. With enough speed acquired for balance, Woody stood on the pedals, and in moments the second lap of the race began. Once again they were on a wind-rushed jarring descent into the depths of hell, but this time the devil was behind them.

Chuck gave a premature sigh of relief. Premature, because as soon as he let it out, Woody turned in front of him and screamed back at the creature in the trees, "Come and get us, motherfucker! Let's see how fast you really are!"

Chuck's sigh of relief turned into a gasp of fright when he realized there were footsteps thudding on the ground behind them. Close footsteps. Too close. He squeezed his eyes shut and buried his face in Woody's back, afraid to turn, afraid to see what it was that pursued them down the hillside.

"Hang on!" Woody screamed, as if *that* needed to be said, and Chuck's balls were banged yet again against the metal passenger seat when Eagle struck another pothole. His feet slipped off the axle rods, and for one brief, horrible moment Chuck saw himself tumbling off and being scooped up by whatever it was that chased them. Scooped up and torn to ribbons by those scrabbling claws he had heard in the shadows. Woody must have sensed it too, for he reached around with one hand and pulled Chuck closer to him, holding on until Chuck regained his perch.

With Chuck's arms safely wrapped around him again, and pretty much squeezing the life out of him in the process, Woody poured every ounce of his strength into pumping the pedals. He could hear the footsteps behind them, too, but the *hillside* here was so steep and so cut apart by erosion and scattered with big rocks he didn't dare turn his head to look.

To Chuck, he yelled, "Can you see it? What does it look like?"

Chuck didn't give a shit *what* it looked like. He was perfectly happy staring at the darkness behind his closed eyelids, smelling the comforting aroma of sweat on Woody's shirt, feeling Woody's heartbeat beneath his hands, thudding away as hard and as frantically as his own. But soon, even in his fear, curiosity settled into Chuck. Between the nut-crushing ride and the feel of Woody's ribs being squeezed to mush beneath his clutching fingers, he began to wonder. What *did* the creature look like? What *was* it they were up against?

And most importantly, Chuck wondered, *just how fucking close is it? How long before it reaches out its arm or leg or whatever the hell it is and plucks me off this bike like a frigging tulip?*

Chuck used up most of next year's willpower in the simple act of getting his eyes open. After that, the rest was easy. Latching himself to Woody's back like a leech, he twisted his head around, and the moment he did, he felt his bowels loosen and the hair on the back of his neck, and most of the skin besides, crinkle up in fear at what he saw.

There was a hand not more than six inches from his face! An ugly hand. With long dirty nails protruding through some sort of horrific growth that encircled the fingertips like a bubbling froth, only hard, like stone. *They're just like Cathy said they were*, he had time to think, before a bump in the path gave his aching balls another jolt of pain that shot all the way up to the top of his head.

Then he heard himself screaming, "Faster, Woody! Faster! It's almost got us!"

Woody tried to sneak a peek and almost lost his grip on the handlebars after the bike struck another rut. "What is it?" he yelled at Chuck, concentrating once again on the uneven trail, trying to swerve around all the crap in his path. "What does it look like?"

Chuck wasn't about to get into long descriptions here. He had enough shit going on trying to keep his seat, keep his head away from that groping hand, and keep his balls securely tucked away in his nut sack, where hopefully they would still be in some sort of working condition when puberty *did* finally kick in, assuming he was still alive to see it.

He could hear the creature breathing behind him now, panting away like a steam engine. Thought he could even smell it. Like something dead. Like roadkill maybe, rotting on the side of a sunbaked highway, just like Cathy said.

And as the downhill slope took a sudden dip and Eagle soared out into the open air before coming down hard with a rattling bang, practically jarring the braces off Chuck's teeth and making him bite his tongue damn near clean off, he felt the faintest touch of those nasty fingers brushing the back of his neck. Groping. Trying to get a grip.

And then the creature was simply gone. Vanished. Chuck almost fainted with relief.

They had reached a turn in the canyon more than a mile from where they started. Suddenly there were houses up ahead, and cars, and a couple of people walking a butt-ugly dog and carrying a humongous bag of dog poop, and the boys realized they had made it back to civilization.

Eagle bumped hard over a curbstone, and the boys suddenly felt smooth, hot asphalt beneath her wheels. Chuck didn't know where the hell they were. He couldn't remember ever having seen this street before in his life, but looking back up the hillside from where they had come, he saw the roofline of Woody's house way off in the distance and the branches of the jacaranda tree in Woody's backyard poking up behind it.

Chuck was about to pee his pants with relief and exhaustion and the wearing down of adrenaline, but he wasn't so exhausted as to not feel surprised to hear Woody laughing in front of him as he slammed on the hand brakes and slid them to a perfect stop in the middle of the street.

"*Fuck you, asshole!*" Woody screamed into the canyon behind them, and the two morons walking the butt-ugly dog turned to stare at them like they had just fallen out of a spaceship or something.

Woody saw them staring, and with a grin on his face said, "Bug off, dipshits."

They bugged off, shaking their heads and dragging their pathetic-looking dog along behind them.

"And for Christ's sake, buy that poor mutt some mange medicine and an antidiarrhetic!" Chuck screamed at their retreating backs, causing both boys to hoot with laughter.

From the scrub and junipers that abutted the street, which the two boys had just flown out of like a couple of startled pigeons, they heard the sound of another's laughter joining in with theirs, floating out to them from the brambles.

"Looks like Willow Man enjoyed the chase," Woody said, turning to Chuck with that triumphant grin still tattooed across his face.

Chuck clutched his balls and moaned. "Glad somebody did," he said before a grin started spreading across his own face as well, but only after he looked down at himself and saw he was still standing and still alive.

"Hell of a ride, Woodrow. A hell of a ride."

Woody nodded, his hair sticking straight up off the top of his head and his face still smeared with muck and blood and snot and God knows what else.

"We've gotta kill that fucker, you know. If it's already dead, then we have to kill it again. That's just the way it is, Chuck."

Chuck stretched, farted, and gave himself a little shake to get everything settled back into place.

"I suppose we do," he finally said. "But not today, Woody. Please God, not today."

THE FIVE of them were sitting behind Woody's house enjoying the shade of evening and the feel of cool crisp grass against their legs while they played strip poker with a beat-up deck of cards Jeremy had found on a bus bench on his way back from the barber. No one was really stripping, of course, although more than one of them wanted to. They were merely keeping track of who was wearing what when the game began and what (in their imaginations) had been removed as the hands progressed. Chuck was already down to an imaginary pair of skivvies and one sock, and for some reason he was embarrassed by the fact. Cathy, alone, was still fully clothed, in real life as well as imagination. She played poker like Doc Holliday, with laser-like concentration and cutthroat coolness. Consequently, she hardly ever lost. It was a skill she learned from her folks, who hosted weekly poker games in their dining room and took their poker more seriously than most people take their health care. With a five-cent minimum and a fifty-cent cap, she had seen her dad rake in thirty or forty bucks on more than one Saturday night, and it was a talent she had worked hard to emulate. Judging by the outcome of this particular poker game, she had succeeded exceptionally well.

"What happened then?" Jeremy asked, pulling a four of spades and a six of hearts from his hand and throwing it on the discard pile, leaving himself a nine, ten, and Jack of clubs. He liked the long shots.

"Then I felt its fingers on my neck," Chuck answered, his eyes widening in fear at the memory. "They're just like Cathy said they were. Hard as rocks. Covered with lichen or barnacles or something. Yuck."

"Barnacles only grow in the ocean," Cathy said, patient as a schoolmarm, all the while staring at the three queens in her hand and wondering what the chances were of getting, great God in heaven, a fourth.

Chuck stuck his hands on his hips and glared at her. "Well, excuse me, Marlin Perkins. I'm the witness here, and I say they were barnacles. Anyway, they were ugly, and they were hard, and I hope to God I never feel them again."

"Tell us what he looked like, for Christ's sake," Bobby said. "You still haven't told us what he looked like."

Woody tossed his cards to the ground, tired of the game, tired of the arguing. Still angry at himself for not looking back and seeing the creature when he had the chance.

For some reason, Chuck had been reluctant to divulge this particular piece of information to anyone, even Woody. He had managed to keep the horror and the ridiculousness of it locked away in a secret vault inside his head for most of the afternoon, but now he figured it was time to let it out. Maybe he would sleep a little better tonight, knowing his nightmares were being shared by the others. And besides, he was holding crap and he was already down to his underpants and one sock and even the thought of *imaginarily* losing either one of them made the blood rush up the back of his neck and sear the top of his head. Maybe if Cathy were damn near imaginarily naked too, it wouldn't have bothered him so much. But as things were—

He threw his cards to the ground. "I quit."

"You mean you fold," Cathy said.

"No, I mean I quit."

Cathy's eyes flashed. "But I'm holding three queens here!"

Chuck cast her a look so filled with insincere sympathy even a tree could have seen he was being sarcastic. "Ah, gee, ain't *that* a shame."

Bobby reached out and plucked the cards from *everyone's* hands and threw them on the ground between them. "Fine," he said. "The game is officially over." He turned to Chuck. "Now tell us what you saw, or I personally am going to do to your neck what the monster didn't get a chance to do. Namely, wring the damn thing."

Cathy giggled. "Like a chicken?"

"*I'm not a chicken!*"

Cathy looked stunned by the ferocity in Chuck's voice but tried to laugh it off. "Whoa there, Chuck. I never said you were."

"*Yes, you did!*"

Bobby poked his palm with the fingertips of his other hand in the international sign for "time out." Patiently, as if it was really a matter of very little consequence, he said, "No, she didn't. Nobody thinks you're chicken, Chuck. We just want to know what it was you saw. You did see it, right? I mean, you did drag your eyeballs out of Woody's shirt long enough to take a peek, didn't you?"

Jeremy stifled a laugh and immediately said meekly, "Sorry."

Cathy reached over to lay a gentle fingertip to the swollen cut on Woody's lip. "Whatever it was you saw, whether you really saw it or not," she said, "you're lucky to be alive. What the hell possessed you guys to go down there, anyway?"

Chuck rolled his eyes in Woody's direction, envying the attention Cathy was bestowing on Woody's injury, wishing he was the one with the fat lip. "Dipshit here wanted a formal introduction," he said, tilting his head to Woody. "Drug me along as interpreter, I guess."

"Seemed like a good idea at the time," Woody said, a sheepish grin beginning to spread across his face until the pain in his lip killed it dead. "I wanted to know what the bastard looks like. I wanted to know what it is we're fighting here. What's so wrong about that?"

"Nothing," Bobby said, "except it should have been all of us together going down there. It's too dangerous splitting up like that. Cathy's right. You're lucky to be alive."

Even without him saying a word, they all sensed it when Chuck stiffened up like a Popsicle. They quizzically turned to him and were surprised to see his eyes bulging out of his head like a couple of Ping-Pong balls. He was staring at the cards on the ground. What Woody saw there, he would see again almost seventeen years later, as he stood in his parents' garage gazing at a forlorn and dusty Eagle propped in the corner.

Every card thrown to the ground between them was an ace of spades. Every one.

"Holy shit," Jeremy said. "How did that happen?"

Bobby gave a wry chuckle. "Spooks," he said. "You gotta love 'em."

Woody felt a chill crawling up the back of his neck. He turned to Jeremy and asked, "Where did you say you found those cards?"

It took most of Jeremy's concentration just to form the words and actually say them out loud. At the moment he was looking even more like a mirror image of his brother than usual. Bulging eyes. Gaping mouth. An idiot's expression if there ever was one.

"Bus bench. On Juniper."

"By the canyon, then."

"Yeah. Right next to it."

Cathy began frantically wiping her hands against the legs of her shorts. "Aw, Jesus. *He* touched those cards. *He* left them there for you to find."

"We don't know that," Woody said, but he didn't sound too sure of himself when he said it.

Bobby stretched out his arm and flipped over the one and only card out of the whole deck that was lying face down. What he turned over was not an ace of spades, but a Joker.

With a sharp intake of breath, Chuck gasped, *"That's what I saw!"*

Everyone looked at him, at the fear on his face, at the expression of utter disbelief, then rolled their eyes back to the Joker lying on the ground before them. It took a moment for the realization to hit, but when it did, it hit them all at the same time. This wasn't a Joker they were looking at. It was *him*. Willow Man. Between the silly, drooping jester's hat with the bells dangling off the ends and the red and black checked clown suit with the frilly collar and the scepter raised against his shoulder, was a face unlike any Joker's they had ever seen in their lives. Cold eyes stared out at them, filled with hatred, but touched by sly humor, too. A cruel, leering mouth spread itself wide in a spiteful grin, and where the frilly collar met the skin of the neck, they saw a seeping wound that tore across the throat like a fault line splitting the earth. The fingers that held the scepter were tipped with bulbous outgrowths of flesh, and through them, long ragged claws protruded.

As they stared, speechless, at the card lying there in the grass in front of them, an ant tentatively crawled up over the edge of it on its way to somewhere, just another ant on a mission for the good of the colony, gathering food maybe, or simply trying to find its way home. As it stepped up onto the playing card lying in its path, the leering mouth beneath the jester's hat opened wide and a greenish tongue shot out, impaling the ant and drawing it into the foul darkness behind the thin cruel lips. Horrible jagged teeth flashed in the shadows, smashing and grinding the poor ant to the consistency of peanut butter. They saw the workings of the mangled throat as the creature in the ridiculous costume swallowed its prey with a gulp, for all the world like a goddamn frog in a jester's suit sucking down a mosquito. They even heard the little brass bells on the jester's hat tinkling merrily as the creature happily swallowed the ant mush with the relish of a starving man downing a Quarter Pounder with Cheese.

Cathy blanched. Chuck and Jeremy gasped. And as they leaned in to look closer at the face on the playing card, they saw one rheumy eye beneath a dangling arm of the jester's hat wink at them in a parody of amusement, as if to say, "If you liked that little trick, stick around. I've got a million of 'em."

Woody reached out for the cards, but Bobby got there first. He scooped them up in his hands, his face red with anger. Taking the time to gather each and every one of them in his trembling fingers, he stood, his back ramrod straight, and carried them to the edge of the canyon, just past the rosebushes. From there he flung them out into the shadows of evening as far as he could throw them.

As the cards scattered in the air and disappeared into the gathering darkness with a flutter of sound, like the wings of tiny birds—or bats—he turned back to the others and said, "Tomorrow we kill it."

And while Woody stared at Bobby standing there next to the roses, so handsome in his determination as he gazed back at them, so sure of himself, so convinced what they were doing was right, a surge of desire rushed through Woody.

And a surge of fear.

The fear was not for himself or the others. Like his desire, Woody's fear was for no one but Bobby.

At the moment, Woody couldn't imagine this would be the last time he would see his friend, his lover, with the rising moon over his shoulder and the purple twilight on his face. He did not know it would be the last time he would see Bobby's summer-tanned face and bright eyes amid the riotous colors of his mother's roses. He did not know that tonight, in the darkness of his room, scented by the warmth of their young bodies, heated in lust, a figure would stand in the shadows at the foot of their bed and watch as the two boys clung to each other. And when the passion flowed from them, lighting each boy's face with a happiness that was a misery to the creature as it trembled there in the darkness only inches away, Woody did not know that on this day the beast had finally decided to make one of them its own.

Later, while the boys slept, one's face on the other's chest, legs entwined, Woody did not know a hand came out of the shadows and stroked their hair, or that a bulbous finger touched the softness of their lips to feel the stirring of breath, the stirring of life—the life this creature in the shadows no longer carried within itself but still envied with every fiber of its being.

And *had* Woody imagined these things, he would not have believed them. At thirteen, he still knew only the good life offered. And he was in love. Perhaps that was enough to explain why he let his premonition of fear pass away from him as he sat there in the grass now with his friends, looking at Bobby's face in the twilight. His fear passed from him as easily as any of the other inconsequential thoughts that constantly bombarded his thirteen-year-old mind.

But tomorrow he would remember.

Tomorrow his sorrow would begin. And that sorrow would stay with Woody for many years, until love touched him once again, right here in the moonlight of his parents' backyard with the familiar scent of his mother's roses filling the air and the moon hanging high in the eastern sky above his head.

Woody would be a grown man then, but Bobby would not.

Bobby would remain a child forever.

Willow Man would gleefully see to that.

CHAPTER ELEVEN

"HE WAS dressed like a joker that day. A jester. Remember? Jesus, I still get goose bumps thinking about it." Chuck ran a hand through his thinning blond hair and stared out over the canyon. In the darkness, it seemed more than a canyon, he thought. It was an abyss. Bottomless and black. He took another long pull from his beer and held Cathy snug against him, shaking his head, remembering. "It was like he was playing a game with us that summer. One big happy costume party. But somehow those silly clothes he wore the day he chased me and Woody down the hill made it all even more frightening than it already was."

"And he's still playing his little game," Woody said. "Tonight he was the Marlboro Man. The cowpoke to beat all cowpokes. Rolling his little cigarette. Ten-gallon hat. Denim vest. Boots. Big-ass belt buckle." And then another thought struck him. "Even by the water today. I don't think I saw him the way he really is. I think I saw him the way he *wanted* me to see him. Dressed like a bum. Those dirty rags he was wearing were just another costume."

"Maybe," Chuck said. "But it's not the clothes he wears that worry me. I've thought about it a lot over the years. What we saw that day down in the canyon. When he was under the trees, when we were damn near blinded by the sun and couldn't really see what it was we were looking at. Those two red eyes I saw low to the ground. They were an animal's, I know they were. He only took human form when he left the trees. When the chase began."

Chuck looked around at the others, his face pale and handsome in the moonlight. All residual effects of the many beers he had consumed seemed to have left him completely. "I think he can be anything he wants to be, guys. I think he transforms himself into whatever he thinks a kid might want to see. A shape shifter. Maybe that's how he lures kids to him. And maybe he knows what scares kids most. I've always had a thing about clowns. Always. Maybe he knew that. Maybe that's why he chose to be a court jester that day. A court jester's like a clown, right? And once he draws you in, he feeds on your fear. It really is a game to him. A *deadly* game."

Jeremy spoke from Woody's side. "Then why is he still playing at it? We're not kids anymore. And it isn't just kids he preys on now. He killed Woody's parents too."

"He only did that to get back at me," Woody sighed, staring back over the years, the ache of his parents' deaths burrowing into him once again. "And Bobby. He killed Bobby for the same reason. I think it's me he really wants. I think it's always been me. I'm probably endangering you guys right now just by having you with me. Maybe you should go. Let me try to deal with this on my own. I carry enough guilt over my folks' deaths, and Bobby's. I don't want to be carrying it for any of you as well."

"No," Jeremy said, laying an arm across Woody's shoulder, resting his strong hand against the nape of Woody's neck, feeling the tension there but feeling the warmth there too, the softness. "Whatever happens, we're in this together." He closed his eyes for a moment at the sensation of Woody relaxing beneath his touch, knowing he was giving comfort, but knowing too that Woody was giving him so much more. This was where Jeremy had wanted to be his entire life. Standing here, next to Woody, feeling Woody's skin beneath his fingertips. Feeling the tremolo of Woody's heartbeat mixing with his own. He had loved this man since they were both children. He wouldn't lose him now. And he would let no harm come to him either. He could never replace Bobby in Woody's heart, but he could give himself. And maybe, just maybe, that would be enough. Woody's sadness and Jeremy's own sense of incompleteness had gone on long enough. If Woody would let him in, maybe they could both begin to heal.

Cathy's voice was as soft as the moonlight beaming down upon her. "Smell the roses? I remember the day Woody's mother planted them. She was out here on her hands and knees for hours in the broiling sun. Then Woody's dad came home and dropped an ice cube down her back. She squealed like a little girl and chased him into the house. We didn't see either one of them again for hours." Cathy laughed. "We knew what they were doing."

"They had a good marriage," Woody said. "They really loved each other. I still can't believe it ended the way it did." Even in the darkness, Cathy could hear an edge come into his voice. There was still pain there. Too much, maybe. But how could there not be? Cathy couldn't imagine how she would feel if her own parents had died as Woody's had. And losing Bobby too—it was *all* too much. For Woody. For all of them.

"But it *hasn't* ended," Chuck said. "The creep's still here. Still playing his silly-ass games. I think maybe Bobby wasn't enough for him. I think maybe Bobby's death just whetted his appetite for more."

A silence fell over them as they stood among the rosebushes, breathing in their scent, staring down into the darkness of the canyon, thinking about what Chuck had said. They could see nothing down below but the treetops, shimmering in the moonlight as they swayed and rustled in the wind. The wind that constantly seemed to traverse this hillside as it wended its way toward the ocean only a couple of miles away. Maybe Willow Man was a permanent fixture too. Like that never-ending wind, maybe he never really left this place. Maybe he had been here forever. Maybe he would always be here.

A sudden exhaustion swept through Woody that was almost mind-numbing. Worrying about the show, the adrenaline rush of actually *doing* the show, seeing his parents the night before, seeing Willow Man this afternoon, seeing his old friends tonight, the recording contract—all of it. Add eight or nine beers to the mix, and it was a miracle he was still standing. He rocked on his feet for a moment before giving in and letting his head fall to Jeremy's shoulder. He smiled in the darkness as he felt Jeremy's arm pull him in, just as Chuck had pulled Cathy in, taking him into his space, making Woody feel wanted there, making him feel this was the one place he was supposed to be. Again, Woody was amazed to note how tall Jeremy was. Chuck, too. As kids they were pipsqueaks. Now they towered. Funny what a little time and a few hormones could do.

And speaking of hormones—

Woody felt the softness of the blond hair on Jeremy's arm brush his cheek, and turning his face to it, he laid his lips against Jeremy's skin, taking in the scent of this man he had previously known only as a boy. Feeling the hairs tickle his nose. Feeling Jeremy stiffen slightly before drawing him in even closer. In the darkness, Woody felt Jeremy's lips in his hair, pressed to the crown of his head. Woody felt his pulse quicken even as a twinge of guilt coursed through him.

Come to me, Bobby, he thought. *Let me see you. Let me hear your voice. Tell me everything is okay. Tell me what I'm doing, and what I'm feeling, isn't wrong. Tell me it isn't betrayal.*

But only the wind responded. And the pounding of Jeremy's heart beside him.

"He's not here," Jeremy softly said, seeming to know the thoughts running through Woody's head as clearly as he would know his own. "Bobby's gone. You have to let him go."

A tear crept over Woody's eyelash and cooled the skin on his cheek. "No. He's here. He's always been here. I just need to know he's all right. That he's—happy." He didn't speak to Jeremy of his own guilt at the desires rushing through him at this very moment. How could he? It was a feeling too new to speak of.

In the moonlight, through the blur of his own tears, he could see the dark smudge of the tear-shaped birthmark on Jeremy's cheek. He fought the urge to lay his lips to it. Too much had happened already tonight. The past two days in this city had taken a toll on him that was damn near crippling. He couldn't face another revelation. Soon he would leave. To another gig in another city. What was the point of starting something he couldn't finish? He ached to give himself up to Jeremy completely. He could feel Jeremy's longing for him. Knew now that Jeremy had wanted him since they were children. Knew too he could love this man if he allowed himself the freedom to do so. Hell, perhaps he loved him already. For Jeremy certainly loved Woody. Woody could sense it in every movement Jeremy made, every word Jeremy spoke.

Still—Bobby was out there somewhere. Was he watching? Did he know the thoughts running through Woody's head? Could he feel the desire beginning to build in Woody at the touch of Jeremy's arm against his face? At the clean warm smell of him in the darkness. So close. Jeremy stood inches taller than him now. Woody felt encompassed. Protected in Jeremy's shadow. Safe in his space. It was a place he suddenly wanted to stay in. He thought maybe this would be a good place to be for the rest of his life. He had been alone long enough, hadn't he? Perhaps fate had brought him back to San Diego for this one thing. Love. Maybe he would find it here, where before he had thought nothing resided but pain and sorrow and memories that tore at you like a scythe. Funny that amid all this misery he should find Jeremy standing there, still waiting after all these long years for his childhood fantasy. And funnier still to Woody was the fact that the fantasy would be him.

This old life was one surprise after another, you had to give it that. One minute you're sweeping fish guts off a rusty trawler, and the next thing you know, your agent tells you that you have a recording contract. One morning you wake up with your heart torn out by the roots, and the next thing you know, that same old heart is filling up with love so fast you think maybe you can't stand it. Jesus, was there ever any downtime? Does a person ever get a chance to just sit back and *enjoy* life, or does it keep hitting you over the head until you don't know what the hell you are doing, and don't even much care anymore. Is it like this for everybody, Woody wondered. Is it always just *too much*?

Then a more mundane thought struck him like a two-by-four to the back of the head. He turned his face to Jeremy's in the darkness. "What the hell do you do? I mean, what is it you do for a living?"

Jeremy grinned. "Investment banker."

"No shit?"

Chuck laughed from the shadows of the jacaranda tree where he had taken Cathy for a little one-on-one. "My brother always was better at spending other people's money instead of his own. The guy has the first nickel he ever made."

"So do you," Cathy said.

"Yeah, but it's the *only* one I still have. Spent all the others as soon as they came in."

"And what do *you* do?" Woody asked, embarrassed now that he had been so wrapped up in himself he hadn't learned the basics of what his old friends were up to with their current lives. Hell, they could be serial killers for all he knew. Or evangelists.

"I write tech manuals," Chuck said. "Boring, huh?"

"Tech manuals for what?"

"Computers."

"Once a nerd, always a nerd," Cathy said. "Computers he knows. But give him anything else with moving parts, like say a vacuum cleaner, and he's a complete imbecile. Weird, huh?"

"What about you?" Woody asked Cathy. "What do you do?"

This time it was Jeremy who laughed. "She's my assistant."

"I'm his secretary."

"Assistant. And she assists her little ass off every day of the week. I wooed her away from the place she was working shortly after she started dating Chuck. Best thing I ever did. I couldn't get by without her."

"Neither could I," Chuck said with a leer in his voice. "And her ass is only the beginning of her many talented parts."

From the darkness beneath the tree, Woody heard the sound of a slap followed by an immediate, "Ouch!"

Ass comment aside, Woody was impressed. And more than a little embarrassed. "So I guess that makes me the only one without a real job."

Jeremy laughed. "Yeah, but you're the one raking in the real dough."

"Not yet," Woody said. *Maybe not ever*, he thought, *if Willow Man gets his hands on me.*

And no sooner had this thought entered his head, than a hand came out of the darkness and pressed itself against his cheek. An icy hand, as cold and hard as steel. There was no gentleness in the touch, and Woody knew immediately it was not Jeremy's hand that touched him.

He spun. There was no one there.

"What?" Jeremy asked, sensing Woody's sudden tension. Then he too felt cold fingers slide beneath his shirt. As those cold fingers, as rough and hard as rusted metal, raked through the hair on his stomach and began to burrow inside the waistband of his trousers, he jumped back. "*What the fuck!*"

Cathy shrieked from the darkness when unseen hands lifted her skirt and thrust themselves roughly between her thighs to touch her where she had once been touched so long ago as a child. She slapped at the feel of those icy scrabbling fingers and was stunned to find there was nothing there. She fought the urge to run, just as she had on that night so many years ago. Even in her sudden fear, she knew better than to make that mistake again. She stood her ground, clutching her skirt tight around her, spinning this way and that, trying to pierce the darkness with her gaze to see where the attack was coming from, but she could see nothing.

It was Chuck who roared loudest of all when hard callused hands, two of them this time, tore at his trousers, digging their way past the tightness of his belt, one burrowing downward to squeeze his testicles like a vise and the other groping for his sphincter, hot fingers trying to worm their way inside to the very core of him, pushing at the tender flesh there, pressing inward, unforgiving, unrelenting. A bellow tore out of him like a raging bull.

Cathy reached out for him to help, not knowing what was happening. For a second, the horror in her lover's voice made her forget her own. But in his fear and outrage, Chuck swept his hand wildly through the darkness, accidentally striking her face, driving her to the ground. Chuck bellowed again, this time in shock, appalled by what he had done, and as he dropped to the ground to take her into his arms, to plead with her to forgive him, he realized those delving, crushing hands had left his body. Only an ache remained where those probing fingers had tried to pierce him.

He pulled Cathy to him and buried his face in her hair. "Oh, God, I'm sorry, baby. I'm so sorry."

Cathy's voice was a tremor. "It was him. He was here. He—he groped me."

"He's gone now," Chuck breathed into her ear, taking in the smell of fear on her body, burrowing his hands into that lush mane of hair, holding her to him, not yet prepared to tell anyone he too had felt those unforgiving hands pawing at him. Not yet prepared to face it himself. "I didn't mean to hit you. I—I panicked. I couldn't see in the dark. I'm so sorry, Cath. Are you all right?"

"Wife beater," she mumbled, trying to stem the flow of tears threatening to rise up, as much from her aching jaw as from the shock of what had happened.

Chuck gave her an uneasy grin, which she couldn't see in the darkness. "I can't be a wife beater, babe. We're not married," he said. "Not yet."

And it was the "Not yet" that finally brought a feeble smile to Cathy's lips. "Don't worry," she said, clutching his broad shoulders and pressing her face to his chest. "I still love you, left hook and all. You big prick."

"Big prick? You really think so? I'll take that as a compliment," Chuck said, attempting to regain some composure, shooting for a little humor, even as he tried to wrap his mind around what had just happened. Between his love for this woman and the memory of those icy fingers digging at his backside and that viselike grip squeezing his nuts like a couple of soup cans in a trash compactor, he wasn't sure if he should be laughing or crying or tearing the jacaranda tree up by the roots and hurling it into the canyon. Finally, he turned to see what Woody and Jeremy were up to, wondering if they too had endured the same horror he and Cathy had.

"You guys okay?"

Jeremy's voice sounded lost. Confused. "Jesus, where's he gone?"

"Who?"

"Woody."

They all heard footsteps slipping and sliding down the slope to the canyon, a tiny avalanche of stones rattling along in front of them.

"Ah, Christ!" Jeremy said. "He's going down there!"

And suddenly Jeremy was gone, too, rattling down the hill in Woody's footsteps. Chuck pulled Cathy to her feet. "Do we let them go, or do we tag along like a couple of idiots? It's your call."

Cathy laid a gentle hand to Chuck's cheek, "We have to go," she said. "We have to stay together. The last time we split up—"

"I know. Come on, then. Idiots it is." Chuck took her hand and led her carefully down the steep hillside in the darkness, following the sounds of Woody and Jeremy up ahead. "So much for my new loafers," Chuck groaned, stumbling in the dirt, tripping over roots, sliding over rocks. "Just bought 'em, too. Shit."

"Stop whining," Cathy said, her hand latched onto his arm, allowing him to guide her through the shadows across the uneven ground. Even the moonlight didn't seem to reach this place. Then she realized the air was cooler here. They were beneath the willow trees already and still headed downhill, into the very depths of the place she once swore never to enter again. *So much for resolutions,* she thought. And she too said, "Shit."

"There they are," Chuck said. "By the old clubhouse." He could see Woody and Jeremy standing there in the moonlight. It took a considerable stretch of the imagination to call what they were standing beside a "clubhouse." In reality it was nothing but a couple of posts sticking out of the dirt with shards of latticework hanging off them like old bones poking out of a rotting carcass. The mud they had spent hours slathering over the thing sixteen years ago was nothing but a memory now. Annual rains had swept the structure clean, and torn it to pieces besides. It looked more like the ancient skeleton of some poor prehistoric creature, unearthed by the forces of nature, than a man-made, or child-made, structure.

Chuck and Cathy stepped out of the shadows beneath the willow trees and into the moonlit glade that had always been their congregating point back when they were kids. From here, they had been safe from prying eyes, human ones at least. No windows looked down on this part of the canyon. It was as secluded as a desert isle. Still was. And in the darkness of night, it felt more than secluded. It felt—primordial.

As if to boost this impression, wisps of mist began to flow across the ground, issuing from the trees, sliding out toward them. Ankle high, it glimmered like quicksilver in the moonlight, creeping toward them, fingers of fog that followed the slope of the earth, moving downhill, slowly, as lava would move, burying the ground beneath it, hiding stones, the roots of scrub, coating the canyon floor in a layer of grayish wavering movement almost hypnotizing to watch. As it slid across their shoe tops, they felt the coolness of it on their feet, or imagined they did. All connection to the ground beneath them seemed to be lost. It was as if they were puppets, floating inches above the earth, held aloft by invisible strings.

Cathy's calm voice shattered the illusion. "Um, guys, I don't think this is fog. I think it's something else."

"It's ectoplasm," Jeremy whispered. "I think it's ectoplasm."

Neither Woody nor Jeremy had turned at the sound of Cathy's voice. "Do you see them?" Woody asked, in a voice as falsely calm as her own. "Do you see them there beneath the trees?"

Cathy took a tentative step forward, dragging Chuck along behind her by the shirttails like a determined mother dragging a reluctant child into a doctor's office. And like that child, Chuck wasn't happy about it at all, but he followed. Then Cathy took another tentative step through the ankle-high mist, and another, until her shoulders brushed Woody's.

"What?" she asked. "See what?"

It was Jeremy who answered. Breathless. Awed. "The people. Dozens of people."

What Cathy had thought to be mist swirling through the willow and pepper trees, suddenly became shapes to her. Human shapes. There was the faintest glow to them as they milled about among the trees, glimmering either in the moonlight or with a translucence that shone from within their misty forms. There was no sense of urgency in their movements. No sense of haste. They simply moved. Brushing past each other. Never leaving the shelter of the trees. Most were children, but there were adults there, too, looking just as lost, just as sad as the others. Many of the figures were unclothed, as naked in death as they had been when they came into life. None of the misty figures seemed to sense one another's presence, as if they moved alone, unseeing of anything but themselves. Cathy watched as one child, a boy, she thought, no more than ten, raised his gleaming hands before his face and studied them, turning them this way and that as if marveling at the light that came from within them. There was no emotion on his small face, nor even much sign of curiosity. He merely stared at the hands extending from his arms as if they were things he had never before seen. Slowly he lowered them and resumed his pacing, back and forth, between the trees. Alone, even among the others. Seeing nothing but himself. Knowing nothing but his own presence.

As the child's misty form passed through the gnarled trunk of an ancient pepper tree as if it wasn't there and resumed its listless pacing on the other side, Cathy's heart skipped a beat. She raised a hand to her throat and felt her own pulse, stricken with sadness by what she had just seen.

"Who are they?" she asked, her voice faint, hushed with pity. "What are they doing here?" She tried to pick out the little boy again, but the child was lost to her, hidden among the other moving bodies, all endlessly pacing. Eerily silent.

Woody shook his head. He couldn't begin to explain the presence of all these restless souls, here in the place where the five of them had played so often as children. Why had they not seen them then?

"They're dead," Chuck said. "They're all dead. This must be like purgatory or something. They're just hanging around waiting for the bus to heaven. Or hell. Or wherever they're destined to go."

"No," Jeremy said. "They're children." The words he spoke seemed wrenched from his throat, torn by sadness. "So many of them are children. Children don't suffer purgatory. Look at their faces. So emotionless. So empty."

And in the milling throng of lost souls, most of them so young, Woody spotted a familiar face. It was Bobby's mom. Her long hair, streaked with gray, which he remembered so well, wafted about her vacant eyes. Her jaw was slack, her shoulders slumped as if wearied by the endless unrest. The outlines of her body were misted and hazy, but he knew it was her. When she turned to begin another weary round of pacing, her movements so apathetic, so *spent*, he saw the left side of her face was torn away, as if by gunshot. Murder-suicide, Cathy had said. But who had pulled the trigger? Was it Bobby's dad, or had Bobby's dad been guided by another? And at that instant, Woody knew who these people were.

"These are Willow Man's victims," Woody breathed. "My God. He killed them all."

Solemn and stunned, Jeremy stood behind Woody and wrapped his arms around Woody's chest, holding him close, pressing his chin to Woody's shoulder, as if needing the feel of him.

Woody felt a tremor in Jeremy's body when he spoke. "It can't be. There must be thirty people here."

"More like forty," Chuck said, his voice just as hushed, just as stunned.

Cathy's mind could not fully grasp what she was seeing. She merely continued looking for that one small boy, as if he alone had sparked the sadness inside her. That there were so many of them was beyond her power to comprehend. But that one small face, so emotionless, so alone, had plucked her heart from her chest and left it bleeding at her feet. Anger began to rise in her at the unfairness of it. What might that child be doing now if he had not fallen victim to the creature that dwelt here in this awful place? Would he be playing still? Would he be grown? Had he been pacing this canyon for years, or had his life only recently been stolen from him? Did he understand what had happened to him, or was he mindless now, without thought, without memory? She hoped so. God, she hoped so. To be endlessly roaming this canyon was bad enough. The thought that he might be frightened and confused and wondering where his family was, and why they had deserted him, was more than she could bear to think about.

"Can't we help them?" she asked. "Isn't there something we can do to let them rest? Death shouldn't be like this. Death should be sleep. Not an endless, tormented wandering. Death shouldn't be this—sad."

As Cathy's words dwindled away to silence, Chuck pulled her into his arms, and standing behind her, continued to take in all the misery he saw in front of him.

Amid the ceaselessly pacing souls, the eerie light emanating from their formless bodies cast a continuously moving glow among the trees. It almost pushed back the shadows but not quite. As he stared, Woody saw one figure stop and turn to face him. Neither adult nor child, but somewhere in between, it stood there gazing at him as the others moved to and fro around it, and sometimes passing *through* it. It raised a hand and reached out to him. Through the mist, he could see terrible wounds on its face, its arms, its body, for this figure, like many of the others, was unclothed. It twisted its battered face into a parody of a smile, and Woody saw gentleness there.

And in Woody's eyes gleamed the sudden light of recognition.

A great wail tore out of Woody's throat as he stared at the suddenly familiar face staring back at him, so still among the throng of moving faces around it. So young and sad. So *mutilated.* He remembered the feel of that face against the flesh of his stomach. He remembered the feel of that body beneath his hands and the feel of those lips against his own. He could hear the voice it once used to tell him they would never be apart, that they were destined to be together forever.

Woody reached out his hand to this presence before him. And for a moment, a smile began to twist his lips.

"Bobby," he said, taking a step forward. But then a darkness rose before his eyes, numbing all thought, leaving nothing but sadness in its wake, covering him like a veil. It was the darkness of grief.

Woody stumbled to his knees at Jeremy's feet, and let the grief devour him completely.

"THEY'VE GONE," Jeremy said softly.

Cool hands stroked Woody's brow and pushed his long hair away from his face. Soft hands. They were Cathy's.

Woody opened his eyes. His three friends hovered around him, and above their heads the August moon shone down on Woody's face like a spotlight. He winced at the brightness of it. Remembering, he turned his head to look toward the trees, but there was no longer any movement there. No longer any light. The spectral images they had seen were gone.

"What happened?" he asked. "Where did they go? Bobby was there. I saw him. He reached out his hand to me. Did you see him?" His voice rose to a higher pitch, took on an edge of desperation. He sat up, straining to see his friends' faces in the moonlight. "Did you see Bobby? *He was right there!*"

Cathy's fingertips brushed his cheek. She made a shushing noise, trying to calm him. He pushed her hand away and rose to his feet, swaying for a second as nausea took him. Remembering the wounds on Bobby's body. The sadness in Bobby's eyes. The valiant attempt Bobby made to smile through those horrible injuries on his face.

"Did you see what the fucker did to him? *Did you see?*"

Chuck tried to calm Woody with the gentle timbre of his voice. "We saw what happened to him a long time ago, Woody. We're the ones who found him. Remember?"

"But *tonight?* Did you see him *tonight?*"

"No," Jeremy said. "We heard you speak his name, but we didn't see him. Are you sure you didn't imagine—"

Woody's eyes narrowed. His mouth tightened. His words were clipped. Terse. Still the nausea ate at his guts like a cancer. "I know what I saw. His mom was there, too. His folks didn't just die from a murder-suicide. Willow Man got them. Just like he got Bobby. He must have. Why else would his mom be here?"

"Let's go inside," Chuck said. "I need to get away from this place. We can talk in the house. We can have another beer and talk."

"No," Woody said, brushing at his clothes, shaking his hair away from his eyes. "We need to find them again. I need to talk to Bobby. I need to help him."

All eyes turned to Jeremy when his voice, numbed by shock, awed to a whisper, stopped them in their tracks. "You don't need to find him, Woody. I think he found you."

And turning, following Jeremy's gaze toward the trees, they saw a lone figure standing in the shadows. As before, light emanated from it like fog-enshrouded neon. The clean lines of strong young limbs were blurred with luminescence, but even in death the boy was as beautiful as he had been in life.

"Bobby," Cathy said, swallowing a sob, seeking out the depths of his eyes, the gentleness of his face, rather than focusing her attention to the wounds on his naked body. Those wounds she had seen once before. They had tortured her dreams for years. She didn't need to see them again. "Bobby," she said again, hearing the sadness even in her own voice.

Bobby stepped from the darkness of the trees and into the moonlit glade, and as he did so, the luminescence of his body seemed to fade as if darkness was what it fed upon. He looked suddenly more alive. Less spectral. He stared intently at Woody, no one else, as he moved slowly toward them, this boy whom they had all known as a child and who had not changed one iota in all the ensuing years but for the wounds that still lacerated his body. His movements were fractured, slightly off-kilter, as if he was unused to leaving the safety of the trees, unused to the feel of solid earth beneath his feet. He tore his eyes from Woody's face only long enough to take a brief glance upward at the moon, then he lowered them and once again gazed upon Woody's face as he slowly continued his approach.

Stopping an arm's length away, as if afraid or reluctant to draw too near, he spoke the same words that Woody's mother had spoken. "You're so handsome," he said. "I knew you would be." And just as Woody's mother had done, he forced a smile to appear among the savage wounds on his face.

Woody's breath caught to see the effort it took Bobby to make that smile appear. He took a step closer, but Bobby lifted his hand, motioning him to stop.

"Do not come near me," Bobby said, casting a fearful glance back into the trees. "He will know. Willow Man will know."

Woody stopped. Brushing tears from his eyes, he asked, "Are you in pain?"

Bobby's smile grew wider. "The only pain I feel is the pain of missing you. I knew someday you would come. I've feared it ever since I came here."

"Feared it?"

"It's you he wants, Woody. No one else." He made a vague gesture back toward the trees, to what they had all seen there earlier. "The rest of us meant nothing to him. He murdered us only to injure you or to ease his own boredom."

Finally, Bobby pulled his gaze from Woody's face to look at the others. Cathy. Chuck. Jeremy. And when his eyes fell on Jeremy, they stayed there, delving deep, studying the face and how it had changed from the way he remembered it in childhood. He seemed especially intent upon the birthmark on Jeremy's cheek, as if he thought it might have faded by now, disappearing with time. It seemed to please him that it was still there.

After a moment, he offered Jeremy a weary smile. "I'm sorry," he said. "I kept him from you, didn't I?"

Jeremy felt a great wave of sadness wash over him, seeing his old friend, seeing what he had been reduced to. He understood Bobby's words all too well, understood what Bobby meant without a moment of reflection.

"It's all right," Jeremy said. "You loved him, too. And your body was ready for love. Mine wasn't. Don't hate me for wanting now what I wanted so badly back then. His heart is still yours, Bobby, but he'll find no happiness there. He has to let you go. You know that, don't you? He has to live the life he's living now, not the life he had with you. I think I can make him happy if he'll let me. If *you'll* let me."

And suddenly the sight of Bobby's wounds was too much. Jeremy turned away, staring back toward the hillside, back toward the house where he could see lights glimmering through the foliage. He spoke his final words to the darkness, unable to look at Bobby any longer and ashamed to look at the others, especially Woody.

"I've wanted Woody my whole life, Bobby. Please don't keep him from me now."

As he stared off into the darkness, Jeremy heard only silence. That, and the soft snuffling sound of Cathy quietly crying. The silence, but for Cathy, was deafening. At last, Jeremy turned to see if Bobby had even heard the words he had spoken.

His eyes opened wide at the sight of Bobby stepping closer, as naked as he had been that day they found him, unashamed now of both his beauty and the injuries that had taken his life. His stride was still stiff, oddly wrong, and taking Woody by the hand, Bobby led him to stand in front of Jeremy. Woody's eyes had not left Bobby's face.

But when Bobby reached out and clasped their hands together, Woody's and Jeremy's, holding them gently for a moment, pressing them tight, enjoying the feel of human warmth, which he had not known for so many years, Woody felt his gaze inexorably drawn from Bobby's face to center itself in Jeremy's eyes. Bobby's touch had been as cool as silk, ethereal, but Jeremy's was strong and warm, and when Jeremy tightened his fingers over his, such hope beamed out from Jeremy's eyes, and such love, that Woody felt his breath leave him. His heartbeat seemed to still for a fraction of a second, as if revving up to start anew. And maybe it was. Maybe the curtain had finally gone up on the second act. Maybe for Woody, life was about to begin again.

We'll see, he thought. *We'll see.*

Bobby backed away then, and all four of his old friends watched him turn and go. As he neared the trees, the light that emanated from him grew stronger, his outline beginning to blur with the radiance of it, just as it had when they had first seen him.

And before he disappeared into the shadows, like a ball of light fading to black, he turned to face them one last time.

"Leave this place," he said to them all. And to Woody alone, he said, "Jeremy will make you happy. Let him. Love him like you loved me. I'll come for you if you don't."

And with a sad, secretive smile, Bobby took one step backward and was lost among the trees.

CHAPTER TWELVE

"THE MUSICAL intro has gone on *way* too long," Woody declared, trying to ignore the familiar tingling in his toes. Jeez. What a time for stage fright. "Too much buildup, you know. Too many drum rolls. The opening number will be a total clusterfuck. Can't be helped. That's just the way it is."

Jeremy stood at the foot of the bed, gazing down at Woody lying there looking worried as hell in nothing but a pair of pin-striped boxer shorts that were about three sizes too big for him. Woody liked his undies roomy, it seemed. Jeremy thought he had never seen anything so sexy in his life.

"What the hell are you talking about?" Jeremy asked, lifting Woody's foot from the bed and massaging it with both hands. He let his fingers roam over the instep, the heel. He felt the brush of reddish-blond hair that covered Woody's legs from ankle to groin and kneaded the sharp, rock-hard curvature of Woody's calf muscle. Jeremy stopped there for fear of rushing things, understanding Woody's need to talk. Jeremy also understood his own reluctance in leaving the fantasy world he had been living in for so many years. After all, he was about to dive headfirst into reality here. This was his *dream* lying before him now, in the flesh, so to speak, and Jeremy wasn't entirely sure he was ready for it either. What if things went badly? What if he couldn't get it up? What if he couldn't get it *down*? Ah, Christ.

"I'm talking about us," Woody said, as if Jeremy didn't know. "I'm talking about you. I'm talking about me. I'm talking about *tonight.* If you've really wanted to have sex with me since the day you got your first boner at fourteen, don't you think I'm bound to be a disappointment? It's just me you're about to jump in the rack with, you know. I ain't Brad Pitt. I think maybe in your mind you've built me up to be a little teensy bit more exciting than what I really am."

Jeremy grinned, finally gathering the courage to slide his hand over the trim hardness of Woody's knee, stroking the firm thigh, feeling the warmth and the strength there, the incredible softness. Feeling the excitement build within himself, he decided to throw caution to the wind. "Fuck it. I'll take that risk," Jeremy said, eyeing Woody's pinstriped crotch like a kid peeking through a candy store window at a really big chunk of divinity. His favorite.

"Caveat emptor," Woody said with a shrug, but he smiled as he said it.

Jeremy stopped staring at Woody's near-naked body long enough to look doubtfully at Woody's childhood bed. "I'm not sure we're both going to fit on that thing."

Woody grinned. "Never fear. The human body is remarkably adept at fitting itself into tight spaces."

Jeremy gave a Groucho Marx eyebrow wag. "In the words of my moronic brother, is that like a *homosexual innuendo?*"

"No. I just mean I can scrunch over a little bit."

"Oh."

Woody could hear Cathy and Chuck speaking softly through the bedroom wall. He had ensconced them in his parents' room, not thinking the muted sound of their voices might bring back memories of his folks speaking softly to each other as they had done so many times when he was a child. Years ago he had heard other noises coming from that room, too. Sexier noises. He and Bobby both had. And by the cooing tone of the voices he was listening to now, Woody figured it wouldn't be long before *that* memory replayed itself as well.

Woody lay back, tucking his hands behind his head, feeling decadent and considerably less jittery as the first stirrings of arousal began to thunder through his body. He studied Jeremy, standing there at the foot of the bed in tiny red briefs that left very little to the imagination, still holding Woody's foot like Indiana Jones cradling a relic he had long sought and damned near died attaining. For the hundredth time, Woody was astounded by the transformation a few years had made in Jeremy's body.

The thirteen-year-old pipsqueak had blossomed into a 6-foot-3 Adonis with tightly rolled abs and long, well-muscled legs, tanned a golden brown from long hours surfing San Diego beaches, something Jeremy had loved to do even as a child, although back then a boogie board was about all he could handle. Like on his legs, a soft, tawny down sprinkled Jeremy's stomach and chest. As he massaged the tense muscles of Woody's calf with his strong fingers, Woody could see the muscles ebb and flow in Jeremy's upper arms, see the tendons stand up like tree roots along the golden expanse of his forearms, and when he rested the sole of Woody's foot against his flat, warm stomach, Woody closed his eyes for a moment at the tactile sensation of it.

There was no question Jeremy was gorgeous, but it was not his looks that appealed to Woody right then. Well, not completely. It was also his sweetness. His honest, open expression. There was so much *hope* shining in Jeremy's crystal blue eyes. So much *longing* as he looked down at Woody lying there before him like an offering. Woody remembered the words Jeremy had spoken to Bobby and wondered what it was about him that made Jeremy want him so. During all his years away, Woody had thoughts of no one but Bobby. It seemed incredible to Woody that Jeremy had spent those years longing for *him*. He was certainly no prize. He drank too much. He had fits of depression. He always seemed to be chugging along on the Bipolar Express like some goofy half-ass tourist: up one minute, down the next, looking out a grimy window at his life passing by and not really caring that it did. Sometimes it was all Woody could do to pull himself out of bed in the morning. Only by sheer luck and considerable willpower had he freed himself from drugs, but who knew when he might backslide even at that? Jeremy didn't look as if a drug stronger than aspirin had ever entered his perfect body.

Woody abruptly pulled his foot away and sat up on the edge of the bed. "I'm not sure I can do this, you know. I keep seeing Bobby's face in front of me. Why was he still out there, Jeremy? Why were they all still out there?"

Jeremy dropped down beside him, their bare legs brushing, his arm reaching out to encircle Woody's waist, almost relieved to have the momentum of their first sexual gambit interrupted. As he spoke, Jeremy looked through the window that opened up to the canyon below. At this late hour, the darkness was complete. Jeremy could smell the roses in the yard, smell the sage and pepper trees farther down the hillside, even hear night birds warbling an occasional song in the treetops far below. But he could see none of it. And he was glad he couldn't. He would be as happy as a fucking clam if he never set foot in that canyon again. And he wished to God Woody wouldn't set foot in it again either. There was nothing but heartache for Woody, for any of them, down there. Who knows? Maybe they had it all wrong. Willow Man hadn't tried to harm any of their little group yet, had he? Not *this* year, at least. But even as he thought that, Jeremy knew it was wishful thinking. And more than that, it was stupid. Willow Man would take every one of them out in a heartbeat if he thought it would help him get his hands on Woody. The only thing Jeremy didn't understand was why the hell Woody was still hanging around. Or maybe he did.

"You think you can free Bobby from that place, don't you?"

"I have to try. Bobby doesn't deserve to be hounded by that miserable fuck for the rest of eternity. Cathy was right. Death shouldn't be like that. Bobby suffered enough when he was alive. His parents. The way he died. Now should be the time when he can sleep. When he can forget it all."

Woody turned to stare into Jeremy's eyes, so clear and open and caring. There was sadness on Jeremy's face as he listened to the words Woody spoke, and Woody's heart ached to see it there. He raised his hand and laid a fingertip to the birthmark on Jeremy's cheek. That perfect teardrop. It seemed to speak of Jeremy's longing for him through all the years of his growing up, and afterward too, when Jeremy's life became like every other adult's life, with work and hobbies and distractions. That perfect teardrop indelibly etched in his skin was a reminder, maybe, of everything Jeremy *didn't* have. Woody had always thought it so strange he had spent his entire life loving the memory of a child. But Jeremy had done the same thing. Woody was Jeremy's memory, his one great longing, just as Bobby had been Woody's. Did Jeremy still see him as a child? Was he really in love with the man Woody had become, or was it only the echoes of what Woody had once been?

That Woody could conceivably wake up one day to find himself loving this man was beyond dispute. And Bobby had been right. Jeremy would do everything in his power to make him happy. Woody knew that. But Woody also knew until Bobby was freed from the eternal misery he suffered, he himself would never be happy. Sooner or later, he would drag Jeremy down into his own well of sorrow, and there in that dark place Woody knew so intimately, and had even learned to cope with after a fashion, Jeremy would be destroyed.

Woody rested his hand on Jeremy's forearm, feeling Jeremy tremble slightly beneath his touch. Feeling his own desire rising up yet again. "I don't want to hurt you."

Jeremy's eyes sparkled. "So you like it rough, do you?"

"You know what I mean."

Jeremy sighed. He hooked a fingertip under Woody's chin and pulled his face toward him. He gazed into the depth of Woody's blue eyes and saw everything there he always knew he would. Kindness. A gentle humor. And beneath all that, a glimmer of the sadness Woody seemed to live with every day of his life. But he saw desire there, too, and this prompted Jeremy to lay his fears aside and press his lips to Woody's. Softly. Without hesitation, but without passion either. The kiss of a friend. A kiss meant to comfort, not to overwhelm.

With open eyes, they tasted each other for the first time, and slowly the tension in them both began to wane. Jeremy's eyes closed first, then Woody's, and gradually the feel of that kiss given in friendship became something more. It was, suddenly, all either of them knew. As they fell back on the tiny bed, their hands began to move, languishing in the feel of each other's skin. A shoulder. A bicep. The warmth of a hip. Unhurried. Undemanding. The kiss, still as gentle and sweet as rain upon their lips, seemed to go on forever. And as Woody's lips slowly parted and the kiss began to speak of more than friendship, Jeremy felt himself being welcomed into the place he had longed to be for as long as he could remember.

As their movements became more heated, they dropped all pretense of uncertainty and began to let themselves go. Lips and hands began to move more insistently over previously unknown places, discovering wonders they both needed but perhaps never truly expected to find so quickly. They found themselves opening up to each other completely, all hesitation forgotten. Desire awoke within each of them like a clamoring of clarion bells ringing out across a previously silent hillside.

In moments, a pair of tiny red briefs and a pair of pinstriped boxer shorts went sailing across the room. Woody gave himself up completely to the feel of Jeremy's velvet body next to his. He burrowed his face, his lips, into warm places, urgently seeking out what Jeremy was more than happy to give. Eyes wide open, Woody savored every square inch of the man beneath him.

Awkwardly twisting around on the tiny bed to face the other direction, Woody pressed his face to Jeremy's stomach, and feeling Jeremy's pubic hair tickling his chin, he smiled. Gently lifting his head, he licked away the glistening drop of moisture from the tip of Jeremy's cock. And as Jeremy trembled beneath him and raised his hips in a silent pleading for Woody not to stop, Woody took the heavy shaft into his mouth at the same moment Jeremy did the same for him. They relished each other for what seemed an eternity, the taste and scent and heat of each other's flesh blinding them to everything in the world but each other. And just as their movements were becoming frantic and they were both about to explode like a couple of teenagers, Jeremy pulled away, slid his cock from Woody's warm mouth, spun around atop the bed, and pressed his lips there instead. Tasting Woody. Tasting himself.

"Woody—?" Jeremy whispered, a tender pleading in his voice, mouths still pressed together, hearts going a mile a minute.

Woody understood the plea immediately.

"God, yes," Woody breathed, his whole body shaking now.

Gently, Jeremy rolled Woody over onto his stomach. Sliding his lips down Woody's spine until he found what he was seeking, Jeremy moistened Woody's opening with his tongue, taking his sweet time about it, lingering and tasting until he was shaking like a leaf, just as Woody was. And when Woody rose up to meet him, pressing his ass against Jeremy's eager mouth, spreading his legs, pleading for more, pleading for *everything,* Jeremy repositioned himself and, with excruciating slowness, gently slid his long cock into the deepest realms of Woody's body. Pressing his lips to the back of Woody's neck, Jeremy laid claim to everything beneath him. Woody closed his eyes then, stunned by the feel of Jeremy inside him, the hardness, the gentleness and longing in Jeremy's touch, the sweetness and the beauty of the piercing. Reaching around, Woody pulled Jeremy in as deep as he could. And moments later, as he felt Jeremy's hot seed spilling into him, heard Jeremy's gasp of pleasure as he held Woody tightly in his arms and impaled him over and over again while he came, Woody's own seed shot out of him like buckshot. As hot as fire. Woody, too, gasped and laughed and groaned as his trembling climax overwhelmed him. Feeling Jeremy's breath against his ear, feeling the length of Jeremy's body, so soft but for the hardness of that one part that had burrowed itself inside him, Woody turned his head to seek out Jeremy's lips. They held that kiss until Jeremy softened and slid away from him. Again, Woody gasped at the sensation of it.

When their heartbeats slowed and the perspiration began to cool on their skin, Jeremy gave him a gentle poke in the ribs. "Too much buildup, huh? Too many drum rolls?"

Woody's eyes were closed. His heart still thudded wildly at the memory of Jeremy's cock buried deep inside him. Wanting to feel it again, even now.

"Maybe I was wrong," his voice fluttered. Turning to press his face into the warmth of Jeremy's neck, he draped his leg across Jeremy's hot stomach and smiled when Jeremy's strong arms pulled him close.

And as sleep gradually overtook them both, Jeremy dredged up the words he had longed to say since he was old enough to understand their meaning.

"I love you, Woody. I've always loved you."

Woody merely nodded, clutching Jeremy more tightly, unsure of what to say. He knew he could love Jeremy too. Maybe he already did. But it was too soon to speak the words. Too soon. He breathed in the scent of the man, enjoying the feel of Jeremy's broad hands cradling him like the child he once was but would never be again. Remembered the feel of this man shooting his seed deep inside him. The heat of their lovemaking. The amazing tenderness.

"Clusterfuck," Woody mumbled with a smile.

Then he slept.

And at that moment, as all thoughts of Bobby left Woody's mind for the first time in years, two soft brown eyes peered through the bedroom window from the darkness outside. Looking into the lighted room, those gentle eyes took in the two naked bodies wrapped in each other's arms on the tiny bed. If anyone had been awake to hear it, an aching sigh could have been heard, like a stir of wind in the eaves. Bobby shimmered there in the darkness, alone in the night, still aglow with the light of death, which never seemed to leave him. Sadly, he turned away, moving back toward the canyon. Tears were beyond him now, but had they not been, they would have fallen from those soft brown eyes as he drifted toward his place among the others. Back to where he had been for so long. At least now, perhaps, Woody would never join him there.

Take him, Jeremy. Take him far away. That thought echoed again and again through Bobby's mind as he saw the gleam of bodies ahead. The bodies of others like himself. Lost souls. Forever restless. Forever wandering. Murdered. Abandoned.

And from the darkness he heard the sound of another soul, laughing at the thoughts in Bobby's head. Knowing everything Bobby felt. Knowing everything Bobby had seen.

"It won't make any difference," Willow Man said to him now, like a tiny spiteful voice niggling at the back of his mind. "Nothing you do will make any difference at all. Woody is mine. You'll see. I'll kill them all before it's over, but Woody will suffer the most. If he thinks he's well-fucked now, wait till I get done with him."

Bowing his head, shearing away from the sound of that cold, malicious voice, so evil, so viciously *amused*, so *threatening*, Bobby slipped back into the trees, cowering, trying to lose himself among the lights of the others.

Once again, he was just another tortured soul. Wandering. But with a glimmer of hope now, burning inside the light that enveloped him. Just a glimmer.

Maybe Woody would escape. Maybe with Jeremy, Woody would be safe. Safe from *him.*

And then a cold, iron hand gripped Bobby's wrist. Twisting. Squeezing like a vise. Bobby hissed in pain.

Come with me, you little shit, the cold voice said.

If death had not stolen them, Bobby's tears would have fallen yet again, but not in sorrow for himself this time, nor even in the pleading for Woody's safety. No, this time his tears would have fallen in fear. The same fear that had become his only world since the day his life was taken. Bobby knew it well, that fear, for not once in all the long years since the world abandoned him had it left his side.

And tonight, as punishment for leaving the canyon, for stepping away from the shadowed prison Willow Man had decreed for him, as he had decreed for all those he had robbed of life, the taking of Bobby's own life would be revisited. Relived yet again. Every blow. Every cut. Every scream. And Willow Man, Bobby knew, would relish every torturous moment of it.

Bobby steeled himself against the coming pain, but even in his growing terror, he managed to dredge up a smile, remembering how handsome Woody had grown to become. As Bobby had always known he would.

Then, with a roar of possession, and a slash of fungus-coated talons, Willow Man tore the smile from Bobby's face.

"YOU SHOULD be happy for them."

Cathy spoke softly, remembering what Bobby had once told her about listening to Woody's parents making love in this very room. She had heard the moment when climax reached the two men in the other room, or thought she had. She smiled now in the darkness, her head burrowed comfortably onto Chuck's chest, idly wondering if Jeremy was as adept at the art of lovemaking as his brother was and wondering, too, if they had heard her own climax only moments before. She had always been a squealer, and Chuck made her squeal better than anyone.

"I *am*," Chuck said. "I *am* happy for them."

But she didn't believe him. He seemed to think Woody was going to drag Jeremy down into some abyss of misery, like the one he had apparently been living in his entire life.

"I just think they're rushing into it, is all. What's the hurry, for Christ's sake? They haven't seen each other for fifteen years."

"Sixteen."

"Whatever."

Cathy sighed. They had been through this earlier in the evening, before the act of sex steered them onto another siding. Now they were back again, right where they started. "Chuck, Jeremy has been in love with Woody since they were kids. It's not the gay thing, is it? Is that what's bothering you?"

Chuck expulsed a little burst of air, as if patience was something he was quickly running out of. "You know that's not it. I came to grips with Jeremy's homosexuality a long time ago. I suppose I wasn't even that shocked to find out Woody was the same way. Hell, everybody to their own thing. You are what you are."

"Then what is it?"

"I—I don't know. I think maybe it's this place. I think maybe it's everything we've seen here. I just can't see any sort of lasting happiness for *anybody* as long as we're hunkered down inside this goddamn house with that goddamn canyon sitting outside like hell's waiting room. Those people we saw tonight. You know, if that had been a movie, I would have thought, Jeez, that's a little far-fetched. But it was *real*." He buried his fingers in the depths of her hair and pulled her closer. "I love you, Cath. I don't want anything to happen to you. I don't want anything to happen to *any* of us. Woody included. But you heard what Bobby said. He said we should leave. He said we should get the hell out while the getting is good."

"He didn't say that."

"He might as well have. Cathy, Bobby understands what's happening here. We don't. If he says we should run like fucking rabbits, then I'm pretty well inclined to agree with him. But no, here we are, *double dating*, for Christ's sake, everybody happily spraying sperm all over the place like a bunch of Roman orgy hounds."

"You heard them too."

"Yeah, I heard them. Maybe Willow Man heard them too. Ever think of that? If it's Woody he's so damned set on getting his hands on, don't you think maybe he might be working himself into a little fit of cosmic jealousy right now? Planning his attack? And maybe even going for my brother first, since he's the one Woody's with? I don't like any of this, Cath. I really, really think we should get the hell out of here."

"Ssh," she cooed. "Go to sleep."

Lazily, she trailed her fingertips across Chuck's stomach, enjoying the feel of the fine hair there, enjoying the heat of him, the familiar texture of his flesh. In the darkness, she let her fingertips continue downward, rustling the tangled mass of his blond pubic hair. She could hear it crackle like crepe paper, could feel Chuck's hips move beneath her hand as he enjoyed the sensation of her touch. Reaching farther, sliding her face along his stomach now to better get where she was going, she cupped his testicles in her warm hand and heard the slightest intake of breath. He shivered. The hand in her hair gripped her more tightly, gently urging her face closer to where he wanted it to be. To where *she* wanted it to be.

In a husky voice, he said, "You expect me to sleep while you're doing that?"

"No," she said calmly. "Not yet."

Sliding farther, she felt the weight of his penis, already lengthening once again. It pressed itself to her cheek like a kiss. And smiling, she returned the kiss.

"You're waking a sleeping giant," he said. "Again."

"It's not *that* big," Cathy giggled.

Her tongue traversed a path along the length of his erection, ever upward, lingering at the tip, licking the slit, tasting the moisture already gathered there. Chuck wasn't even trying to hide his shivering now. As his hand slid down her bare back and reached beneath her, she moaned, opening herself up to him, letting him go where he wanted to go. When his fingers entered into her, gently seeking, and her mouth opened wide to encompass his cock, all thoughts of what lay in the canyon outside their bedroom window were lost in the immediate needs the nearness of their two bodies always brought them.

His orgasm was so swift and so powerful it stunned them both. She held him in her mouth until the last drop of semen had spilled from his body, and even then she did not let him go. As he pressed her face more urgently into him, and as his fingers continued to move inside her vagina, she felt her own orgasm surging up, and with a cry, she let it go. Her hot juices flowed across his hand like nectar from warm fruit just plucked from a sun-drenched tree. Her vulva engulfed his fingers as her own lips engulfed him, urgently. The muscles of her vagina contracted, over and over again, clutching him, letting him go, clutching him again, as the orgasm shuddered through her. Then, surprising them both, another.

"My God," he said, his voice nearer a croak than a whisper. "You're the most incredible woman I've ever known."

"Yes" was all she said. All she *could* say. Her heartbeat thundered inside her like that horrendous machine they had seen once, deep in the bowels of Hoover Dam. And as she slowly calmed, as her breathing and her heartbeat eased, she raised her head to him in the darkness. She could feel him smiling at her, his fingers still deep inside her where he knew she wanted them to be. Still savoring the taste of his come, she pressed her lips to his.

"What did you mean, when you said what you said down in the canyon?" she asked, still breathless from her orgasm.

"Why? What did I say?" His voice sounded a little more like himself now. But there was still passion in it. Still wonder at the workings of this woman leaning over him.

"You said you couldn't be a wife beater because we weren't married. *Yet*. What exactly did you mean by that "*yet*" part?"

Even in the darkness, she sensed his grin. "I should think it would be pretty obvious, Cath. Jeez, what do you need, a printed invitation?"

"No, but I'd like to hear the words."

"What words?"

He immediately tensed when her fingers tightened around his scrotum like an octopus squeezing the life out of some poor unfortunate clownfish that had wandered into its path.

"*What the hell are you doing?*"

Innocently, she said, "Waiting for the words." Her fingers tightened even more. She scraped his balls together like a pair of dice and gave them a little shake like she was about to toss them across the room.

"Jesus! All right! I love you! I want you to marry me! *Let go of my nuts!*"

And in the next room, they heard Woody say to Jeremy, "Gosh, I never heard my folks say *that* to each other."

"Congratulations!" Jeremy called out through the wall. "I'll get you a toaster!"

"I was coerced!" Chuck cried back.

And for the first time in sixteen years, laughter rang out through the house on Highview Lane, as it had when happiness truly lived there. The sound of it carried out past the windowsills to the canyon below, and there, where night slowly crept toward dawn, a creature with red burning eyes cocked its head to the side, listening.

The red eyes narrowed, becoming two sparks of angry light in the darkness. At its feet, which were as fungus-riddled and deformed as its hands, a young boy who was very nearly a man lay sobbing as the creature scraped its claws through the wounds it had inflicted so many years ago. The boy's flesh was gone now, but still it lived in memory. It could be seen. It could be touched.

It could be felt.

And its injuries, the creature knew all too well, could be improved upon. Reopened. Reawakened.

As the creature peeled a swath of skin from an unblemished cheek, just as it had done for the first time sixteen years ago, Bobby let out a wail of pain. He did not plead for relief. He knew there would be none.

You went to him. You told him to leave.

Bobby didn't answer. He was too buried in agony to form words. Only an unending scream of anguish escaped his lips.

Relishing the sounds of misery, the tormented cries, the creature smiled. Soon, it knew, another would be singing this song of pain. Not the miserable creature beneath it now, but the other. The one it had always wanted.

And roughly flipping his victim over, pushing Bobby's face into the hard ground, the sharp stones digging at Bobby's wounds, causing him to cry out yet again, causing him to wail in anguish as he had the night he truly died, the creature splayed those strong, young legs wide and drove himself into the sweet bowels of this boy who was very nearly a man, and as Bobby screamed, the creature roared yet again his roar of possession.

His seed, when it shot forth, was like a welling up of maggots, a surging, burrowing mass, ravenous, hungry for the taste of flesh. They tore into Bobby and gnawed their way deep inside where, even in death, such pain could not be borne. In the anguish of it, Bobby's mind blessedly drifted away to calmer shores. To a place where Willow Man did not exist. A place where pain did not dwell and horror was just a memory.

With his prey inert beneath him, Bobby's pain having taken all semblance of awareness away from him, and taken with it, too, the joy that pain gave to the one atop him, the creature pulled his misshapen cock from the boy in disgust and stood and walked away.

Leaving Bobby to bleed and die, yet again, in the dirt.

Until the next time he was wanted.

CHAPTER THIRTEEN

THAT MORNING, the last morning Bobby would ever know in life, the children gathered up their dimes and quarters and took the #2 bus downtown. By nine o'clock the temperature was already in the nineties. Today, the weatherman said, all records would be broken for the month of July. Usually at this time of year, San Diego would be the one pleasant spot in a country seared by summer heat, a relatively cool oasis, drawing thousands of tourists to the zoo, the Wild Animal Park, the museums, the beaches. But not today. The tourists who were already here were holed up in their air-conditioned hotel rooms praying for rain, and the ones sitting in airline terminals in Boise, Idaho, and Huntsville, Alabama, and a dozen other places, all packed and waiting to come here, stared morosely at the Weather Channel on airport TV screens and listened to nattily dressed weathermen going on and on about the heat wave that had gripped the West Coast, probably were wishing they had booked that cruise to Alaska instead. Damn the cost.

By nine thirty, when Woody and his friends climbed aboard the big red #2 bus in single file, solemnly dropped their coins in the slot, and took transfers for the return trip home, most workers were already sitting at their desks or standing behind their counters, sweltering in the heat and waiting for five o'clock to roll around so they could wend their weary way home and swelter there.

The children expected to find the bus empty. Instead, they were met with a sea of faces, almost all old, almost all women, blissfully soaking up the air-conditioning, going nowhere really, just there to cool off. They would ride to the end of the line, gossiping with each other along the way as if attending a coffee klatch, get off, swelter for a few minutes while they waited for the return bus to come, then flash their Senior Passes and climb back on, heading back to where they started. Some of them spent the entire day riding back and forth, going nowhere, simply to escape the heat. Perhaps, Woody reflected, seeking a comfortable place to sit was really what old age was all about.

In the heart of the city, the sidewalks were almost deserted due to the steadily rising temperature. The children disembarked at Broadway and Twelfth Avenue and walked the three remaining blocks to the main branch of the San Diego Public Library. There they politely asked for the microfilm room and were directed by a pleasant old lady in horn-rimmed glasses to an area in the back.

An adult might have been momentarily stymied by the mechanical workings of the microfilm monitor, but these were children of the eighties. They had grown up with mobile phones and pagers and every other electronic marvel that had popped up in the last ten years. In mere seconds they had this analogic dinosaur figured out and were eagerly scrolling through past issues of the *San Diego Union-Tribune*, concentrating on the month of May, ten years earlier.

They found the headlines almost immediately. "Death from the Air. A Rain of Bodies. Flight 182 Goes Down in Park Canyon. Pilot's Last Words." The stories were endless, continuing on for days and days. And in the Sunday edition of the paper that week, they found a full page printing of tiny photographs, laid out neatly row after row, a memorial to all the people who had lost their lives that day, both in the air and on the ground.

"It wiped out six houses," Chuck said, reading furiously. "Jesus. Some of the people who died weren't even on the plane."

A chill crept up Cathy's back when she read the pilot's last words transmitted to the control tower at Lindberg Field. "We're going down. God help us all." She wondered what he was thinking at that moment. Did he blame himself for the death of all these passengers in his care or did he think only of the people he would leave behind? His wife, maybe? Or his children? Or did he simply think of himself? Did he carry a hope until the very last second before the plane struck the ground and exploded into fairy dust that he would somehow survive, or did he stoically accept his fate, considering it a risk of his profession, a risk he thought he would never run, but now here it was, staring him in the face?

God help us all.

"Guess God wasn't listening," Woody muttered, reading over Cathy's shoulder.

Jeremy studied the rows of tiny photographs, lingering for a second on each face, humbled by the fact that each and every one of them was as dead as cheese. There were women here, and children, too, more than a dozen of them, but it was the men he concentrated on. With almost one hundred and fifty people dead, there were enough faces here to pretty well cover every facet of male humanity. Young, old, in-between. Handsome, ugly, smiling, glum. Some looked uncomfortable in their poses. Others were peacocks, preening their feathers, strutting for the camera. Jeremy figured those peacocks wouldn't be looking so pleased with themselves if they had known where this photograph they were currently posing for would eventually end up. On a roster of the dead.

"I think he's middle-aged," Cathy said. "Not too young. Not too old."

"You don't know that," Woody said.

No, I guess I don't, Cathy thought. *Not really.* But she figured it was true nevertheless. She remembered the cruel hands pawing at her in the canyon, probing, uncaring. They were too strong to be old, too unhesitant to be young. He had known what he was doing, she thought. He had done it before.

Woody turned his attention from Cathy's monitor and studied the one Bobby was looking at. He rested a hand on Bobby's shoulder as he read the words Bobby was reading, or tried to. Bobby was scrolling through articles so quickly it was almost impossible to keep up with him, as if he knew exactly what he was looking for.

And maybe he did.

"Wow, look at this," Bobby said, the tenseness in his voice drawing every eye to him and to what he was staring at on the screen. Just a blurb, really. A short four-paragraph news byte buried between pictures of the crash site and a woman's first-hand account of seeing a body, or the major components of one, crash through her bedroom window as she stepped from the shower.

Two photographs accompanied the article. One, that of a fat man with mean little eyes who looked like maybe he drank too much. And another. The other was of a relatively young man, probably in his midthirties, nondescript, like a schoolteacher or an accountant, with fine pale hair that looked as if the faintest breath of wind would blow it right off his head. The fat man looked grim while the other was smiling.

It was the other photograph Bobby laid his finger to.

"This guy was a prisoner on the plane," he said in a library hush. "The fat guy was bringing him back to San Diego to stand trial."

"For what?" Jeremy asked, moving closer and laying his hand on Bobby's other shoulder, mirroring Woody.

"Oh, shit, this has got to be him," Bobby went on, excited now, leaning forward in his chair, staring at the monitor as if trying to glean every ounce of information out of it he could.

"Why?"

"He was a child molester. It says here he was arrested on sixty-four counts. Sodomy. Kidnapping. Oral rape. Trafficking in child pornography. Battery. Crossing state lines to avoid capture."

"With boys?" Cathy asked.

Bobby nodded. Rereading. Absorbing. "Yep. Strictly boys. Teenage boys."

"Murder?" Woody asked.

Bobby shook his head. "No. It's not on the list of charges. Guess he hadn't worked himself up to that yet."

"Still hasn't as far as we know." It was Chuck. Later they would all remember his words.

"Willis James," Cathy read, suddenly feeling the healed scratches on her back crawling back to life, the nerve endings there doing a little tap dance on her skin, as if in remembrance of the all-out dance marathon they had entertained her with only a couple of weeks earlier. An encore, if you will. Highlights of a past performance. A revival of their greatest hits. Breathlessly, she said, "His name was Willis Earl James."

She tried to picture this meek little man as the one who had grabbed her in the canyon, the one who had torn her shirt from her body and dragged his claws across her skin. The one who had recoiled at the feel of her vagina in the darkness. Appalled. Expecting a boy, but getting her. She tried to picture that milquetoast face spitting words of hatred in her ear as he pushed her away. She couldn't do it.

"I don't think that's him," she said. "He looks like a bank teller."

"What the hell does that have to do with it?" Bobby hissed. "Who cares what the hell he looks like? It's what's inside that counts."

"Yeah," Chuck said, his mind on lunch. "Like a burrito."

Cathy gave him a heated glare. "Oh, do shut up."

"Sorry," he said, feeling the blood rush to his face in embarrassment and turning away before Cathy saw it. Of the six monitors in the room, Chuck noted, four were occupied. Two by him and his friends, one by a nondescript fiftyish woman who worked there, and the last by a man who looked like maybe he had just wandered in to escape the heat and was simply going through the motions of doing a little research for the sole purpose of enjoying a few minutes of free air-conditioning.

The woman gave the children a friendly shush now and then when they got too loud, but the man seemed to be ignoring them completely. With a khaki sun helmet pulled down low over his eyes like Stanley Livingston taking a break from discovering the source of the Nile or something, the man might even have been asleep for all they knew. Oddly, he wore a mailman's uniform. So why the hell wasn't he delivering the mail, Chuck wondered. Too hot? So much for the mailman's credo. How'd it go? Through rain, sleet, snow, and heat like a fucking furnace, or something like that—

Bobby tapped the screen in front of him, dragging Chuck's attention away from the lazy-ass mailman.

"This *has* to be him. Our guy *is* a ghost. He died in the plane crash just like Chuck and Jeremy's dad said he did. He preyed on kids when he was alive, and now that he's dead, he's preying on *us*." Bobby twisted his head around to look up at Woody. "But what the hell for? It's not like he can do anything—*sexual*, is it? I mean, if he's dead, the plumbing isn't working, right?"

"Plumbing or no plumbing, what he did to me seemed pretty sexual," Cathy said, shivering at the memory. "I think if I had been one of you guys, things would have ended up a whole lot different than what they did. And even if he *can't* do anything sexual, he's still strong. Look what he did to me. Look what he did to Wilbur. If he can kill a dog, he can kill a kid."

Jeremy agreed. "And he doesn't have to worry about the law this time either. Unless the ghost of Wyatt Earp is out there somewhere rounding up wayward spooks with a posse of other dead guys, Willow

Man can do anything he wants. Who's going to stop him? Who's going to punish him? He not only got away with what he did in life by being on that plane and dying with everybody else before the law got their hands on him, but now he's so far beyond the law it doesn't matter *what* the hell he does. That must be a pretty tempting position for a dead pervert to be in. Jeez. He's immortal and he's crazy and he likes dicking around with young boys. And here we are, playing on his doorstep nine days out of ten. How fortuitous is that?"

Chuck grinned. "Fortuitous? Good word, bro."

This time the librarian at the other monitor wasn't so pleasant. Her *Shhuuushh!* split the air like a hatchet and drew five stunned young faces in her direction. When she had their attention, she gazed suspiciously at each of them, going slowly from one to the other until she had made a full circuit. She didn't look like she much cared for what she saw.

"What in the world are you children talking about? Sex? I thought I heard you talking about sex. And why are you reading about that horrible plane crash?" she said, glancing at their monitors. "It's summer. You should be outside *playing!*" It was clear by the inflection in her voice what she really meant was "You should be playing anywhere but *here,* and if you don't drag your little asses outside pretty damn quick, I'm going to *throw* them out!"

Chuck pointed his finger at a sign on the wall by the window. A happy little sign printed in happy little colors. It said Learning is Fun.

"We're learning," he said. "Bug off."

Her voice turned to ice in a heartbeat. "You're annoying the other readers."

Chuck looked at the dozing mailman. "Who? Him? The only person annoying him is *you.*"

The librarian popped up from her chair as if someone had lit a firecracker under her ass. Her voice was a sibilant whisper, her whole body shaking in outrage. "I want you children out of here *now*. We don't tolerate unruly people here. If you can't be courteous and *quiet,* you can just—"

A calmly resonant voice interrupted her tirade.

"There's a cancer growing inside your cunt. A big one. I can smell it."

The blood drained from the librarian's face as if someone had just pulled a stopper from her throat. Ashen, she turned to the mailman sitting three monitors down. *"What did you say?"*

The mailman didn't raise his head. Nor his voice. He merely continued to sit there, scrolling idly at his own monitor, obviously not too interested in what he was digging up, his face all but hidden by the outlandish pith helmet perched atop his head like a dishpan.

"I said you have a tumor growing inside your cunt. You don't douche enough. That's why it always smells like a possum crawled up there and died. That's why the cancer started growing. I put it there to teach you a lesson. Remember," he said, pointing his finger at the same sign Chuck had pointed to, then wagging it gaily in the stunned woman's face, "learning is fun. So leave the little tykes alone."

The children were as stunned as the librarian. Only Chuck had the urge to grin, but even he was too amazed to let it unfold.

The librarian's face, mousy at best, was all but racked with horror. But looking at her, Woody thought he saw a glimmer of something else there, too. A dawning of understanding, perhaps. Had she had trouble down there lately? Had the thought begun to enter her mind that maybe, just maybe, there was something wrong, that perhaps she should see a doctor and have it checked out?

She opened her mouth to speak, or perhaps to scream, when the mailman butted in yet again.

"It's that damned vibrator you use. You could tear up a fucking street with that thing. What the hell do you power it with anyway, a *car battery*? Is it *nuclear*? Just because you prefer women but never had the guts to act on that preference, although I have to tell you, the first time a dyke got a whiff of your snatch she'd probably go right back to men. What was I saying—oh yeah—just because you prefer women doesn't mean you have to fuck yourself with a piece of equipment that was made to shatter concrete just to get your rocks off. There must be somebody out there desperate enough to tackle that smelly hole of yours."

The woman's scream finally made it to the surface, and when it did, it shook the rafters. There was no fear in that scream; it was one of pure unadulterated anger.

"You fucking animal. Get out of my library. I'm calling the post office to report you."

Calmly, the mailman said, "Better call the janitor first."

The woman was apoplectic now, spittle forming at the corners of her mouth, her eyes flashing, her face the color of terra-cotta tile. The blood had returned to it in one mad surging rush. Woody figured her blood pressure should peak any second, and then she'd probably fall over dead. Pissed off to death. Probably be a first among librarians, he thought. Usually they just died of boredom. Or bookworms.

"What the hell are you talking about?" she shrieked. "I don't need a janitor, I need the police. What the hell are you talking about? Why are you saying these things? I don't know you. I don't—why do I need a janitor?"

The man slowly lifted his hand from the dial of the microfilm monitor and pointed a long finger at the woman's feet. "Tell him to bring a mop," he said, then calmly put his hand back on the dial and continued to scroll. The children could hear him now, humming softly to himself. He was humming "I Fall to Pieces," an old Patsy Cline hit. A decade and a half later, Woody would still find it impossible to sing that song, no matter how many times someone requested it. The mere thought of it took him back to this day. To the last day he spent with Bobby. To the last day he knew innocence.

To the first time he saw human blood. Quarts of it.

All of them, Woody, Bobby, Chuck, Jeremy, and Cathy, and even the librarian, looked down to where the man had pointed. The children were shocked by what they saw. Cathy even gasped. But it was nothing compared to the reaction of the fifty-year-old librarian, who by now was beginning to look like she had been dragged through a lunatic asylum and, like a sponge, absorbed every single symptom to be found there among the babbling, blathering, blithering inmates.

A thin trickle of blood was seeping down her support-hosed leg, making a little dogleg turn at the ankle, then spilling over her orthopedic shoe to form a tiny puddle on the floor.

Her hand flew to her mouth. "My God. I'm bleeding."

The mailman said, "You ain't seen nothing' yet."

And no sooner had he said it than the trickle became a stream, the stream became a torrent. The blood didn't even bother traveling down her leg now, it spilled out from beneath her shapeless plaid skirt like oil from a busted oil pan, splattering out across the floor around her. The children jumped backward to avoid the rush of it. The mailman coolly picked his feet up off the floor and propped them on the edge of his chair.

"God, what a mess," he mumbled.

It was only then that Woody made the connection between what was happening to the woman and the faceless man three monitors down. But even as the realization hit him, he couldn't take his eyes from the blood gushing from the woman, painting everything around her red. Her skirt was soaked in it now. Rivulets spread across the floor in every direction. Toward the door. Toward the wall. Toward the desks. She stood there, staring down at that horrible growing pool, at her life spilling out of her like cherry Kool-Aid. Her trembling now was not from anger but a growing weakness. Woody could see the dizziness in her eyes. Waited for her to fall. Wondering vaguely which way she would go. Forward. Backward. Straight down in a heap.

The woman was too frightened to scream. She suddenly didn't seem to have the energy for it. With a face as pale as paper, her eyes pulled away from the bloody mess surrounding her, still spilling out, the pool still growing, and her gaze came to rest on the mailman sitting unconcernedly at his monitor, still humming Patsy Cline's greatest hits, still calmly twiddling the dial on his monitor, occasionally peering a little closer at the screen to see what had popped up, as if not a thing of interest was happening anywhere in the world except for on that tiny little lighted area smack in front of his face.

"Who are you?" the woman tried to say, but the words wouldn't come. They stayed inside her head. Unheard, except by her.

And as darkness began to encroach on her senses to carry her away from it all, her mouth opened wider and this time a scream did emerge, but a weak, timid scream, as if her heart really wasn't in it.

It should have been, though, for from beneath her skirt a bloody mass of tissue as big as a five-pound meatloaf suddenly tore itself from her body and slid to her feet with an audible splat.

The mailman tsked without looking up. "Tumor. What'd I tell you?"

A scream from across the library floor, over by the main desk, brought people running. By the time the woman gushing blood was beginning to run on fumes, her tank being about empty, more than a dozen people were standing around watching as she finally sank down on her haunches and then folded up like a pocket knife, chin to ankle.

"Limber little minx," the mailman said, and when Woody turned to look at him, his chair was empty.

The mailman was gone.

"MASSIVE HEMORRHAGE, my ass," Bobby said, sipping his Coke, trying not to throw it back up. "It was *him*. Willis Earl James. A.k.a. Willow Man. He was sitting right there with us all the time. He was there when we *got* there. He knew where we were going, and he put himself there to meet us."

"He knows too much," Woody said, looking nervously at the beads of sweat on Bobby's brow, the slight tinge of panic in Bobby's sweet brown eyes. He supposed if he had a mirror handy, he would see the same tinge of panic in his own. But his own fears he could deal with. Seeing it in Bobby, however, was more than he could bear. He reached across the table and laid a hand over Bobby's, not caring what the others thought about it. "It's all right," he said, soothingly. "He didn't hurt us. We're all okay."

Still downtown, they were sitting in a McDonald's across from City College. Five pale faces soaked in sweat, their T-shirts stuck to their bodies. They hadn't just strolled into the place, they had *dived* in after running six blocks from the library as if the hounds of hell were hot on their heels.

If Bobby's eyes were sprinkled with panic, Jeremy's were all but inundated. His hands were shaking as he wiped the sweat from his face with a handful of paper napkins. "Yeah, we're all okay *now*, but how long is *that* going to last? If he can do what he did to that librarian anytime he wants, when's he going to take it into his head to do the same to us?"

"That poor woman," Cathy said, staring through the window at the traffic passing along the street. It looked like any other day out there, but she knew it wasn't. Things had changed. The world had suddenly shifted a little off-kilter, and only she and her friends knew it. "He killed that lady just to scare us. Just to let us know how much power he has. Jeremy is right. One of these days, it's going to be one of us. We have to do something. But what?"

Chuck alone had ordered food with his Coke. A sleeve of fries. It was all he could afford. He was eating them now as if he hadn't eaten in a week. "Maybe she wasn't real," he said, chewing lustily, sipping at his drink between bites. "Maybe that woman was just one of his little tricks. An illusion." He said it again as if wishing with all his heart it was true. "Maybe she wasn't, you know—*real*."

After seeing what they had just seen, watching Chuck poke one ketchup-soaked french fry after another into his mouth was making Woody want to puke, but he didn't say anything. Everybody dealt with fear in their own way. Chuck did it with food. He always had.

Woody's patience, however, didn't extend to what Chuck said. "How can you say she wasn't real? You saw the paramedics carting her dead body away, didn't you? You saw everybody standing around staring at the blood, didn't you? Jesus, Chuck. How real do you want it to be?"

Chuck looked crestfallen by the vehemence in Woody's voice. He glanced down at his hands on the tabletop and said meekly, "I was just hoping is all."

Cathy reached out and laid her own hand over one of Chuck's. "It's okay. We all hope it. We just don't think it's true. We have to face the facts. Things have been building up to it for a long time, and now it's finally happened. He's finally killed someone."

"At least it wasn't one of us," Bobby said. The panic seemed to have left him now. He looked calmer. More determined. His eyes centered on Woody sitting across from him. Among all the other emotions Woody saw there in the depths of Bobby's eyes, he still detected love for himself, and that gave him heart, just as the feel of Woody's hand had given Bobby heart earlier.

Their two hands were still clasped on the tabletop for everyone to see, but no one had mentioned it. No one seemed to notice. That great mass of cancerous tissue spilling from the woman's body like a bloodied fetus and tumbling to the floor with that horrendous *splat* was still too real for them. Too near. In their minds they saw very little else, although each and every one of them wished the hell they could.

Jeremy's attention was drawn through the restaurant window to a man across the street. He was running in circles on the college lawn, arms stretched out wide to either side like a kid playing airplane, swooping and dipping, heading straight for a while, then banking steeply in one direction or the other. People steered clear of him like he had the plague. He wore sweats, like a jogger, although any jogger wearing sweats on a day as hot as this one had to be nuts, and Jeremy figured that's what he was. Another of the mindless whackos who survived somehow on the streets of San Diego, hand to mouth, bumming a quarter here, a nickel there, sleeping in doorways, messing up the landscape and pooping in the gutters.

Jeremy tore his gaze from the man and concentrated on his Coke.

"Maybe we should tell your dad," Bobby was saying to Woody.

But just the thought of it caused fear to flash in Woody's eyes. "No. If we drag anybody else into this, Willow Man might go after them. It's our problem. We have to deal with it on our own."

"But we're *not* dealing with it," Cathy said. "We're just letting things happen. And things are getting worse all the time."

"We're not going back into that canyon," Chuck said. "Ever. We'll just stay the hell away from the place, and maybe all this stuff will stop happening. If he doesn't see us, maybe he won't think about us."

"But he doesn't *stay* in the canyon anymore," Woody said. "Now he goes anywhere he wants. If we don't go to him, then he'll come to us. Like he did today." He too had noticed the man doing his strange little dance across the street, and he was watching him now, but he wasn't really focused on him. There were always one or two crazies around. This one was no different from all the others. He was a part of the urban landscape. Like a fire hydrant. Or a mailbox. You saw them, skirted around them at a slightly accelerated clip, then forgot about them.

"How does he do what he does?" Bobby asked. "Where does he get his power from? Can all dead people do what he does, or is it just him? Do they have to be evil, or can *good* dead people do *good* stuff? Even if they did, I don't suppose we'd ever know about it. Bad shit makes headlines, good shit just sorta gets swept under the rug, racked up to luck." He struck his fist against the tabletop and a pimply-faced boy behind the counter gave him a dirty look. Bobby lowered his voice a fraction. "I wish we knew how to stop him! I wish we knew how to *kill* him!"

Chuck dug a chunk of ice out of his cup and held it in his hand, feeling the coldness of it against his palm, and then he popped it in his mouth and noisily crunched it into water. "Well, we'd better figure something out. Otherwise it's us who're going to be getting killed, and frankly, I'd sort of like to see what this orgasm stuff is all about at least once before I depart this miserable planet." His eyes opened wide and he cast a nervous glance in Cathy's direction as if he suddenly remembered she was sitting there listening to him. Or so he thought.

But Cathy hadn't heard a word he said. She raised her chin toward the man across the street. "What the heck is that guy doing? Why is he bothering all those people?"

All eyes turned to see what she was talking about.

The man playing airplane on the lawn had broadened his game to include dive-bombing passing pedestrians. Head tucked into his chest, arms straight out at his sides, he raced toward one person after another, veering away only at the last moment. One girl dropped her book bag in shock. Another ran up onto the lawn to get away from him.

When the man chased the girl across the grass, they could hear her squeals of fright as she disappeared around the corner of a building. More than one person had stopped to watch. An older man, possibly a teacher at the college, raised his hand to admonish the man, but slunk away when the guy in sweats stopped dead in his tracks and glared at him, eyes narrowed, fists clenched at his sides as if priming himself up to do a little neck wringing just for the hell of it.

"Guy's nuts," Woody said. "Let's go home."

He started to rise, but Bobby pulled him back down. "Wait. Look."

A slight young man, Asian, with spiky black hair and headphones draped across his ears, who appeared to be about the same age as them but must have been older because he carried college textbooks under his arm, was standing off to the side watching the scenario unfold. When the crazy guy in the jogging suit spotted the young man, trim and handsome in white tennis shorts and open shirt, he turned his full attention to him, spreading his arms wide yet again, running toward the boy, circling close, occasionally reaching out and brushing his hand across the boy's chest as he circled around, letting his fingers linger on the taut tanned flesh.

The young student held his ground, never taking his eyes from the man, but not recoiling either. He seemed about to turn and walk away when the crazy dude grabbed the boy's books and flung them out into the street. Even from inside the restaurant, they could hear the guy hoot with laughter at the stunned look on the student's face.

Angered finally, the young man pushed the crazy fucker away from him and stalked out into the street to gather up his books, which were scattered across two lanes. Traffic reluctantly slowed to accommodate the boy, and someone blasted a horn, but the boy calmly scooped his books off the asphalt, ignoring it.

When he had gathered everything up, the man in the jogging suit yelled out to him. "Heads up!"

And as the boy stopped what he was doing to look at him, a car struck him head-on, flinging his body and his books across the remaining two lanes. Tanned young legs and arms, curiously graceful, wheeled in midair as the boy sailed up over the sidewalk and smashed into the plate glass window Woody and his friends were looking through. A bloodied arm came to rest on the sill, ribboned by the splintered glass. Screams echoed through the restaurant.

The five children scrambled away from the window just as a huge sliver of glass high above their heads shivered in its frame before falling loose and crashing down onto the boy's shattered body. Blood spurted like McDonald's Extra Zesty Ketchup across the floor and onto the tabletop where they had been sitting.

The young man opened his mouth once, like a fish out of water, eyes unseeing, unknowing, then lay still in his bed of broken glass and bloodied textbooks. All the worrying the guy had done about his GPA was now moot and would forever remain so.

Woody felt the piercing of fingernails on his forearm and turned to see Cathy squeezing his arm, staring past him with eyes the size of grapefruits. Her words were barely audible. "Oh shit, Woody. We gotta go. We gotta go."

Woody didn't know what she was talking about. He looked back down at the young man, his stillness telling Woody everything he needed to know, and when Cathy's fingernails tore his skin, drawing blood, he finally whirled on her.

"*What?*" he hissed, rubbing his arm after yanking it from her grasp.

It was Jeremy who answered. He motioned to the door leading in from the street. "Christ, Woody. It's him."

Woody finally turned to see what the rest of his friends were staring at. "Him who?" he started to say, but the words crawled to a halt at the spot where his tonsils hooked onto his throat, then lay there in a lump like a lodged chicken bone.

The man in the jogging suit was standing inside the door, the only unmoving figure in the place. Everyone else was either running toward the dead young man or *away* from him, their Big Macs forgotten, the only thing on their minds, depending on the type of people they were, was to get the hell out of there fast or to get as close as they could to the mayhem and check out all the blood. Woody and his friends had been of the first variety until Cathy stopped them dead in their tracks.

The crazy guy in the doorway seemed to be enjoying all the confusion. He swerved his head to the left, then to the right, grinning broadly, watching all the hubbub, even emitting a gurgling giggle at the sight of a young woman crawling across the floor, delirious with shock, trying to get away from it all, then he slowly faced forward and rested his gaze solely on Woody's startled face.

"You," the man said, that evil grin still smeared across his face. And in the faintest of whispers, he said it again. "You."

Woody felt his heart thudding inside his chest like a war drum, and in his ear, he heard Bobby speaking softly. Matter-of-factly. "It's Willow Man. Cathy's right. We gotta boogie."

And the next thing Woody knew the five of them were vaulting over the McDonald's counter, scattering straws and napkins and soda cups and ketchup packets and God knows what else from one end of the joint to the other, hurdling through employees who were standing around stunned by what had happened, racing past the grill, the deep fryers, the walk-in freezers and storage closets, and finally throwing themselves through the back door and out into the blinding, searing sunlight. The heat hit them like a wall of flame, but they didn't stop to complain about it. In fact, they were two blocks away before they felt it at all. It wasn't until Cathy begged them to slow down that they actually stumbled to a halt.

Collapsing against a lamppost, Chuck tried to draw some air into his tortured lungs. "I can't take much more of this," he gasped, clutching his heart like an old man on the cusp of a massive coronary. "Jesus! People are dying all around us. It's like a horror movie or something. What the hell is he going to do? Kill everybody until there's no one left but us?"

Bobby looked back in the direction they had come. "I don't think he's following us."

Cathy rolled her eyes and spat a pigtail out of her mouth. "Yeah, well, we didn't see him follow us to the library or to McDonald's either, but he sure as hell did. I don't think you ever see this guy coming. I think he just wishes himself to be some place and, bam, there he is."

In the distance they could hear sirens converging on the place they had just left, saw the red flash of a fire truck screaming through traffic two streets over, followed quickly by a white boxy ambulance and two police cars, red and blue lights glittering across their roofs. Faintly, they could hear the sound of a woman wailing, a high-pitched keening that seemed to reverberate through the heated air like a yodel across the Alps. Perhaps a relative of the boy. Or a friend. Or some panicked office worker who didn't expect to see a slaughtered Chinaman on her way to slurping down a few thousand McCalories for lunch.

Woody remembered the young man, so handsome only moments before, heading off to class with his dreams banging around inside his head like so much flotsam bobbing on the tide. What was he studying? What had he intended to do with his life? Woody supposed it didn't much matter. His dreams were now as dead as he was.

As dead as they were *all* going to be if they didn't figure out what to do, and how to get away from this fucker.

Bobby was intently staring at him, he noticed, as if hearing his thoughts. But if Woody could have entered into Bobby's mind, he would have heard only one word echoing there. "You."

Bobby seemed to be gathering up his courage to speak. "He was talking to you, Woody. Didn't you hear him? He was only talking to you. Why did he do that? Why did he pick you out of all those people and direct that one word to you?"

"Maybe Woody's the one he wants," Chuck said. "Maybe it's Woody he's really after."

Quietly, Woody said, "I think maybe I've known that all along."

"Bullshit!" Cathy spat, her face going from fear to anger in the space of a second. "You don't know anything of the kind!"

Woody felt a twinge of gratitude lighten his heart as he looked at the fury on Cathy's face. It was nice to have friends who got all pissed off if you were the least bit threatened by a dead pervert. Seemed to make the effort involved in having friends on the active roster worth all the trouble of keeping them there.

"She's right," Bobby said. "And even if it *is* you he wants, he'll have to deal with us first."

From the exertion of running two blocks in the blistering heat, not to mention everything else that had happened that day (and it wasn't even noon yet, for Christ's sake), the birthmark on Jeremy's cheek had turned a fiery bloodied magenta, like a freshly etched tattoo, hot off the needle. "Listen to you people! What the hell are you talking about? We can't even protect ourselves! How are we going to protect Woody?"

"Well, we have to try!" Cathy railed.

Jeremy blinked. He hadn't meant to sound like such a baby. Hell, of *course* he would protect Woody. He would protect Woody before he would protect *anybody*. Being secretly in love with the guy probably had a lot to do with it, he told himself, if love was what it really was. A bead of sweat rolled off the tip of his nose and splattered the sidewalk.

His voice, when he spoke, was a mixture of remorse and embarrassment, with a peppering of righteous indignation. "Well, of *course* we have to try! Who the hell said we wouldn't *try*? Did *I* say we wouldn't try? I'm just saying how the hell are we going to do it? *That's* what the hell I'm saying! So get off my ass, Cath, before I cram my Keds up your ass and pull the laces out your ears. *Jeez!* What a *bitch!*"

Cathy opened her mouth to scream right back at him, and then she grinned. "You're not wearing Keds. You're wearing Nikes."

Jeremy's anger and embarrassment fell away from him as quickly as it had come. Timidly, he grinned back at her, and his braces flashed in his cherubic face like a glint of sunlight off a chrome bumper. "The principle's the same. Brand names don't matter."

"They matter to me," Woody said. "I prefer Reeboks."

Then they were all laughing, although they felt pretty guilty about it, and pretty soon they plopped themselves down on the curb to take stock of the whole sorry situation, but before much stock was taken, Bobby pulled his bus transfer from a trouser pocket and checked the time imprinted on it.

"Shit, guys, unless you want to walk home, we'd better get to a bus stop *now!*"

"I'm not walking home in this heat," Chuck stated.

"Me either," Cathy said.

"What about the dead kid?" Jeremy asked. "Shouldn't we go back and tell the cops what really happened?"

Woody shook his head. "They'd never believe us. Hell, *I* wouldn't believe us. Let's just go."

And the next thing they knew they were once again flying down the street, panting, stumbling, soaked in sweat, heading for Broadway and their last chance for a free ride home. As they ran, each of them in their own way thought of the handsome young student lying back there dead on the sidewalk like a broken, battered toy. Then their minds turned to the poor librarian folded over in a pool of her own blood with that god-awful mass of tumorous flesh lying beside her, both lives taken by the thing that haunted them. Each of them wondered if they would be next. Each of them but one. That sole exception could think of nothing but Woody's safety. And the feel of Woody's body, back arched, coaxed to the brink of orgasm, trembling beneath his hands. Even in the midst of dead librarians and slaughtered college students, that memory brought a smile to Bobby's lips.

Chuck pointed up the street. "There's a number 2!"

They dredged up a last burst of speed and hit the bus stop just as the bus pulled up beside it.

Woody first, they fumbled for their transfers and began climbing onto the bus. When Woody stopped in front of them as if someone had suddenly nailed him to the steps, they plowed into each other like a bunch of Keystone Kops, heads banging together, stumbling to a halt.

"What's the holdup?" Cathy grumbled from the rear.

But Woody didn't hear her. He was staring at the bus driver, all decked out in his neat little uniform, one hand on the wheel, the other resting casually over the slot where the transfer was supposed to go. Woody's hand had stopped in midair when he saw the fungus growing on the driver's fingertips, burying the nails completely beneath bulbous masses of infection that Woody even thought he could smell. It was the bittersweet stench of pus oozing from an infected wound.

When he raised his eyes to the driver's face, he saw the same person he had seen in the library, the same person he had seen playing airplane on the college lawn. It was the timidly smiling man in the photograph. The child molester. The one who had made, and was still making, their summer a living hell. Dead for years, he was still here, making a grand old comeback so to speak, and by the look on his face right now, he was having a dandy time doing it. As the light of recognition lit Woody's face, the bus driver smiled like a benevolent old uncle grateful to be remembered. Then a long green tongue shot forth from the man's mouth and snatched the transfer from Woody's hand. The driver's throat swelled up as he rolled that monstrous tongue back into his mouth and gulped down the transfer slip, for all the world like a gecko snapping up a dragonfly.

Grinning, the driver said, "Next stop, hell."

And before his friends behind him knew what was happening, Woody had pushed them back out onto the street as the door began to whoosh inward.

As the bus door slammed shut in front of them, they saw the driver give them a friendly little finger wiggle of good-bye before the bus lurched back out into traffic, barely missing a car that was creeping past on the left. And as the bus pulled away, they heard Willow Man, a.k.a. bus driver, a.k.a. mailman, a.k.a. crazy jogger dude, scream out at the passing car, "Watch where you're going, you stupid motherfucker! I got the right-of-way here! I got the fucking right-of-way!"

A burst of acrid exhaust fumes struck them in the face, and they heard the driver cackling gaily as the bus rumbled off down the street.

The scrolling billboard in red neon pebble lights on the back of the bus that usually read Park Canyon #2, now read, Walk—Don't Ride, Shitheads.

And then the bus was gone, lost in traffic.

CHAPTER FOURTEEN

WOODY LAY in the darkness of his old room. Even after so many years, the scent, the *feel* of it, were still as familiar to him as his music. He listened to Jeremy quietly breathing sleep sounds beside him. Jeremy's lean warm body, so close, so comforting, was now as familiar to Woody as this room, this house, every song he had ever sung. Woody had explored every inch of Jeremy's body, as Jeremy had explored his, before the temporary waning of passion had lulled them both to sleep. Even now Woody felt a sense of contentment surround him like a soft, billowy cloud. He had awoken from sleep when Jeremy, unaware, draped an arm across Woody's chest to snuggle closer, never waking, as if laying a claim to this man he had loved since childhood even as he slept.

Woody pressed his face into the velvet softness beneath Jeremy's bicep, touched his lips to the tender flesh there, feeling the heat of it against his face, feeling a pulse somewhere beneath the skin pounding out the rhythm of Jeremy's life, a soothing drumbeat Woody closed his eyes to better feel against his cheek.

Jeremy's warm breath, scented with sleep, swept over him, and Woody found himself again becoming aroused, remembering Jeremy inside him, remembering Jeremy gasping with the orgasm that shot deep into Woody's body, remembering his own orgasm rising up to meet it. Their hearts had been racing then; now they were calm. Woody knew if he let himself go, if he pushed away everything else that was happening to him, to *all* of them, and then he would be content to stay right where he was at this very moment for the rest of his life. Wrapped in Jeremy's arms. Letting Jeremy's love for him take him to that place he had not visited for so long. But he had felt this way with Bobby once, and the creature that had destroyed that love was still out there, maybe waiting for the perfect time to reach back into Woody's life and destroy this one too. It had taken everything Woody had ever loved. Bobby. His parents. It had stolen the happiness from his life, and now that happiness was once again being offered, Willow Man might very well reach out for it yet again, laying his own claims to Woody as he had done so many times before.

Woody knew beyond all doubt he would not survive another loss like that. This was why he had lived so long not only in fear of the past, but in fear of the future as well. Fear that love would find him again and as quickly be stripped away.

Well, here it was. When he had least expected it, love *had* found him again, and it was lying next to him at this very moment. It didn't take a psychoanalyst to dissect Woody's feelings. Woody could dissect them perfectly well on his own. He knew love when it hit him over the head. He had, after all, been hit in the head with it once before. In this very room. In this very bed. And with another he had known practically since infancy.

Bobby had even given his blessing to this new love, all but throwing Woody into Jeremy's arms, not that it wasn't already where Woody wanted to be. It didn't take a psychoanalyst to figure that out either. But still, mixed with the contentment Woody felt lying in Jeremy's arms, and the excitement too, wondering where this new relationship would take them—if Woody allowed it to take them *anywhere*—there was still a hammering of guilt pounding away at the back of his mind. A sense of betrayal. He had loved Bobby, loved the *memory* of Bobby, for so many years, it seemed like treachery now to move on to someone else as if Bobby had never existed.

Woody knew he was not the first to feel this way. Millions of people lose loved ones. Millions of people, after the first horrible throes of grief subside, gather up the broken bits of their lives and forge new ones. They open their hearts to new partners. They let their sadness retreat to a place where it still might be remembered but no longer dictates how they will live their lives. Woody's grief was nothing special. And Woody's love for Bobby had been nothing special either. Not really. It was simply love. Like the love of those millions of others who suddenly find themselves alone, then pull themselves up by their bootstraps and shake off their pain to begin again.

Woody felt ashamed to think he had allowed himself to live in mourning for so many years, afraid to seek out new relationships, unwilling to open himself up to anyone else. Perhaps he had thought no one could be all the things to him Bobby had been. And perhaps they couldn't. But to simply give up, to accept the sadness of Bobby's loss and let it carry him through the rest of his life, was an act of weakness. He could see that now. The man beside him had *made* him see it.

Jeremy.

Woody remembered the tow-headed little kid with the "I'm With Stupid" T-shirt and the braces that glittered like sparks of fire when the sunlight hit them just right. Then he remembered the feel of Jeremy's hands on his body, the feel of Jeremy's lips surrounding his cock, the velvet softness of Jeremy's back, the smooth strength of his long tanned legs, the taste of him. The soothing warmth of Jeremy's arm holding him now was like the closing number of the show they had performed together earlier, Woody thought. A winding down of tension, a lowering of sound, easing the audience out with something mellow. A ballad, maybe, or a simple love song. Closing the night with a whimper instead of a roar. A gentle abatement of passion to where, in the calmness and the silence that followed, love could truly settle in.

Before sleep took him again, Woody found himself thinking of ways to make this relationship work. Occasional treks back to San Diego between gigs to be with Jeremy. Meeting Jeremy on the road in other cities. It would be awkward, but he supposed it could be done. Yet it didn't seem right somehow. People who love each other should be together. Always. They shouldn't be forced into long absences, meeting in strange motel rooms, garnering a few precious hours together before rushing back to their own lives, waiting for the next meeting, the next rendezvous. Counting hours and days alone, wondering what the other was doing, wondering when they would see each other again. And if this recording contract panned out, Woody supposed he would be away for even longer stretches of time. Months on end, maybe. Jesus, did he really want to live his life like that? Was his music that important to him? But what else was he qualified to do? He couldn't go back to sweeping up fish guts and chipping rust for a living, and outside of his music, that was about all that was on his resume at the moment.

Christ. I'm so fucked-up, even happiness is a problem.

In the darkness, he smiled. He supposed he got that worry gene from his mother. And the moment her face entered his mind, he heard the tinkle of high keys on the piano in the living room, a discordant little jingling of sound, as if a cat had pranced across the keyboard.

But Woody didn't own a cat.

His eyes popped open wide, and he knew beyond all doubt the shit was starting up again. He felt Jeremy tense beside him. He had heard it too.

Again, the happy tinkle of piano keys played out through the darkness, not a jumble of disconnected notes this time, but a melody. "Chopsticks." Someone was playing "Chopsticks." And playing it badly.

"Aw, Christ," Jeremy whispered. "Now what?"

They both jumped in the bed when the door eased open and Cathy poked her head in. In the moonlight, they could see Chuck standing behind her, his pale hair sticking up at all angles, peering over her shoulder into the room as if wondering what he would see there, like maybe he was hoping they were still bonking away and he might catch a glimpse of the action. But he was casting a few nervous glances behind him at the same time.

Cathy, calmer, seemed to be taking this new wrinkle in the night's proceedings in stride. If she felt fear at that moment, her voice wasn't registering it. She sounded almost happy. "Guys, I think you'd better come and see this."

Since he and Jeremy were still stark naked, Woody opted to leave the light off while they stumbled around in the dark looking for the underwear they had excitedly cast away a couple of hours earlier. Cathy giggled when Jeremy stubbed his toe on the nightstand and mumbled a curse.

Finally dressed, after a fashion, the important points of their bodies covered, at least, with one pair of pin-striped boxer shorts and a tiny pair of red briefs, Woody and Jeremy followed Chuck and Cathy down the long hallway toward the living room, all four of them padding softly on naked feet. Cathy was draped in a sheet—apparently she couldn't find her clothes in the dark either—but Chuck was as naked as the day he was born and apparently unconcerned by the fact. As they approached the living room, Woody had time to take stock of the fact that Chuck's body was remarkably like Jeremy's, long and lean, only slightly less muscled, but still nicely put together, as beautiful as his brother's. Woody no longer had to rely on moonlight for this assessment because in the forward part of the house, every light was burning.

There seemed to be a party in progress. He heard suddenly the laughter of children, and mixed with the discordant sound of that inept version of "Chopsticks" still being pounded out on the piano, he heard the old hi-fi in the corner grinding out a Beatles tune. His mother's favorite song. Norwegian Wood. Woody still incorporated it into his show sometimes, and whenever he did, he always thought of her.

As they approached the doorway leading into the living room, Woody realized it was not electricity radiating the light, but the same ectoplasmic glow they had seen surrounding the dead souls in the canyon. Here, in the confines of the house, it glowed brighter. There was no mist here as there had been among the trees, only that pulsating, wavering light that brought everything into perfect focus. The light of reality. Only there was no reality here. This was a memory. Woody recognized the scene the moment he looked into the room.

It was his sixth birthday party. He remembered the enormous sheet cake with the plastic cowboys and Indians and a little covered wagon on it made of spun sugar. It was a store-bought cake, not one his mom had made, and it came from Charlie's Bakery over on Juniper Street, delivered that morning in a big pink box with Woody's name on the lid. He recalled the sweet taste of that rock-hard little wagon when his mother presented it to him alone since he was the birthday boy. He had gnawed away at it while his mother and another woman doled out cake on paper plates to the dozen or more kids who had been sent formal little invitations a week before. He remembered them coming to the door, gifts in hand, all decked out in their Sunday best. And his best friends were there, too. Bobby, Chuck, Jeremy, Cathy. The other kids were just filler. For Woody, the party centered around the five of them. Even then, theirs was an exclusive club where others might peek in now and then, but no one else was invited to stay.

Unbreathing, his eyes alight with memory, Woody watched his mother, still young and pretty at this stage in her life, bend over a small boy and wipe icing from his face with a paper napkin that had colored balloons printed on it. The boy was squirming beneath her hands like a trout, but she was relentless, not stopping until the kid's face was shining like a new pair of shoes, as uncomfortably clean as it was when he walked through her door.

As he had done so many times during the course of their years together, Woody cast his gaze around for Bobby, seeking him out among the laughing faces of the other children, finding him finally, sitting at the piano by the front window. He was the one pounding out "Chopsticks."

It had rained that day, Woody remembered, and even now, looking past a young Bobby pecking away at the damn piano, adding to the din, he could see the water lashing at the picture window beside him. The party was supposed to be held in the backyard, but at the last moment, not liking the looks of those black thunderheads moving in from the ocean, Woody's mom had moved everything inside. Not too happy about it either, Woody remembered, grinning now. Having a dozen cake-smeared kids rampaging through her clean house was not high on the list of her most favorite things on a Saturday afternoon. He could see her even now, staring around her with a slightly bewildered look in her eyes, a forerunner of panic, as she continually herded the kids like cattle, trying to keep the destruction centered in one room.

Chuck and Jeremy wore matching jackets and little neckties that were obviously choking the shit out of them, but the cake seemed to be easing their pain. With their hair plastered to their heads with what looked to be Crisco, toothless grins lighting their angelic faces (they had only recently lost their baby teeth so their braces had not yet been screwed into their heads), they were scarfing down slabs of cake like cavemen attacking a mastodon carcass, crumbs flying everywhere. His mother looked on, dying, Woody figured, to drag out the Hoover and suck the whole lot of them into the bowels of the thing and restore her house to its pristine beauty. And silence.

Cathy, also six, but looking very mature on this day with her thick red hair pulled into a fat bun at the back of her head held in place by at least a dozen barrettes of varying colors and shapes, and wearing a party dress of red and white stripes and shiny black slippers with white socks, was sitting next to Bobby on the piano bench, happily swinging her legs and feeding him cake as he played.

No one in the room looked up to see the four almost naked adults staring in at them from the hall.

"Holy crap," Jeremy whispered, digging his chin into Woody's shoulder. "It's your birthday party. I gave you a bike horn."

Woody could only laugh. Too many memories were flooding through him for speech.

Chuck laughed too. "Yeah, bro, but only after you cried and whined and pleaded with Mom to let you keep it for yourself. She finally had to go out and buy you one just like it. What a brat you were."

"Thanks. I love you too."

Cathy nudged Woody, making him jump. "Look at your mom. She's about to have a cow."

Woody saw his mom was looking just as miserable as she had a few moments earlier, only now her eyes were focused on the kitchen door leading out to the garage.

For the first time, Woody realized they were one partygoer short. His own little six-year-old body wasn't present, and like the glowing image of his mother, he too turned his attention to the kitchen door.

He tried to think back. Had he gone to the garage that day, and if he did, what the hell had he gone there *for*? Why was his mother looking so suspiciously in that direction? It was his very own birthday party, so why wasn't Woody in the living room scarfing down cake and ice cream with the rest of the little brats?

His mother took a step toward the kitchen door, and Woody found himself reaching his hand out, silently pleading with her not to go out to the garage. Not knowing what she would find there, but knowing it couldn't be good, whatever it was.

At the piano, Woody heard a crash. His mother heard it too, and turned, momentarily forgetting about her search for her son. Cathy had dropped her plate of cake onto the keyboard, and she and Bobby were alternately laughing their heads off and looking at Woody's mom with a certain amount of fear in their eyes, like maybe she would come over there and toss their six-year-old asses through the picture window for being so goddamn clumsy. And she did rush to their side, but not to evict, not to berate, not to pick them up by their ears and toss them out into the street, but to clean up the mess. Resignedly. Tsking her displeasure, but being nice about it, scraping the gooey mess off of her beloved ivory keyboard even while she told Cathy to go get herself another piece of cake and try to be a little more careful with it this time. Woody's mother then asked Bobby very sweetly, please God, to stop pounding out his ham-handed version of "Chopsticks" before she had a nervous breakdown and took off screaming down the street, all semblance of sanity gone forever. Kaput.

And while the low piano keys pounded out what sounded like a death march as Woody's mom dabbed them clean, thunderously atonal beneath the fingers of a woman who could play Strauss waltzes without a single mistake, Woody stepped out into the room and headed for the kitchen door. No one noticed him there, this all but naked man in the middle of a children's birthday party, decked out in pinstriped boxer shorts, riding low, barely hanging onto the bulge of his pale ass, fuzzy legs poking out beneath, his broad tanned back tinged to blue in the ectoplasmic light. Nor did they notice his friends, themselves all but naked, except for Chuck who truly *was* naked, leaning in from the hallway door, whispering frantically for him to stop.

Woody crossed the kitchen and grasped the doorknob gingerly, as if expecting it to be hot, and then, without thinking too much about it because thinking too much always seemed to be his downfall, Woody pulled the door open and stepped into the garage.

His gaze fell immediately onto his own little six-year-old self, all dolled up like the rest of the kids, in his Sunday suit, sitting on the edge of the Kenmore washing machine, dangling his legs like Cathy had done at the piano bench. He was puffing determinedly at a long cigarette that looked supersized and totally out of place sticking out of his innocent little face. The man standing in front of him with his hands resting on Woody's thin thighs was a stranger to the adult Woody, but the young Woody seemed to know him well enough.

The man was dressed in his own version of Sunday clothes. Muddy patent-leather shoes. Ragged gray socks that were all too evident beneath trouser legs that rode high on the calf. High-water pants, Woody's dad would have called them. They were shiny and faintly green with age, tattered at the cuffs. The man's suit coat, which didn't come anywhere close to matching the trousers, was tight across the shoulders, looking ready to split apart at any second. Dirty shirt cuffs poked out, all but covering his hands while the jacket sleeves rode high above the wrist. He looked like he had dressed in the dark from someone else's closet, then wallowed around in the dirt for a few hours.

The hair on the man's head was a pale, mousy brown, streaked with blond or gray, and looked so fine and listless that a gust of wind would likely blow it right off his head.

As the young Woody puffed away at the cigarette, looking greener all the time, his face beginning to match the patina on the man's pants, his eyes continually stared down at the man's hands as they kneaded his legs, stroked his thighs, and occasionally wandered uncomfortably north to where even a six-year-old knew they shouldn't go.

"Again," the man was saying. "Take another puff. Draw it deep into your lungs, boy. You'll thank me for it one day. I'm teaching you how to become a man. Real men smoke. It's a fact of life. You don't want to grow up to be a pussy, do you?"

At any other time, the word "pussy" might have brought a giggle to the boy's lips, but right then he was too busy trying not to throw up or run screaming into the living room where he knew his mom was probably looking for him. He couldn't remember how he had let himself be drawn into the garage with this man. He had seen him at the party, standing quietly in the corner, watching all the children like maybe he was going to write a book about them or something, but no one else seemed to notice he was there. His mom hadn't offered the guy any cake. Not one child took a moment to stare in his direction. It was almost as if the man didn't exist except in Woody's eyes.

And when the man wiggled a finger at him, luring him to follow, Woody couldn't understand why he had. But there he was, trying to smoke the lighted cigarette the man had handed him and wondering how the heck he was going to get away from the guy and back to his party. He hadn't even had his cake yet, except for the little sugared wagon, which had made him thirsty.

The adult Woody, with his pinstriped boxer shorts riding low on his hips and his long hair falling to his bare shoulders, stood in the doorway with the same look of mistrust on his face as the child wore on his. Same face, same look, but separated by a span of almost twenty-five years. The child had become a man, and now they were thrust together again from opposite ends of a lifetime. But only one was aware of it. Woody knew instinctively the child could not see him standing there. Just as those inside the house had not seen him as he walked among them, following his mother's gaze to the kitchen door, leading him to this place, this moment.

"Who are you?" Woody watched his young self ask the man, obviously leery but trying not to show it, his boyish eyes almost hidden behind the curtain of cigarette smoke that wafted around his head. Squinting against it. Trying not to choke. "Where did you come from?"

"I live right here," the man said, touching the boy's temple with a long finger that had something wrong with it. A growth of some sort almost buried the fingernail from view. Like dried mud. He took the boy's hand then and pressed the child's small finger to his own forehead. "Just like one day you'll live right *here*."

"It's cold," the boy said, running his small fingers freely across the man's forehead as if mesmerized by the icy feel of it.

"Yes," the man said, closing his eyes at the boy's touch.

"You mean I'll live with you inside your head?"

The man's eyes popped open. "You betcha."

The child didn't appear too thrilled with the idea. "You mean I'd have to leave my mom and dad?"

"Either you'll leave them, or they'll leave you."

"Why?" There was true fear on the boy's face now as he withdrew his hand from the man's temple and rubbed it on his jacket as if trying to erase the coldness he had felt. "Where would they go?"

"People die, kid." The man gurgled up a chuckle that sounded like some vile substance bubbling up through the ground from the belly of a volcano, and it smelled that way, too. Like sulfurous vomit, spat up by a dying planet. There was something unholy in the stench of the man's breath. Woody could see the boy recoil from the reek of it.

"You don't know the truth of the world, yet," the man went on. "You're just a baby. You haven't figured out yet that people die. They do it all the time. They leave their kids. They leave their pets. Shit, they just *leave*. It's called death. Ever hear of it?"

"Y-yes. That's when people go to heaven."

The man's hands were stroking the boy's thighs again, lingering, narrowing his eyes at the warmth he felt there, testing the firmness of the young flesh. "You have nice little legs," he said now.

Woody wished the man would stop touching him, but he wanted an answer to his question even more. The man didn't seem to be listening to him anymore. "Don't they, mister?"

A flash of anger crossed the man's face, as if the child had slapped him from his reverie. "Don't they what? Who the hell are you talking about?" But even as he said the words, his gaze did not leave the boy's body, did not range upward to the boy's face.

"Dead people go to heaven, don't they?" the child persisted, squirming under the man's touch, taking another tiny puff from the cigarette the man had given him, more to ease his own discomfort at the feel of those ugly fingers on his legs than because he wanted it. In fact, the cigarette was making him really, really sick.

Finally, the man's eyes reluctantly rose to the boy's face. "Not many make it to heaven, kid. Most of 'em just burn. Or they hunt while they're waiting to burn. That's what I do. I hunt. You're the prey."

"I pray every night," the child said. "Mom told me I had to."

"Nice segue, kid, but you're screwing around with two different words. Not very bright, are you?"

Not understanding what the man was talking about, the child ignored the insult. "But you're not dead."

A cruel smile twisted the man's face, and the six-year-old Woody could have sworn he saw the man's eyes flash red like the brake lights on his daddy's car. "Someday I'll show you just how dead I'm not."

At the sound of footsteps moving closer, the man slowly turned, never taking his hands from the child's legs, and faced the adult Woody standing behind him.

"You remember now, don't you?" the man asked, still smiling that leering smile, his face still contorted with lust.

"Who are you talking to?" the child asked, but the man ignored him, letting his eyes burrow into Woody's as Woody stood there in his ridiculous boxer shorts, those cold, murderous eyes tearing themselves away from Woody's face only long enough to take in his body, his long legs, the promising bulge beneath the thin fabric of his shorts. There was hunger in the man's eyes. Hunger for the boy. Hunger for the man.

"This is the day your long love affair with cigarettes began," he said. "Remember, Woody? I tried to make you a man, see, but somehow it just didn't seem to take, did it? You grew up to be a faggot anyway. How did it feel when the little twin stuck his dick up your ass tonight? Not so little anymore, is he? Did you like it? Oh, don't look so surprised. I was there. I watched it all. Was even tempted to join in a time or two, but I didn't want to interrupt a burgeoning love affair. I'll take him from you, Woody. All those plans you were working out inside your head won't amount to crap in the end. You'll find no happiness in this world. I won't let you. All your happiness will come with death. With me. You'll see. It won't be so bad. Maybe a little pain now and then, but hey, into every death a little rain must fall."

Such anger surged up in Woody that his words flooded out of him in a roar. "Take your hands off him!"

"You mean take your hands off *you*," the man said, grinning so broadly Woody could see blackened teeth and something green moving around inside his mouth like a snake. "Pronouns can be such a mystery sometimes, can't they?"

This is all an illusion, Woody told himself. *Calm down. Don't give him your anger. That's what he wants.*

Woody tried to force a smile to his lips. "You weren't here on the day of this party. I would remember it if you were. What are you playing at? What exactly do you want from me?"

The man seemed amused by Woody's attempt to be calm, to be rational. "Oh, but I was here. I couldn't give you a replay of the action if I hadn't been here to witness it." He patted the boy's leg beside him. "And you were right here where you're sitting now. Feeling my hands. Wondering what I was going to do. You were afraid that day, Woody, but you tried not to show it. I have to give you credit for that. Such a little man you were. All innocent and bright-eyed, so beautiful it would have taken my breath away if I had had any to be taken. You sat right here, puffing away at the cigarette I gave you, trying to look mature, wanting to get away but not really knowing how to go about it, never knowing that at any second I could have ripped the clothes from your body and cracked you open like a melon. I could have torn the life right out of you in a heartbeat. And, oh, how I wanted to."

"What stopped you, then?" Woody asked, trembling now in his anger, but wanting to know the truth too. Wanting to know why this creature had spent a lifetime tormenting him. "Why didn't you kill me when you had the chance? It would have been better than killing all the others you've taken from me."

"No," the man said, turning back to the boy and laying a hand against the smooth cheek while his other hand still rested on the child's leg. "You were too beautiful to kill that day. Too—intriguing. I wanted to give you time to ripen. To mature. I wanted to see how you would turn out. I wanted to see your body grow so that the day I *did* take you, you would feel the pleasure of it. I wanted to be the first to touch you on the day you understood passion, but you found another person for that, didn't you?"

"Bobby—" Woody said.

"Yes. Bobby." The man spat out the word as if it left a bitter taste in his mouth. "I waited too long, you see. Wasn't keeping my eye on the ball, no pun intended. Bobby took what should have been mine. The first taste of you. But he paid for it in the end. You remember what I did to him, don't you?" The man eyed Woody again with a look of pure glee. "You remember how he looked when you found him. I know you do. Maybe that's the first thing you remember every morning of your life when sleep falls away and awareness kicks in. I hope it is. I hope that image never leaves your head. In the end, Woody, that's what will happen to you too. You and your friends. I'll take you all before it's over, and there's nothing you can do to stop me. And I think maybe tonight will be the night it happens."

"Then do it," Woody screamed. "Finish it now."

Willow Man laid his diseased fingertips to the boy's chin, then slid them lower, moving to encircle the boy's throat with his icy hand. Woody saw his own six-year-old eyes open up wide in surprise. And fear. And at that moment, he did remember. Willow Man *was* there that day. He *had* lured him into the garage. He *had* picked him up and sat him on the edge of the washer, teasingly offered him a cigarette, then stood before him stroking his legs as he watched Woody ineptly puffing away, the fear in him growing stronger with every passing second until—

"Where did you get that cigarette?"

Woody's mom was across the garage and slapping the cigarette from his tiny hand before he even knew she was there.

"What have I told you about smoking? Just wait until your father gets home. If he doesn't whip you to within an inch of your life, I will! And I may just whip him too, for leaving his cigarettes around for you to get at!"

Tears leaked from the boy's eyes. There was a different fear in them now. "Daddy didn't—"

Woody watched the scene unfold before him, remembering it all now. Seeing not only the fear in his young face, but seeing the confusion there too as he wondered what had happened to the man who brought him there, wondered why his mom hadn't seen him. He had disappeared like magic, leaving Woody to face the music alone—disappeared as if he had never been there at all.

And as Woody watched his mother drag his young body back into the house after angrily throwing the cigarette into the service sink by the washer, hearing it sputter out with a hiss as angry as her own, he understood that maybe it had been all too much for his six-year-old brain to grasp, and in not understanding, he had buried the memory so deep inside his head he had never, until this moment, let it out again.

Stunned by that realization, Woody, as if in a dream, followed the memory of his young self and his mother back into the house. There he found now only silent darkness until Chuck, still naked, flanked by his brother and the woman he loved, flipped the light switch, illuminating an empty room.

"Looks like the party's over," Chuck said, studying the look of wonder on Woody's face but not daring to ask what it meant. Not really wanting to know. "Can't wait to see what happens next," he lied. He figured he could wait an eternity for what was going to happen next and not mind waiting at all.

"Now it begins," Woody said, turning his gaze to Jeremy's sweet face, remembering the night behind them, the joy of it, the passion, the awakening *love* that seemed to come out of nowhere and hit Woody smack between the eyes. He wondered if they would ever see another night together, the two of them. It seemed doubtful, considering the words Willow Man had spoken to him only moments before. *"I'll take him from you, Woody. I'll take him from you—"*

"Now it really begins," Woody said again, scooping Jeremy into his arms. Fearing his loss already.

CHAPTER FIFTEEN

In the only bed they had ever shared together, Bobby lay naked in Woody's arms. The electric fan perched on the dresser slowly turned its head back and forth as if gazing out across the room, this way and that, filling the hot night with a comforting rush of sound and cooling the perspiration from their young bodies. With their passions spent and their thirst for each other slaked, at least for the moment, they both had time to think about everything that had happened that day. The librarian, folded up like a pocketknife in a pool of her own blood, that horrible glob of bloody flesh, as big as a cat, that had gushed from her body and lain there obscenely beside her head. The boy at the college, his body broken, gasping for one more breath like a dying fish before the darkness of eternity took him, a blood-spattered calculus book splayed open at his feet. The sound of splintering glass as the shattered window crashed down onto his dying body, tearing into his flesh, finishing the job good and proper.

Willow Man. Idly spinning the dial on the microfilm monitor, taunting the librarian with truths and lies as he sat there so seemingly unconcerned. And later, doing his macabre little dance on the campus lawn, hooting with laughter as the Chinese boy's books went sailing out into the street. Speaking that one word, "You," in McDonald's, his insane stare resting solely on Woody's face. His long green tongue snaking out to grab Woody's bus transfer as he sat there in his busman's uniform, swallowing the transfer down with a satisfied gulp.

Woody remembered the fear he had seen on his friends' faces that day. They were all beginning to understand the power Willow Man wielded. The power to follow them anywhere, the power to be anything he chose to be, the power to do anything he wanted to do. Free from the restraints everyone else in this world labored under, Willow Man could kill anyone he chose. Anytime. Anywhere. Today, he had taken great pains to make those truths abundantly clear to them, and Woody and his friends now accepted that knowledge beyond all doubt. They had seen it with their own eyes. They were believers.

But it was the reckless *joy* Willow Man took in everything he did that frightened Woody the most. Like an untended child in a toy store, Willow Man just went assholing along, having the time of his life, never once looking back at the destruction he left in his wake.

All those shattered lives he left behind were merely broken toys to him. With their destruction, he simply and uncaringly moved on to the next. Then the next. Blithely working his way toward his ultimate goal.

Them. Woody and his friends.

Or maybe—just Woody.

Both boys were as tired as they had ever been in their lives. The traumas of the day kept bombarding them, over and over again, horrible images that filled their heads until they could think of little else. Their hour of sex had merely blinded them to those images for a little while, for in each other's arms they saw only themselves, needed only themselves. Nothing else in the world existed at all. But now that their craving for the taste of each other was satisfied, those images came rushing back. The blood sluicing out of the woman in torrents. The Chinese boy's mangled body sailing through the air like a rag doll flung aside by a petulant child. Today they had caught their first true glimpse of human death and the sadness of it left them breathless. And compounding it all was that long, miserable walk home from downtown in ninety-plus temperatures and ninety-plus humidity. They hadn't dared try to board another bus, even if they could have snuck onto one with their expired transfer passes, figuring Willow Man would be at the wheel of that one, too, waiting for them with that sappy, evil grin on his face, playing his little game, taking them to God knows where. Taking them to a place, maybe, from where they would never return. A place where transfer passes and bus tokens and transit schedules didn't much matter.

"Next stop, hell," Willow Man had said, and Woody believed him.

Woody pressed his lips into Bobby's mop of brown hair, breathing in the clean scent of it, feeling it tickle his eyelashes, his nose. Bobby's warm hand rested atop his stomach and his smooth face lay against his chest. When Bobby spoke, his lips moved against Woody's skin, soft and gentle now, where before they had been so eager. Their lovemaking tonight had been the best yet. Between the horrible images of the day behind them, the memory of everything the two boys had done with each other only minutes before filled up the remaining corners of Woody's mind, making him as happy as he could ever remember being. At this moment, Woody knew, his love for Bobby had reached a zenith. Where it would go from here, he couldn't imagine. Even the day's ordeals couldn't dampen it.

"Woody?" Bobby said quietly.

"Yeah?"

"I think we should leave. Just run away."

Woody thought about that. "Where would we go?"

"I don't know. Anywhere he isn't, I suppose."

"Willow Man?"

"Yeah. Willow Man."

Their whispered voices seemed to echo through the darkness, even as the import of Bobby's words seemed to echo through Woody's mind like the tolling of a great sad bell.

"We can't do that, Bobby. What about our families?"

Another note of sadness tolled out. "My folks wouldn't care," Bobby said in a voice so crushed in misery Woody's heart ached to hear it.

"Maybe not, but mine would. And they would care as much about losing you as they would care about losing me. My family is yours now. Maybe they always have been. Forget about your mom and dad. Just think about mine." And after a moment, he added, "Just think about us."

Bobby raised his head to try to peer through the darkness at Woody's face. "That *is* what I'm thinking about. Willow Man is going to take us, Woody. I know he is. Either one of us or both of us. And either way, it means we'll never be together again. If we get away from this place, maybe we can spend our whole lives together. I look pretty old for my age. Maybe—maybe I could find a job someplace. Maybe I could—"

Woody pressed his lips to Bobby's, silencing him. He let the kiss linger a long time before he finally pulled away.

"No. We belong here. He doesn't. He's the one that has to leave, not us. Maybe if we just don't go into the canyon anymore—"

"It won't make any difference," Bobby said. "You know it won't. He can go anywhere we go. He proved that today."

"Then if we leave, what makes you think he won't just follow us to wherever we end up? We could go a million miles away, and maybe he would be right there when we got there, waiting for us. I don't think we *can* run from him. And if we have to face him, I'd rather do it here. Maybe we should talk to my folks."

Bobby sighed. "They won't believe us. You know they won't."

And Woody knew he was right.

He pulled Bobby more snugly into his arms, tucking Bobby's head into the crook of his neck. "Try to get some sleep. We'll decide what to do tomorrow. We'll talk to the others. Maybe they can think of something. Cathy's pretty smart. Maybe she can figure it out."

Bobby let himself be drawn into Woody's arms, savoring the comfort he always found there but still feeling the fear welling up inside him like a distant gathering storm, ever growing more dark and ominous, threatening and thundering on the horizon.

"It won't make any difference," Bobby said, closing his eyes, squeezing them tight, trying to force himself to relax, trying to lose himself as he had done so many times before, in Woody's scent, in the warmth of Woody's skin.

And just as desire began to once again build up inside him, Bobby felt his body grow slack with weariness, and muttering, "I love you," into the darkness, he finally drifted into sleep.

When Woody echoed the words right back at him, Bobby didn't hear, but even from that place where sleep had taken him, a tiny smile turned his lips.

Soon, both boys slept, neither seeing the figure standing in the shadows at the foot of the bed.

Neither knowing this was the last time they would ever hold each other and whisper those gentle words. But Bobby was right. Even had they known, it would have made no difference.

The figure standing at the foot of the bed knew this all too well. And the creature who was once a man, smiled now in the shadows, and when he did, the stench of his breath filled the tiny room with the odor of a charnel house.

THE MOON hung low in the western sky when Bobby opened his eyes. He could see it through the bedroom window, hanging there like a big fat movie prop, looking totally unreal, as if it were made of plasterboard and strung from a proscenium on a sound stage as a backdrop for some crummy second-rate horror flick. Something with werewolves, maybe, or vampires. It glowed faintly orange in the black sky. A moon like that was called a harvest moon, he remembered Woody's dad telling them once, although he couldn't remember when.

Bobby gently eased Woody's arm from across his chest and sat up on the edge of the bed, staring at that big orange moon through the open Batman curtains. As his gaze took in the immensity of that humongous moon, as if someone in God's production crew had screwed up and hung it too close to the earth, Bobby's mind began to see something else. Not a moon, but a face. Not the face he used to imagine seeing there as a little kid either. Not the face of the Lady in the Moon, sitting at her dresser mirror combing her long pale hair, admiring herself for hours as the moon slowly crested the sky and sank away to morning. The face he saw now was a living face. A face he knew. A wisp of white cloud against the dark sky surrounding it looked like long flowing hair, black but streaked with gray. Like his mother's hair.

With a little gasp of surprise, Bobby realized it *was* his mother's face he was staring at now. Familiar lines of care were firmly etched into her face from long years of sadness brought about by too many battles, too much drinking, too many hours of trying to hold herself together through one more day, one more bottle, one more fight. Bobby could see the emptiness in her eyes that always greeted him on the mornings when he awoke in that house. Those mornings were fewer and fewer now, since Woody's folks had welcomed him into their home. Lately his mother's eyes were always dulled by sickness. But there was shame to be found there too. Sometimes, in the depths of her illness, Bobby thought his mother was about to reach out to him, to stroke his cheek as she used to do when he was small, say a tender word. But then the shame got the better of her and she left the movement unfinished, finally turning away, blocking Bobby out. Then she would climb back down into that dark cavern of misery she had, for a moment, tried to pull herself out of.

It had been a long time since Bobby felt his mother's cool fingers caress his face or stroke his hair. And every day, he missed the feel of it. She had drunk away her love for him just as surely as she had drunk away her life, leaving nothing behind but the sagging outlines of a woman who longed for nothing more than the peaceful oblivion of death to ease her from her pain.

And from her all-consuming shame.

Her failure as a woman was echoed in her failure as a mother. The torment she endured because of it shone out in those weary lines etched so deeply into her face, and in the dead expression in those once happy eyes.

Bobby remembered a time, when he was small, when happiness could be found in that face. When her laughter rang out through the house. When those soft hands *did* caress his face, when words of love *did* leave those lips and direct themselves to him. But those days were long gone. Perhaps even his mother had forgotten them. Perhaps they lived only in Bobby's memory now, and if Willow Man took him, maybe they would not live even there any longer, but be lost forever. He supposed it wouldn't matter then. What mattered only to him would matter to no one else after he died. Hell, they mattered to no one else *now*.

Bobby knew the anger he always showed toward his mother and father when anyone mentioned them was just a defense mechanism he had perfected over the years to stem his own pain. In making others believe he didn't care, he could sometimes make himself believe it too. For a little while.

And in truth, Bobby felt very little love for his father. They had never been close. It was, Bobby knew, his father who had brought his mother down to the place she dwelt in today. His furies. His drunken rages. Oftentimes Bobby wished his father would die and leave them in peace. And this wish was not an act. He did wish it. Perhaps with his father gone, his mother could return to being the woman she once was. The *mother* she once was. But Bobby suspected, deep in his own heart, it was too late for even that. His mother was lost. To him. To everyone.

She had gone too far down the lonely road she now traveled to ever find her way back again.

So when Bobby rose from the bed and moved to the window, looking down into the yard that hovered at the edge of the canyon, and saw his mother standing there among the roses in the moonlight, gazing up at his face as he peered down from the window high above her head, he didn't think it strange to see her there. And he didn't think it strange when she raised her hand and silently beckoned him to come to her. Perhaps it was with one last hope of saving her from herself that he chose to go.

Bobby crept from the bedroom like a thief, holding his breath as he opened and closed the door behind him. Not wanting to wake Woody's parents. Not wanting to share this moment with anyone. Even Woody. If his mother had come to him in the darkness, it could only be because she wanted to plead with him to forgive her for the years of pain she had caused him. And Bobby *would* forgive her. He still loved her enough for that.

He stole through the house as silently as possible, not realizing he was still naked until he opened the back door and felt the cool night air wash across his genitals. But it was too late to worry about that now. His mother wouldn't care if he came to her naked. She would only care that he came.

The grass felt cool and damp beneath his bare feet as he crossed the yard to the figure of his mother, still standing there among the roses, dressed in a long flowing nightgown he had never seen her wear before. Although no wind moved the heavy heads of the roses at her waist, her hair seemed to billow out, continuously, framing her face in constantly flowing movement, beautiful to watch. Swirls of black and gray. Like the restless willow trees behind her.

"Mom?" Bobby said.

At the sound of his voice, she silently turned, moving away from him, gliding smoothly down the steep incline leading into the canyon. He heard no rocks beneath her feet. Heard no footfalls echo in the darkness. He thought, *how graceful she is*, as she slid away from him, entering that part of the canyon where no moonlight ever pierced. Down to where the darkness was always absolute. Down to where Willow Man lurked. Endlessly.

But Bobby's mind refused to dwell on Willow Man now. His thoughts were filled only with his mother. He followed her down the cliff face, his naked feet slipping on dirt and stones, causing little avalanches to precede him as he went. *I'm so clumsy*, he thought, remembering how his mother had traversed this very same path as silently as the passing of a cloud while he sounded like a herd of buffalo thundering down a mountainside.

Bobby watched as his mother approached the trees at the base of the canyon. Willows. Pepper trees. Eucalyptus. All rustling gently in that nonexistent wind that still lifted the hair around her head and fluttered the pale gown about her legs. But on Bobby's naked body he could not feel the air at all. Only the coolness of night touched his skin. Windless. His hair didn't move atop his head as hers did. It was as if he walked upon a different plane than she. And suddenly uneasiness settled into him.

When his mother reached the trees and stepped into the shadows, disappearing from view, Bobby called out, "Wait!" but she was already gone.

Uncertain now, tempted to go back, to run from this darkness that seemed suddenly to lie over him like a shroud, he called out once more into the shadows beneath the trees. "Mom?"

And he heard her laughter as he remembered hearing it as a child. A happy lilt of joyous sound, as pretty as tiny wind chimes tinkling in a breeze. He had heard that sound so many times when he was little that now a smile crossed his lips to hear it again.

And unthinking, he stepped into the shadows beneath the trees, into the darkest part of night, losing himself to the moonlight, seeking the laughter.

Seeking his mother's love. Just like the child he really was.

But in the seeking, Bobby found something else. And what he found, there in the shadows, *or what found him,* froze his heart in fear.

Hours later, when his pain had taken him to a place where he knew his life must surely soon end, he thought of his mother one last time, remembered the tinkling sound of her girlish laughter, and only then did he realize she had never been there at all. It had been *him* all along.

And as the creature atop him spread Bobby's bare legs wide and tore into him yet again with his vile, reeking cock, as Bobby felt the white heat of his own blood moving in rivulets across his thighs and felt something deep inside him tear apart like aged cloth, forcing a scream to his lips he was too weary and too weak to utter, Bobby understood at last the dark cavern of forgetfulness his mother constantly sought to find. He understood the darkness's lure. Understood its beauty.

Bobby's only surprise was it would be him who reached it first.

At the moment when his eyes closed gratefully in death, it was not his mother's face that Bobby saw, but Woody's. And even as the pain of everything the creature had done to him took all semblance of sanity away from him, and as he felt his limp, still body being borne high into the air in the grip of those cold, cruel hands he had learned to know so well in the last few hours, and even as he vaguely wondered, disconnected, why he was being lifted up so high from the ground, to where and for what purpose, Bobby still pulled the strength from his young heart to carry a smile to his torn face, remembering Woody, remembering everything he and Woody had meant to each other, before that black cavern of hopelessness, and silence, *and death,* surrounded him.

And when Bobby opened his eyes for the very first time on the other side of life and saw Willow Man there, waiting for him, stroking his foul, misshapen cock and eyeing him hungrily, Bobby knew he would find no peace even in death.

Woody, Bobby thought, as Willow Man leered his evil grin and came for him yet again. *Don't follow me here—*

WOODY DIDN'T open his eyes until a swath of morning sunlight had crept across the floor of his room, climbed up the side of the bed, and laid itself across his face. At first, in those quiet seconds when sleep turns to languid awareness, Woody thought it was the heat of Bobby's arm he felt against his cheek. But when he opened his eyes, he realized he was alone.

Bobby was gone.

Hearing a murmur of voices outside in the yard, he pulled himself from the bed and strode naked to the window, looking down. Cathy and the twins were there, sitting in the grass beside the roses, talking quietly to each other, but Bobby was not among them.

Woody quickly scooped up the clothes he had worn the day before from the floor and pulled them on, and as he did so, he saw Bobby's clothes still lying there in a tangled heap at the foot of the bed. He quietly pulled open his bedroom door and crept down the hall to peer into the bathroom. It was empty.

He could hear his mother and father speaking quietly from behind their bedroom door, moving around, dressing for the day. Carrying his shoes in his hand, Woody tiptoed past their door and checked out the living room and kitchen, wondering all the while where Bobby could have gone. Stark naked, he certainly couldn't have gone far, Woody thought. And then the first tingle of fear began to crawl across his scalp.

He warily pushed open the back door, trying to avoid the squeak of the hinges his father always meant to oil but never got around to, and with one footstep, Woody entered into the day that would torture him for the rest of his life.

Cathy and the twins looked over at him as he plopped down on the back steps and squeezed his feet into his sneakers. But it was Cathy alone, who saw the look of fear in Woody's eyes as he raised his head to gaze at them.

"What's wrong?" she asked. Her gaze traveled to the door he had just exited, then back to Woody's face. "Where's Bobby?"

"I don't know," Woody said. "He's gone. He must have left in the middle of the night."

"Maybe he went home," Chuck said, but not one of them believed it. It took an act of Congress and four guys with bazookas to get Bobby to go home. He hated going home, and every one of them knew it.

"He didn't take his clothes," Woody said, the first boilings of panic beginning to register in his voice, now that he heard his own thoughts spoken aloud. "Wherever he went, he's naked. Why would he do that?"

And as if the Great Puppeteer had just pulled each of their strings at the same time, they all turned to look down past the roses into the canyon.

"No," Jeremy said, as if suddenly hearing the thought that had entered each of their heads. "He wouldn't go down there by himself. He was the one who always warned us about staying together and never going down there alone. He wouldn't do it himself, would he? I mean, for Christ's sake, *would he,* Woody?"

"Is there an echo out here?" Chuck asked, trying for a little humor to mask his own fear and getting nothing back but disgusted looks from the others. "Would he, Woody? Would he, Woody?"

"Shut the hell up, peckerbrain. This is serious," Cathy said, then turned to Woody. "Are you sure he's not in the house? Maybe he was showering. Maybe—"

"No," Woody said. "He's gone."

"Then we have to find him," Jeremy said, a simple statement of fact every one of them knew was the truth, and once again their eyes slid toward the canyon, less frightening now in the light of day, but still a fearsome place inside their heads.

Woody knew in his heart they would find Bobby there. And he knew in his heart, already, that Bobby was in trouble. Somehow Willow Man had lured him out of the house in the middle of the night, lured him out of the house, and lured him down there, down to where Wilbur lay rotting in his shallow grave, where bats could come together like a wave of black water and dive-bomb innocent heads as their owners sat around a campfire eating peanuts and shooting the shit. Down to where, in the cool hours of nighttime, moonlight did not reach and darkness was as absolute as a mathematical equation. Down to where the malevolent power that had tormented them through all the days of this long, hot summer had taken up residence, and where it had first seen them, the children it chose to one day make its own.

Perhaps that day had finally come.

Woody realized he was trembling, but he managed to bury his fear somewhere deep inside the love he felt for Bobby. His determination to rescue Bobby from whatever horrors Willow Man had decided to inflict on his friend, his lover, was the sole thought inside Woody's head at that moment.

He ran a hand through his sleep-tousled hair and, with a look of grim determination plastered across his face, set out to do what he knew he had to do.

What they all knew they had to do.

Not one of them sought out weapons, sticks or stones or baseball bats, for this was a rescue mission, not a battle. And even if Willow Man was down there, perhaps holding Bobby in some sort of weird-ass ransom for God-knows-what, how would any sort of weapon help them? Willow Man's powers were so far beyond theirs that nothing short of a nuclear weapon would turn him away. And maybe even that wouldn't do it. He did, after all, live in a totally different world than they did. His world was the world of the dead. He only came here to visit. To taunt. And sometimes to kill.

Please, God, Woody thought, *don't let him be killing today. Not Bobby. Please, God, not Bobby. Not now. Not ever.*

Later, he would remember that prayer, and after this day he would never pray again.

They saw the first drops of blood on the big chunk of granite that covered Wilbur's shallow grave. Woody remembered how it had taken all of them, working together, to roll that rock into position in the hope of protecting the dog's small body from scavengers. Not so much for Wilbur, but for themselves. They had seen enough of the Pomeranian's tortured body to last them a lifetime. They didn't want to see it again. Twice was more than enough.

"It's blood," Jeremy whispered, then seeing the horrified look on Woody's face, quickly added, "but it could be from anything. A possum, maybe. Or a squirrel."

"It's Bobby's," Cathy said, and Woody nodded his head in agreement, knowing she was right, feeling his heart sink like a stone inside his chest.

Woody raised his voice to the trees and called out Bobby's name, and when he did, the echo of that one word seemed to reverberate back at him like a gunshot, then fall dead in the hot, still air. The silence around them was so profound each of them could hear the heartbeats of the others.

"Where are the birds?" Chuck breathed into the silence. "I don't hear any birds."

"Maybe they got scared off," Cathy breathed back at him.

"By what?"

Cathy merely shook her head. "I don't think I want to know." Her words were barely audible.

Woody stepped around the blood-spattered stone and approached the shadows beneath the trees, his friends following close behind, none of them wanting to find themselves alone in this eerie, unearthly silence. In her dread at what they might find, Cathy reached out and grasped Chuck's hand. Chuck's heart gave one tiny lurch of surprise before he wrapped his fingers around her small, cool hand, the hand he had dreamed so many times of holding, and together they followed Woody into the shaded part of the canyon where they knew Willow Man dwelt. Jeremy, needing an anchor of his own, laid his hand on Woody's shoulder, then reached behind him and took Cathy's other hand.

And thus bonded together into a whole, like one body with one fear and one great thundering heartbeat, they let the gloaming beneath the willow and pepper trees swallow them up.

A thousand thoughts raced through Woody's mind as he robotically placed one foot before the other, over and over again, as he moved farther into the depths of the canyon, leaving the sunlit glade behind, feeling the gloom of this place burrow into him like cold water seeping deep into sun-parched ground. Steeling his courage, his resolve, he thought of Bobby's voice whispering to him in the darkness of his room. Soft words of love. Words of commitment. He remembered Bobby's body shuddering at the moment when his seed spilled out of him, pressing his hips to Woody's face, grindingly eager yet always gentle. Woody was still stunned by the beauty of that moment when he first accepted everything Bobby offered him, longing for more, never wanting the moment to end. Loving the taste of Bobby's come. Loving the feel of Bobby's thrumming body trembling as the come exploded out of him. And later, as their thudding heartbeats calmed, he remembered Bobby telling him they should run away, leave everything behind, their families, their friends, Willow Man—everything. Run away and build another life for themselves far away from this place where the threat of separation seemed to be always hanging over their heads. Where the threat of death seemed to hang there too. Like a blade.

Woody realized now that Bobby had been right. They should have left. Bobby had understood the danger there better than Woody had. Bobby had seen Willow Man's true purpose more clearly than Woody ever imagined.

"Ask me again," Woody silently told the wavering image of Bobby's face that hovered in his mind. "Ask me again, and I'll go." But he knew it was too late. Bobby would never ask again.

Through vision dimmed by tears and darkness and dread, he saw more droplets of blood scattered across the ground in a place where the dry, summer-seared earth had been torn apart as if in battle. Dark scars of upturned dirt, like drag marks, were etched into the ground. And looking closer, he saw four tiny trenches, as if desperate fingers had torn through the earth, seeking a hold, being pulled away. Violently. Relentlessly. And in one of the tiny trenches he saw a glitter of white, and leaning closer in the gloaming light, made out the outline of a human fingernail, bloodied at the root, lying there like a seed neatly placed in a planter's furrow.

"Oh, God, no—" Woody whispered. And when Cathy and the twins bent down beside him to see what he was looking at, Woody felt the chill travel up each of their spines, felt the fear suddenly rampaging inside their heads as it had in his own.

Cathy turned away from that pitiful little piece of Bobby's body and bit down hard into the heel of her hand, trying to stifle a sob. The pain made her gasp, but it gave her strength too. It cooled the fear, replacing it with something else. Determination, first. Then anger.

The three boys jumped when she screamed out at the trees, at the shadows hanging over them like a heavy black blanket, so stiflingly hot even the air did not stir around them.

"Let him go, you son of a bitch! Pick on somebody else for a change! What the fuck is wrong with you? What the fuck do you think you're doing?"

And when nothing but silence echoed back at her, she screamed out again, this time even louder than before.

"Don't worry, Bobby! We're coming for you! Woody's here! Woody will make things right! Woody won't let anything happen to you!"

And suddenly she was crying, looking down again at that small splintered fingernail lying in the dirt. Imagining what it must have felt like to Bobby to have it torn from his body. Imagining the pain Bobby must have endured. The pain, perhaps, that he was still enduring at the hands of this creature. She knew as well as the rest of them what sort of animal they were dealing with. She, like them, had watched it kill without any compassion at all for the suffering it caused. The old librarian. The Asian kid. If Bobby was at its mercy now, then it was beyond any of their powers, she suddenly knew without a shred of doubt, to save him. Even Woody wouldn't be able to do anything. And Woody was the person Cathy looked up to more than anyone else in the world. Bobby she loved. The twins she put up with. But Woody was her rock. If Woody had no strength in this place, in this situation, then what hope was there for any of them?

She saw, through tears of anger and hopelessness, Woody staring at her as if he understood her thoughts. There was such a look of sadness on his face, the same sadness, the same hopelessness, she knew was on her own face, that she had to look away before the pain in his eyes crushed her into the ground like an ACME safe falling from the sky and flattening Wyle E. Coyote into the desert sand.

"Help me," Woody said, his voice that of a small child. "Help me find him." And as the words passed through his lips, a single tear glittered for a moment from his lash, then fell skittering down his cheek.

Chuck and Jeremy went to him then. Jeremy stroked his arm while Chuck rested a comforting hand on Woody's shoulder.

"We'll help you," they both said in unison. And Jeremy added, "If Bobby's here, we'll find him."

Cathy joined the circle of her three friends, missing the fourth, praying as Woody had prayed that he was all right, but knowing beyond all doubt if Bobby was here, then he was no longer among the living. The words she had screamed into the trees were for her own benefit, not his. She knew, even as she screamed them out, that Bobby wouldn't hear. Bobby was gone. As dead as Willow Man. All they could hope for was to bring his body home. Not back to the parents who didn't care for him. It was not for them she would do what she had to do. What they *all* had to do. She would do it for Woody. Without Bobby, Cathy knew, a little bit of Woody would die as well. And maybe not just a little bit. Maybe *all* of Woody would succumb to the grief of losing his best friend. And losing, Cathy suspected, even more than a friend. A lover, maybe, for she had seen the way they looked at each other, the way their hands sometimes brushed when they thought no one was watching. She didn't condemn them for it. She understood it completely, possibly even more than they did, for she carried in her child's body a woman's heart. And to a woman's heart, love is not a mystery at all.

She brushed the tear from Woody's cheek with her fingertip, and gripping his hand, turned to the trees they had not yet walked beneath. "Come on, then," she said. "Let's bring Bobby home."

Somewhere above the shadows that enveloped them, a summer sun was burning brightly, but its light did not pierce this dark place. On other days, when they had been in this part of the canyon, the light was dim, the canopy of treetops filtering it down to a gray twilight, but today, this early in the morning, with the sun barely over the horizon and shielded further still by the tall canyon walls, the darkness was almost complete.

As they passed a stand of scrub, its branches dead and lifeless, rattling like dried bones when they brushed against it, Chuck saw a tuft of brown hair dangling from a thorn. He reached out his hand to touch it, then drew back. When he opened his mouth to mention it, he found he couldn't speak the words, didn't *want* to speak the words, so he let the others pass it by without knowing. But by the tensing of Cathy's sweaty hand, once again resting in his, he knew she had seen it too.

In a hollow of ground, like some forest creature's lair scooped out of the earth after years of wallowing and lurking, they found the scattered bones of many small animals, as dead and lifeless as the scrub. In the midst of the bones, they saw a red collar and a small brass bell such as might have been hung by loving hands around the neck of someone's pampered cat. Unknowing, the children had stumbled upon the place where Willow Man had first tested his strength and honed his skills. This was where he had taken the small creatures he had hunted and killed as his powers began to grow, back at a time before he had set his sights on bigger game. It was in this hollowed-out spot of ground that Willow Man worried the bones of those first tiny victims, and where he had first seen the children who stood there now. And in the seeing, coveted. And lusted.

It was in that place his fascination with Woody and his friends truly began. It was there he brought the first of them to join him in death.

The children stood mute, stricken breathless by what they were seeing.

There was blood everywhere. Not the blood of the small slaughtered animals, their bones now as dry as old pencils in a forgotten pencil box, but *fresh* blood. It glistened in the few dapples of sunlight that filtered through the canopy of treetops overhead. It filled the hot, silent air with a feral stench, the stench of a battleground after the fighting has ended, where sundered bodies lay seeping their life's fluids into the battle-scarred earth. Where the echoes of dying screams are lifted by the wind and carried away to memory. In the oppressive silence of this dark, evil place, not even an insect hummed. The only sound to be heard was that of four trammeling heartbeats, galloping in fear inside four young chests.

And then in the silence, they did hear a sound. A gentle tapping, like water slowly dripping in the dead of night from a leaky faucet.

Their bodies unmoving, their feet nailed to the earth in fear and dread, the children swiveled their heads this way and that, eyes as bright as diamonds, seeking out the source of the sound. It seemed to come from everywhere. And nowhere.

When a droplet of blood spattered across the toe of Woody's sneaker, they all looked up, and there behind a tangle of branches above their heads, they saw Bobby's mangled body, wedged high against the trunk of a great willow tree like the prey of some big cat, carried there for safekeeping. One still arm hung downward, stripped of flesh, *flayed,* and from the fingertip of that fleshless hand, the blood was slowly gathering until the weight of each precious drop pulled it away, carrying it to the ground with that gentle tapping sound as it splattered onto the bed of small bones beneath it.

Bobby stared down at them through sightless eyes, so filled with the remnants of terror that Woody thought for a moment the boy still lived. But Bobby's wounds told him otherwise. His naked body was scored in a dozen places where strips of flesh had been peeled away. His mouth hung wide in a silent scream that in the stillness, Woody thought he could still hear echoing through the trees. On Bobby's face, still sweetly innocent even in death, circles of flesh had been bitten away, gouged out by gnawing teeth.

Woody turned away from the sight of that beautiful, battered face, pushed his mind away from everything he had just seen, and with an emptiness welling up in him already he would soon recognize as grief, he sought comfort in the living. He found it in Jeremy's eyes, no longer looking upward, but staring into Woody's eyes now, as Woody's stared back at his. They each sought comfort in the other. They each tried to push this ghastly reality back to the place where it belonged, back to the world of childish games and imagined horrors. Back to the place where Willow Man was just a figment of imagination to be dragged out for a few hours of amusement during the course of a long, dull summer when they could find nothing else to occupy their minds.

Even the events that had happened the day before, in the library, on the street outside McDonald's, they might have, with time, begun to think of as another part of the game. Unreal. Imagined. But now they knew beyond all doubt that it *was* real. Every moment of it.

And with that realization, their childhoods ended. The death of one of their own brought adulthood crashing down on them in the space of a second.

Death was no longer something to talk about in whispered voices around a campfire. It was here among them. Now.

Bobby had been the first in their little group to meet death head-on. In this stifling hot place that still reeked of blood and misery, the imagined echo of Bobby's screams still roared through the canyon like distant thunder inside their heads. Each of them standing beneath Bobby's twisted, bleeding body, naked, grotesquely splayed in the treetop high above their heads, obscenely tortured and lifeless but for the agony etched on his face, would be forever changed because of it.

Until lured there sixteen years later, not one of them would enter the canyon again.

LATER THAT night, after the long day was behind him, Woody would weep in his mother's arms for hours while his father stroked his hair and offered meaningless words of consolation, humorless for once, stricken numb by the pain so clearly written on his young son's face. It was a pain that echoed in his own heart too. Woody had been right in telling Bobby his parents would miss him if he left, for they were as brokenhearted as Woody at what had happened. Woody's mother, while almost insane with the anguish of finding a long-dead skeleton in the canyon a few weeks earlier, had now taken on the role of consoling mother to her grieving son. She buried her own sorrow and her own shock in the act of comforting him, and in doing so, she proved her strength to Woody at last. While before he had only seen a slightly neurotic but loving woman with a penchant for going off the deep end at every little crisis that popped up, but whom he loved with all his heart, he now saw a tower of unbending strength and a bottomless well of loving compassion. And as she comforted Woody, she comforted her husband as well. On this night, when death had reached out to touch them all, all roads in this house led only to her. She was the one both Woody and his father reached out to for solace when solace was most sorely needed, and Woody's love for his mother was multiplied many times over by the time this night ended. As an adult, when he thought of her, it was inevitably memories of this night that came first. The gentleness of her touch. The soothing kindness of her words as she attempted to ease a young boy's grief. And the strength to balm her husband's sorrow as certainly as Woody's own.

It was not until this night, the night after Bobby's death, as he lay on the sofa with his head in his mother's lap and felt her teardrops dampen his hair, felt her cool fingers stroke the nape of his neck as Bobby's had once done, that Woody came to understand which person held the true reins of power in his family. At a moment of crisis, such as this one, there was no hesitation at all, in either Woody or his dad, to relinquish those reins into his mother's hands. If she was crushed by Bobby's death, as Woody knew she surely was, she kept her own pain hidden long enough to assuage the pain of the men who meant the most to her. Woody. His father.

Later, she would weep into her pillow and scream out in silence at the injustice of it all, but for now, she held her emotions in check, gave of herself where she knew she was most needed, and Woody would never forget it.

The tiny enclave of police and press that had shown meager interest in the finding of a fleshless skeleton in the canyon, on this day had become a determined army, appalled by a child's mutilation, a child's rape. They were rabid to find the person or persons responsible, each and every one of them as shocked and as furious as if the child had been their own. The police spouted placating words to everyone involved, orating endlessly to the media, assuring the city they would find the murderer, and find him quickly, but Woody and his friends knew they never would. How could they? Their manhunt was centered in the wrong world. *This* world. The world of the living. Willow Man, they knew, did not reside here.

The children didn't tell the police all they knew about Bobby's death because they knew they would not be believed. They listened to the cops swaggering and boasting of their own prowess, nodded mutely at the reassurances offered them by all the grown-ups involved, then backed away, back into their own little worlds of grief, each of them knowing in their hearts Bobby's death would never be avenged and accepting that fact as best they could.

A week later, after the first storm of police activity began to wane and even San Diego's Finest began to suspect the culprit who had perpetrated this horrible crime might never be apprehended, the children came together one last time. Not in Woody's backyard or anywhere near the canyon, but in the city park, two miles away. There they sat by a man-made lagoon as evening shadows began to lengthen. Surrounded by ornate architecture and the smiling faces of a thousand grateful tourists (the heat wave had finally broken), they sat quietly on a park bench and watched the koi swim to and fro among the lily pads.

They were each of them still numbed by what had happened. They saw Bobby's mangled face a hundred times a day, but at night he was *always* there, the sound of his screams tearing them from their sleep.

Woody had slept less than any of them. He carried dark smudges beneath his eyes these days that never seemed to go away. Worried about him, his parents had even begun to speak of selling the house and moving to another part of the city, but Woody had pleaded with them not to. He wasn't sure why. Perhaps because Bobby's memory resided in that house. Abandoning the memory would be like abandoning everything he and Bobby had once shared.

Sometimes on those nights when sleep was farthest from him, Woody would stand at his bedroom window in the dark and look out at the moonlit canyon, remembering the games he had once played there with his friends. But it was the other thoughts that tortured him most. Thoughts of him and Bobby lying in each other's arms, breathless and happy after their physical needs were momentarily quieted, the taste of each other's passion still on their lips, speaking softly of their love for each other. Planning their futures. Planning their lives. Lives they would spend together.

Thoughts of Bobby's funeral, too, were always with Woody now, as he lay in the darkness in his lonely bed.

The closed white casket Woody's father had paid for. The faces of Bobby's parents, tearless, standing at the graveside watching the casket slowly sink into the ground, looking more uncomfortable than inconsolable, isolated by their shame, embarrassed, perhaps, that they could not afford to bury their own son. Woody's mother, remaining close to Woody through all that long day, her hand never once leaving his. His father's sadness. The plaintive music of the organ at the funeral home. The long line of cars wending its way to Cedar Lawns, with the hearse that carried Bobby's body clearing a path through the noontime city traffic.

Woody didn't speak a word that day to anyone. He could find no words to say. Nor did he weep. His tears had already been shed. His friends, too, like Bobby's parents, stood tearless at the edge of Bobby's grave and watched that gleaming white casket silently carry Bobby away from them for the last time, deep into the bowels of the earth where they hoped he would be safe, where, unlike them, they hoped he would truly sleep. Where maybe, just maybe, the miseries of his death might be finally forgotten.

In the park, Cathy's hand rested on Woody's as they silently watched the koi languidly swimming back and forth in the still water. The twins, one at either side of them, were as silent as the fish.

Finally, Woody spoke.

"Have any of you seen Willow Man since that day?"

"No," Cathy quietly said.

The twins shook their heads, muted by the sadness in Woody's voice.

Woody turned his weary eyes to each of them in turn, studying their faces, trying to sort out the thoughts ranging through his head, trying to make some sense of the doubts that had, over the past few days, begun to creep into his thinking.

"Did we imagine it?" he asked softly. "Was it just another game like the ones we used to play when we were little? Cops and robbers. Cowboys and Indians." As his words began to flow, he found it impossible to stop them. "Does Willow Man really exist, or did we make him up? Was Bobby killed by a ghost or by some weird sicko fuck from *this* world? In the library that day, was that woman really there? Did that boy really die on the sidewalk? Did we really see the things we thought we saw, or were we just playing at being afraid? Suddenly I can't understand anything that happened to us this summer.

It's like I dreamed it all. Is that what it was? Did I dream it? Did we all dream it?"

Jeremy was frightened by the look of emptiness he saw in Woody's eyes. They were those of a person teetering on the brink of insanity, he thought. The eyes of a person hanging by his fingertips on the fragile edge of reason. It tore at Jeremy's heart to see Woody this way, but he also knew Woody would have to somehow find a way to cope with the truth of it all. For that's what it was. Truth.

Cathy, too, was stunned by everything Woody said. How could he think it was all a game? Was that the only way he could find to deal with Bobby's murder? She knew now he had loved Bobby. They had *all* loved Bobby, of course, but Woody's love for Bobby was an adult love. A real love. She could see the loss of Bobby tearing at Woody like Willow Man's teeth and claws had torn at Bobby. Sorrow was eating Woody alive, but she could think of nothing to say that would ease his pain. Finally, she turned away from those weary, pleading eyes and looked down at her shoe tops, such sadness rushing through her she could only wonder why she didn't cry.

Chuck alone was truly angered by Woody's words. They had gone through an ordeal of fire, and now the leader of their little group suddenly seemed to think it was all a figment of their imaginations. Chuck spoke without thinking, as he usually did, but this time he knew his words made more sense than anything any of them had said all day. He had no knowledge of Woody's deep love for Bobby, had never suspected it, wouldn't have believed it if he had. What Woody was saying now, in Chuck's eyes, was tantamount to an act of treason. They had lost a battle, but the war was still being fought. Willow Man would be back. He didn't doubt it for a minute.

"What the hell is wrong with you, Woody? You act like you're the only one who lost a friend. How can you think we imagined all this shit? Bobby's not here, is he? Do you see him anywhere? No you don't, because he's laying six feet underground up on a hill in that fucking graveyard, and if we don't watch what the hell we're doing, one of these days the rest of us will be laying up there with him. Just a game we were playing? Bullshit! Willow Man's as real as we are. And he isn't finished yet. In fact, I think maybe he's just getting started! He'll come after one of us next, and what will you do then, Woody? Keep thinking it was all a dream? Will you just keep on thinking that until there isn't a frigging one of us left? Look around you. This world we're living in isn't the only one. There's another world out there, and if we don't watch our step, we're going to find ourselves in it. Just like Bobby. And let me tell you something else. We can't just keep hanging around, shooting the shit, and waiting for Willow Man to come after us. We have to do something. We have to take a stand!"

Chuck was shocked to see the glimmer of a smile cross Woody's face. "So it *was* all real," Woody quietly said.

"Yes, asshole, it was all fucking real!"

Cathy laid her fingers to Chuck's arm. "Chuck, cool it."

Chuck shook her off. "No! He has to understand! He has to *know!*" He faced Woody again, all but trembling in his rage, not understanding that glimpse of a smile on Woody's face and not caring that he didn't understand it. All he knew was it was really pissing him off. "What is it you think Bobby died of, Woody? You think he died of old age or something? Jesus Christ! You saw what that fucker did to him. Do you think a living man would do something like that? Well, okay, maybe there are some real twisted shits out there that might tear a kid to shreds, but that's not what happened here and you know it. Willow Man did it! No one else! He tried to grab us that day on the bike, or have you forgotten that too? He's been chasing us all summer, you stupid twit, and now that he finally caught one of us you want to rack it up to a figment of your imagination! If Bobby heard you saying that, he'd be doing flip-flops in his grave, and I wouldn't blame him one goddamn bit! What the hell are you smiling at?"

"I thought I was going crazy," Woody said. Suddenly there was more life in his eyes than had been there all week. "I really thought maybe I was going crazy. This kind of stuff happens in movies. It doesn't happen in real life. And even if it did, it wouldn't happen to normal kids like us."

"You're not normal! You're a fucking moron!" Chuck railed, flinging his arms through the air like a windmill. Then he clutched his chest and lowered his voice and said, "Jeez, I think I'm having a heart attack. I can't take all this excitement. I'm not built for it."

Woody laughed. He honest to God laughed. Chuck looked so shocked at the sound of it that Woody laughed again. Jeremy and Cathy simply sat on the sidelines and watched the two of them as if they were spectators at a show they didn't quite comprehend.

Then, before he knew it was coming, a flashback of Bobby's mangled body hanging in the treetop like some grotesque Christmas ornament erased the smile from Woody's face in a heartbeat.

Woody pulled his gaze from his friends' faces and watched the koi for a moment, glittering in the sun like the twins' braces. Then he looked around him. At the park. At the arboretum off to his right. At the art museum in front of him with huge banners flanking the front doors proclaiming the works of Monet on display there until August 25. Watched the tourists and the locals milling about. Leading their children. Walking their dogs. Living their lives.

Suddenly, Woody knew what it must feel like to be a magician on stage. To know all the tricks. To know how they worked. These people he saw going through the motions of enjoying a simple Sunday afternoon, heading to the zoo, heading to the hot dog stand, heading to wherever they thought they might wile away a few unpressured minutes of relaxation, were merely spectators in this world. Only he and his three friends sitting beside him now actually knew what lay beneath it all. Only they knew how the trick worked. Woody hoped none of these people would ever know the fear of being hunted, never know the horror of having a friend or a lover torn to pieces, never know what they saw in this world was only the icing on the cake. For in a place where sound did not carry and eyesight did not reach, where even imaginations could not delve, somewhere on the other side of life, true terrors lurked. They *did* exist. Woody knew that now. He supposed he had always known it. The horror in Bobby's empty, lifeless eyes had shown it to him.

And he knew, too, that he couldn't bear to see it again.

Beyond all doubt, he knew his friends sitting beside him now on this hard stone bench, feeling the California sun on their necks and listening to the monkeys in their cages, living out their own dull existences behind metal bars and concrete moats in the zoo a stone's throw away, were in danger this very moment because of him. Somewhere in this throng of strolling passersby, Willow Man watched and waited. Seeking an opportunity to make his presence known yet again. Who would he kill this time? Would it be another stranger, like the librarian, like the student? Would it be the mime performing antics beneath the palm tree over by the fountain? Would it be the lady smelling the hibiscus blossoms on the other side of the lagoon? Or would it be one of them?

"Woody?" Cathy said, stirring Woody's thoughts away from death and back to life. Her gaze was still troubled by the confusion she had sensed in him only moments before. But that confusion, she also sensed by the determined look on Woody's face now, had been abruptly resolved. "What are you thinking?"

"I'm thinking," Woody said, "that summer's over."

Jeremy alone knew immediately what Woody meant.

"You're thinking we shouldn't see each other again," Jeremy said. "You're thinking that since Willow Man is really after *you*, you're putting the *rest* of us in danger."

Woody saw such sadness there in Jeremy's eyes he had to turn away. Had to block it from his mind. From his heart. Had to *steel* his heart for what he had to say next.

But in the end, he knew he needn't say the words at all. Jeremy had said them for him.

Woody bent and picked up a small stone from the ground and chucked it into the lagoon, scattering the startled koi in a dozen different directions. *That's us,* he thought. *That's what* we *have to do. Scatter.*

And without saying another word to any of them, Woody stood and walked away.

CHAPTER SIXTEEN

"WE ALL knew why you did it," Jeremy said now, dressed again in the trousers and shirt he had worn to the concert, his bare feet, strong and tanned, propped up on the coffee table as he sipped at the cup of coffee Woody had poured for him, poured for *all* of them, since no one figured they would be getting any more sleep tonight anyway.

Dawn was still an hour or so away, and he and Woody were sitting in the living room, watching the black of night turn to silver gray outside the picture window by the piano. Music from the Met was playing softly on the hi-fi in the corner. "*Rigoletto*" Jeremy had said, unapologetic, as if he figured *everyone* listened to opera in the morning, and if they didn't, they damn well should.

"You deserted us because you thought it was the only way you could protect us from *him*."

Woody was sitting next to Jeremy on the sofa, his own naked feet tucked under him, wearing only a pair of khaki cargo pants that, like everything else he seemed to own, looked way too big for him. Jeremy was stroking Woody's bare shoulders as he spoke, and Chuck and Cathy were in the kitchen, trying to scrounge up enough food for a breakfast for four. Woody could hear Chuck grumbling about the lousy coffee and the goddamn faggoty music, and Cathy was telling him to shut the hell up before she stuffed his head down the garbage disposal.

Just another day in paradise, Woody thought, and inwardly he smiled to himself once again at the contentment he found having his old friends around him. Supporting him. Simply being there when he needed them most. The feel of Jeremy's warm hand on his back, massaging his neck, stroking his tense shoulders, gave Woody another sort of contentment, but it was tempered by the words Willow Man had spoken to him earlier. *"I'll take him from you, Woody. I'll take him from you—I'll take him from you—"* The words echoed in Woody's mind like a bad song, the kind you can't get out of your head but wish to God you could.

Jeremy hooked a finger under Woody's chin and dragged his face toward him, gazing deep into Woody's eyes to see, after everything that had happened tonight, what he might find there. What he saw didn't seem too bad. Woody looked tired, but Jeremy didn't think he would be needing an IV of antipsychotic meds or a massive regimen of therapy anytime soon. In fact, Woody seemed less wearied and stressed out than any of them. Jeremy suspected Woody was used to sleepless nights, and in that suspicion Jeremy was right.

"Will you be able to sing tonight? What time's your show?"

Woody gave him a gentle smile. Reassuring. "Same as last night. And don't worry. I could be up for a week and still do the show. In fact, I *have*. Just plug me in, pour a beer and a couple of diet Cokes down my throat, and the music comes out, doesn't matter what condition the body is in. What about you? Do you work today?"

Jeremy spread his arms wide, like Jesus pontificating to the masses. "What? And miss all this? Not on your life. Time to drag out one of those 'sick days' I keep accruing and never using. Cathy too. We're here until you throw us out."

Pushing all thoughts of work from his mind, Jeremy ran a light finger down the line of soft hair on Woody's stomach that trailed from his chest all the way down to his navel (and beyond), enjoying the feel of it. But it was the "beyond," and the memory of all he had discovered there only a few hours earlier, Jeremy couldn't shake from his mind. In fact, he would have happily burrowed his face into Woody's "beyond" right then if his brother and his best friend weren't still piddling around in the kitchen less than ten feet away. He was tempted to do it anyway when Woody brushed his hand along Jeremy's thigh, stirring the hair there, making goose bumps pop up along Jeremy's back and making the head of his cock poke up inside his trousers to see what was going on.

Woody saw the flash of hunger in Jeremy's eyes, and at the same time, he felt his own cock stir in anticipation. He grinned. "Two minds with a single thought," he said.

Jeremy lifted Woody's hand from his leg and pressed his lips to it. "You're not going to leave again, are you? You aren't gearing yourself up to do a reprise of what you did the last time we were all together, I hope. I mean, come on, Woody, that dramatic exit bit might work once, but it loses some of its oomph if you do it too much. So don't even think about it, okay? Don't think about it and don't do it."

Woody grinned. "You've loved me your whole life, and I've only been in love with you," he checked his watch, "for about three hours, and already you're giving orders?"

Jeremy blinked. "*What* did you say?"

"I said you've—"

"No. The last part. What was that last part?"

"About the orders?"

"No, asshole. The part about you loving me."

"Oh, that."

"Yeah, that."

Cathy squealed in victory from the kitchen like Marie Curie discovering radium. "A can of lasagna!"

And Chuck grumbling right back at her. "Who the hell eats canned lasagna?"

"Fine," Cathy snapped back. "Lay me some eggs and I'll make an omelet."

"I've got some eggs for you, baby."

"Shut the hell up and keep looking. And put that thing away before I throw it in a skillet."

"Kinky. So you like bratwurst, do you?" Chuck muttered.

"Looks more like a vienna sausage." Cathy giggled.

Chuck sounded mortally offended. "Jeez, babe, no need to be unkind. Give it a minute. It always rises to the occasion with the proper motivation."

"Well, motivate it yourself. I'm busy."

Cathy's giggle turned into a full-fledged laugh, then just as quickly turned into what was supposed to pass for a squeal of anger but didn't quite make it. "For God's sake, it's dripping! Put that thing away!"

Chuck sounded sincere when he said, "I'd rather not."

Woody turned to Jeremy. "I'm not sure I want to eat anything that comes out of that kitchen this morning."

"Fine," Jeremy said. "We won't. Let's go back to bed, and then you can tell me what I thought I heard you say a minute ago but now you're too chicken to say again."

Now it came right down to it, Woody wasn't sure he *could* say it again. Or even that he *should*. Once again the humor faded from his eyes.

"I'll take him from you, Woody—"

"Jeremy—"

Jeremy interrupted before Woody could even begin to find a way to put his feelings into words. "I know what you're afraid of. I know what he said to you. But I'll take my chances with our dickhead ghost if you will. We're not kids anymore. We're not helpless."

"We're not?" Woody asked, feeling that old familiar anger rising up in him yet again. "What sort of defense do you think we have? It's no different than it was when we were kids. We can't even see what's coming at us half the time."

"Well, he's not going to lure us into the canyon like he did Bobby. None of us are *that* stupid."

"Bobby wasn't stupid."

"I didn't mean that, Woody. You know that wasn't what I meant."

"I know."

Cathy stood in the doorway. "Got any bug killer?"

"Why?" Jeremy asked, tearing his gaze from Woody's face. "Have you finally decided to exterminate my nitwit brother?"

Even at four in the morning, Cathy was beautiful. She was wearing a ratty plaid bathrobe she had dug out of some closet or other, and Woody seemed to remember it belonging to his father maybe a couple of decades back. Her face was free of makeup, and she had her long red hair pulled back in a ponytail.

"No," she said in a little-girl voice. "I saw a roach."

Woody shrugged. "The house has been empty a long time. If there's a can of Raid lying around, it's probably as old as we are. Just ignore it. Maybe it will go away."

Cathy appeared hesitant. Uncomfortable. She did everything but shuffle her feet. "I don't know, Woody, it's pretty goddamn big."

And as if on cue, Chuck piped up from the kitchen, "There's *another* one! Christ, what is this? Wild Kingdom? The Discovery

Channel? Animal Planet?" They could all hear him do a little barefoot tap dance on the kitchen floor.

"Maybe there's a flyswatter someplace," Woody said.

Chuck stuck his head through the door. He was only wearing a snow-white pair of BVDs. As a child, modesty and shyness concerning his own body had always been big on Chuck's list of character traits, Woody reflected, but apparently it wasn't anymore. He had also always had a thing about bugs, and by the look on his face right now, that hadn't changed much at all.

"Flyswatter, hell! Get an elephant gun. These things are *huge*."

"Maybe they're hungry for bratwurst," Jeremy said, trying not to laugh at the mortified look on his brother's face.

Chuck's eyes narrowed, and his words came out in a seething whisper. "Don't just sit there. Do something."

"Fine," Woody said, rolling his eyes and shaking his head. "We'll do something."

With Jeremy at his heels, Woody followed Chuck and Cathy back into the kitchen. On the counter, he saw Cathy's can of lasagna, a jumbo-sized bag of potato chips, and a frozen pizza. Breakfast. Climbing up the counter *toward* their breakfast was the biggest cockroach Woody had ever seen in his life. Four inches long and as ugly as sin. Woody wouldn't have been surprised to see a can opener and a jar of bean dip in its paws, that's how goddamn big it was.

"Holy crap!" were the only words he could formulate in his surprise.

"Holy crap indeed!" Jeremy echoed at his back.

"Where's the other one?" Chuck asked, looking nervously around.

"Probably getting himself a beer. Or calling for takeout. The pickings are pretty slim," Cathy said.

Woody laughed. Looking around for a weapon, he finally settled on a saucepan sitting on the stove. He gripped it by the handle, crept up to the roach like a great white hunter closing in on a sleeping rhino, and smashed it flat with a resounding clatter that made everybody jump. Roach guts squirted across the cupboard door and the flattened body of the disgusting creature tumbled to the floor with an audible thud, its long hairy legs doing a death curl, even as it fell.

Woody thought maybe he might puke, but before he got around to it, Cathy shouted, "There's the other one!"

The second roach, as big and ugly as the first, was halfway up the refrigerator door, and as if it knew it was suddenly the center of attention, it scurried sideways and disappeared through the rubber seal that lined the door.

"Hope he's wearing ear muffs," Cathy said.

"Might want to see about having that door relined," Jeremy added.

Chuck was jubilant. "The cold will slow him down! I'll kill *this* fucker myself!"

In two strides he reached out and yanked open the refrigerator door. What happened next was so mind-numbingly unbelievable that none of them could take it in for a moment.

From inside what was once an almost empty refrigerator, save for a couple of beers and a tub of margarine, an avalanche of black roaches tumbled to the floor. Hundreds of them. Every one of them as big as a Maine lobster. As they hit the floor, they took off running. Across the floor. Along the baseboards. Up the cupboard doors. The sound they made was like a buzz of swarming bees, angry, boiling, sibilant, filling the air with a shriek of skittering noise that was almost electric, like a power line dancing in the wind, spraying sparks.

Cathy clapped her hands to her ears, then decided the hell with the noise and took off running into the living room, dragging a bellowing Chuck along behind her.

Woody felt a thousand tiny feet scurrying across his bare instep and kicked out, dislodging them, sending them flying in a dozen directions. He grabbed Jeremy's arm and practically hurled him through the kitchen doorway in front of him, then just as quickly slammed the kitchen door closed behind them.

Breathless, they all stood staring at each other, wondering whether to laugh or scream or barf or just get the hell out of the house before that avalanche of roaches battered down the kitchen door and came clattering after them.

Jeremy tore off his shirt and, dropping to his knees, stuffed it into the crack beneath the door.

Satisfied it was good and tight, he casually looked up at the others and said, "Maybe we should just eat out."

If there was any humor in the situation for Chuck, he was having a real hard time finding it. "Maybe we should just *get* out! What the hell are we doing here, smashing bugs and worrying about breakfast! Are we all nuts? Let's just go! Let's get the hell out of here before Willow Man comes back and has *us* for breakfast!"

"They're just bugs," Cathy said, trying to calm him, and maybe trying to calm herself as well, rubbing the goose bumps from her arms even as she spoke.

Chuck didn't buy it for a minute. He stood there with his hands on his hips, dragging his BVDs down almost to the point of impropriety and not giving a shit that he did, glaring at Cathy, then glaring at each of them in turn, like Woody's mom spotting grout in a shower stall and moving in for the kill.

"*Just bugs?* Do you honestly think those were just bugs? That was Willow Man playing another one of his stupid mind games! Cockroaches don't swarm! Cockroaches don't grow to be two fucking feet long! Cockroaches don't hang out in the refrigerator having snowball fights in the freezer and ice skating on the butter!" He aimed a trembling finger toward the picture window and the approaching dawn outside. "Our long dead friend, Bobby, stood in that canyon not more than two hours ago and told us to get the hell out of here while we could. So why are we still here? Someone please tell me. Why the fuck are we still here?"

Jeremy crossed the room and, clutching Chuck by the shoulders, gave his brother a little shake. "We're here for Woody," he said quietly. "And we're here for Bobby too. We're here because sixteen years ago, things were left unfinished, and now it's time to clear the slate. We've all lived with this hanging over our heads for too long. What we just saw in that kitchen isn't real. We all know that. It's just an illusion. One of Willow Man's illusions. And you're right. He's still playing his little mind games. But now is the time for it all to end."

"And exactly how do you intend to end it?" Chuck asked, noticeably calmer now but still rigid, still wide-eyed. "Exactly how are you—are *we*—going to *do* that, little brother? Enlighten me."

Jeremy smiled, knowing the tide had turned. Chuck was still one of them. Still a brother. Still a friend.

"Beats the hell out of me," Jeremy said with an exaggerated shrug. "But don't worry, we'll figure something out."

Chuck nodded as if he expected no other answer than the one he got. "That's what I thought. Oh well, as long as we're all agreed that we have no plan and none of us have the vaguest idea what the fuck we're doing, then I guess I'll stay. You'd all be toast without me anyway. But tell me, please, just what the hell are we *hoping* to do? What, exactly, is the impossible outcome we're hoping to achieve with this plan we don't have? Just so I know," he added lamely.

Woody stepped up and gave Chuck's cheek a gentle slap. "We're going to free Bobby from the fucker's clutches so he can rest in peace for the rest of eternity. Bobby, I mean, not the fucker. Then we're going to send Willow Man into a death that even *he* can't crawl back out of, and then Jeremy and I are going to get married and live happily ever after. You'll be best man at the ceremony. Later that same day, you'll marry the little redheaded bimbo here, and I'll be best man at *your* ceremony. That way we only have to rent our tuxes for one day. Simple enough for you?"

Chuck twisted his face into a wry grin and thought about it for a moment. "Works for me," he finally said, then headed for the bedroom to don some clothes, scratching his ass and mumbling along the way, "As long as I know—"

From behind, Jeremy pulled Woody into his arms and pressed his lips to the back of Woody's neck. "That's a *great* plan, babe! I love weddings. *And* honeymoons. *And* happily ever afters."

Cathy shook her head at the lot of them. *Men.*

WITH HER ear pressed nervously to the kitchen door, Cathy stood and listened.

"Hear anything?" Woody asked.

"Nope. I think they're gone."

"Well, good."

"Yeah. Roaches suck. Especially ones the size of hamsters."

Tucking back a long tendril of hair that had worked its way out of her ponytail, she faced Woody with a solemn look on her face. Tilting her head at Chuck's retreating backside, she said, "He'll be all right. Chuck gets overly dramatic at times, but he's not a coward."

"I know," Woody said. "It's just like when we were kids. He might rant and rave when he finds himself in a bad situation, but he always comes through in the clench." After a moment, Woody added. "I'm happy for you, Cath. And I'm happy for Chuck. I think he spent most of his thirteenth year pining for you. Got so I was sick of hearing about it." He laughed. "The funny part was he never thought you knew. Thought he was being all sneaky about it. Men are such nimrods, to coin one of your old phrases."

Cathy wrapped her arms around Woody and held him close. "I'm happy for you too. I think maybe you've been doing your own pining, and I think maybe it's been going on way too long. Bobby's death was difficult for all of us, Woody, but I know it hit you the hardest. Just like Chuck with me, Jeremy has always loved you. Maybe now we can all get down to the business of being happy. If we survive the night, that is."

"Do you think we should leave? Do you think we're biting off more than we can chew here?"

"No. I think Jeremy was absolutely right. We have to at least *try* to help Bobby. It breaks my heart to think of him out there right now. Wandering. Alone. Still in the grips of the bastard who murdered him. He's suffered long enough. *Too* long. The four of us have finally found happiness, or at least we're working on it. Now it's Bobby's turn."

"But *how*?" Woody asked. "How do we give it to him?"

"We burn it," Jeremy said, standing at the picture window with his back to the room, his strong naked back rigid as he stared out at the approaching dawn. His three simple words crashed into the room like a truckload of bricks. Woody and Cathy swiveled their heads to stare at him as he spoke again. "We burn the canyon and everything that's in it, right down to the ground."

Jeremy continued to gaze through the glass while his words echoed through the silent house. Over his shoulder, Woody could see a pink dawn lighting the sky at the edge of the horizon, coloring it in unbelievably beautiful colors, like a child's crayon drawing of what that child thought a sunrise was supposed to be but rarely was. Well, here it was. The most beautiful dawn Woody had ever seen. It was burning in the sky like fire.

Like a sign.

The echo of Jeremy's words tore his mind from the colors, from the beauty, dragging him back to the dark and the fear and the creature that pursued them all.

Jeremy spoke as if speaking to himself alone. "Willow Man draws his power from the shadows under the trees, or at least it always seemed like he did. If we burn down the trees, the willows and all the rest of them, he'll have nowhere to hide. Nowhere to rest. Nowhere to lie in the dark gnawing old bones and plotting out his little games."

Jeremy turned, facing them. His handsome blue eyes shone bright, his fists clenched into knots of sinew and bone at his sides. There was a tremor in his body, almost like the tremor that comes at the moment of climax, but this was the tremor of a different sort of excitement. The excitement of an *idea*. The excitement of a *plan*.

"My God," he said, as if the words he had spoken had come from another's lips rather than his own, as if the idea had come from another's mind, not his. "It might work. He would have nowhere to keep Bobby and all those other poor souls prisoner. You saw them. They wander endlessly there beneath the willows. Last night Bobby could barely tear himself from the shadows to speak to us. That's Willow Man's realm. That's where he rules. We can take it from him, guys. We can leave him homeless and wandering, like he left Bobby. Like he left all the others. And with the shadows gone, with their prison destroyed, maybe the others can leave too. Maybe they'll find themselves free to go where other dead people go. Where they're *supposed* to go. Heaven, hell, who knows? But at least they'll be free of *him*. They will—*progress*."

And beneath the brightness of Jeremy's eyes, a timid smile appeared. Weak at first, then growing, spreading out until it transformed his face into a thing of utter beauty, like the sky behind him. Jeremy's eyes sought Woody and burrowed into the love he saw on Woody's face, and into the confusion, too, seeking some sort of indication that Woody understood, that Woody *believed*.

"If we believe it, it will happen," Jeremy tried again, unsettled by the silence that thundered around him. And unsettled, too, by the fact Woody and Cathy were staring at him as if he'd just climbed off the bus from Crazyville with an aardvark on his shoulder. "It's all an illusion, remember?"

Cathy frowned. "Bobby's death was not an illusion."

"No," Jeremy said. "But maybe Willow Man's power is. Maybe there's something evil in the shadows beneath the willows that brings it to him. Maybe it's not Willow Man we're battling at all. Maybe it's that ancient evil that's always been there in that goddamn canyon. Maybe it's using him just like he's using us."

"You're talking out of your ass," Cathy said. "Willow Man was real. We saw his picture that day in the library back when we were thirteen years old. We know what he was in life before the plane crash, and we know what he is in death. If his power comes from the shadows, and we attempt to destroy the shadows, he'll try to stop us."

Jeremy nodded his head. "Of course he will!"

In the doorway behind them, Chuck was hopping on first one foot, then the other, pulling on a pair of socks. "Are you people nuts? You can't set fire to the canyon. You'll burn down half the city, not to mention Woody's house. We'll have so many lawsuits on our hands the ABA will make us honorary members. We'll spend the rest of our lives in prison, and the sort of sex they have in prison isn't exactly my cup of tea, if you know what I mean. It might be okay for *you* boys, but not me. Forget it. Think of something else."

Woody stood there considering everything the two brothers had said. Just like when they were kids, Chuck and Jeremy seemed to be opposite sides of the same coin. Even then they could never agree on anything, always taking opposing sides to every argument that popped up. But this time, Woody suspected, they were both right.

Like Jeremy said, Willow Man *did* always return to the canyon. He *did* always go back there, back to the shadows beneath the willows. That was his center. That was where he laid in wait, where he made his plans, and maybe Jeremy was right. Maybe that was where he renewed his strength, where his power truly blossomed. Why else would he keep Bobby and all the others there? Was it only in the umbra of those stifling, sepia shadows, where the sun did not penetrate and where even the endless wind that tore through the canyon never reached, that Willow Man could find the strength to maintain his hold on the people he had murdered?

And the bastard was just getting started. He had committed his first murder sixteen years ago, beginning, as far as they all knew, with the librarian, if you discounted the poor little yappy Pomeranian with the stake driven through its heart. First the librarian, then the student outside McDonald's, then Bobby. Since then he had taken how many others? Woody's parents, certainly. And Bobby's, too, probably. There must have been thirty souls in the canyon last night, and many of those were children, for they all knew that was where Willow Man's hunger truly drove him. How many more children would he kill if they left this place and turned their backs on Bobby and all the others? Willow Man was not mortal, which meant the killings could go on forever. They might *never* stop.

If they set a fire in the canyon, that endless wind would carry it all the way down to the ocean. Flames would sweep down the hillside like a screaming freight train, destroying everything in its path. Trees, wildlife, everything. Without the trees the shadows would be gone. And without the shadows—

But Chuck was right, too. The fire would not take only the trees and the wildlife, it would take many homes as well. At least it *might*. Woody wondered if that was a risk he was willing to take. How many children lived in those homes that abutted the canyon? How many of those children played in this canyon just like Woody and his friends had played in it when *they* were kids? *Does Willow Man watch them as he once watched us?* Woody asked himself. Was it only a matter of time before Willow Man reached out his disfigured hands and snatched them from life like he had snatched Bobby? Would those children one day find themselves endlessly pacing among the other lost souls that Woody and his friends had seen there the night before? Would those children have to relive their deaths over and over again, waiting for the man who killed them to once again pluck them from the crowd of lost souls and tear at their bodies a little more? Feed on them as he fed on them in life? Torturing them yet again, and again, and again—

Woody blinked, realizing Chuck's face was hovering there, only inches from his own. There was such an incredulous look in Chuck's eyes Woody almost laughed.

But Chuck wasn't laughing with him. "You're not seriously considering doing what my moronic brother suggested, are you? My God, you are!" He turned and grabbed Cathy by the shoulders, shaking her until they all heard the sound of rattling teeth. "Christ, honey, do something! Talk them out of it!"

"It might be the only way," Cathy quietly said.

Chuck jerked his hands from her shoulders like they were red hot. Then he laid his hands to the sides of his own head as if he had the world's biggest headache all of a sudden. "I don't believe this!" He whirled on Woody, clutching Woody's shoulders like he had clutched

Cathy's a moment before, shaking him until Woody's long hair tumbled over his eyes. "No one will believe why we did it! You know that, don't you? To them we'll be nothing but arsonists. And murderers, too, if the fire gets out of hand. Is that what you want? We all loved Bobby, but this—but this—Are you honestly willing to give up your own life to help someone who has already lost his own?"

And hearing that question, Woody understood it all as clearly as he had ever understood anything in his life.

"Yes," he said sadly. Sad for the desperate look on Chuck's face. And sad for other things too that might be lost. His music. His career. His friendships. And most of all, his future with Jeremy. But at that moment, all Woody could truly see in his mind's eye were the horrible wounds on Bobby's once-beautiful body, and the lost look on Bobby's mutilated face in that unearthly light as he stood before them in the canyon only a few hours before, telling them to leave, telling them to save themselves. Telling Woody to accept Jeremy's love and to live his life as best he could. Telling him, in so many words, to forget everything he and Bobby had shared sixteen years earlier, and *that*, friends and neighbors, ladies and germs, was something Woody knew he would *never* be able to do, no matter *what* happened.

"Yes," Woody said again. "I'm willing to do that. I'll give up *everything* to save Bobby from one more minute of suffering. I have to, Chuck. I won't be able to live with myself if I don't."

Chuck mutely nodded, as if he'd expected nothing else, and releasing Woody, he turned to his brother and asked, "What about you?"

Jeremy shied away from his twin's accusing look and stared back out through the window to the ever-nearing dawn. "I can't see any other way, bro. Willow Man has to be stopped. But whatever Woody decides, I'm with him one hundred percent."

"So am I," Cathy said. "Help us, Chuck, please. Bobby was your friend too. But even *more* than Bobby, think about all those kids out there Willow Man is watching right now. He'll take them, Chuck. If we don't stop him, he'll take them all, one by one. You know he will."

Peering into Cathy's eyes, Chuck's face softened. The lines of panic in his forehead smoothed themselves out as if by magic. What was a frown of desperate anger and despair slowly twisted itself into a pathetic little self-deprecating smile that seemed to amuse Chuck as much as it heartened Cathy.

"I never could say no to you." He smiled.

And Cathy nodded. "Not since we were kids."

"It would surprise the hell out of you if I said no to you now, wouldn't it?"

"You bet."

"Well—then I guess I won't."

"So you'll help us?"

"I suppose I will. But I don't like it."

Jeremy came across the room in two long strides and ruffled his brother's thinning hair, so like his own he might have been standing in front of a mirror. "None of us like it, Chuck. But we have to try *something*. If it doesn't work and we don't end up dead or in prison, we'll try something else."

Chuck shook his head. "I can't believe people actually pay you to manage their money. You can't even map out a simple ghost-killing strategy without turning it into a felony. I must be insane."

"You are."

"So-o-o—" Chuck said, glancing around at nothing in particular and heaving a long, interminable sigh, finally settling his gaze on Woody's face and wondering for a moment at the glistening of tears in Woody's eyes. "Who's got a match?"

THE CANYON was as dry as they remembered it as children, perhaps even dryer, for the coast had seen very little rain the previous winter. In the headlines only yesterday, as Woody sat outside the coffee shop on Juniper Street being fawned over by the fruit cup waiter and sipping his six-dollar cup of cappuccino, he had read of the mayor's pleading for water conservation, dangling the threat of water rationing once again over the populace's heads. Even restaurants were refusing to serve water with a meal unless it was expressly asked for, which, in Woody's mind, was the very pinnacle of inanity considering the fact that untold thousands, hell, *tens* of thousands, of San Diego citizens were gaily watering their lawns every morning.

Looking around, Woody could see the dry winter and the burning hot summer had combined to make the canyon a tinderbox. The morning sun, not yet over the horizon, afforded them just enough light to walk by but not enough to truly identify the parched and brittle flora crunching beneath their feet. The terrain, however, was as familiar to them as it had been when they'd played there a decade and a half before. Some things, it seemed, were never really lost to memory, no matter how young the mind was that first absorbed them.

Once again, they followed Woody's lead. Sixteen years ago, it would have been Bobby forging the path, taking command, but now the job fell squarely on Woody's shoulders, and the others seemed grateful to follow him, wherever they ended up. Each of them knew Woody was not only leading them through the canyon, but he was leading them toward whatever remained of the rest of their lives. How they would spend it. How happily, or how unhappily, they would be in living it. What they were about to do was indeed a crime, especially here, in Southern California, where brushfires took homes every single year, and since many of those brushfires were started at the whim of arsonists, it was a crime harshly punished by the law. But what was arson compared to murder, and how many children might be spared Bobby's fate if Willow Man could be driven from this place? Perhaps the authorities would never believe why they had done what they did, but they themselves would know, and that would have to be enough.

But more than those faceless yet-to-be-murdered children, it was Bobby they truly wanted to help. They had known him in life. Known of his goodness. They had, each in their own way, loved him, Woody most of all. But what they had seen last night on this very spot, what had stepped from the shadows and spoken to them, was only a sad remnant of the boy they once knew; the last dregs of a young life cut short by the cruel creature who died in this place thirty years ago and dwelt here still. And that creature did not merely survive here, it was growing, its malevolent powers becoming greater with every passing season.

Standing in the glade with the willow trees looming ahead of them in the grayness of approaching dawn, Woody could sense the evil festering there in the shadows beneath the great flowing trees, with their long slender leaves whipping about their heads like prairie grass in the hot, never-ending wind that tore through the canyon day in and day out. Where did that wind come from, Woody wondered? And where did it end? Did this great rent in the earth act as a wind tunnel, sucking the sun-heated air from the world of men who lived in the sunlight along its verge? Did the wind flow through this place until it reached the ocean and then dissipate in the vast empty spaces of water and sky, or did it carry its evil onward, touching other shores, dragging its malevolence along with it to infest other lives, other cultures? Was the evil centered here alone, or did it spread out its arms from this one place, carried by the wind, to deliver its misery to faraway locations Woody could not even imagine?

But it was not the wind, Woody knew, they had come here to battle. It was Willow Man. Yet maybe, just maybe, the wind would help them in their fight, driving their cleansing fire into every crevice, around every turning of the canyon's winding path, reducing the willows to ash and embers and freeing the shadows that lingered beneath them. And in freeing the shadows, freeing the souls that lingered there as well. Freeing Bobby. Freeing Woody's parents. Freeing the nameless child Cathy had seen looking so lost, seeking, forever seeking, for the world he once knew, the faces he once loved and who once loved him. Would those restless, tortured souls move on to their rightful places once the shadows that bound them were opened up to the wide California sky? Woody could only hope so. Perhaps, even when it was all over, he would never really know, but still he had to try.

For that child.

For Bobby.

And for the living, too, the yet unmurdered. And for Jeremy, Chuck, Cathy. And himself. Like Bobby, they had all lived in torment long enough. As Jeremy had said, the time to end it was now.

At the edge of the shadows, in the deepest part of the canyon where the willow trees began, where to Woody's ears, in Woody's imagination, the rustle of their leafy heads seemed to fill the air with the sounds of a restless, sleeping giant, tossing and turning in his bed, Jeremy laid a hand on his shoulder and quietly said, "Woody, stop."

Woody tilted his head to lay his cheek on the hand that touched him, feeling once again the warmth of it, the gentle strength. Then he turned and smiled as Jeremy's arms surrounded him, pulling him close, whispering into his ear the very words Woody most needed to hear.

"Whatever happens, this is the right thing to do. I know it is. We *all* know it is. And we'll see it through with you to the end, no matter what that end might be. Just answer one question first."

"What is it?" Woody whispered back, already knowing.

"Do you honestly love me?"

And Woody's words met Jeremy's on the edge of that awful darkness without a heartbeat of hesitation. "Yes. Help me do what I have to do, and I'll spend the rest of my life proving it to you. We can make it work if we try. I know we can. But not while Willow Man still exists in this world. He'll never give us a moment's peace, Jeremy. You know he won't. And he'll make good on his promise. Sooner or later, he'll take you from me."

Woody burrowed his face into Jeremy's broad chest and listened for a moment to the heartbeat racing deep inside, ignoring the uncomfortable silences coming from Chuck and Cathy, not caring that they heard every word he spoke. "I can't let Willow Man do that to me again, Jeremy. I've lived too long without love in my life. I won't let him take it from me now."

Chuck cleared his throat. "If we're going to do this, guys, we'd better get started. The sun will be up soon, and frankly, if we're going to set fire to the city, I'd like to do it with as few living witnesses as possible."

Woody gently pushed himself from Jeremy's embrace, and turning, he faced the gathering of shadows that hovered there in front of them. It was like a silent wall of darkness, those shadows. Soundless. Seemingly solid, seemingly impenetrable.

"Don't hem and haw around," Woody said to himself. "Just do it." And taking Jeremy's hand for courage, he strode fearlessly into the very depths of the darkness. He could hear the footsteps of his friends following close behind, and in the space of a moment, the light of the coming dawn was little more than memory. The lightless gloom of Willow Man's realm settled around them with a hush, deadening all sound of wind and morning, all scent of sage and dew, all song of bird and insect. As the shadows closed over them, it seemed everything good and clean in the world had been stripped away, plunging them into the very maw of despair. *Evil Central*, Woody thought, feeling the darkness engulf him. *This is the place where all pain is born.*

It was there that Willow Man dwelt, and Woody knew, suddenly and beyond all doubt, the creature was there with them now. Waiting. Knowing they were coming. Just as eager to finish the game as they were.

Suddenly the still air reeked a foul stench, as if Death itself had stepped into the shadows with them. They were not surprised when a harsh, rasping whisper greeted them from the darkness.

"Welcome to my humble abode, you little shits."

THE VOICE seemed to come at them from every direction. But it was not the voice of Willow Man that greeted them. It was the voice of Woody's father. Woody recognized it in an instant, and turning, saw his father standing by the twisted trunk of a tall willow. His father's face, lit by that blue ethereal light they had seen the night before, was as gnarled by time and misery as the skin of the ancient willow. He was ravaged still with the wounds that had torn him from life, the same wounds Woody had seen in his dad's grocery store on the day the policeman asked Woody to identify the body.

And again, when the ghost of his father opened his torn lips to speak, the stench of death and corruption spilled out, tainting the air, pervading the gloom around them. Cathy coughed and turned away from the sickening smell, but Woody continued to sadly stare at the man who had once been his father. His heart was so overwhelmed with grief and pity that the stench, which flowed from those sweetly remembered lips, did not reach him, did not even register in his mind. He saw only the blood still seeping from decade-old wounds. Saw only the pain still lingering there on his father's face, as if, even now, his father felt the bite of the blade that had sliced into him, over and over again.

"Dad—"

The voice that was once his father's was now like the cold hard clattering of stones in a tin bucket. Metallic. Toneless. Raw. "What are you doing, son? What is it you think you're doing?"

"We've come to free you," Woody said, swallowing his grief, fighting back the tears, trying to block the memories from his mind of the happy hours he had once spent with this man. Steering the car while his dad worked the pedals. Playing stickball on the street. Listening to the old man's ribald jokes at the dinner table while his mother looked on, tsking at the language his father used, trying not to laugh herself, hiding her smile behind her napkin.

His father sadly shook his head. Accusing. Bewildered. "We've been hurt enough, your mother and me. Don't hurt us anymore, son."

Woody unclenched his jaw and tried to slacken his stance. "Relax," he told himself. But his heartbeat thudded like an overworked engine inside his chest, his pulse pounded in his head, and he felt the first icy droplets of sweat slide down his ribcage. *What the hell was he doing?* The trash bag in his hand, which he had packed earlier with gasoline-drenched rags, seemed suddenly too heavy to hold, and he dropped it to the ground. Jeremy, standing beside him, immediately snatched it up and clutched it to his chest like a father cradling a child.

"That's not your dad," Jeremy said. "It's him. Don't get sidetracked, Woody. You know what we came here to do."

"No—"

The figure took a step toward them and reached out two withered hands. Dead branches on a dying tree. They could hear the crackle of tendonless bones snapping and popping like twigs crunching underfoot as the fingers groped the empty air, reaching out for Woody, beseeching, imploring, but then one hand veered away from Woody's startled face and pointed an accusing finger at Jeremy, who took a step backward when he saw it aimed in his direction.

The voice spat out venom like a viper. "You keep your mouth shut, you cornholing little bastard! Fucking my son in my very house! Sucking away at his cock like a great slobbering pervert! How was it? Did his ass taste sweet when you flipped him over and plumbed it with your tongue? Did it taste like candy or last week's caca? Was it tight enough for you? Did it fit your seeping cock like a glove, or was it as loose as a fucking coat sleeve? How was it? Answer me!"

Jeremy narrowed his eyes and spat words right back at that evil, accusing face. "It was beautiful, you twisted piece of mindless toe jam!"

And the creature that Woody knew now was *not* his father threw back its head and howled with laughter. The stench in the air grew so heavy, so fetid, that all four of them staggered backward as if slapped in the face. As Willow Man roared out his maniacal laugh, past the parted lips that looked like Woody's father's but were not, they could see something moving, like a great green snake. It twisted and coiled there in the putrid darkness, and Woody remembered the bus driver on that long-ago day in the city, snatching the bus transfer from his hand with a long green tongue, like a lizard. Like a fucking lizard.

The laughter ended as quickly as it began. The creature with Woody's father's face suddenly pouted like a child. It turned its great rolling eyes back to Woody, and as it did so, it puckered out its swollen, bloodied lips until the decade-old wounds on its face tore even wider with a sound like rotting cloth being pulled apart. New blood flowed across the creature's chin, onto the filthy, mildewed shirt it wore, splattering the ground at the creature's feet. As the droplets hit the ground, they skittered off like frightened bugs, each and every one of them a living entity.

"Jesus, son! Getting fucked in the ass without a condom? What the hell is wrong with you? Don't look so surprised. I was there, you know. Saw it all right down to the last gasp. Nasty old Mr. AIDS might be gnawing his way up your colon right now! Chomping away, happy as a clam. Christ, boy, this time next year you might be looking even worse than I do! What do you have to say about that?"

Woody shook his head. "I say you're not my father."

And the creature roared out in laughter again, and as it did, they could all hear the sound of watery bowels spewing forth a stream of vile excrement. What had been a stench before, now became a miasma of such mind-numbing filth that the four of them closed their eyes against the reek of it.

"Why, damn, boy, I guess you're not as dumb as you look. Fucking A ditty-bag *right* I'm not your father! He's rotting with the other corpses back in the trees. Wanna see him? Wanna see how he really looks these days? How about your dear sweet momma? She's back there too. Still sucking your old man's wienie too. Gads, I don't know how she does it without puking her guts out. He's way beyond the point where Dial and a little deodorant will help, if you get my drift. I mean, that fucker *stinks!* Of course, your old lady's not much better. Wanna see 'em?"

"No," Woody said, amazed at his own calmness. Amazed he still had a voice. "I just want to see you die."

The creature blinked. Innocent as a baby. "Sorry, kid. Been there. Done that. What else you got?"

Grabbing the bag of gasoline-soaked rags from his brother's hands, Chuck stepped forward and placed himself between Woody and the creature, holding the bag out in front of him like a talisman. "We've got *fire*, you miserable murdering shit, and we're going to burn your little castle of death right down to the ground!"

Willow Man settled his gaze on Chuck for the first time, scanning his long frame from head to toe before speaking. He seemed to like what he saw. "So you're the straight one," the creature grinned. "The only pussy poker in the whole damn bunch, huh? Castle of death? Pretty poetic for a straight dude. You sure you don't like a taste of the old wanger once in a while yourself? Don't tell me you haven't thought about it. Don't tell me the thought of dropping to your knees in front of old Woody here or having Woody drop to his knees in front of you hasn't once entered your mind."

"*Shut up!*"

The creature spat up a gurgling chuckle. "Oops. I seem to have hit a nerve. Well, maybe before the day is done, I'll break you in myself. Give you what you've always wanted. How would you like that? I'm not prejudiced. I don't mind plowing a straight furrow now and then. Straight guys always squeal so much louder than queers. That's 'cause they like it more. Seeing as how it's happening *behind* them, they don't think they're actually *involved*, so they really let themselves go. You understand what I'm saying? Oh, yeah. I can see it in your eyes. You understand."

Chuck was trembling with anger, but trying not to show it. He cocked his head to the side and stared back at the creature with wide, hate-filled eyes. "Don't you think I'm a little old for you? You like kids, don't you? That's your *thing*, isn't it? Hurting people that are too little to fight back?"

"Like Bobby, you mean? He wasn't so little, believe me. Ask Woody. He knows. That boy had a beautiful, long cock on him, he truly did. Thick and succulent. Yummy. Woody knows. He tasted it himself every chance he got. You should have heard the kid scream when I tore it off. Gnawed that fucker right off at the root with little Bobby flailing and screaming beneath me. Blood shooting everywhere. Phew! What a head trip! Get it? *Head* trip?"

Woody felt his heart plummet inside his chest, once again thinking of the misery Bobby endured at the hands of this—*thing*.

Willow Man seemed to sense Woody's thoughts and, turning his evil, grinning face back to his, reached out a hand once again, fleshless and groping, aflame with that blue ectoplasmic light that flashed a little brighter with every movement the creature made. Like a welder's sparks.

"Come with me, Woody. Come with me, and I'll let the others go. Otherwise none of you will ever leave this place alive. I'll torture them, Woody. I'll torture them all forever. You know I will. You don't want that. All you want is to be with Bobby. And he wants that too. He's waiting for you just inside the trees. Come with me. Come with me now."

Woody hesitated, looking past the creature, hoping to see Bobby's face staring back at him from the darkness, but he saw only shadow. Heard only silence. And if he were to see Bobby there in that endless night beneath the looming willows, he knew it would only be a vision, a memory. A *wish*.

"Bobby's dead," Woody finally said, turning his attention back to the present, back to Willow Man's face, grinning now at the hesitation it saw in Woody's own.

"Not while he's with me," the creature said. "No one is ever truly dead when they're with me. You should know that by now. I can give him back to you, Woody. You know that's what you've always wanted. Give yourself to me, and I'll give Bobby back to you. What's left of him, anyway. I'm offering you a one-time deal. Take it or leave it."

Again Woody hesitated. For one horrible moment, he thought, *Yes, I can do that*—

But Cathy had heard enough. Seeing the faltering look in Woody's eyes, and knowing he was weakening, she stepped firmly forward and snatched the bag of rags from Chuck's hands.

"The time for talk is over," she flatly stated, her voice as cold as a winter gale, her jaw firmly set, her mind made up. "I don't want to hear any more bullshit from any of you! Let's just end this now!"

And pulling out a cigarette lighter she had swiped from Woody back at the house, she tore open the bag and began flinging the gasoline-soaked rags in every direction, blinking back tears from the fumes, her hands shaking with anger but still determined, still doing what needed to be done. When the trash bag was empty, she tossed it aside, and holding the last gas-soaked rag in her left hand, with her right she pressed her trembling thumb to the lighter and a tiny flame of true light pierced the unearthly darkness that surrounded them. The sharp flame almost blinded them all.

Willow Man's eyes opened wide when that tiny flame burst into life. He raised his hands to block it from his sight, as if the pain of it pierced his head like a knife. Bellowing in outrage, he struck Cathy across the face with one of those snapping, fleshless hands, and Cathy crumbled to the ground as if the world had suddenly fallen out from under her feet. As she did so, the lighter went tumbling off into the underbrush, its flame extinguished.

Chuck cried out, "*No!*" and flung himself at Willow Man, wrapping his hands around the cold, lifeless neck of what no longer looked like Woody's father, but looked now like the postman they had seen at the library sixteen years earlier. Like the crazy fucking dancing dude they had seen outside McDonald's when they were thirteen years old. Like the insane bus driver with the lizard's tongue and the spiffy little busman's uniform, all ironed neat as a pin with razor sharp creases in the pants and perky little shirt cuffs reaching down to those diseased fingertips laden with what they had once thought to be fungus, but what Chuck knew now was nothing but rot. Rotten flesh on a long-dead body. Just as it was supposed to be.

Willow Man roared in fury at the feel of Chuck's fingers digging into the age-old wound on his throat where that sliver of metal had torn into him as the plane plummeted to earth so long ago. In his anger, the creature lifted Chuck's flailing body high into the air and flung him away like a doll. Chuck screamed until the trunk of a willow knocked the air from his lungs. He slid to the ground, moaning, clutching his chest.

Through his pain he suddenly felt another's hand inside his own, and opening his eyes, Chuck saw Bobby bending over him. The true Bobby. His wounds gone. His face as flawless and handsome as it was at thirteen.

"Run," Bobby whispered, then raising his voice, he yelled out to all of them, "*Run!*"

Woody stood rooted to the ground, staring at Bobby, so beautiful again, so undamaged, so *whole*, but then he caught movement in the shadows behind Bobby, and he gasped to see his mother standing there. Her face, too, was as sweetly perfect as he remembered it the last time he had seen her in life. She smiled at him now and made that little shooing motion he remembered her making with her fingertips when he was a child, trying to get him out from underfoot, telling him to scoot, telling him to go outside and play. She had things to do.

As Woody gasped at the memory, he saw Cathy shaking herself awake beside him, preparing to run, preparing to flee this place as Bobby wanted them to do. Seeing Cathy was okay, Jeremy pulled his brother to his feet, then spun toward Woody and clutched his arm. With Cathy helping him, he dragged Woody and Chuck back the way they had come, wanting nothing more than to scramble back to where the morning sun was lighting the world, back to the place where light reigned instead of darkness, where clean healthy air would fill their lungs instead of filth.

But they all stopped dead in their tracks, Willow Man included, when they saw the young boy, the boy they had seen wandering aimlessly and sadly through the trees the night before, the boy they didn't know, step from the shadows and pick up the cigarette lighter Cathy had dropped in the bushes.

Still naked, as he undoubtedly was at the moment of his death, he stood before them clutching the lighter. His injuries were gone, his eyes no longer empty, but innocent, as a child's should be. With a tiny smile twisting the corners of his boyish mouth, he awkwardly flicked the lighter into flame and, bending down, carried the flame to the one remaining gasoline-soaked rag lying at his feet.

With a *whoosh!* the rag ignited, lighting the boy's face. The flames pushed back the shadows that surrounded him, and from the trees, Woody saw other figures emerge. Suddenly they were all there, all the ones Woody and his friends had seen the night before. The ones held captive in this terrible place: Bobby's parents and unnamed strangers, and there among them, Woody's true father as well, alongside his mother. They all stepped forward into the light. Each of them carried one of the rags Cathy had flung about earlier, and holding them over the flames, they ignited each and every one of them, and when the rags were burning brightly in their hands, they tossed them into the trees in a dozen different directions.

The acrid smell of burning gasoline filled the air and the darkness was quickly replaced by smoke. As the flames of those countless burning rags ate into the underbrush, the flames grew stronger, reached higher, until the shaggy plumes of the very willows themselves burst into bright orange fire above their heads.

As the trees twisted and groaned in the flames, Willow Man screamed out his fury from the very midst of the inferno. His clothing, as rotten as his heart, burst into fiery flowers so quickly he didn't realize he was on fire until the flame touched his precious skin. It gnawed into him just as he had gnawed into the flesh of those standing around him, his victims, watching, smiling, feeling no pain from the fire themselves, only a great cleansing as pure morning sunlight began to filter in through the ravaged treetops. It was a sight so lovely they stood motionless among the flames, gazing up at it in wonder.

But soon even the sunlight was hidden behind the thick plumes of smoke that now filled the canyon. As Woody watched, he saw the bodies of his parents and all the other nameless victims begin to fade. Like smoke themselves, they dissipated into the air in wispy tendrils of mist. Woody heard what sounded like a gentle, contented sigh as they disappeared completely into the haze.

Bobby's was the last face Woody saw, smiling sweetly at him through the flames, before he faded away like all the others.

Soon there was no one left standing but Willow Man himself, screaming and doing a macabre little dance of pain, writhing in agony as the flames seared his flesh and his clothing drifted down in fiery tatters to smolder at his feet.

Before Woody could say good-bye to Bobby one last time, Jeremy tore him away. Frantically, Jeremy pushed Woody away from the wall of fire rising up before them, and together, the four of them fled the place where death had ruled so long. As they ran along the path back toward the house, back toward the *world*, they heard a long anguished cry of misery echo from the canyon walls around them. Willow Man. Screaming out his tortured death, just as his victims had once screamed out theirs.

Soon, even that screaming wail of outrage and anguish was lost to the ear, replaced by the thundering roar of windswept flames, as the canyon erupted into a great tunnel of fire. And quickly, very quickly, that tunnel of fire forged a path of destruction through the very heart of the city.

But the wind that fed the fire and swept it along between the winding canyon walls also kept it low to the ground. Nothing survived that lay before the flames, but those flames did not climb to the crest of the canyon. They did not work their burning tendrils into the homes standing above them, defenseless. The fire, contained by those steep stone walls and herded by that endless screaming wind, moved with the speed of a galloping horse. It tore down the hillside, following the path of the winding canyon, and in its wake, the willows and the pepper trees and the sage and the eucalyptus all succumbed to its hunger. What was once green and lush to the eye, but shadowy and dark beneath, became nothing more than a twisting tongue of fire reaching out for the next bush, the next tree, until it bisected the city with a pulsing red scar of flame that finally wound its way to the ocean shore. There it slowly faded to ember and then to smoke.

And by the time the flames were doused by the sea, hours later, the day was over.

Dawn had turned, once again, to night.

CHAPTER SEVENTEEN

WOODY'S HOME, like all the others along the canyon's rim, survived the blaze. Only Woody's mother's roses, standing as they did on the very brink of the canyon's edge, were seared lifeless by the heat.

"They might recover," Cathy said, but Woody doubted it. It seemed only fitting they should finally die, now that his mother was truly gone. After all, it was only because of her that they had ever existed at all. Maybe roses needed a rest from life, just as people did. And now perhaps Woody's mother had truly found that rest. His father, too. And Bobby. All of them.

The four friends stood by the blackened blossoms and stared down into the canyon where, as the darkness of night settled around them, they could see splashes of red embers still sprinkled here and there. A few charred tree trunks poked up from the desiccated earth, casting dark silhouettes in the smoky moonlight, but they were limbless and smoldering, as dead as his mother's roses. The only shadows to be seen, other than those of the barren, lifeless stalks of trees, were the shadows of clouds passing across the moon, the normal shadows of evening. The great canopy of willows, which had always billowed there in the depths of the canyon, was gone now for the first time in memory. Only in Woody's mind did they still exist.

And for a moment, from the silent, empty canyon, Woody imagined he heard the laughter of a child trailing up into the sky among the smoke. The playful laughter of freedom, joyous and lilting. He imagined it sailing high, heading home. Even if it was all imagination, the sound of it, real or not, made him smile.

"We did good," Chuck said, staring out across the blackened canyon, surrounded by his friends. "Not a fucking tree in sight."

"The poor animals," Cathy said, still holding an ice bag to her cheek. Willow Man's fist had done a number on her face, and it still pained her. But being woman, and being stronger than a man in many ways, as she would be the first to tell you, the pain didn't overwhelm her because she wouldn't let it. The ice bag was for the swelling, at Chuck's insistence. "Can't have you looking like a chipmunk for the rest of your life," he joked, but the joke didn't reach his eyes. He looked truly concerned, and Cathy loved him all the more because of it. "And don't worry," he reassured her, "the animals will come back. Nature always triumphs in the end."

Jeremy kept a leery eye on the myriad assortment of emergency vehicles, all flashing their colored lights and still sounding their sirens as they moved back and forth along the canyon's edge, dousing hot spots with fire hoses. The police were keeping civilians away from the rim and out of the firemen's way, and all the while they were looking, Jeremy suspected, and rightly so, for the moron, or morons, who *ignited* this holocaust.

And each and every one of those morons was with Jeremy right now.

Standing in Woody's arms, Jeremy shook his head as he stared at the destruction laid out before them. "I have to tell you, Woody. You really know how to show a guy a good time. If we can accomplish all this on our first date, imagine what we can accomplish with the rest of our lives."

Woody laughed. "Yeah. Just imagine."

The acrid stench of cindered woodlands still burned Woody's eyes, but he tried to ignore it as a sad smile spread across his face. He stared down the sweeping hillside into the canyon for the very first time since childhood without fear of what lay beneath him. With the willow trees gone, now in the distance, almost two miles away, he could see the glint of seawater sparkling in the light of a newly risen moon. It was a view as new and precious to Woody as the knowledge that Jeremy loved him. Even in the midst of all this destruction, Woody couldn't stop thinking how amazing that was.

Due to the poor air quality in the city, for which Woody figured he was pretty much solely to blame and didn't much give a fuck who knew it, except maybe the police, Woody's show had been canceled for the night. And possibly the next night as well. Many citizens were hunkered down in their closed-up houses with their air purifiers cranking out ozone to beat the band, trying to survive the lack of oxygen in the air, and probably hoping the arsonists who were stupid enough to bring the city to its knees like this would be quickly captured and hung up by their Buster Browns. But Woody figured if there was a God—and since Evil was a certainty (Willow Man alone was proof of that), then God would most assuredly have to follow right along behind—and if that God was just, as they had all been raised to believe, then He would surely allow no punishments to be doled out for what had taken place this day. As Jeremy told him earlier, before the conflagration began, they were doing the right thing. And they *had* done the right thing. There was not a single doubt in Woody's mind about that. He would have been happy to suffer the consequences for their actions if it came right down to it. Just knowing Willow Man was destroyed would be incentive enough for that. But he was equally happy to think they had actually gotten away with it. And *more* than happy knowing no one was injured in the process. No one *living*, at least.

Woody supposed he would never actually understand the true source of the evil that had raised its head there and continued to reach out for them through all the long years since their childhood. Was it the shadows in the canyon that created the evil or Willow Man himself? At this point, he supposed it didn't really matter. Both were gone. The shadows, like Willow Man, had been seared from the earth. They could no longer hurt anyone.

Woody reached out his hand once again, for maybe the hundredth time that day, and found Jeremy's hand right there waiting for him. Through this long, miserable day, Jeremy had not once left Woody's side. Never before in his life, even in the days of Bobby and their awakening passion, had Woody felt so secure in the knowledge that he was loved, and even now, after all they had been through together, the knowledge humbled and all but overwhelmed him.

They were each of them as weary as they had ever been in their lives, their faces smudged with soot, their hair brittle and reeking atop their heads from the heat and the smoke, their clothes stained with ash and fit for nothing but rags, but in their hearts they were exultant. They had faced their tormentor head-on and emerged triumphant. But more importantly, they had freed Bobby and the others from an eternity of misery at the hands of the creature they had come to know as Willow Man.

The echo of Willow Man's screams when the flames consumed him still thundered inside their heads, but they felt no pity. No regret. Children would sleep safely in their beds tonight because of what they had done. And those who had fallen victim to him in years past, would at last find peace themselves. Heaven? Hell? Nothingness? Who truly knew what awaited them, but now, at least, it would not be endless eons of torture and fear. They would never again feel that foul breath on their bodies, hear that cold laughter as they screamed out their suffering at the hands of the evil being that had torn them from the world, then left them in the shadows to await his pleasure yet again. And again.

Woody wished for nothing more than peace for Bobby and his parents. If peace was heaven, then so be it. Perhaps their souls had returned to their bodies resting asleep in the earth where the world of men had buried them years ago. Or maybe they were still here, peacefully sleeping in the hearts of those they left behind. Either way, they were at rest, and Woody was content to know he and his friends were the ones who had made it happen.

At last, Chuck turned away from the canyon. He looked down at Cathy's face resting against his chest, her arm wrapped tightly around his waist, still holding on as if anchoring herself to the world of the living.

"I could sleep for a week," he said, smiling down at her, pressing his lips to the top of her head. "How about you?"

"A month," she said. "Maybe two. But first a shower."

"I'll wash your back," Chuck said, and Woody and Jeremy watched as the two of them turned toward the house. Before they walked away, Cathy reached out and touched each of them gently, first Jeremy, then Woody, caressing their faces with her long, cool fingers, smiling at the knowledge they were as weary as she and looked every bit as wrung out.

"Get some rest," she told them. "Don't stand out here all night."

Jeremy grinned. "Yes, Mama."

And to Woody alone, she said, "The house is safe. The fire is over. Bobby and your folks are free. We did a good thing today, Woody. Don't ever doubt it."

Blinking back a sudden onrush of tears, Woody nodded. "I know."

Tugging her gently away, Chuck led Cathy to the back door, the one that squeaked because Woody's father always meant to oil the hinges but never got around to doing it, and as they disappeared inside the house and the screen door banged closed behind them, Woody turned to see Jeremy gazing at his face, a tiny smile playing at the corners of his mouth.

"What?" Woody asked.

Jeremy gave his head a little shake. "Nothing. It's just—I never really thought we would survive today. When we walked into the canyon this morning, I knew—I *knew*—we would never step out of it again alive."

"And still you were willing to do it." Woody said.

"There weren't many other options on the table."

"And now that Willow Man is gone, you're thinking you're stuck with me. Too many promises made in the throes of passion."

Jeremy clutched Woody's hand a little tighter. He brought it to his lips. "Nope. Those promises I intend to keep. And if you know what's good for you, so will you."

"What is it, then?" Woody asked. "What's with the worry lines etched across your forehead? You look like my mom surveying an acre of dirty carpet."

Jeremy laughed, but it quickly faded, and he turned away from Woody and stared back at the canyon. Between them, the silence hung heavy for a moment before he said, "I'll never be Bobby, you know. I can never be everything to you that Bobby was. I'll try to make you happy, Woody, but I can never be anything more than what I am right now. I'm not Bobby. I'm just me. I want you to—understand that."

Woody moved closer to him, smelling the ash and smoke on his clothing, feeling the heat of Jeremy's body next to his own, longing for him even now. He wrapped Jeremy in his arms and pressed his face into Jeremy's neck.

"I never want you to be anything more than what you already are. I think maybe even Bobby never loved me as much as you do. We had our moments together, Bobby and I. Wonderful moments, we surely did. But we were so young that *every* moment was amazing. I never felt safe with Bobby like I do with you. We were always afraid someone would find out how we felt about each other, or discover what we were doing together on those hot summer nights behind my bedroom door. There was always turmoil. The hiding. The sneaking around. There was passion and love there, too, but we were too young to really accept it for what it was. Too young to say, 'fuck you, world, this is who we are, this is what we want.' I'm all grown up now, Jeremy. I'm not afraid anymore. My parents are dead. Bobby's gone. I have no one but myself to make an accounting to. No one but myself—and you. All I can do is what I think will make me happy. And what makes me happy is having you standing here with me at this very moment, looking worried as hell, maybe, and smelling like a week-old campfire, but being here nevertheless."

Woody held Jeremy at arm's length and gave him a little shake to get his attention, as if he didn't already have it. "I've avoided relationships for fifteen years, and now I've fallen head over heels in love in a single night and day."

"With my dick."

"No, with *you,* nimrod." Woody paused for a second, answering Jeremy's smile with one of his own. "*And* your dick."

Jeremy reached out to brush the hair from Woody's forehead, and as an afterthought, he kissed a smudge of soot on the tip of Woody's nose. "I guess we'll be okay, then," he said, pulling Woody close and giving him a little crotch-to-crotch action by way of sealing the deal. "As long as you stop setting fires. Arson is a crime. But I have to say, Woody, it really has been a hell of a first date. I'm duly impressed."

"The arson was your idea. And it *has* been quite a first date, hasn't it?"

"Oh, yeah. We set the town on fire. Literally. We surely did."

From inside the house, they heard Chuck break into a bellowing, off-key version of one of Woody's ballads, quickly followed by Cathy screaming for him to, please God, shut the hell up before she came over there, ripped his head off, and threw it out the window.

"I guess maybe we *will* be okay," Woody grinned, drawing Jeremy more snugly into his arms, holding him tight and giving him a little crotch-to-crotch action right back. He felt such a rush of desire when he did it almost buckled his knees. "I guess maybe we'll be just fine, you and me."

EPILOGUE

AND BECAUSE of Chuck's caterwauling, or Cathy's hollering, or simply because of the brittle, heat-charred jacaranda branches rattling in the arid breeze above their heads, neither Woody nor Jeremy heard the whimper of pain and torment coming from the crawlspace under the house behind them, a mere susurration of sound that barely escaped into the night from the musty cavern beneath the floors.

For there cowered the remnants of the creature that had been Willow Man. With its beloved canyon shadows burned away, and its sweet, captive victims freed by the flames forever, it was to this filthy hole that it had been forced to retreat. Alone and diminished, it had come here, to the only refuge it could find.

It gnawed at its diseased fingertips as it trembled in the blackness in fear and fury. The humans standing outside his shameful lair, planning their futures, plotting their love, infuriated it even more.

Seething with impotent rage, the creature hunkered in the dust, trying to ignore the agony of its beloved flesh, seared by the ravenous fire the humans had unleashed. In a single night, they had taken everything from it. No, not from *it*. From him. *Willow Man. I am Willow Man*, he screamed soundlessly into the shadows.

He froze. Suddenly a familiar hunger tore through him. A familiar need.

I must feed. To grow strong I must feed. And once I'm strong, I'll begin again. Yes. Willow Man will begin again.

His lips spread wide in a wicked leer. His hand, the fingers tipped with pestilence, snatched through the darkness to seize a roach racing across the dirt. He tossed the wriggling roach into his gaping maw and, slavering insanely, chewed it to a pulp.

Suddenly he stopped and listened. He heard words, words spoken by a familiar voice. Yes. It was the boy he once hungered for—the boy who had become the man he now despised more than any other.

Willow Man peered from beneath the back steps. Two men were standing in each other's arms at the edge of the canyon. *His* canyon. A soot-scented breeze stirred their hair. Their handsome faces glowed pale and happy in the moonlight.

"I guess maybe we *will* be okay," Woody said, his voice gentle with love and hope as he held the twin in his arms—the twin Willow Man should have killed long ago. "I guess maybe we'll be just fine, you and me."

"We'll s-see about that," the creature hissed among the shadows, fluttering the cobwebs with fetid air, sending the spiders scurrying in fear.

Willow Man licked the taste of cockroach from his lips, all the while longing for sweeter meat, firmer flesh. "Oh, yes-s, my fine young gentlemen. We'll just fucking s-s-see."

JOHN INMAN has been writing fiction since he was old enough to hold a pencil. He and his partner live in beautiful San Diego, California. Together, they share a passion for theater, books, hiking and biking along the trails and canyons of San Diego or, if the mood strikes, simply kicking back with a beer and a movie. John's advice for anyone who wishes to be a writer? "Set time aside to write every day and do it. Don't be afraid to share what you've written. Feedback is important. When a rejection slip comes in, just tear it up and try again. Keep mailing stuff out. Keep writing and rewriting and then rewrite one more time. Every minute of the struggle is worth it in the end, so don't give up. Ever. Remember that publishers are a lot like lovers. Sometimes you have to look a long time to find the one that's right for you."

You can contact John at john492@att.net,
on Facebook: http://www.facebook.com/john.inman.79,
or on his website: http://www.johninmanauthor.com/.

Coming soon to
DSP PUBLICATIONS

'Til Darkness Falls

By Pearl Love

A malicious deception.... An ancient curse.... A timeless love....

Brian Macon is a worn-out homicide detective whose job and life hold no meaning until he meets a gorgeous German man who turns his world upside down. Alrick Ritter has a poet's soul, a master cellist's skill, and a sniper's deadly accuracy, and though constrained by sinister forces to be a killer-for-hire, Alrick wants nothing more than to be with Brian. Helpless to resist the call of their hearts, Brian and Alrick begin a cautious affair, keeping secret the reality that places them on opposite sides of the law. But an ancient danger threatens to destroy their love.

Three thousand years ago in the burning sands of ancient Egypt, Prince Rahotep and his devoted slave, Tiye, were robbed of their lives, betrayed by a powerful woman's mad hatred and the cruel humor of an evil god. Now, destiny has reunited the lovers, joining them in an unquenchable passion even as a twist of fate casts them as potential enemies. Will Brian and Alrick be able to overcome the centuries-old curse to secure the love that should have always been theirs? \

http://www.dsppublications.com

Also from DSP PUBLICATIONS

Eagle's Blood

By A.J. Marcus

Brock Summers is a Colorado Parks and Wildlife Officer who loves his job and takes it very seriously. When he discovers a video of golden eagles being shot and learns of a nest in trouble, not even a blizzard can stop him from trekking up the mountain in an attempt to rescue them.

When Brock returns with the one eaglet he manages to save, Landon Weir, the local wildlife rehabilitator, patches up the bird and the injury Brock suffered during the rescue. Though they have been friends and colleagues for years, they discover a shared passion for protecting wildlife and vow to work together to protect the majestic birds from the criminals preying on them. It isn't long before another video of eagles being killed comes to their attention. They must face inclement weather, a dangerous mountain, and armed poachers if they want to ensure the eagles'—and their own—survival.

http://www.dsppublications.com

Also from DSP Publications

Erasing Shame

By Yeyu

The son of a Han traitor who had let the Xianbei Mongols invade the borders, Jiang Shicai swears to restore his family's honor, hoping to better the Hans' lives through peaceful means. He believes violence is never the answer, but to gain respect, he finds himself fighting for the Xianbei.

Ten years later, an annoying but handsome playboy, Dugu Xuechi, arrives as the incompetent new military inspector of Shicai's region. Shameless, irresponsible, and obnoxious, Xuechi tests Shicai's patience almost every second. Despite their mutual dislike, Shicai finds himself drawn to the capricious man, especially when he sees the resemblance between Xuechi and his deceased best friend. Yet Xuechi's self-destructive behavior and refusal to accept help require attention that distracts Shicai from his goal for peace--and it doesn't help that Xuechi is Shicai's strongest political opposition. Haunted by a childhood promise he never had the chance to fulfill, Shicai must choose between his feelings and his values.

http://www.dsppublications.com

Also from DSP Publications

Ghost

Wolf's-own: Book 1

By Carole Cummings

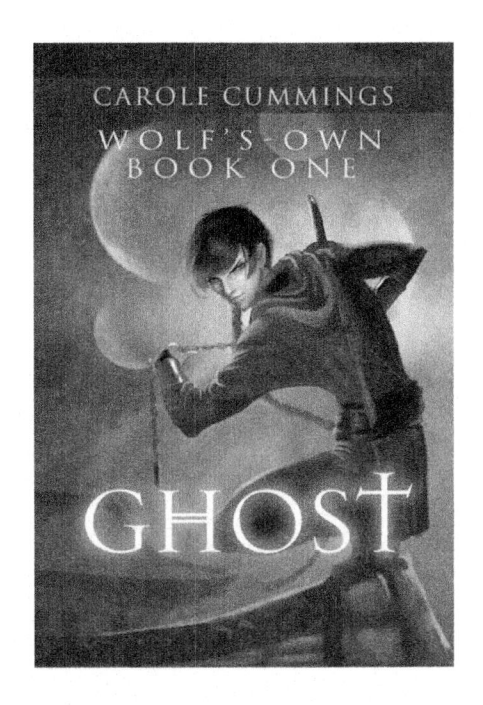

Untouchable. Ghost. Assassin. *Mad.* Fen Jacin-rei is all these and none. His mind is host to the spirits of long-dead magicians, and Fen's fate should be one of madness and ignoble death. So how is it Fen lives, carrying out shadowy vengeance for his subjugated people and protecting the family he loves?

Kamen Malick means to find out. When Malick and his own small band of assassins ambush Fen in an alley, Malick offers Fen a choice: *Join us or die.*

Determined to decode the intrigue that surrounds Fen, Malick sets to unraveling the mysteries of Fen's past. As Fen's secrets slowly unfold, Malick finds irony a bitter thing when he discovers the one he wants is already hopelessly entangled with the one he hunts.

http://www.dsppublications.com

Also from DSP Publications

Dreamlands

Dreamlands: Book 1

By Felicitas Ivey

The Trust and its battle-hardened recruits are fighting a horrific war, a war between the humans of this world and the demons of the Dreamlands. In this shadowy battle, Keno Inuzaka is merely a pawn: first an innocent bystander imprisoned and abused by the Trust, then a captive of a demon oni when taken to the Dreamlands.

But oni Samojirou Aboshi treats the human with unexpected care and respect, and the demon only just earns Keno's trust when a team from the Trust arrives to exploit the Dreamlands' magic.

As the war spreads across both worlds, Keno is torn between them. If he survives, he faces a decision: go home and carve out a new life under the Trust's thumb… or stay in the Dreamlands and find freedom in love.

http://www.dsppublications.com

Also from DSP Publications

Third Eye

By Rick R. Reed

Who knew that a summer thunderstorm and his lost little boy would conspire to change single dad Cayce D'Amico's life in an instant? With Luke missing, Cayce ventures into the woods near their house to find his son, only to have lightning strike a tree near him, sending a branch down on his head. When he awakens the next day in the hospital, he discovers he has been blessed or cursed—he isn't sure which—with psychic ability. Along with unfathomable glimpses into the lives of those around him, he's getting visions of a missing teenage girl.

When a second girl disappears soon after the first, Cayce realizes his visions are leading him to their grisly fates. Cayce wants to help, but no one believes him. The police are suspicious. The press wants to exploit him. And the girls' parents have mixed feelings about the young man with the "third eye."

Cayce turns to local reporter Dave Newton and, while searching for clues to the string of disappearances and possible murders, a spark ignites between the two. Little do they know that nearby, another couple—dark and murderous—are plotting more crimes and wondering how to silence the man who knows too much about them.

http://www.dsppublications.com

Also from DSP Publications

Infected: Prey

Infected: Book 1

By Andrea Speed

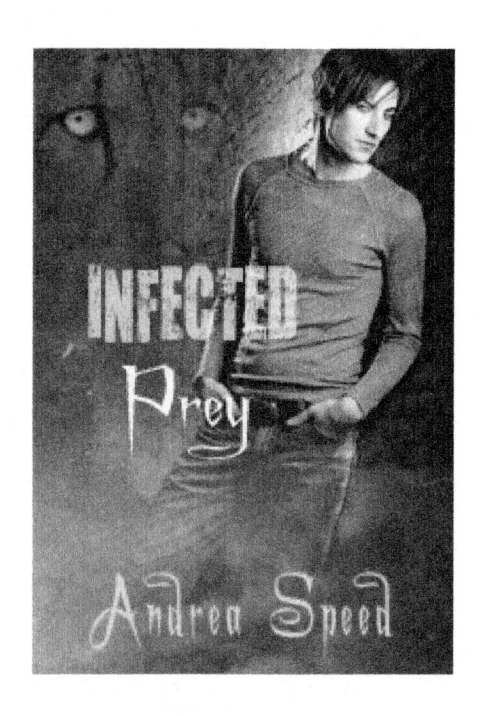

In a world where a werecat virus has changed society, Roan McKichan, a born infected and ex-cop, works as a private detective trying to solve crimes involving other infecteds.

The murder of a former cop draws Roan into an odd case where an unidentifiable species of cat appears to be showing an unusual level of intelligence. He juggles that with trying to find a missing teenage boy, who, unbeknownst to his parents, was "cat" obsessed. And when someone is brutally murdering infecteds, Eli Winters, leader of the Church of the Divine Transformation, hires Roan to find the killer before he closes in on Eli.

Working the crimes will lead Roan through a maze of hate, personal grudges, and mortal danger. With help from his tiger-strain infected partner, Paris Lehane, he does his best to survive in a world that hates and fears their kind… and occasionally worships them.

http://www.dsppublications.com

Coming soon to
DSP PUBLICATIONS

Desert World: Book 1

Desert World Allegiances

By Lyn Gala

Livre once offered Planetary Alliance miners and workers a small fortune if they helped terraform the mineral rich planet. People flocked to the world, but then a civil war cut the desert planet off from all resources. Half-terraformed and clinging to the edge of existence, Livre devolved into a world where death was accepted as part of life, water resources were scarce and constantly dwindling, and neighbors tried to help each other hold off the inevitable as the desert fought to take back the few terraformed spaces.

Temar Gazer claims to be the victim of water theft. His claims could be a simple misdirection intended to help him escape a term of labor after his criminal prank caused irreparable damage to a watering system. However as the only member of the council arguing against a short-term slavery sentence for Temar, Shan Polli can't escape the fear that something darker is happening. The more he investigates Temar's story, the more he finds that his world is not as free of politics or danger as he had assumed. Together, Shan and Temar must get to the bottom of the conspiracy before time runs out for the entire planet.

http://www.dsppublications.com

For more great fiction from

DSP PUBLICATIONS

visit us online.
WWW.DSPPUBLICATIONS.COM